# Ghost of the Past

## BAKER CITY: HEARTS & HAUNTS 4

# JOSIE MALONE

GHOST OF THE PAST
Copyright © 2022 by Josie Malone

ISBN: 978-1-955784-89-4

Published by Satin Romance
An Imprint of Melange Books, LLC
White Bear Lake, MN 55110
www.satinromance.com

Published in the United States of America.

Cover Design by Lynsee Lauritsen

*Ghost of the Past is dedicated to the Evergreen Writers Critique Group, my sister writers who helped in so many ways to make this book the best it could possibly be. As the saying goes, "Friends are the sisters we choose for ourselves." Thanks again. I couldn't have written this book without you.*

# PART 1

# CHAPTER ONE

*Baker City, Washington ~ August 2014*

"I'm done coming second in your life, Durango Hawke."

"Say again, babe. I didn't get that."

"You heard me." Heather McElroy shifted on the corral rail where she'd perched so he could snap her photo with his new camera, the one she'd given him for his birthday back in March. She eyed the tawny-haired man twenty feet away. Six foot six in his socks, broad-shouldered, narrow-hipped, he carried himself like the Marine he'd been for six years before he became a soldier of fortune. She'd followed him far too long.

"Let me spell it out for you, Hawke. I love you, but it's my turn now. I've been offered a great job and a recording contract. I'm going to Nashville in time for the Labor Day show."

"We've talked about this. It'll have to wait. I need you here to run Hawke Construction when I'm on a mission for Nighthawke."

"Not my circus, not my monkeys." She took a deep breath, longing to slug him when he didn't listen to her. *But I'm an adult, so I won't even if I hate it when he mocks me.* "I'm not doing it, not anymore. My life has been on hold long enough. I told you I didn't agree with rescuing the company

3

when your father ran it into the ground while we were in Afghanistan, but you had to save the day one more time instead of letting it go into bankruptcy."

"The people who've worked there all these years didn't deserve to lose their retirement when it went down in flames, and I was the only one that could borrow money from the extended family in Texas."

He didn't get it.

"You did what you had to do because you always have to be the hero, but that's not my deal. I've always dreamed of being a country singer and now I have a shot. I'm going to Nashville in two weeks."

She watched the storm build in his navy eyes. Irritation made his rugged, handsome features harder for her to resist. Blue jeans, boots, and a faded, sleeveless chambray shirt increased his resemblance to a Madison Avenue cowboy. But there was nothing plastic about her man!

*At 28, almost 29, I have three combat tours behind me. I've been working part-time as a horse trainer while I rebuild my career as a country singer in the local bars. We were supposed to move to Nashville as soon as he found a manager for Hawke Construction, but the damned jarhead didn't even look for one. He's too freaking busy hunting for his brother, the family favorite. It's not like Durango doesn't know how much I love music. It's my turn, damn it!*

She shook her head, long copper strands floating in the warm breeze. "I'm through nursing you after your stupid adventures, and I'm definitely done picking up the slack at Hawke Construction when you're off in South America. You wouldn't hire a manager, so I did."

"Thanks for the support." Sarcasm laced his bass rumble.

Deliberately, she focused on his bandaged left shoulder as he adjusted the camera. Any lower and the bullet would have hit his heart. As cantankerous as he was, though, she hadn't asked but knew he'd taken out the attacker. She wouldn't let Durango see how he affected her when he lowered the Nikon and strode toward her.

"I mean it." She raised her chin. "No more system support, Hawke, when you return to Colombia on one more suicide mission. I'm going to Nashville. Someone else will have to patch you up. Just remember, doctors are required to report gunshot wounds, and all cops aren't stupid. One might not believe you were hit in a drive-by shooting at a construction site."

"Don't threaten me." He stepped closer. "I've never taken your crap. It's why we've stayed together this long."

"I won't be here when you return this time."

4

Her ultimatum didn't appear to faze him. His face was expressionless, a mask that hid any and all emotion. She reached for the emerald engagement ring on her left hand, began to slide it off. "I mean it. I'm done waiting on the sidelines."

"Watch it, Heather Marie. You don't want to piss me off."

"I'm not scared of you." She shrugged, but stopped toying with the ring. She'd wait. "Save the macho act for the bunch of mercenaries you run with or one of your cousins. Don't try to placate me or act like you think I'm cute when I'm angry. I'm serious."

She didn't want to know how many soldiers of fortune died in the South American jungles. It was bad enough knowing he might.

He was pretty annoyed with her. She could tell by the edge in his deep voice and the tight line of his strong jaw. He moved nearer, boots soft on the summer grass. Did he think he could intimidate her into silence?

*No way! Too bad, too sad! After all those tours as a combat nurse in Iraq and Afghanistan, does he honestly think his tantrums frighten me?*

He stopped in front of her. The shirt left unbuttoned and open because of the injured shoulder revealed his neck and tanned, muscular chest. Her gaze narrowed on part of the bright red scar that she could see, one that she knew slashed from his right shoulder in a diagonal six-inch line toward his left nipple.

The injury two years ago had been her introduction to his illegal, dangerous hunt for his younger brother. Granted, Durango was morally right when he tried to save the day and his bro, but damn it, she wanted him home, safe with her in Tennessee—not getting himself killed, pursuing a dream and a man who was most likely dead.

She pointed to the healed wound. "Remember when I stitched that with an upholstery needle and dental floss? I cleaned it with alcohol first. You yelled like a stuck pig. Without anesthesia, I know everything I did must have hurt like hell. You fainted from the pain."

"Yeah, I passed out. Your nursing hurt worse than being stabbed. Your point?"

"You didn't learn anything, not from the cause or the cure. You still think you can change clothes in a phone booth. I'm not Lois Lane to your Superman." She trembled when he moved suddenly and gripped the fence, resting large hands on either side of her. "I'm right, damn it."

"You always tell me so." He leaned nearer, brushed a kiss over her lips. "It's why we fight so much. You're all spit and vinegar. It makes me horny as hell when you start issuing edicts, Empress. You're my pretty little tyrant."

She tried to turn her head, but he caught her chin in calloused fingers. "Don't. I'm not in the mood, especially when you make fun of me."

*Of course, it's all too easy for him to get me in the mood.*

"I won't force you." He chuckled. "I don't have to, and we both know it. This is your pride talking. It's why you've slept on the couch for the past three weeks. It's cold comfort at night, isn't it? I've missed you hogging the covers."

"As if you really cared. If I believed that, you've got oceanfront property in Arizona like the song says." Heather trembled when he feathered his thumb over her lips. Of course, he didn't have a clue that she wasn't actually sleeping in the living room. She sat up nights, drinking vodka while she watched insipid late night movies. Enough booze and she wouldn't dream about dying kids who should be anywhere but in the military trying to survive in a war zone.

"You've ignored everything I said," she went on. "You won't admit how wrong you are. And you didn't say a word when I moved out of the bedroom until I took away the television. Then, you bitched because you missed laughing at *Walker, Texas Ranger,* and your war movies."

"I'm not stupid. If I said I needed you every minute of every day, you'd figure you won. And did you think I wouldn't find the small flat-screen on the kitchen table? You weren't even watching it. You just stole it for spite."

The mockery in his voice grated. She'd fallen in love with him before she knew what the word meant. She trailed behind him as a child, adored him as a teen, and followed him to war as a woman. She didn't make a secret of her feelings, unlike him. He'd never said he loved her, not once in all these years.

"Come on, babe. Don't be this way. You know how bad I *want* you." The warmth in the dark blue eyes left no doubt of the way he *wanted* her. "I like having you in that big, brass bed or anywhere else I can take you."

She glared up at him. "Want in one hand, Marine, and crap in the other. See which fills up first."

"Wow, can you talk dirty, *Empress.* Is this when I make you beg for me or later?"

She pushed him away, jumped off the fence. "You son of a—!" She stopped, aware of how he felt about name-calling. "You're damned right about one thing. I'm too good for you. I'll find a real man, one not afraid to stick and stay with me when I get to Nashville."

"Don't go there." His fingers gripped her shoulders. "You belong to me. You have since the day you were born. You'll always be mine."

"Kiss my butt." She wrenched free, stalked across the yard. She'd collect her purse and jacket, then hitch a ride into Baker City. From there, she could find a friend to take her back to their place in Lake Maynard.

The scent of flowers drifted from the overgrown rose garden in front of the old Victorian house where her grandparents had lived. The four hundred–plus acre farm waited for her uncle to return. Fenian McElroy had disappeared on a covert Army mission back in 2011 with Durango's brother, Waco.

There was little hope her uncle would come home to claim his inheritance. After all, the US wouldn't even admit they had troops in South America fighting the drug lords. The American government knew how to fight secret wars. The blood of its soldiers was currency to politicians, and too much attention was taken up with the war in the Middle East. Durango might not have learned the lesson, but she had long before her uncle and his younger brother died.

"You don't get it, Hawke. These trips of yours scare me half to death and they won't do any good."

"Nothing frightens you." He caught up with her. He didn't sound quite so amused when he trailed one finger down her neck to the gold chain she always wore along with the special four-leaf clover he'd given her as a gift on her sixteenth birthday. "I won't let you leave me."

She glared up at him. "In the past, you were everything to me. I have dreams and I'm going to follow them. I told you already. I'm done waiting."

"You want me." He nipped her ear, kissed the spot below it. "You're too damned proud to admit it when you're in one of your snot-slinging, foot-stomping hissy fits. You figure if you don't let me make love to you, I'll kowtow to your demands."

"I'm not that manipulative. Even if I were, you'd deserve it. You walked into the house leaking blood like a saturated surgical sponge and terrified me."

"You didn't show it. You fixed me up." He pressed another kiss to her neck. "You're one in a million and way too good for me."

"At least we agree on something, jarhead." She stepped away from him, headed toward the blanket she'd spread on the grass. "Let's go home. Your idea of a picnic on the old McElroy homestead was just another try to get me in the sack."

"We haven't eaten yet and I still want to take some pictures of you with my birthday camera." He followed her.

"I'm not in the mood," she repeated, her back to him. "I'd have more luck talking to a rock. No wonder your mother claims, 'Bigger is dumber' and acts like you're a monster because you're not a scrawny little runt. For once, she's right."

"Funny. You never say that in bed," he shot back. "You always beg for more."

She whirled to confront him. He was right behind her. Surprised, she fell back a step, the blanket beneath her shoe. "I won't sleep with you until you're home for good."

He grinned down at her. "Wanna bet?" He hooked a hand around her neck. "I haven't given you a birthday present yet."

"My birthday isn't until next week. You'd better be here and packing to go with me to Nashville." When he didn't answer, she stiffened. "I said *no*."

"I heard you." He brushed her lips with his. "I fully intend to get started on your present today."

"Oh, really? What do you plan to give me?"

"What do you think?" He lowered his head. "The same thing I've given you for the past eight years, multiple orgasms. I'm going for a new record, twenty-nine of them, one for each year."

She shuddered, trying to ignore the heat in her face. "It's physically impossible. I'll die of exhaustion."

"You haven't yet." He laughed. "Let's check it out."

She hesitated. She wanted him as badly as he wanted her. She'd ached for his touch, longed to go to him, but forced herself to maintain a safe distance. Would surrender work any better? Could she entice him to stay home with her?

It was worth a try. At five foot eight, it wasn't much of a stretch to tiptoe up and tease his mouth with hers. "Want me?"

"You know it." He pulled her tight against him. "I've missed you."

"Not enough to come out to the living room and charm me."

"It wouldn't have worked until you stopped ranting and raving."

"I don't have tantrums."

"When I got home, you tipped a table full of food on me. Laredo hit the door a-running."

"That was the plan," she said in her sweetest voice. "I couldn't let your youngest brother see you were a bloody mess. If I had, we wouldn't be arguing. You'd be in a hospital, then jail. You got off easy."

He snorted. "Says the woman into payback. Vengeance is always yours. You do enjoy trying to make me suffer."

"I'm not that petty."

"You'll go to hell for lying." Durango kissed her brows. "You threw your engagement ring at me for a week straight. I kept putting it back on your finger."

She tipped back her head and met his gaze. "I didn't ask for it. I offered to bring you a jar of petroleum jelly so you could shove it where the sun doesn't shine."

Another laugh before he dropped a kiss on her nose. "You make me glad to be alive, except when all you give me to eat is potato soup."

"It was good for you."

"I hate the stuff. Then you made peanut butter cookies for dessert." He stroked her hair. "How many times have I told you that peanut butter makes me gag? And you refused to make me chocolate chip ones, no matter how many times I asked."

"Making you miserable was the least I could do after you scared the hell out of me."

"You went for two and a half weeks without speaking to me, even when you were changing my bandages. Must have been a new record." He rested his chin on top of her head. "You're an ornery woman, Heather Marie McElroy. My ornery woman."

"As if you'd want any other kind." She closed her eyes and leaned against him, relishing the hard, solid feel of his body. Did he realize how close he'd come to dying? Tears burned her eyes. She blinked them away, determined not to reveal the weakness. He couldn't handle it when she cried. She'd learned that eons ago. "You're mine."

"I always have been." His mouth claimed hers. "Ever since we were kids."

When the kiss ended, he lifted his lips a few inches from hers. Before he spoke, she slowly slid his shirt down the muscled arms, letting it fall onto the grass. "I've given you all of me." Deliberately, she reminded him of the 4-H pledge they'd exchanged as teen sweethearts. "Head, heart, health, and hands. I want all of you."

"You have me. We'll get married as soon as I bring Waco home."

"He's gone. We have to let him and Fenn go."

"I don't believe that. I'll keep looking for the two of them."

"All right, lover. You think what you need to think." She stopped him with a kiss, then said, "I wish there were another O'Leary who talks to the dead in Baker City, someone who could find Waco and Fenn for you, but there isn't, and your brother means more to you than—" She paused. His little brother was the family favorite and no matter what Durango did, his parents still wouldn't love him, but he didn't need to hear it again. "No, I won't say that. I won't spoil this moment, but I agree we'll both do what we have to do."

---

As soon as he parked the rental car in the driveway, he knew she was gone. October leaves covered the unmown lawn and weeds shared space with the bright marigolds in the flowerbeds. Rolled-up newspapers littered the front porch. Envelopes overflowed from the small mailbox beside the screen door. Proof of her departure from his life as if he hadn't gotten a clue when she didn't come to the airport to meet him.

"I don't need this crap, Heather Marie," Durango muttered aloud.

He left the bouquet of yellow roses, the box of her favorite chocolate-covered macadamia nuts, and the small sack from the jewelry store on the passenger seat. He'd expected her to be angry. She always got mad when he left on a trip to South America, but this tantrum was ridiculous for a twenty-nine-year-old woman. She'd bitch that she was done waiting for his selfish, lazy ass and she wanted her dreams too. But, why couldn't she understand he didn't have a choice either?

Then again, maybe she really hadn't left the state.

He reached into his back pocket, pulled out his wallet, and flipped to the last picture he'd taken of her. Vibrant red hair cascaded to her narrow waist. High cheekbones, a pointed chin, and huge green eyes. The regal glare made him think of an absolute ruler, but there was nothing tame about his Heather. She was wild, feral, and downright vicious at times. *My kind of woman, long on guts, short on self-preservation, my pretty tyrant. She'd charge hell with a bucket of water.*

It was the low, rich taunting voice he always missed most. She might tear strips off him with her words, but that voice was saturated with sex. He wanted to fall into the photo, grab her and hold her forever. He'd just hold those curves against him. She was the perfect size for him, heart-high. In the picture, she leaned against the corral rail, the summer wind ruffling her hair.

He'd told her to say cheese. She hadn't, of course. She'd never followed his directions in her entire life. She'd looked him straight in the face, smiled dangerously, and purred, "But babe. I don't want cheese. I want you."

His hands shook when he snapped the photo. It was pure luck, not skill it'd come out this good. He'd assumed their wild lovemaking meant everything was great between them. She'd stopped calling the hunt for his brother the definition of insanity. She'd even driven him to the airport, kissed him goodbye like they were going to jump back into the sack, not like they'd just left it.

How was he supposed to know she really intended to leave him?

He flung open the car door, stalked to the trunk, and removed his duffel bag, a leftover from his stint in the Marines. He slung the carrying strap over his shoulder, slammed the trunk, and went around the house to the back door.

The kitchen was dark. Daylight filtered through the door behind him. Some came through the window above the farmhouse sink.

What happened to the curtains? He flipped the light switch by the door. Nothing. Had the bulb in the overhead fixture burned out? He turned, saw the note taped neatly to the outside of the breaker box.

*Durango—Call to have the utilities turned on when you want them. That includes the landline. You never phone me, so I won't worry.*

Damn it!

He tore down the note, wadded it into a ball, and looked for the wastebasket.

Gone. He walked farther into the room. The table and chairs were missing too. So were all the appliances, the electric range, fridge, washer, dryer, and dishwasher. No microwave. He grimaced, grateful they'd furnished the rental on their own. At least he wouldn't have to listen to the landlord pitching a major fit.

The cupboards were bare. Another note lay where the dishes used to be. *I gave away the groceries. You had more important things to do than be here for me or the meals I cooked for you.*

"You little witch." He shook his head. He was cracking up. Imagine arguing with a piece of paper.

He stormed through the house, searching the rest of the rooms. She'd stripped the place. The furniture was gone, everything they'd bought together. A manila envelope was taped to the bedroom door, obviously where she'd left her engagement ring. Another note fluttered beside it.

*I got rid of the bed. I didn't want you to share it with someone else. Your clothes are at the cleaners down the street. You can pay them to do laundry for you. I'm outta here. I'm going to Tennessee. So long, lover!*

He dropped the duffel on the floor. He ripped the paper off the door, took down the envelope, tore open one end, and shook out the emerald engagement ring, shoving it into his shirt pocket. He'd save the note inside for later, make her read it to him.

"I'll find you, Heather Marie McElroy," he shouted, his voice echoing in the empty house. "When I do, I'm taking you to bed. Then we're getting married. Enough is damn well enough! I'm done putting up with your tantrums."

He collected the other snotty notes on his way to the back door. He slammed it behind him, pausing to lock the vacant house. A quick stop at the detached garage revealed it was empty. "Where the hell is my truck?"

She'd better not have sold the classic '57 Chevy four-by-four. If she had, there'd be another nastygram, but he didn't see one. Okay, so he'd track her down. *After all this time, I know where she likes to party, even if she calls it "singing for her supper," and it won't be the first time I've dragged her out of a bar.*

Three taverns later, he'd heard the same story from all the bartenders. She hadn't been around since September. Did her folks know her address in Nashville? If they did, would they tell him when he called or would they chew him out for standing in the way of her dreams again? He eyed the CD the last bar manager gave him, then slid it into the player.

The twang of guitars, beat of drums, and finally, organ music slid into a melody. It was an old Dottie West song. "Lesson in Leavin'" was one of Heather's favorites. Why hadn't he realized she was giving him a warning when she sang it before he left two months ago on a vain hunt for his brother?

Okay, so he hadn't found him this time, Durango thought, but he'd keep looking. Heather's husky voice sent chills down his spine. The words echoed through him as a wronged woman sought vengeance for heartache.

---

*Lake Maynard, Washington ~ May 5$^{th}$, 2015*

He'd spent the day on the construction site, too busy working on a new strip mall to check for his messages. Finally, back in his office, he crossed to the desk, picked up the landline, and called the automatic answering service.

Her mocking voice filled his ears. "Durango, sorry I missed you. Happy birthday, lover."

He froze, pressed the button to repeat the message. *It's not my birthday. She knows better than anyone that's in March. What the hell is going on? What game is she playing now?*

# CHAPTER TWO

*Baker City, Washington ~ September 15ᵗʰ, 2015*

It'd been one year, one month, one week, six days, eighteen hours, twenty minutes— Gawd, he wanted a drink. He craved it. Laredo Hawke tasted the imagined whisky, felt it burn his throat, and finally warm his stomach. Hell, it didn't have to be Scotch or his favorite, MacNaughton's. He'd even settle for moonshine the way the Sweeneys brewed it in the foothills above Baker City. Anything to satisfy the gnawing in his guts.

*I'm clean*, he reminded himself. *I've stayed clean and sober more than thirteen months, ever since last August when I promised Heather I'd quit drinking and using for good. I meant it when she bailed me out of the Gray-Bar Hotel and sent me off to rehab one more time.*

At nineteen, he wasn't a kid anymore and jail always scared him. So did the other inmates, all of whom seemed bigger than he was at five foot eight. They figured he was fresh meat. He shuddered at memories of the assaults, trying to force them out of his mind. He hadn't been locked up in more than a year, but he still needed a drink to forget what happened there. This was the longest he'd managed to stay sober.

When he got the message from his mother, Laredo knew better than to refuse to meet the family at the café in Baker City. He'd thought they'd have a meal in the restaurant, but he'd found them in the cocktail lounge. Because he was underage, Pop MacGillicudy wouldn't serve him. If the old man did, it could mean the loss of his liquor license. Heather's cousin, Jassy Sweeney, the waitress and Laredo's girl, would freak. Nothing and no one intimidated her. She was always the first to tell him to find a meeting or to call his sponsor.

Looking across the parking lot, Laredo spotted his older brother parking near the used Ford 150 pickup he'd helped Laredo buy last November. Granted, the former Marine wouldn't fight with him, but hassling Durango was almost as good as alcohol. "What are you doing with my rig?"

"Nothing yet." Durango stalked toward him. "What are you doing in Baker City? I told Pop not to serve you."

"The folks called. They brought Brazos here for her twenty-third birthday. Eli's hounded me for two weeks since Amarillo's shindig, not that she showed up for it."

"Shit, I always forget these damned things."

"Heather sent your gifts, like usual. She's in Nashville, but she never forgets our birthdays. You're still in trouble with the Senator, Mother, and Eli."

"You're a day late and dollar short, boy," Durango replied. "I've been up Shit Crick since I came back alive from Afghanistan. I don't suppose the Empress provided a return address so I could drag her scrawny butt home where she belongs."

"I don't think so, but she still has the same cell phone number."

Feeling safe for the first time that night, Laredo followed Durango toward the restaurant door. "You could try calling her. She always returns our calls, even if it takes a while. She contacted Sean Killian in Liberty Valley and asked him if he'd let me apprentice with him when I finish shoeing school. He said if I were top of the class, he would. When he called me, he said several barns in Liberty Valley want Heather back to train their horses if she ever returns to Washington state."

Durango nodded. "Where are you going? When?"

"Texas. Classes start in two weeks, so I have time to drive there. I appreciate you fronting the tuition, but I promised Heather I'd pay you back when I start working."

"You bet your hide you will. Have you called Uncle Ogden and made arrangements to stay with his family?"

"Yes, and that pissed off the folks nearly as much as you paying another year's rent for Amarillo and her boyfriend, Gino. Mom still hasn't forgiven Heather for saying you were through hearing them call our baby sis a whore and a slut last summer. Amie needed a chance, and you'll keep giving her one."

"That's right. She's doing a good job at Hawke Construction, and she'll start college classes now that she's completed her GED," Durango said. "I'm glad Heather furnished their rental. She's wanted to do something about Amarillo ever since we came back from our last tour and discovered Amie was eight months pregnant."

Laredo nodded, recalling the various family arguments. "You two weren't the only ones who wanted to help her. I was surprised it took until last fall for you to finally put your foot down and intervene."

"What are you talking about?"

"You know already." Laredo shrugged. "Sure, Heather did all the dirty work because you were off working for Uncle Quentin at Nighthawke, but she said it was what you wanted. That you were the one who got me into rehab and your lawyer, George O'Connell, defended me against the DUI charges. He arranged for Amarillo's emancipation and—"

"Sounds about right. Heather runs amok if I'm not around to rein her in."

Laredo ignored the comment and added, "Brazos and I tried to convince the folks that Amie was too young at fourteen to be a mother and to let her get an abortion, but they refused. They wouldn't let us tell you about it when you were overseas."

"I know."

"You've always stepped up for me and the girls, Durango. It meant a lot when you lent me your truck last year, after I wrapped mine around a tree."

"Like I told you then, one ding and your life is over." Durango's smile warmed dark blue eyes. "You better keep going to a lot of meetings, boy."

"I am. It meant a lot when you believed I was clean and sober while I lived with Uncle Ogden."

"I told Dad and Eli it was stupid to bring you back to Washington state and let you run with the same crowd. They didn't listen to me or Heather. Wish she'd show up. She'd better sooner or later."

Laredo followed him through the door, irritated by the lack of affection his brother showed for his fiancée. "You ought to thank God for Heather every day. All she ever talks about when she calls is that you're a real angel and we should treat you with respect. Jassy and I have been together for the past three years. *She* never says what Laredo wants, he gets, and she doesn't make that happen either. Not like Heather."

"Jassy is a sweetheart," Durango said, his tone even—a little too even. "Heather's not. When she does her queen of the world routine, I know to watch for what's coming. She's a pretty little tyrant who will frag me in a heartbeat."

"Frag?"

"Shoot me in the back." Durango entered the cocktail lounge as if it were a warzone.

Maybe it was, Laredo thought, trailing behind the man.

---

Plaintive classic country music poured from the jukebox. Brazos Hawke twirled the straw in her soft drink and wondered how much longer she had to wait for the birthday present from her parents. She would return the gift and use the money to pay for law books.

She eyed her father. Tall, graying, and professionally handsome in his custom-tailored, three-piece suit, he seemed relaxed yet aristocratic. The quintessential chameleon, the perfect politician who said whatever his constituents wanted to hear, who never sullied his tongue with truth.

Only her father, Senator Floyd Hawke, better known as Tex to his thousands of adoring voters, would glad-hand his way around a loggers' bar. Her mother was well turned out in a navy-blue dress and a string of cultured pearls. No hint of silver touched Estelle Hawke's carefully dyed blond hair. Her lovely face didn't have a single wrinkle, compliments of a devoted plastic surgeon. Few believed she actually had five grown children.

Brazos stiffened when Elijah Roberts winked at her. The weasel who served as Tex Hawke's campaign manager and loyal dogsbody had dressed down to come to Pop's renovated barn of a bar and restaurant. She'd opted for jeans and a casual sweater too, but hers weren't as expensive as Eli's.

Of course, she had no doubts about who was more important to her father and who paid for Eli's attire. She'd bet her father wouldn't be shocked if he knew Eli had offered to pay for law school if she shared his bed. The surprise would come when Tex heard she'd turned down his long-time friend.

She counted herself lucky she hadn't ended up pregnant. Like her younger sister, she'd been sexually active forever, not that she'd had a choice as a child and young teen when her father traded her and her siblings for political favors. *No matter what my mother calls me, I am* not *a whore or a slut. I don't know how she has the nerve to say it when she knows what he does. If it'd been me, I'd have found a way to have an abortion. I'm not Amarillo. I'd never play the victim and keep the baby. No priest would have changed my mind.*

She glanced across the room, surprised when she spotted Laredo again in the crowd of loggers and small-town folks. Her younger brother had left earlier, outraged because their father had attempted to buy him a drink. Their parents' refusal to recognize Laredo's drug or alcohol addictions wasn't a shock, since admitting to them would play hell with their father's presidential hopes. So did the fact she was a lesbian. When Durango pushed their younger brother into rehab last summer and paid for it, Brazos had expected a skating party in Hades.

Her eyes widened when she recognized the tall man with Laredo. Durango looked like the giant-size version while Laredo was more the economy package. Both men had tawny gold hair, the color of honey. Durango's had more blond streaks. Even in the subdued lighting of the lounge, she saw his deep tan.

*Why did I have to wait for Heather to tell me how he earned his money? It makes total sense he's a mercenary for Uncle Quentin's company. Durango learned to shoot in the Marines, and he told me once he liked being a sniper. He's always alert, a hunter after prey.*

Durango nodded to their father, then bent to kiss the air somewhere in the vicinity of their mother's perfectly rouged cheek. "Hi, Mom. How are you?"

"For heaven's sake, be careful." Estelle Hawke leaned away, almost falling from her chair. "Bigger boys are always so clumsy. What are you doing here?"

"Watch it, Estelle." Elijah looked around the large room before sipping his beer. "Reporters are everywhere." He smiled with practiced courtesy at Durango. "How are you, son?"

"Careful, Eli." Durango's tone was dark and dangerous. "You don't want anyone to think we're related. That'd really screw up the campaign next year."

Brazos almost choked on her cola. Not just big, brawny, brave, and beautiful, she thought. He also had more brains than most men. If he wasn't one of a kind, she might have stayed straight. Then again, she'd never been drawn to men for affection, love, or sex.

She jumped to her feet and hugged him. Because their parents had major money, she couldn't get financial aid even when they refused to help fund her education. "You're the best. Thanks for the present. I thought it was amazing when you and Heather paid my tuition last year at law school. I never expected you to do it again or to raise the limit on the credit card you gave me. Heather said—"

"I'm sure the Empress told you what's what." Durango shrugged. "Do what she said, darlin'. I can afford it."

"What did she say?" Laredo demanded. "I've been dying to hear."

"For me to go shopping and buy decent clothes for my upcoming interviews at the top law firms in Liberty Valley this year so I get a good internship."

"He's not doing much for you." Contempt shone on Estelle's face, but she remained seated at the small table. "He has that trust fund from Grandfather Hawke. The old bandit made millions in oil and he didn't leave your father a cent. His older brothers stole your dad's inheritance."

"No, they didn't." Laredo stepped forward, his voice filled with sudden fury. "Uncle Ogden told me Grandpa Jackson disowned Dad nearly forty years ago because the old man didn't approve of him. Uncle Quentin was the one who talked Grandpa into leaving Dad's share to Durango. You're angry because he won't sign over his inheritance to you."

Estelle paled, but before she argued the point, Durango intervened. "I don't get the money for another year and a half until I'm thirty-five. Same conditions apply to the rest of you."

Brazos felt the words as if they were a blow and stared at the three people seated around the small table in the corner of the cocktail lounge. Her parents and Eli never told her she had an inheritance waiting in the wings from the wealthy side of the Hawke family.

She gazed up at her older brother. "All of us?"

"Damn straight." Durango studied her, concern in his gaze. "You mean you didn't call Uncle Quentin for help with college? Mom and Dad said they'd told you about your inheritance." He swung around to eye their parents, blocking Brazos in an obvious attempt to protect her. "You asked me not to tell the kids. You said you'd explain it to them. Why haven't you?"

Floyd and Estelle didn't answer. As usual, Elijah Roberts intervened. "It's uncertain. If something happens to your brothers and sisters, their inheritances revert to Quentin and the Hawke trust in Texas. It's why your uncle wants Waco listed as dead, not missing in action."

Rage darkened Durango's cobalt eyes. "Watch it, Roberts. Uncle Quentin raised me from the time I was six. Insult him again and I'll take you out."

"Leave him be." Brazos stepped to the side, standing next to her brother and rested a hand on his arm. "He isn't worth you doing a minute of jail time. I'll call Uncle Quentin and see if he'll lend me enough for my textbooks. I didn't want to put them on the credit card after everything you and Heather did for me."

"I'm sorry. I thought you knew. He'll step up if I can't. I should have told you before, not trusted them to do it."

Tears burned her eyes. Her older brother hadn't received his own inheritance yet. He undoubtedly didn't consider the money as his. If he had it, would he continue risking his life as a soldier for hire?

"It's not your fault. Mom and Dad should have told us. If they'd raised you instead of dumping you on Uncle Quentin's and Aunt Vicky's doorstep when Waco was born, you would have." Brazos kissed Durango's cheek. "You've always thought they were better than they are. They lie, but it's not your fault." She glanced at Laredo. "Did you know?"

"Not for sure. Uncle Ogden told me I had money coming when I was old enough to handle it, but he'd make sure I never saw one red cent of Hawke money to buy heroin."

*He doesn't sound the least bit resentful, but I am,* Brazos thought. *I'll make them pay for everything, all three of them.*

---

Tired of the potshots, Durango headed for the bar. He didn't know how his younger sister managed to snipe at their parents and remain untouched in the onslaught of emotional battering. He couldn't. It hurt worse than a gunshot wound when they rejected him. His father hadn't even spoken to him once tonight. If it weren't for Heather, he'd walk out the door right now.

"Whisky, Pop. What have you heard from her?"

"You know I can't tell you." The old man tending bar poured a shot and passed it to Durango. "She makes me promise whenever we talk. You know, boy, I got standards. Wasn't for the fact I like you, I'd throw out that lying snake, Tex."

Pop seemed to consider the idea for a moment longer, then added, "Along with that worthless Bible-thumper and your mother, who's no better than she should be. I can't stomach any of them. They make my skin crawl with all their hypocritical do-gooder crap."

"Last time you threw him out, Heather said my father had the county health department shut you down for a month." Durango tossed back the whisky and held out the glass for a refill. "I had to sleep alone until you reopened. She told me if you lost your liquor license for good, she'd castrate me in the middle of your parking lot and invite the town to watch. She says she always holds me accountable for what my family does because they don't take responsibility for anything, and I take it for everything."

"Always wondered why you got in the middle of the muck and why you hired George O'Connell to represent me." Pop chuckled before he eyed the group on the other side of the room speculatively. "I ain't had a vacation since then. How old is Laredo?"

"Turned nineteen in June. Still underage for the lounge." Durango accepted the glass Pop offered. "You might ask George to talk to Laredo. Bet he'd sign an affidavit that the old man and Elijah brought him here and offered him drinks. He's trying hard to stay clean and sober."

"I know." Pop grinned. "The boy has guts. I really do like you, Hawke. Not enough to tell you where to find Heather in Nashville, but I'll pay for the food and booze when you two finally get hitched."

"Thanks." The alcohol burned a path to his stomach. "She's as touchy as a teased rattler."

"You don't tease her?" Pop asked, his wrinkled face suddenly expressionless. "I've seen you two squabble like little kids. A body would think after the two of you went off to war time and again, you'd have better things to do than one-up each other."

The truth sliced into him worse than a knife. "I need her, Pop. She means more than anything or anyone in this whole, crazy world."

"I know how you feel." Pop's voice softened and he refilled Durango's glass. "Sometimes, love ain't enough. You tell her?"

"She knows." He stared into the depths of the golden drink. "She's always known. She still left me more than a year ago."

"You'd best say it until she hears you, boy. She thinks you care more for your parents than her. She called in to make sure your sibs had good birthdays, because she knows you're a busy man and your folks won't do anything for them."

"I heard. Heather knows she's everything to me."

"How?" Pop slid the bottle of whisky toward Durango. "You said you didn't tell her. It's hard for a man like you to share your feelings."

"What the hell does that mean?"

"What I said."

Durango waited. No more was forthcoming. Finally, he said, "Did she say if she was going to her folks in Hawaii?"

"They've been pushing for the two of you to stop dilly-dallying and get married. She's as riled with them as she is with you."

Durango nodded. When he called them, his future mother-in-law always ripped him up one side and down the other for not respecting Heather's dreams. It'd been a long trip home from Colombia, and he still wasn't there. His real home was with her, regardless of how angry she was with him. "What am I going to do without her, Pop? How am I supposed to live?"

Pity flickered across Pop's features before it landed in his dark eyes. "She must have told someone else, someone who can tell you. Talk to her friends, her family."

"What family? Her grandparents passed while we were in Afghanistan the last time. Fenn didn't come back from Colombia. She's not with Liz and Art. There's nobody else."

"Bull. Don't you remember anything, boy? The McElroys settled Baker City along with the Sweeneys, O'Learys, O'Connells, Garveys, O'Neills, and the O'Sullivans. Sure, my kin got here later than them, but she's still related to us too. Talk to the other folks who live here. She spent lots of time with Reverend Tommy before she left. He knows where all the bodies are buried around here, and some ain't even dead yet."

# CHAPTER THREE

*Lake Maynard, Washington ~ March 2016*

Durango sat in the Hawke Construction office and contemplated getting drunk. *What I ought to think about is facing the world sober,* he decided with newfound cynicism. He reached in the bottom drawer for the fifth of blended Canadian whisky. Putting the open bottle on top of the desk, he glared across the room at the huge portrait he'd hung on the opposite wall and uttered his usual toast after the last year and a half. "Damn you, Heather Marie McElroy."

What insanity prompted him to choose a frame to enlarge from that last roll of film? Why had he hung a poster-size photograph of the woman who still haunted him? In the picture, she leaned against the corral rail, the summer wind ruffling her coppery mane. High cheekbones, a pointed chin, and huge green eyes reminded him of an ancient queen issuing directives, a beautiful tyrant.

A sleeveless white blouse clung to her breasts and showed off a narrow waist before she'd tucked it into the faded, tight jeans that outlined curving hips and long legs, ending in lace-up riding boots. Wow, he missed her, missed her touch, her kiss, her smile—

The intercom buzzed. He turned his angry attention to it, flicking the switch. "What now, Tia?"

"Mr. Ransom is here for his interview." Patience filled his construction site manager's long-suffering voice. "Shall I send him in?"

"Did I have him on my calendar?" Durango hadn't scheduled any appointments for months. He left his business in the capable hands of his employees while he continued to hunt for Waco and Fenn in Colombia. Granted, it'd been five years since the two Army Rangers were captured by the cartel, but Durango wasn't ready to give up on either of them. He'd look until he had definitive proof they were gone.

"What are you doing?" he heard Tia squawk. "You can't go in there."

Durango reached for the razor-sharp K-bar knife he kept sheathed in his boot. Grasping the handle, he flipped it blade side up, ready for the intruder. The office door opened.

A tall, dark-haired man in a black suit limped into the room. Tia clutched at a muscled arm like a Christmas ornament, still trying to keep him out. He eyed Durango, then spoke in a deep, gravelly voice, permanently damaged from the torture he'd endured. "Tell her you're safe with me, Angel."

Durango winced at the nickname the other mercenaries had given him early on in his career. "Take off, Tia. Ransom's an old buddy from—"

"Where? You didn't say you knew him."

"Afghanistan," Durango lied. "It's been a while."

"Cute." Tia glowered at Ransom, then at Durango. She straightened to her full five feet. Plump and grandmotherly, she didn't look like she could take down or put up a building faster than any of the other construction foremen, but she could. "Wait until I finish with the pair of you, *Angel and the Badman*. You'll be sorry you messed with me."

"Don't you dare," Durango ordered. "I won't let you embarrass me."

"What will you do?" Tia glared at him, sky-blue eyes scornful. "Fire me? You'd have to stand up first. With as much as you drink, we'll have to scrape you off the floor."

"Tia, I'll never hear the end of it from the guys."

"You'll get him killed if you toss that name around." Jeff Ransom lounged into a chair facing the desk. "A lot of guys want the bounty on the Angel of Death. We could have a great funeral, but he wouldn't be here to annoy."

Tia's irritation slowly faded, replaced with concern. "Who is hunting you, Durango?"

"Nobody. Ransom exaggerates."

Tia turned to Ransom. "Are you?"

Jeff shook his head. "A mercenary always makes enemies. I know four governments who'd love to get their hands on Angel and kill him slowly. The US would just turn him over to one of them."

"Great." Tia stomped toward the door. "No wonder Heather left. It must have been like living in the shadow of the gallows." The door slammed shut.

"Wonderful." Durango returned the knife to its scabbard in his boot. He straightened, poured himself a drink. "Well, Ransom."

He deliberately dragged out the name, both knowing it was false. "What are you doing here? I told you to go home and forget me. How did you find me?"

"A slight problem came up." Ransom smiled, but the humor didn't touch his coal-black eyes. "My father's dead. So are my older brothers. My cousins and their business associates want the family enterprises. It's not worth dying to deal drugs, run prostitutes, do human trafficking."

"Especially since you were captured trying to end the drug trade. Why are you here, Ransom?"

"Can't you call me Jeff?"

"That your real name?"

"Close enough for government work." Ransom returned in the same tone. He appeared relaxed, but Durango wasn't fooled. "I'm expendable, Angel."

"Don't call me that. My name's Durango. What are you saying?"

"I want to go with you."

"Stand up. Take off your shirt."

"For Christ's sake, I'm not trapping you. Not after you saved me."

"Do it." Durango waited.

Ransom stood. He removed his jacket, unfastened the striped tie, unbuttoned the white shirt. He removed it. Scars ran across his chest to a missing nipple, and scars banded his wrists. When he turned, more scars covered his back. Slight amusement filled the harsh voice when he met Durango's gaze. "Want me to take off my pants?"

Durango considered the offer. He didn't see any wires or transmitters and decided to take the risk. "No, it's not necessary. All right. So, you're clean. Honest and sincere, but stupid."

Ransom drew on his shirt again, hid the former wounds from the prison camps, at least the physical ones. "Man, you're paranoid."

"Yeah, well, as Gunny used to say, coyotes eat rabbits and rabbits are paranoid too." Durango took a swallow of the whisky. "Want a drink?"

"You told me you only used booze to kill pain," Ransom commented. "You injured on your last trip?"

"Nope." Durango gestured to the photograph. "My nemesis."

Ransom glanced over his shoulder at the large picture. "Then you didn't send her to San Antone? I'd blocked out *how* I escaped since I needed to protect you and your crew. I checked myself into a veterans hospital. My new nurse told me how to find you."

"Really?" The information seemed to take forever to seep into his brain. "What hospital? Why did she send you to me?"

"Told me she was afraid someone might actually listen to my babbling." Ransom paused. "She said she was a visiting nurse, and she got that job to get to me. She's long gone by now. No reason to stay there after I left."

"Maybe so. Maybe no." Durango picked up the phone, dialed a long-distance number for Nighthawke Security. He was immediately put through to his cousin who had three years on him. He'd always been a hero to Durango when they were boys. "Bendigo, it's me. I need your help."

"You got it, boy." The lazy drawl comforted and reassured at the same time. "What can I do?"

"Heather was working at a VA hospital in San Antone." Durango hoped the desperation he felt wasn't revealed in his tone. "Will you check it out? Keep her there for me?"

"No problem. I'm on my way." There was a pause, then Bendigo continued. "I still have friends. Your name comes up and that's not good in times like these. Dad intends to set up a branch office in your neck of the woods and wants you to run it. Watch your back."

"My name?" Durango narrowed his gaze on Jeff Ransom, wondering who had listened to the injured warrior. "All I do is run the most honest construction company I can in Washington state. It's turning a profit and I've repaid the money I borrowed from Hawke Enterprises."

"Right," Bendigo grunted. "I don't want to hear you're in heaven before your time. Got it, boy?"

"Yes." That was all he needed, a warning from the cousin who'd left the CIA and now managed Nighthawke Security in Texas, providing mercenaries around the world. "But Heather?"

"I'm going." Bendigo chuckled. "You could find another woman. You're not that ugly."

"She'd skin me alive. I'd tell her it was all your fault."

"Then she'd skin *me*. She has spunk." Bendigo chuckled again. "Uncle Ogden frets about Laredo. He says the boy plans to marry that gal, Jassy Sweeney, this summer."

"She's good for him."

"Uncle Ogden says twenty is too young especially since Laredo hasn't been clean and sober for two years yet."

"Well, she hasn't told Laredo when the wedding will be yet."

"Uncle Ogden says Laredo needs a woman who will let him be a man and he has a lot of growing up to do. End it now, Durango. Otherwise, I'll saddle up and pay a visit. Create a hell of a stir."

"Okay." Durango's good humor fled. "I'll tell him it's a no-go. You find Heather."

"Only if you keep her from throwing another pot of spaghetti sauce at me."

"Figured you were supposed to be stoic, not whine and whimper." Laughing, Durango replaced the receiver. "My cousin will see if she's in Texas. How is she?"

Ransom glanced at the photo again. "Still beautiful. She has this 'damn your eyes' attitude when she orders the doctors and nurses around. When they talk back, she tells them the 'crap train has left the station' and she's not listening."

The office door flew open. A tiny, curvaceous woman with golden-brown hair stormed into the room. She whirled on Jeff Ransom. "I don't care what he told you. I do the hiring. We're full up."

Durango leaned back in the chair, propping his feet on the desk as he watched the former pilot gape at the young woman, just past girlhood. "Ransom, my sister, Amarillo."

"Amie. I've told you before I prefer that, Durango."

"I forgot," Durango answered, unrepentant. "I should call you 'Cyclone' anyway, little sister, because you move so quick."

"Don't patronize me. I won't stand for it."

"Want my chair?" Ransom asked. "Then we both could, while you sit down, *cara mia*."

Amarillo's deep chocolate brown eyes darkened with fury. "Get out!"

"Not in this lifetime, baby girl." Jeff winked at her. "Cute little thing, isn't she?" He glanced at Durango. "I see the resemblance. She'd fight bear with a stick too."

"And she'd win." Durango swung his feet off the desk and stood. "I'm proud of her." He started for the open door. "I'll let you two argue about it without me. I'm going hunting with Bendigo."

"What about him?" Amarillo pointed toward Jeff Ransom, bewildered. "What do I do with him?"

"Marry me," Jeff suggested. When she made a rude gesture, he smiled. "I can wait."

"Put him on the payroll, Amie." Durango glanced at his baffled younger sister. "She's in charge of the money, Ransom. She makes a dollar do the work of ten. Tia supervises the sites and the foremen, more than half of whom are gals. I need a company manager to keep everything and everyone off their backs. Don't let anyone condescend to them or disrespect them. Even in this day and age, some people like my father and his political cronies can't believe that I let women run the place."

"I'll handle it," Jeff said. "My family does construction work back East. I'll keep you and them from being fragged."

---

*Lake Maynard, Washington ~ May 5ʰ, 2016*

He studied the blueprints scattered across his desk. He had no idea how he'd bring this job in on time, much less for the price Amarillo quoted. He missed Heather. When she ran the construction company, he didn't have these problems. She insisted he figure the costs for upcoming projects.

The telephone rang and he glanced at his watch. Oh-two-hundred hours, two in the morning, civilian time. Who'd be calling now?

He picked up. "Hawke Construction."

"Hey, handsome. What's a good-looking guy like you doing alone in a place like that?"

The husky female voice mocked, teased, and tormented. His hand tightened, knuckles whitening. "Where are you, Heather Marie? Why are we playing this game?"

"You know the answers." Her low tones were still amused. "I come first or not at all. Are you worried, babe? Or have you replaced me?"

"Don't be ridiculous. No woman could replace you. I'll never look for one. Where are you? I'll come there."

"Not unless it's forever. I only called to see if you'd stopped looking for Waco. If you have, I'll take time off and fly to Washington tomorrow to help you pack, and you know how much I hate airplanes."

"I'll stop when I get him and Fenn home. Not before."

"Your parents still won't love or accept you. Give up, Durango. Nothing you do will make them change."

"Not in this lifetime, Heather Marie. Why did you call? It's been a year and—"

"Nine months," she interrupted.

"Eight months, three weeks, five days, ten hours, twelve minutes and forty-three seconds," he corrected. "But who's counting?"

"Just you." Her whisper was almost a sob. "And me."

"Each minute's an eternity. An hour lasts forever."

"Do you honestly mean that?" She sounded dazed by the prospect.

"Didn't you expect that, Empress? You belong to me even when you don't stick around where you should and don't provide system support for me."

"It's a two-way street, Hawke. You need to provide system support for me too. When you didn't follow me to Nashville, I figured you really didn't care, especially after I called you all those names in my last letter." She sighed. "I do love you, Durango. Will you ever tell me that?"

"When you deserve it. Now, cut the crap. Stop hassling me because I don't have a lot of time to chase after you when you're in a snit. I have to find my brother. People are depending on me. "

"Unfortunately, unless I'm happy on a shelf waiting for you to come home between your excursions, I'm not one of them. In that case, you don't *deserve* me." Her tone grew sharper. "I have choices too."

She knew him far too well. The cold tone was meant to cut him to the quick. It never had. Instead, it tended to turn him on. "Keep it up. This autocratic bullshit game will have to end sometime."

"Rot in hell, jarhead!"

He listened to the buzzing dial tone. He'd acted like the macho miscreant she always called him. He'd inherited the money his grandfather left him two months ago, but so far it hadn't helped him find his brother or her uncle.

Durango stood, went across the room to move the large photo. Behind it was the wall safe. The combination was her birthday. He hadn't changed it. He never would. No point to it. She was the only woman he'd ever have in his entire life. He'd known it since he was four years old and waited on her parents' porch for them to bring "his" baby home from the hospital.

Granted, Heather hadn't been that interesting as an infant, but she was fun to watch. When she started to sit up, life became more challenging.

When she started crawling, he chased after her. Things hadn't changed that much. She still threw tantrums, and he still went after her, trying to soothe hurt feelings, hers, and everyone else's. She depended on him. He adored her even if he didn't tell her.

He removed the stack of snotty notes he'd saved when she left. He opened the one he hadn't had the courage to read before, the one enclosed with her ring. "Durango, to train an arrogant, egotistical jackass, you have to get his attention. Do I have yours yet?" The rest of the page contained more insults regarding his intelligence, morals, courage, and sexual abilities.

The foolhardiness thrilled him. If she didn't care, she wouldn't fight him to this extreme. The letter was a red flag, one meant to lead him into the chase. He headed back to his desk, picked up the phone, pressed star-six-nine. A recorded voice announced his call couldn't be completed since she'd blocked his number.

Heather Marie McElroy was a brat, all right. His brat and Lord, she was smart!

---

*Lake Maynard, Washington ~ May 6th, 2017*

Despite all his attempts to be home the night before, he'd failed. The planes from South America didn't run on his convenience or hers. He strode across the office to his desk, picked up the phone, and called for messages.

Her voice was familiar, taunting and so damned sexy. "Happy birthday, lover."

In the background, he heard an old Tanya Tucker song. What was it? Oh yeah! "Love Me Like You Used To." One more smart-ass choice.

"Same day, next year," Heather mocked. "Sorry I missed you. I don't know how you manage to do recon, Angel. You can't find your butt with two hands and a roadmap. See ya! Wouldn't want to be ya!"

He grimaced when the song changed to the one she'd left on a CD for him. Why did she think he still needed a "Lesson in Leaving"? "It's not my birthday," he said aloud.

She knew it better than anyone. Why call on May 5th? What was going on? What was her game?

# CHAPTER FOUR

*Nashville, Tennessee ~ May 6$^{th}$, 2018*

*It's late. I had to work two extra hours, which I didn't expect, and traffic was bad, which I should have. Still, it's only 11:45 in Washington state. I have fifteen minutes before my deadline expires and I want to talk to him. I need to talk to him.*

Heather took a deep breath and pressed the numbers to the landline at his new home. Voice mail picked up, and she listened to his deep voice saying he wasn't available and to leave a message. The last words totally freaked her: "—Heather Marie, I've had it with your crap. Get back here!"

Why did his bass rumble excite her even when he acted like a macho jerk? She had to leave some response. "Forget it, jarhead. You can dream. It won't happen until you come here, and you haven't put me first yet."

She replaced the receiver. She longed to talk to him. Cursing herself as a weak-willed fool, she reached for the phone again and hesitated, and then decided to try the direct line to his office. If he wasn't home, he had to be at work.

"It's about time," a young female voice announced. "Where are you guys? Still on the job site in Oregon?"

"Who the hell is this?" Heather demanded. Had he dared to trade her in on some little chickee? *I'll geld him. He's mine.*

"Heather? It's me, Amie." A hastily caught breath, and then the younger woman lowered her voice. "What's wrong?"

"Easy, kid." Heather adopted the reassuring nurse's tone she used to soothe anxious patients. "Honey, I appreciate you so much. I only call your scumbag bro once a year on May 5th. It's a special day for us. He's so charming. I can't believe he hasn't caught on that you're my favorite spy."

"Why would he?" Amarillo sniffed. "I'm careful. I haven't said a word even when he worries you might be in trouble."

"What kind?"

"He's said more than once the Army might want you back. They can't take you, can they? If they try, call me. I'll come to Nashville and take care of your place."

"Not necessary, but I appreciate it. I finished my military obligation before I resigned my commission. If things change and my BFF Kate or I get orders, we'll let you know."

"All right. I owe you." Amarillo's tone was firm. "If you hadn't rescued me and Maria, they'd be after her by this time. Durango wouldn't help me escape from my parents. You believed everything I told you. You didn't say I was a lying sixteen-year-old hungry for drama."

"After as many combat tours as I've had, I know most men are pigs, except my dad and Durango. Sisters have to stick together. After all this time, we might as well be, even if I haven't married your brother yet."

"You're kinder to me than Brazos ever was. She's so busy being perfect. She never listens."

"She can't, honey. She'd have to admit it happened to her first."

Sudden heavy silence and Heather winced. She should have kept her opinion of Tex Hawke and his hangers-on to herself. Amarillo's folks should have protected her, not thrown a young teen to their sycophants.

"Child molesters are lower than dirt. Phone me whenever you need to and we'll talk," Heather said. "Tell Durango I love him. Wish him a happy birthday."

"It isn't his birthday."

"I know, but I didn't call him then." After a few more pleasantries, she hung up. "Hellfire! Damn him. Damn, damn, damn!"

She should have asked for his new cell phone number, but she'd been distracted by Amarillo's concern. Heather heaved a sigh. Now, she had to wait another year before she talked to him. She didn't know how much longer she could continue without him. Did he worry about the Marines coming after him? Why would he when he finished his time on active duty? He wouldn't be sent back to Afghanistan either.

Tears burned. She had too much pride to let them fall. "Sick, sorry, misbegotten—"

"More bad words," a childish treble announced from the doorway. "Is you super mad, Mommy?"

"No, sweetie." Heather spun around. Frustrated, irritated, and horny as hell. She hadn't graduated to anger yet. She smiled at the little girl in the flowered, flannel nightgown. Her baby looked like an angel, red curls tumbling to her waist. "Did you have a bad dream, honey?"

"No." A big sniff. "Henry got losted." Tears swam in the dark blue eyes, so much like her father's. "I fink the monster under the bed ate him all gone and Toney won't get out of bed and help me look."

"I see." Heather hurried across the room to scoop her daughter into a warm hug. "I'll kick that monster out of our house again and we'll find Henry."

The stuffed pinto pony was a cherished friend who traveled everywhere with the three-year-old. Heather made it before her daughters were born, but Ally was the one who named the creature. "I love you, precious."

"Me too." Ally snuggled close. "Will you tell me and Henry a story?"

"A short one." Heather carried the little girl down the hall. "It's time to sleep. Did you have a good birthday?"

"Yes, but we still don't got our *for-real* pony, Mommy."

Heather smiled against her daughter's hair. "And where shall we keep a *for-real* pony, sugar pie? It can't live in your room."

The question was considered the rest of the way to the bedroom. "Can we have a *for-real* pony someday, Mommy?"

"You bet. What if we go pony-riding on my next day off? It will have to do until we find you a *for-real* pony."

Ally nodded, a huge smile dawning. "We'll share and I won't boss Toney when it's her turn."

"Okay." Heather didn't doubt Ally's pure intentions, but the opportunity to order around her twin was too good to pass up most of the time. "Then it's a date. How will that be?"

"Good, and will you tell us about your favorite pony tonight? The berry one?"

"Of course, I will."

---

*Lake Maynard, Washington ~ April 2019*

Tires screeched. A cloud of dust boiled around the 1957 red Chevy pickup as it bounced up the rutted gravel drive. Heather reined the young horse she rode to a halt and stared at the truck. It stopped in a spray of rock. The driver threw open the door. He vaulted out of the rig.

*I'm not ready yet!*

He reached the wooden fence between the driveway and the pasture. "Heather Marie. Get over here!"

"Not in this life," she shouted. "I told you we're done, Hawke. Bigger is dumber."

The colt danced under her and she forced herself to relax, so he'd calm and stand quiet. She wished she'd worn something more glamorous than a skimpy T-shirt, faded blue jeans, and old western boots. *I didn't expect him to show up, even if his parents do live next door to mine.*

"What are you doing here, Hawke?"

He didn't answer. He scaled the fence and strode through the ankle-high spring grass, menace obvious in each step.

A chill trickled down her spine. She had choices. She could turn, gallop away. He wouldn't be able to outrun the horse. What good would running away do? She'd left him and he hadn't cared enough to follow her. Today meant nothing, she told herself.

Spring sunshine gleamed off his tawny hair, picking out flecks of silver among strands of gold. She remembered how thick it'd felt in her hands, the way it curled around her fingers. She took a deep breath, lifted her chin. "You're trespassing, Hawke."

"Really?" He strode to the right side of the chestnut. "Post a sign, Empress."

"Who'd read it to you?"

Before she evaded him, he grasped her right arm. He pulled her off the horse, toward him. With a strangled yelp, she grabbed a fistful of his denim shirt. She landed against him, but he didn't stagger or seem to notice. Large hands gripped her shoulders.

"You always had more guts than sense." His voice rumbled like thunder in her ears. He lowered his head. "*God*, I've missed you."

His lips claimed hers. She stood, shocked under the onslaught of his mouth. She could fight, respond, or pretend the kiss didn't matter. His lips roved over hers, conquering yet hungry. The kiss stirred too many memories. She'd dreamed about this for so long. The fierce pressure of his mouth demanded surrender.

Her hands shifted. She clung to his muscled arms. Dimly, she knew she had to escape, but she couldn't make her body obey the dictates of her mind. What would it take to destroy the connection between them?

When he deepened the kiss, she yielded. She needed him. His touch brought her back to life, returned her to the woman she'd once been. The sudden knowledge of the weakness jolted her to reality.

"No." She struggled free. "Never again, Hawke."

She flicked a glance toward the chestnut. The colt cropped grass a few feet away, unperturbed by the actions of the humans. She took a deep breath. She hoped she didn't appear as flustered on the outside as she did on the inside.

"Where do we go from here?" When he smiled down at her, she felt heat warm her cheeks. "Not there. When the horse dies, it's time to dismount."

"Sounds like you're having another fit and falling in it." He folded his arms. "What are you miffed about now?"

"Miffed? Are you serious?" She glared at him. "I'm a hell of a lot more than miffed, Hawke. How many years did I waste on you? I followed you to Iraq and Afghanistan, for Christ's sake."

"I told you to wait at home for me. I should have known you'd do the opposite."

"You're right. Next time some man tells me he'd rather join the Marines and go to war than marry me, I'll cut my losses. I won't pack for him and drive him to the airport. Been there, got the T-shirt for *Stupid Woman of the Year*."

"Watch it." He took an angry step forward. "Why did you stay away so long?"

"You worthless, misbegotten jarhead." She lifted her chin. "You were supposed to come after me, show me I mattered to you. I needed to know my dreams were important too, that you cared when I gave up everything for you and put my life on hold. What did you think I'd do when I finally learned I was just a hot piece of tail?"

"You know better." He touched her hair gently. "I looked for you whenever I could between missions. I didn't have a lot of free time. Life isn't like the movies."

"You're right." She glimpsed the confusion he hastily suppressed. "We had something cheap and superficial. Too bad I took 'lust in the dust' so seriously. I ought to have held out for a *real* man."

"Stop sniping. I'm not in the mood to put up with it."

She gestured toward the corral gate. "There's the exit. Don't let the gate hit you in the backside."

Emotion faded from his face, leaving it impassive. "Kicking doesn't get you anywhere unless you're a mule."

"You'd know."

She took a step back, determined not to lose her temper, regardless of how much he provoked her. She wasn't quite ready to ride away and leave him. He must have come from a job site. A light blue denim shirt stretched across his wide chest. Dark blue jeans looked new. So did the steel-toed construction boots. *God*, he looked good. She wanted to jump him, but didn't dare. Sex never had been one of their problems. Life was.

"Nothing to say?" He eyed her. "I'd think you'd have a lot of bitches after this much time."

"What's the use?" She opted for her most haughty voice. "Crying over the past is a waste of good tears. I made a mistake. I looked in the donkey corral for a good stud."

"Okay, that's it." He chuckled, snagged her hand, and pulled her against him. "Third time's the charm, Empress. I've told you not to use that imperious routine on me. This peasant gets uppity."

She shuddered when his arms tightened. One of his hands tangled in her waist-length hair. His fingers splayed on her lower back, pressed her into his rock-hard thighs. She tried to wrench free, failed.

"I can shut you up." He kissed the curve of her neck and shoulder. "All I've got to do is make love to you." He nipped at her ear. "Let's go to the barn. It won't be a first for us. I can't take you in this field in broad daylight. Somebody will call the cops."

"You're scum." She twisted and wriggled, trying to ignore the bulge in his jeans. "Let go of me. I won't sleep with you."

"Fine. You were gone too long. I won't let either of us sleep for two or three days."

"You son-of-a— I said no!" The rage increased when he deliberately mocked her with a shrug and her release. She wanted to knock the smirk off his face, but didn't dare. He'd view it as an invitation. She hated him almost as much as she'd loved him once. "Freaking Marine!"

Amusement lightened the navy eyes. "I'll pick you up for dinner. You can have a long talk while I have a long listen. Any luck at all, we'll make it to a bed, rather than the front seat of my truck."

"I'm busy." She stalked after the horse. "I plan to be busy the entire time I'm here visiting my parents."

"Come on, baby. Don't play hard to get. You want me."

"So what?" She moistened suddenly dry lips. "I've wanted you for the last four and a half years. I'm an adult. I can survive without you. Our affair's over, Durango Quentin Hawke."

"You love me. It's never been an affair, Heather Marie."

"If you cared, you'd have found me." She put up the reins, prepared to jump onto the colt's back. "Do you love me, Durango? Did you ever love me?"

"Don't push it. This hissy fit's gone way too far. I've never made a secret of what you mean to me. You're *my* woman."

"Really?" She rested one hand on the neck, the other on the withers, and belly-flopped onto the horse's back, deftly swinging her leg over until she sat upright. "Your woman? Like your truck? Your weapons? Your furniture? I'm a person, damn it. I want the words. Will you just say them once?"

"No, Heather." He stood like a statue, staring at her. "You won't make me crawl. You don't deserve the words after this stunt."

She caught her breath, determined not to cry. "If I'd stayed, supported your suicide missions, would you say them? Would you tell me you loved me?"

"Those words don't mean anything, and you won't get them from me."

She bit her lip, struggled to maintain control. "What if I had your baby? Would you say them then? To me? To our child?"

For an instant, his composure slipped. "Don't do that to yourself. We went through it twice before you left. Some couples aren't meant to have kids. It's not your fault we lost our babies. Stop hurting yourself with the memories, sweetheart."

She stared at him, remembering those two miscarriages. He'd been with her at the hospital. He hadn't said he loved her, even once. He hadn't held her when she cried over their loss. Thankfully, her mother had been with her and made the difference. Meanwhile, Durango walked out of the room and she'd learned to hide the pain from him since he couldn't handle that kind of emotion.

A sob rose in her throat. She trembled, blinked back the tears. "You win, Hawke. I'm not Sam-I-Am. I won't ask about green eggs and ham anymore."

"What are you talking about?"

"We're finished." She brushed a hand across her eyes. "I should have realized it years ago when you didn't come. You knew I'd gone to Nashville without you. You always knew even if you won't admit it. I thought you'd follow me, put me first for once. I was stupid. That's over."

"No self-preservation? You haven't shared much today. You will, believe me."

"Stuff it." She reached for the pendant he'd given her so many years before, the one she'd worn for eighteen years. She tried to jerk it free. She'd had to hock the gold chain twenty months before when the twins had the flu and she needed to pay for prescriptions.

The black plastic shoelace didn't break. She lifted off the necklace, flung it at him. "You win. Loving you was a complete waste of my life."

# CHAPTER FIVE

Liz McElroy muttered a string of cusswords, the kind she'd forbidden her daughter and the kids in her 4-H group to use. She scowled out the kitchen window above the new farmhouse sink. When she'd heard gravel crunch in the drive and seen her daughter and Durango's embrace, Liz figured a wedding was finally in the works.

"I should have known. Give those two pigheaded twits free choice and they blow it every time. I ought to have smacked their heads together to see if they'd grow brains."

She knew she wouldn't. Why couldn't the two of them see they belonged together? Her heart ached as she watched Durango stride toward the back porch. He wouldn't leave without visiting her. Of course, loyalty to Heather prevented him from criticizing the girl. He thought she walked on water. So why didn't he open his mouth and say it?

Liz knew he hadn't. Heather shared that much of their troubles. *Maybe it's my fault*, Liz thought. *I could have refused when he demanded secrecy about the way we met. He didn't want Heather's pity, didn't want her to see or know about the little boy I met shortly after Art and I moved into this house a few months after our wedding.*

She glowered out the window as he approached the back door. What would it take for him to realize he hadn't done anything wrong? He'd been such a cute little towhead when he was four years old. She'd spotted him as he grubbed for worms in her side yard that morning and thought he

41

might plan to go fishing, and wondered where to find the adult who should oversee him. She'd gone out to introduce herself.

He'd looked up at her with those huge, dark blue eyes that would ensnare a saint and offered a long, slimy brown treat. In the first trimester of her pregnancy with Heather, Liz refused. She struggled not to gag when he ate the worm with obvious hunger and rooted through the grass for another.

She'd taken him into the house, taught him to wash without dry-cleaning on her new towels, and proceeded to feed him bacon and eggs for breakfast. Lunch followed a few hours later. When he brought her a daffodil the next morning, a new tradition started between them. It didn't take her long to learn he lived next door with parents who were too busy to care for a young child.

The knock on the back door still startled her. She went to greet him. "Durango, what a nice surprise. It's good to see you." She hugged him. He towered over her now. "How have you been, honey?"

"I've survived, Dauntless Leader." He leaned down to kiss her cheek. "I saw Heather. When did she arrive?"

"Yesterday, in time for breakfast. I was flabbergasted. We haven't seen her since Father's Day of 2014." Liz stopped, afraid she'd given away too much information, then decided she hadn't. "She hasn't come to visit us at Christmas in four years. Art worries about her."

"Like you don't." Durango's tone was as soft as the hand he placed on her shoulder. "Did she stay in touch with you and Art?"

"Of course." Liz looked up to meet his gaze. "She knew better than to avoid me when she was angry with you. Phone calls, emails, and letters don't make up for her absence."

"I figured the two of you must know where she was." A muscle twitched in Durango's jaw. "I didn't want to make you choose between us, but I couldn't go to her."

"The choices you make today guide your tomorrows. I told you that when you were a boy, Durango, and that doesn't change when you're an adult. My daughter needs to know she is important, that she matters to you, and you're paying the price for not supporting her dreams."

Durango winced. "I have responsibilities here. Moving to Tennessee isn't do-able."

"Then suck it up, buttercup, and quit your sniveling when my daughter isn't in Washington state to hold your coat." Liz hugged him again, before she stepped away. "I worry about her. She doesn't sleep.

We talked for hours last night, but she refused to share anything important."

"She's probably fine. Don't fret too much. She claims life is too short to waste any of it in sleep."

"She doesn't eat," Liz told him. "She smokes. She finished off a fifth of vodka last night. She brought it with her and opened it when she arrived. It didn't faze her at all. That means she drinks too much. Why?"

"I don't know." Durango shrugged. "I'll talk to her. She'd never want you or Art upset."

"It's our job." Liz changed the subject. "Have you had lunch? Shall I make you a sandwich?"

"I didn't come to eat you out of house and home, Dauntless." Durango laughed. "I needed to check on Heather."

"You can do it while you eat." Liz patted his arm, then headed for the refrigerator. "Now, clear off the table for me. Don't touch Art's papers. He couldn't leave his project at the university one more day, or he'd have stayed home to visit with Heather. Put those dishes to soak. I need to wash my china before I put it in the hutch. Tell me what your sisters and Laredo have been doing. Your dad had some stiff competition last time. He barely got re-elected. What's the plan for 2022?"

"He's okay. Brazos is already helping his opponent plan the next campaign."

"Good heavens." Liz removed roast beef, mayonnaise, mustard, and sourdough bread from the various fridge shelves. "That girl has more brass than an old bedstead. Where does she get it? Your mother doesn't have the backbone of a jellyfish."

"Could be from you, Dauntless." Durango winked at her as he ferried the delicate coffee cups to the sink. "You've always stood up for your beliefs. Brazos said she didn't care for the old man's politics. It wasn't personal."

"Horsefeathers." Liz began spreading mayonnaise on the slices of bread. "Tell her to come and see me. I'll get the truth from her."

"I bet you will." Durango paused, then asked. "Did Heather come by herself?"

"Of course." Liz stacked slices of roast beef on the first sandwich. "She hasn't married and isn't seriously dating anyone. I asked. Her Majesty bit my head off for intruding in *her* life. I told her I was too old to quit now. If she'd spill her guts, I wouldn't have to interrogate her."

"You'd do it, anyway. You're a busybody."

"As if you're not here to pump the well."

Durango ran hot water into the sink. "You know me all too well, Liz. Is there anybody else at all?"

"She always had a ton of boyfriends when she was a girl. Things haven't changed even if she's almost thirty-four. She collects admirers as if they're stamps. Remember what I used to tell you?"

"There's safety in numbers."

Silence filled the room while Liz assembled two more sandwiches. She poured a tall glass of ice-cold milk, cut a slab of the chocolate cake Heather baked that morning for her father.

"Go wash up. Don't you dare dry—"

"I know. I know. Don't get dirt on your towels or you'll snatch me baldheaded." Whistling, Durango left the kitchen.

When he returned, Liz waited until he started to eat. "After lunch, you go out to the barn and patch things up with Heather. The two of you set a wedding date. Then you both come tell me. Got it?"

He picked up half a sandwich. "You know I'm willing."

"Is that the right answer, young man?"

"No, ma'am. How am I supposed to convince her?" He focused on the sandwich he was eating. When it was gone, he added, "She's mad at me."

"I love you, Durango." Liz poured a cup of coffee and sat down across from him. "Art does too. We know you'll do what's right."

"Or else."

"Are you being smart with me, young man?"

"No way."

"Very good. What are the rules when it comes to my daughter?"

"Heather's right, no matter what. You and Art are *her* folks. Whatever she wants, she gets."

"Right. And she loves you, so shape up. I want grandchildren to spoil. You and Heather grow up, get married, and give us a bunch. Got it?"

He looked dubious but nodded. "Whatever you say."

"Don't make me come with you and organize it," Liz told him. "If you let her marry someone else and ruin her life, I'll find the foulest, grossest job I can, and you'll do it for the next forty years."

She relaxed when she saw the smile he barely hid and rose to her feet. She left him to eat in peace while she packed a second lunch for him to take along. He used to steal dry dog food from the bag when he was small so he would always have something to eat. She'd insisted he stop because it was a heartache. In exchange, she sent another meal for him to eat later.

There had to be a special hell for people like his parents, who abused him in every way possible. She hadn't known how they could mistreat their own son and claim to be decent, honorable folks. She also hadn't understood how so many reporters were in and out of the house next door and never managed to print one word of the truth she saw.

Had he ever learned she was the one who helped arrange a new life with his uncle in Texas? Liz hoped not, but at the same time, she hoped so too. She didn't want him hurt. He'd suffered enough. When he was six, she couldn't stand it any longer. She kept her actions a secret, not even confiding in her husband. She made calls and found a woman who claimed to be Durango's aunt.

*Yes, I interfered in his life. It wasn't the first time, and it won't be the last. Someone must straighten out this boy and make him happy.*

***

Waco Hawke enjoyed hearing their retired 4-H leader harangue his older brother. The only thing better would have been if they could see him snickering at the two of them. Of course, Liz McElroy would have seized the chance to bitch about his manners or lack of them, but he'd never been one of her favorite people, not like the other Hawke kids.

She'd go to hell and back for the rest of the clan, but only allowed him in the club because of the emotional blackmail Eli Roberts exerted. If she hadn't agreed to let Waco join his brothers and sisters, the longtime campaign manager would have pulled them out of the youth organization.

Liz would do anything for his sibs. She loved the three younger kids, bought them presents, fed them, clothed them, and gave them everything their parents denied them. She always made time for Durango when he visited during the summers. She was a smart woman, so why didn't she see that being Tex and Estelle's favored chick hadn't been a walk in the park? He'd suffered his own brand of torture long before this eight-year imprisonment in Colombia while the cartel waited for a ransom his father wouldn't pay.

Waco floated into the living room and spotted the flat-screen TV. Had he arrived in time to watch the news? He glanced at the remote and turned on his favorite cable news station. A lovely woman with glorious ash-blond hair stared at him as if she knew he was there, listening to her read the latest headlines off a teleprompter. He settled into the recliner, determined to remain as long as possible. Now, if he only had a six-pack of beer, and a pizza, life would be perfect.

―――――――――

A half hour later, Durango strolled out to the four-stall barn. He spotted the one Heather used for the chestnut, the only stall with shavings on the floor and hay in the manger. More proof she was real, and she was home. Relief swept through him again. He wouldn't tell her that he'd called the Red Cross several times to make sure she wasn't in Afghanistan or Iraq, hadn't volunteered for a medical organization, or returned to the Army when Nighthawke Security lost track of her in Tennessee. Because of the demands on his time between hunting for Waco and managing the construction company, he hadn't joined her there, but it didn't mean he hadn't known where she was.

Of course, he couldn't share that! She didn't have a need to know she made him vulnerable. He heard footsteps, swung to watch her enter the barn. He knew when she noticed him. She tensed, wariness in her face.

"Why are you still here?" She held the bridle in one hand. She must have turned the horse loose in the field. "I thought you'd left. What do you want?"

"The same thing I've always wanted. You, baby. Just you and a home here."

"Am I supposed to believe that charm?" She shook back her hair, headed for the tackroom. "Do I have 'Stupid' tattooed on my forehead?"

"No. Try spoiled, haughty, and manipulative. Amazes me it all fits, Empress."

"Really?" She stopped, glowered up at him. "You're not the most stubborn man alive?"

Dark circles under her eyes and the pale features revealed exhaustion. The sight eased his irritation. "I'm obstinate."

"Got that right." She lifted her chin. "You're still hunting for him, aren't you? Mom said there was an O'Leary in Baker City again. Have you asked her to intervene?"

"I know her, but I don't need her."

"Cut the killer stare." She gestured to the empty barn. "Don't play dumb with me. I haven't betrayed you and I won't. Why haven't you talked to the O'Leary about them?"

"Why would I when they're not dead? I just haven't found them yet." He advanced on her. "I've always trusted you."

"Save the charm." Fists planted on hips, she glared at him. "Don't try to placate me, Hawke. I'm the one who patched you up when you got injured on a mission. I went after my dreams and you always knew where I was. I didn't stop loving you."

After everything he'd learned as a kid about what his parents and their political cronies called "love," he didn't have the words to tell her how much she meant to him. "Let's get married."

"Why? So, I can't testify against you when you're caught?"

"Damn it, Heather Marie." He ran a hand through his hair, frustrated. "I don't know how to talk to you. I've wanted to marry you since I was a kid. I planned it from the first day I saw you, wrapped in a blanket in Liz's arms. Sure, you were her and Art's baby, but you were mine too."

She stood silent for one long moment. "You've forgotten what we said about *wanting* in the Army, Marine. *Want in one hand, defecate in the other and see which fills up first!* I won't marry you until I can have you twenty-four/seven, but I won't tell the cops what you're doing either, Angel."

He shook his head, amazed at the insistence. She had to be the most beautiful woman in the world. Add her courage and her loyalty, and she rated even higher. She never settled for less. "You're someone special, Heather Marie McElroy."

"Too damned good for you, Durango Quentin Hawke. I won't take you back unless I come first."

"Don't you know there could never be any woman but you?"

"I hate it when you play the *bigger is dumber* game." She sighed. "You won't cheat on me any more than I'd cheat on you. I'm not talking about that. You're breaking so many laws in South America when you look for Waco and Fenn. The drug lords and governments will kill you if they find you down there, Durango."

"For God's sake, I'm careful, baby."

"Sure, you are. It's why you return with bullet holes and knife wounds." She shook her head. "How gullible do you think I am?"

He chose not to answer. "Now, sweetheart."

"Save the charm, you fool. What do you expect me to do when you're arrested? I was a freaking nurse in the Army." She took an angry step forward. "I'm not a combat expert. I barely hit the broad side of a barn when I use a weapon. How am I supposed to rescue your sorry ass?"

He bit back an appreciative grin, changed his chuckle to a cough. Trust *his* woman to think like that. "You're wonderful."

"I know. I'm glad you realize it at long last."

"I've always known." He strode to her, pulled her into his arms, and held her tight. "You stay home and wait. Anybody asks anything, you play dumb."

"No way. Acting stupid degrades me."

"All right. Freeze the commoners with one of those regal looks, Empress." He kissed her forehead. "You're something, my pretty little tyrant. No other woman would put up with me for a heartbeat."

"I can't either." She leaned against him. "Our war ends while I'm here or I fly home Saturday. I've already booked my flight."

"What if I never let you go?" He tightened his hold. "You're mine."

"It doesn't mean you'll stop riding rainbows, cowboy."

The reference to a classic Tanya Tucker song made the hairs rise on the back of his neck. A new suspicion filtered into his mind. "Before you walk out on me again, explain May 5th."

"What?" Heather pulled back to eye him warily. "I don't know what you're talking about."

"May 5th," he repeated. "What's the significance? You called every single one while you were gone. Why? It's not my birthday or yours. We didn't choose the date for our wedding. Neither of us started or ended a combat tour then."

"What a brilliant detective." She shook her head, copper mane rippling for an instant. "I won't tell you and I'm not apologizing for my choices either."

It had to be bad if she brought up the possibility of seeking forgiveness. He framed her face with his hands, tipped up the arrogant chin so their gazes met and clashed. "Oh, you'll beg my pardon if I think it's necessary. Now, tell the truth. We partied on Cinco de Mayo, but that was it. What happened on May 5th? Why is it important?"

# CHAPTER SIX

She abhorred the way he sounded so calm, so reasonable, so damned patient. It'd serve him right if she told him why she called, but she wouldn't. She watched comprehension dawn in his dark blue eyes, the same color as their daughters'.

"You called," he said slowly as he obviously put two and two together, "on my child's birthday. Right? Why keep the baby a secret? I'd have been there for him."

"You freaking jarhead!" She yanked free. "If you only came because of the baby, why should I waste any more time on you?" She hurled the words at him, pain and fury combined. "Will it make a difference? Will you stay home to be a full-time father?"

"I can't." A pause while he stared into the distance. "Damn you, Heather Marie."

"Oh, sure." She shoved past him. "That's really fair. Blame me because your stupid brother got taken prisoner. Blame me because your parents love him more than they love you. I must protect my baby. You're too busy to be a dad." She headed for the barn door. "You've certainly shown that over the past four and a half years."

"Tell me about him. What does he look like? What color eyes? Hair? Favorite toy? Food?"

The questions stopped her, and she spun to face him. "You don't have a son, Hawke. You never did. You fired blanks."

Awe mingled with a new gentleness in his eyes. "A daughter?" He began to smile. "A little girl? Is she like you? A princess?"

"You have nothing." Heather sniffed and opened the door. "You've got a trip to Colombia, remember? I have twin girls. I came second in your life long enough. They never will."

Before he answered, she stormed from the stable. Halfway to the house, she spotted his younger brother, Laredo, wearing typical western gear down to the cowboy boots. "What are you doing here? Don't you Hawkes remember you have a home next door?"

"It's great to see you too." Laredo laughed and grabbed her in a quick hug. "I bet you've been chewing Durango's ears. Where is he?"

"In the barn." Heather took a ragged breath. "How are you?"

"Still clean and sober," Laredo reported with pride. "I'm apprenticing with Zeke Knight and started building my own shoeing book. Hey, why did it take you so long to get here? I figured you'd be on George O'Connell's doorstep once you had word you inherited the McElroy spread."

"What?" She looked down to meet the small, wiry man's gaze. "Grandpa left it to Fenn."

"Yes, but he had to claim it by 2016. The trust ran out and Durango caught up the back taxes for you. He's been living there since last summer."

"He didn't say a word about the ranch." Rage began to smolder. "George O'Connell didn't do a thing to find me. Some trustee."

"He ran ads in all the Washington state papers." Laredo pushed back his Stetson with a thumb. "I told him he'd do better to place personals in the country music magazines or advertise in the Nashville papers, but he wouldn't listen to me. Guess I haven't lived down my wild past as a drunk and a druggie."

"It's not your fault, Laredo. It's me. George hates my guts. He thinks I treat Durango like dirt."

"For a lawyer, George runs short on brains." Laredo winked at her. "If it was me, I'd tell our Dauntless Leader and your dad about the McElroy place."

"Of course, I will, but I'm going to the O'Connell law office in Baker City right now." Heather took two steps toward the house, then froze. "Wait a second. Mom will tear off George's ears, cook them in one of her special sauces, and serve them to him. You're a nasty, mean, little bugger, Laredo. I like that."

"I learned from the best, sis." He patted her shoulder. "Get someone for backup. You need a witness. Want me to call Zeke and rearrange our shoeing schedule for the afternoon?"

"No way I'm messing with either of your agendas. Good shoers are hard to find." Heather hugged Laredo quickly. "I have an old friend who will jump at the opportunity to help make Durango jealous as hell."

"Can't do better than that." Laredo sauntered in the direction of the barn, calling, "I'll keep him company for a while before I visit Dauntless and have lunch."

"Thanks, I owe you."

"Not hardly. It's the other way around."

---

Heather studied the cards in her hand. *I have three queens and I'm not going down without a fight.* She glanced across the kitchen table at her parents. Dad could be bluffing, but she wasn't sure about her mother, the family cardsharp.

"I'll raise." Heather tossed in two pinto beans. At a taunting look from her mother, she threw in a third.

"Too rich for my blood." Art McElroy dropped his cards face down on the table. "I'm out. It's after one in the morning. What are you two trying to prove?"

"I want answers," Liz said. "Your daughter's too proud to talk about her problems, much less admit she has any."

Art flinched. "Couldn't you tell your mom what she wants to hear, Rusty?"

"I've tried, Dad." Heather wrinkled her nose at the childish nickname her uncle had given her years ago, but didn't criticize it. "She's the one who wants truth."

Art ran a hand through silvered red hair. "Liz?"

"I want to know why she's so thin. She needs to put on at least twenty pounds. She's too tense, too defensive, and far too worried. If she were a horse, I'd lock her in a stall, so she'd be forced to rest, eat, and stop living on her nerves." Liz narrowed hazel eyes. "Why did you swear me to secrecy about where you lived in Nashville? Why did you tell me not to give your address to Durango? Shall I continue?"

"Do what you want, Mother. You will anyway."

"I need a beer." Art pushed back from the table, stood, and went to the refrigerator. "Rusty, what's the story with you and Durango? Have you finished making the poor boy jump through hoops?"

"Damn it! Will you quit choosing him over me?" Heather caught her breath. How had that opinion escaped? "I'm sorry. He pissed me off today."

"Any particular reason? Did he fail to scrape and bow? Or was he breathing again? Sometimes it doesn't take much to enrage you." Art crossed to the window that overlooked the driveway. "Better come to a decision, Rusty. He's here."

"Try to remember your manners this time," Liz said. "You're too old to expect people to put up with your hissy fits. I don't want to be embarrassed tonight, not like I was this afternoon. You left with Mr. Ransom and I had to explain to Durango where you'd gone. You're not a teenager anymore and it wasn't a cute stunt, then."

"Yeah, right." Heather lifted her chin. "You could have kept your mouth shut, Mom. Durango called Jeff on his cell phone to give him the curfew speech and tell him what time I had to be home. It almost ruined a lovely afternoon."

Art choked on the beer. "Oh, I'm sure you found a way to pay Durango back for what you considered his arrogance."

"Definitely." Heather opted for her sweetest tone. "He'll be fighting with George very soon."

"Heather, that's unfair." Liz frowned. "I wanted to discuss George's irresponsible behavior with him. He should have contacted your father and me when you inherited the McElroy farm. He had our address and phone numbers. He didn't do the right thing. He knows better after ten years in our 4-H club. We taught morality and he should have learned it."

"You can still chew his ears, Mom. George called me a slut. He said I couldn't be without a man for nearly five years since Durango and I have such a love-hate thing." Heather left out the part where the attorney asked *who* fathered her children. It was her fault. Excitement over owning the ranch she'd always loved caused her to mention the twins.

She knew better. She'd intended to tell their father first before she let out the news to everyone else. Well, technically, she supposed she had, although he was the one who'd figured it out today when he confronted her about the phone calls on May 5$^{th}$. "Durango can deal with his best buddy in Baker City."

"He'd better." Controlled rage flickered in Art's fierce gaze. "If it weren't so late, I'd call Dick and discuss his son's manners with him. I'll go see George in the morning."

"Now, Art." Liz struggled to regain her calm. "We decided to retire from the 4-H club after most of the kids were grown. They're adults. Let's give Durango a day to sort out this mess before we handle it."

"I'd still like to kick George O'Connell's butt," Art grumbled. "All right. I'll let the kids settle their squabbles."

"For twenty-four hours." Their concern touched Heather, although she couldn't make herself admit it.

"We worry about you, honey." Liz leaned across the table to pat Heather's hand. "You're so prone to fits and starts. Durango is a good, steady man. He'll keep you centered. You need to marry him."

"For *God's* sake, Mother!" Heather leaped to her feet, threw down the cards. "Stop comparing me to a horse!"

She went to the liquor cabinet, took out a fifth of vodka. She grabbed a water glass from the dish rack next to the sink. She filled the tumbler halfway with alcohol. She took a swallow.

The vodka warmed her. It eased the lump in her throat, made it possible to breathe again. She wouldn't cry. The booze never judged, never found her wanting.

Now she could sip it. She wished she had a cigarette, but she had smoked the last one shortly after dinner. She loved her parents. She really did. So, why did they make her crazy? She hadn't wanted to listen to more of their nagging about how wonderful Durango was so she'd kept the twins a secret from them. It'd undoubtedly come back and bite her in the butt.

A light tap sounded on the back door. Durango sauntered into the kitchen without waiting for an invitation. He acted as if he were a member of the family.

She drank more of the liquor. It provided an illusion of control, something she desperately needed now. She swept a scathing glance over him.

He'd dressed up to come here. Black jeans, a black western shirt, and a black denim vest made him appear like a midnight cowboy or the *Angel of Death*, the other mercenaries called him. His battered black boots didn't do a thing for the ensemble, but showed he chose comfort over style.

"What's the occasion?" Heather eyed him over the glass she held. "Who died, Angel?"

"Nobody yet." His tone held a warning. He shook hands with Art, went to kiss Liz's cheek. Spotting the cards on the table, Durango added, "Poker, huh? Give it up, Empress. You can't win against Dauntless. You may as well strip your soul and confess all your sins."

"Want to take a turn, Angel?" Heather waved to the cards she'd tossed on the table. "We open on guts, play for truth. Enliven the game, why don't you? Let the folks know where you go, what you do, and why I really left."

Durango crossed to her, cupped her elbow, and guided her to the back door. "I prefer privacy when you snarl at me."

"What makes you think I care what you like?" Heather saw the embarrassment on her mother's features and surrendered. "Why not? We fight better without an audience, anyway."

On the porch, he closed the door behind them. She looked up at him. "What's the matter? Don't you want me to do some oversharing, Angel?"

"You're an evil woman." He bent, touched her lips in a soft kiss. "When you get nasty, I get hot. Baker City is a half hour away, but we can go to a motel here in Lake Maynard."

"In your dreams." She shuddered when he slipped a hand around her neck, tangled his fingers in her hair. "I don't want you touching me."

"Liar." He removed the glass of vodka from her hand, poured the rest of the alcohol on the grass, put the glass on the porch rail and turned to loom over her. "Stop threatening me. One more bitchy word and I'll carry you out of here. It won't be the first time. Your folks will be glad to see us reconcile."

She shoved at his wide chest. "All right, you win, Angel. Whatever you say."

"Right." He chuckled, lowered his head, and his mouth claimed hers.

She ordered herself not to respond, but she couldn't avoid it. She laced her arms around his neck, let her lips part beneath the pressure of his.

When his tongue began to explore her mouth, she remembered she wanted to keep her distance. She tried to bite him. Her teeth grazed his tongue, and she tasted blood before he lifted his head. "Keep your hands off me."

"Are you through sniping at me?"

"Yes. God, I hate you." She pulled free, fully aware he released her. She stomped back into the kitchen. She longed to swear at him when he followed. However, she didn't want to hear another of her mother's lectures. "You freaking Marine."

He grinned down at her, putting the empty glass in the sink. "Behave."

She ignored the command. Who did he think he was? She despised the amusement she saw in his eyes. "Leave me alone."

"In a minute." He reached in his shirt pocket, drew out a jewelry case, and opened it. "Come here."

"No." The gold cloverleaf glinted up at her, newly strung on a thick gold chain. "I don't want it."

"It's always been yours." He put it around her neck, fastened it. "You threw it at me for the last time today."

"Bull." She trembled at the feel of his calloused fingers on her skin. The chain was shorter than the previous one. The 4-H emblem rested in the hollow of her throat. "I'll pawn this chain for major bucks like I did the last one."

"Heather Marie!" Liz gasped in shock. "How could you sell a gift Durango gave you? It's scandalous. I raised you better. If you don't like a present, return it. When you end a relationship, you always offer to give back the jewelry."

"It's okay, Liz. She had a good reason to sell the chain." Durango feathered his thumb along the line of Heather's jaw. "Or two. Besides, we're not finished unless one of us stops breathing."

"I'll do it again," Heather warned him.

"I know." He smiled, mischief in the dark blue eyes. "This time I had the clasp fixed so it won't open. The chain's shorter. You'll have to cut it to remove it and it will lose value. If you need money, call me or Amie and we'll send it."

"That's not necessary, Durango." Art rubbed his jaw as he studied the two of them. "If Heather needs help, she can always call me or her mom."

"Except Heather has too much pride to ask either of you for it. She'd die first." Durango reached in his vest, pulled out several folded bills.

Heather spotted the number on the top one. It was a hundred-dollar bill, and there had to be at least a dozen or more in his hand. Did he think he could buy her? "Forget it. I don't need anything of yours."

"I didn't ask." He put his arm around her waist, tucked the money in the back pocket of her jeans. "You've already got three things that are mine, whether you admit it or not."

"You son of a—" She stopped, unwilling to hear more censure from her parents. She yanked out of his hold, grabbed her purse off the counter. "I'm out of smokes and here too."

"Are you coming back?" Liz pushed away from the table and stood. "Or are you running off for another five years?"

"In the morning, Mother." Heather waited until she'd opened the door and was on the back porch. She glanced over her shoulder. "I won't pay extra to change my flight home. I need the bucks the Wallaces are paying me to train Flash. It's not as if your perfect, wonderful Durango Hawke coughs up any child support."

"What?" Art started toward her. "Heather Marie, wait right there."

"I told you I wanted the truth." Liz hastily crossed the room to stand between the men and the back door. "I knew she had a good reason to constantly be on her cell phone calling or texting her best friend in Tennessee. Your daughter never even called Durango that often before she left him."

Heather glanced past her mother to meet Durango's furious gaze before bolting to the rental car. "Payback's hell, jarhead. Enjoy it. I will!"

# CHAPTER SEVEN

Durango sat in his office at Hawke Construction. He'd given up heavy drinking when he finally learned his troubles swam better than they drowned. He hoped Heather would come to the same conclusion soon. He stared at the huge photo across from his desk. The picture taunted him as much as the woman herself. "Damn you, Empress."

What made him think their problems would end if she came home? It cut to the quick when he listened to Liz and Art chastise him. He'd tried for two hours to convince them he didn't know Heather was pregnant when she walked out on him. Yes, he knew where she lived in Tennessee but he couldn't go after her. While he didn't share what he did for Nighthawke Security, he did tell them he had to put those jobs first. He had to find his brother.

The lectures only ended when the cat walked on the remote, turning on the TV in the living room, and a cable news show started. Grateful for the distraction, he'd escaped from the house.

Heather barely shared anything about their daughters. They were twins, born on May 5th, and they'd be four years old next week. Did they play with dolls? Did they like animals? What did they want for their birthday? So many questions and no answers. If he went to see her, would Heather tell him more?

Could he live without her? The idea tempted him. Life with her was as close to hell as he wanted to get and a heartbeat away from heaven. He remembered Ransom telling him more than once that courage had boiled down to mere survival when he was captured. It was what Durango decided to do now. He'd hang on.

Sooner or later, he'd go to her. He knew it. However, he'd delay the heartbreak a while longer. He hadn't expected this when he opted to look for his brother rather than follow her to Nashville. Why did she think he deserved to be treated like scum by her parents? She knew how close he was to them. Of course, they never would have kept his kids from him. If they'd known about the twins, they'd have told him, so it stood to reason that they didn't.

---

Jeff Ransom eyed the closed door, then glanced at the young secretary again. "He busy, Laurie?"

She frowned, light blue eyes concerned as she filed a broken nail. "He said to leave him alone. If anybody wants anything, I'm supposed to transfer the call to you, but this is the first time I've seen you today. When your voicemail was full, I referred everything else to Amarillo."

"Fine. Write a memo to that effect, detailing the business you sent to her. Copy those files and forward them to Tia so she can add the new projects to the schedule." Without waiting for a response, Jeff tapped on the office door and entered.

"What do you want, Ransom? Company falling apart? Did Denver call from Nighthawke Security with a crisis?" Durango scowled from behind the bare desk. "Get out."

"Make me." Jeff limped to one of the visitor chairs and sat down, slouching comfortably while he straightened the pleats in his black slacks. He switched to the Spanish the two of them used most of the time. "You got trouble, boss. What do you want me to do, Angel?"

"About what?"

"*La Capitana*." Jeff waited until Durango recognized the reference to Heather. "She showed up at my door early this morning and I cooked her supper. She stayed and made me breakfast and we talked until lunch."

Durango's jaw tightened, and he clenched one fist. "She sleep on your couch?"

"No. In my bed and I slept on the couch." Jeff leaned back in the chair. The action pulled up a jacket sleeve, revealing a scarred wrist. "You saved my life when you broke me out of that prison, Angel. She saved my soul when she sent me to you."

"So you've said before."

"She wants me to marry her and raise your kids." Jeff watched the other man stiffen, death in the cobalt eyes. "I didn't refuse. Figured it'd be better if she thought I was agreeable. It'd keep her from finding someone else. You've got to do something, boss."

"Really?" Durango leaned forward, the threat imminent. "I could kill you. Make her a widow before she's your wife."

Jeff controlled the impulse to laugh. As a prisoner, he'd learned truth was always the first casualty and he didn't have a problem lying to get what he wanted. Durango needed to sort out his differences with the captain. "My life is yours, Angel. Take it if you want. First, promise to look after Amarillo and Maria for me."

"Have you been messing with my sister?"

"My intentions are purely honorable, *jefe*. I love your sister. I want to marry her and adopt Maria. Could you please take care of *La Capitana* for me?"

"You'll be lucky if I don't castrate you, but it'd be too little, too late." Durango pointed to the office door. "Leave before I forget you're my best friend. Next time I see Amarillo, she'd better be treating you like you walk on water."

"Might be a problem. She saw *La Capitana* kiss me."

"You're the one who fixes things here at Hawke Construction and at Nighthawke Security. Go fix this," Durango ordered. "I'll take care of Heather."

"*Muchas gracias*, Angel." Jeff rose and then sauntered toward the door and the reception area.

Now, Jeff would go to the accounting department and hassle Amarillo. Having her older brother in her face would make up for the short paychecks in the past two months. She'd been trying to send him running ever since he arrived in Washington state. Despite the rotten stunts, he didn't plan on going anywhere.

He really did intend to marry the little varmint. She hadn't agreed to even date him yet, but he'd keep after her. He couldn't take no for an answer. Like her brother, she was lethal, and she made Jeff feel safe in an extremely dangerous world. First, he had to arrange Durango's happiness.

*I owe the Angel of Death that! I don't have any limitations. It's how I make everything run smoothly here, but Durango doesn't need to know. He has more integrity than anyone else around. I don't. I buried mine along with my pride and morality during the five years the cartel held me.*

Silently, Jeff admitted he admired Durango. The man refused to lie. He'd rather lose the woman he loved than admit to a convenient subterfuge of agreeing to give up the hunt for his brother, then pretending to leave on a business trip when he went to South America. Pure foolishness.

Luckily, Angel had Jeff to smooth the trail.

Whistling, he limped toward the elevator and Amarillo. She was his future, even if she didn't know it yet. Of course, once he shared the story he'd told her older brother, she'd probably come after him with that combat knife he'd taught her to use a few years ago. It'd brighten up the afternoon.

---

Using her seat and legs, Heather urged the colt forward. He minced one step, then another as if he walked on raw eggs. He flicked his ears, and she felt him tense underneath her. She wondered if he'd rear, buck, or crowhop, but it hadn't been his style when she rode him for hours yesterday.

He spooked frequently whenever he saw something that startled him, newspapers, the UPS truck making deliveries, vehicles on the road or in the driveway, birds, rabbits, the wind blowing tree branches, puffs of cottonwood blossoms, and even the family cat when she stalked moles. Heather sighed. She had today and tomorrow to finish training him so his teenage owner could successfully ride him.

*Then, I'll be on the first plane to Nashville. Durango Hawke can rot in hell or Colombia.*

She didn't know what angered her more, his presence or his absence. He'd avoided her since Tuesday night—okay, it'd been early Wednesday morning, and it was Thursday now. She'd be flying out Saturday afternoon and they still hadn't settled anything. What was she going to do?

And how was she going to work things out with her parents? They were totally disappointed in her for not sharing the news of the twins with them and they took turns lecturing her. How could she say she didn't trust them not to put Durango first? Oh sure, her mother claimed that Heather was her favorite, but –

Flash took advantage of her distraction. He leaped sideways, then galloped toward the fence. Heather dropped deeper in the saddle, sitting back further on her butt. She slid her left fist down the reins. She reached with her right hand, caught that rein, and pulled the horse's head around toward her right knee. At the same time, she applied pressure with her right leg, so he ended up disengaging his hindquarters and coming to a halt.

It wasn't the first time she'd forced him to cross his hind legs when he was in motion so he couldn't run, or rear, or buck. However, he didn't seem to learn the lesson she was teaching. He kept trying to bolt with her. She loosened fractionally on the reins and sent him forward again.

Three steps and he repeated the stunt. She did the same thing, bringing him to a halt. He knew better, but since he'd irritated her, this time, she brought his nose closer to her leg. Instead of signaling him to walk around the ring, she spun him in a tight circle to the right. Then, she switched to holding the reins in her right fist and yarded him around to the left.

When he wanted to walk, she didn't let him. Spin left, spin right, spin left, spin right. Finally, he lowered his head a little and began to lick and chew on the bit. She accepted the victory and eased her grip. They started around the ring again, Flash almost stomping his hooves. She might have won the battle, but he wasn't happy about surrendering.

Tires crunched on the gravel and she glanced quickly at the driveway. She didn't know who drove the brown Ford pickup in the lead, but she recognized Durango's classic truck behind it. It was about time. Of course, she wouldn't say so. She returned her attention to the chestnut gelding.

Another circle and Flash plunged ahead. This time, Heather did what she considered a hard stop. She slid her left fist down the reins, pulling all the slack out with her right hand. She yanked as fiercely as she could, putting so much pressure on his mouth that Flash halted and then backed five steps. This time, she booted him in the ribs and sent him around the corral at a fast trot. Another kick and he shifted into a gallop. She let him run two laps before she did a slide stop and backed him again.

Flash didn't care for that either, but this time, when she requested a walk, she got it. Since he paid attention on the left track, it was time to change to the right one. She turned a circle and started going the other direction. Three steps forward, and he sprang toward the middle of the corral.

Sighing, Heather sat deep in the western saddle, collected on the reins, and reached for the right one. Time to disengage the hindquarters again. She did and he stopped. Spin left, spin right, spin left, and right again.

Durango stood at the gate. "What are you trying to prove?"

"I'm training this stupid son of a jackass." She held the horse still. "Is he a relative of yours?"

"Looks like he's doing the same thing that got him sent to the kill-pens in Eastern Washington." Laredo rested his elbows on the top rail, one boot on the bottom. He must have been the driver of the brown pickup. "Arena work bores Flash in the Pan, sis. Take him out for endurance riding and he's a champion."

"What are you talking about?" Durango demanded.

"I've been apprenticing with Zeke Knight and he knows every horse in the Baker City area, plus most of the ones in Liberty Valley." Laredo jerked his head toward the Warmblood-Arabian cross. "Flash belonged to one of Nina Armstrong's students. If Nina hadn't been murdered last fall, she'd have helped his original owner find a suitable home for him when the gal got a new prospect to do the Tevis 100-mile in a day challenge."

"And what happened to Flash?" Heather petted the horse's steaming red neck. "How did he end up waiting to go to slaughter in Canada?"

"His owner tried selling him as a kid's mount because she didn't want anyone heavy riding him, even though he's a big fella and can safely carry 250 pounds all day long and buck the person off at dinner time." Laredo shook his head ruefully. "Every horse isn't suitable for children."

"And the Wallaces?"

"They were saving money by rescuing him out of the kill-pens," Laredo said. "Of course, that's not their story. They claim they were doing a good deed. Zeke told them to train their kid for endurance contests, but cross-country trail riding isn't her thing. She wants a 4-H show prospect."

"Then buy her one," Durango snapped, impatient. "Heather, don't you know someone who rides endurance?"

"You know full well I've been out of the area for damn near five years, but Mom could make some calls. First, we have to get the Wallace girl a show-ring horse. Laredo, can you and Zeke find one?"

"Sure, but didn't you hear me? They won't spend the money."

"Yes, they will if I want him. Thanks to our grandfather, I have more bucks than the Rockefellers." Durango climbed through the fence. "Bail off, Heather, and let me ride him."

She looked him up and down, assessing his weight and size. He was a big man, but Flash wasn't a small horse. Laredo was right about the draft horse cross. The 17-hand, sturdily built gelding could carry Durango all day and half the night.

"Get down, I said. Pronto. I'm done talking."

"I'm still thinking about it."

His frown deepened. "I'm not waiting to see if he throws you."

"He hasn't done that yet."

"Doesn't mean he won't," Laredo said cheerfully. "Go back far enough and Flash has enough Quarter-horse in him to make a rodeo happy. When he's pissed, he bucks like a bronc fresh out of the chute and nobody lasts eight seconds."

Heather eyed him quickly. "Shut up, Laredo. Your brother doesn't need to hear you."

Durango snagged the western belt she wore, pulled her from the saddle, and into his arms. "Enough already."

"Who the hell do you think you are?"

"The guy who lived without you for too long." He held her tight. "I've told you before, Empress. Nothing and nobody hurts you, not four-legged or two-legged critters. Got it?"

She stared up at him. He hadn't said he loved her, but she obviously meant a great deal to him. But it wasn't enough to stay with her or go with her to Tennessee. She wouldn't settle for less, not again. "Damn you, Hawke. Sweet talk doesn't train this horse. I don't want him believing he's beat me."

"I told you. I'll ride him."

"Well, don't get injured. I won't put you back together. I'm leaving on Saturday and you're not stopping me. I have to be home by May 5th for the twins' birthday."

"I know." He kissed her quickly. "Get out of the way and remember, you belong to me."

"Whoa!" Laredo held up his hand. "Wait a minute. What twins?"

Heather lifted her chin and narrowed her eyes, glowering at the younger man. Time to share the truth since Durango obviously hadn't yet. "I was pregnant when I left your jerk of a brother. He didn't come after me, so I didn't tell him or anyone else in your family."

"Makes sense. Some news shouldn't be shared, especially around the Hawkes." Laredo eyed his brother. "I've never said before you're an asshat, but I'm saying it now. Comes to you and Heather, I'm on her side. Always!"

Touched by his loyalty, she walked toward the fence, spotting her father coming from the barn. He stood next to Laredo. She couldn't let them see how Durango affected her, especially when he was willing to provide Flash with a good home. "Macho jackass."

"Which one?" Art snickered. "Flash or Durango?"

"Both." Heather waited while Durango led the horse to the middle of the corral and adjusted the stirrups for his longer legs. "Sometimes, it takes a few minutes for him to get going."

"I can handle it." Durango tightened the cinch. "Start your excuses for what you did to George on Tuesday. I've told you before not to cause fights between my friends and me."

"What did he do?" She wasn't going to admit how much George O'Connell's insults hurt. "Did he whine at you about what a whore I am? He's lucky I haven't reported him to the bar association for being such an incompetent attorney. He certainly didn't have Grandpa's best interests in mind when he took money as a trustee."

"Don't push me. You and George should have grown up by now. He's pushing forty and you'll be thirty-four this summer. Neither of you is a spring chicken. He'll apologize and so will you."

"Like hell. I won't explain anything to the likes of George O'Connell. Let him think what he likes."

"The peasants get tired of cake." Durango chuckled. "And you will apologize to me and George. He's not up to your games. *Noblesse oblige.*"

"I don't grovel. Not to you or your scummy pals. After you finish showing off, take care of Flash."

"Guess I'll have to teach you how to say *please*. I'll bet you've forgotten how to thank people too."

"Not people. Just men who think they're God's gift to the world." She stormed in the direction of the house. Behind her, she heard Laredo's laughter.

"Well, she told you, big brother! I know, I know. Shut up, Laredo! But if she needs someone to hold her coat when she kicks your tail, I'm available. And I hope you told George to watch his nasty, lawyer mouth or I will."

# CHAPTER EIGHT

Liz glanced out the kitchen window and spotted the three men coming toward the house. From experience, she'd planned on serving sandwiches, coffee, and homemade cookies when they hit the kitchen. Art led the way inside, and she gestured toward the adjacent bathroom. "Wash up. Don't dry-clean on my towels and lunch will be ready when you are."

"Lunch was hours ago," Laredo said, but he took the lead. "Thanks, Dauntless."

"I know how hard you boys work and you can always eat again." Liz saw concern rising on Durango's face and added. "I sent Heather to shower and change before we go to your sister's office to sort out this business. I've already told you what Art and I want."

He nodded. "It's not necessary. I'll pay for whatever Heather needs."

"Good. You know as well as I do, she won't ask for anything." Liz carried the platter of grilled cheese sandwiches over to the table. "I'll see to it you support her and your children."

"Whatever you say." Durango followed his brother.

She drank coffee while the three men ate and heard all about the plan to buy the former endurance champion munching hay out in the stable. "Laredo, you should contact Zeke and get a line on a suitable show horse first."

"Durango's going to buy Flash so the Wallaces can use the money to get a horse for their kid," Laredo said.

"That won't work. They'll take his money and then go low-budget for their kid. They've already revealed they're not interested in the best horsy interest of the child. It means another horse will suffer. If it's not sold to a decent home, it'll be off to the kill-pens."

"So, what's your suggestion?" Art asked.

"The boys find a top-of-the-line, fully trained prospect. Durango buys it and then offers to swap for Flash because he really likes that horse. If they say they thought he already had a big Warmblood mare, he tells them, Cinnamon isn't getting any younger. It makes sense he'd want a replacement for her."

A fierce frown twisted his mouth and landed in Durango's eyes. "Nobody could replace Cinnamon. She's mine for her entire life."

"Yeah, but you're weird that way, bro. Dauntless is right. Most people would either send off a twenty-five-year-old horse to slaughter or put her down, not keep her until she dies of old age."

"And he'll throw in a year's board at Mindy MacGillicudy's place, for boot." Art selected one of the largest chocolate chip cookies. "As well as show lessons with the new owner for the kid."

Liz nodded. "Now, you have a good swap-ortunity, like they say on television. I'll look forward to hearing how the strategy works when I get back."

As if her words were the catalyst, they heard voices in the living room as the flatscreen came to life. "Damn that cat," Liz muttered. "She's making me crazy when she finds the remote and turns on the TV. That cable news show just repeats the same headlines every half hour. It's annoying."

"It's not the cat." Laredo selected another half sandwich. "I saw her sleeping in a sunbeam on the porch after hunting moles. Your place had renters for the last five years. Did you have the O'Leary do a walk-through checking for haunts when you came home?"

Liz shared a glance with her husband, then shook her head. "No, but we've only been here a couple of weeks. I'll call her when we get back from Tennessee."

Her words captured Durango's attention. "Why are you going there?"

"To meet our granddaughters," Art said, his tone even. "Four years of not knowing them is long enough. You may have other things to do, things more important than your children, but we don't."

"Wish I could go with you," Laredo added, "but I can't leave Zeke in the lurch at the start of showing season. Too many horses need shoes and he can't all the work by himself. I'll have to visit in the fall when things slow down."

---

The law firm of Shultz, Estrada, Danford, and O'Brien was in one of Everett's largest office buildings near the Snohomish County Courthouse. As they rode up in the elevator, Heather eyed her mother. "How many times do I have to tell you I don't want Durango's money? I never did. I want him."

"My mind's made up. He agreed to support you and his children. I spoke to him again while I was waiting for you." Liz nodded in satisfaction. "He didn't dare change his mind. He knows he must do what your father and I think is right. Or else."

"I don't believe this. You made Brazos agree to see us at the last minute today. You bulldozed Durango into giving up money without even meeting my babies. He doesn't know them. Don't you ever get tired of winning through intimidation, Mother?"

"Why should I?" Liz considered the notion. "It works so well. And just because I'm talking to you, don't think I'm not figuring out a way to kick your tail from Baker City to Tacoma for keeping the girls a secret from me and your father for almost five years. I should at least have been there when you had them and helped take care of them when you went home from the hospital."

"I'd appreciate it if you didn't teach your tactics to your granddaughters," Heather said. "Dallas is already a little bossy britches."

"She must take after me, and I never doubted Durango was their father."

Heather struggled to ignore the heat rising in her cheeks. Of course, her children's names gave away their parentage. She'd named them for their two uncles who hadn't returned home from Colombia, but she'd intended to share those names with their father first. She didn't know when she'd speak to him again, but it would have to be before she returned to Nashville on Saturday afternoon.

When they stepped out of the elevator, she realized the law firm took up the top three floors of the skyscraper. "Wow, Brazos has done well for herself. How did you get her to agree to see us on such short notice? I wouldn't think she'd knuckle under to emotional blackmail. How am I supposed to pay her?"

"You're not. Durango's responsible for all legal fees. Brazos and I already discussed it. She said she owes you a lot. I don't think she'll take advantage of him."

"I used his money to put her through law school," Heather nodded and explained. "I was pissed at him, and I meant to irritate him to the utmost. I hold the monopoly on harassing him so she better not put the screws to him."

"Watch your mouth, Heather Marie."

"Yes, Mother." Heather mimicked Dallas' tone of reluctant obedience and saw Liz flinch. Trying to dismiss her guilt, Heather led the way into the reception area and gave their names to the young woman behind the desk. "I'm sorry you had to work late."

"We have evening hours on Thursdays, so I usually do." The receptionist blinked and then smiled. "Most of the associates are here catching up on cases, and Ms. Hawke is waiting for you in the conference room."

The receptionist ushered them to the appropriate location. Two walls held huge windows that revealed views of Port Gardner Bay. Tiny sailboats moved back and forth across the blue water. There were evergreen-shrouded dots of islands in the distance.

"How beautiful," Heather said. "I can't believe you manage to do anything except stare out these windows."

Brazos laughed and rose from her chair at one end of the large, antique table. She was a tall, statuesque blonde wearing a navy pinstriped suit over a lighter sky-blue blouse that matched her eyes. She waved to the other two walls that held an assortment of bookcases and legal texts. "I have a cubicle here because most of the time I'm in Lake Maynard at our branch there, but I was in court today. I do most of my research in here."

"Thanks for fitting us into your busy schedule." Heather suffered through the younger woman's fierce hug. She didn't mind helping Durango's younger siblings, but why did they have to be so touchy-feely? She never had been one to enjoy stray kisses or embraces.

"I know better than to tell Dauntless, 'No.'" Brazos hugged Liz and lingered in the woman's arms. "How are you and Art? Is it good to be home?"

After a few minutes spent chatting, the door to the room opened. A slender, black-haired woman entered, encumbered by a tray that held a carafe of coffee, cups, saucers, and a platter of pastries. Brazos' smile warmed as she went to help the newcomer.

"Liz, Heather, this is Natasha Hollister. She agreed to let me bring home the paperwork on this matter."

"It's not a hardship, only an inconvenience." Natasha's polite smile didn't touch the cool, gray eyes.

Heather suppressed a sigh. It didn't take a genius to add two and two and come up with four. "I appreciate it. I'm involved with Bree's, okay, Brazos' older brother and he's a major pain in the—"

"Watch your potty mouth, Heather Marie." Liz accepted the cup of coffee Brazos poured and headed for one of the elaborately carved chairs.

Brazos pointed to another seat. "Heather, staring out windows doesn't help with a solution. It just avoids the problem."

"You're right." Heather took a cup of coffee from Natasha. "I didn't know I was pregnant until after I'd left Washington state. And when they were born, I didn't share I had twins for a reason."

"What was it?" Brazos began to stack the papers she'd obviously been working on earlier. "Will you tell me?"

"Your jerk of a brother was supposed to come after me and sweep me off my feet. He didn't. I wanted to know I meant more to him than anything else in the world. I don't."

"Actually, you probably do." Brazos pulled out a legal pad and pen. "He's afraid to show it. I'm the first to admit he's an insensitive, politically incorrect lout who is emotionally stunted by our narcissistic parents. Those are his good points."

"You got it." Heather relaxed in the chair and felt as if she could breathe for the first time in days. "Thanks, Bree."

"It's all right." Brazos glanced swiftly at Natasha and the other woman nodded. "Actually, we have the same kind of problem. We need your help."

"What's wrong, honey?" Liz asked.

"Do you remember Zeb Steele, Heather? He was one of your patients in Iraq."

"Sure." He'd been more than that, but she decided not to admit it yet. "Why bring him up?" Heather propped her chin on her fist. "Are you writing a book? Leave out that chapter and make it a mystery."

"Don't be rude," Liz said. "Was he a nice boy, Heather?"

" 'Nice' and 'boy' are two words that could never be applied to Zebulon Steele." Heather smiled reminiscently. "Try a hunk and a half who kicked Durango's butt in a brawl. It was lovely."

"I hope you had a good reason for arranging the fight." Liz eyed Heather sternly. "What was it?"

"Your darling Durango deserved each and every bruise." Heather sniffed. "When he found me in Iraq during my first tour in '07, he hauled me off to my quarters and—"

"I think I'm too young to hear this," Liz interrupted.

"Then you shouldn't have asked." Heather shook her head. "He spanked the living daylights out of me because I dared to show up in a warzone without his permission. He's lucky I didn't file charges, and neither did Zeb."

"You'd have to report what happened, every excruciating detail." Liz sighed and shook her head. "You've never dealt well with embarrassment. Frankly, if I'd thought it'd do any good, I'd have locked you in your room until you came to your senses and agreed to stay home, where it was safe. Still, Durango had no business putting his hands on you like that. He deserved the comeuppance he received."

The support amazed Heather. She found herself smiling at her mother. "If my girls ever try joining the military, we'll lock them up." She looked at Brazos. "So, what does Zeb have to do with the pair of you?"

Natasha took over the conversation. "Zeb's a shirt-tail relation, an uncle of sorts. He stayed in the Army until last Christmas when a jeep accident forced him to take a medical retirement. He's been interfering in my life ever since."

"How?" Heather studied Natasha's lovely porcelain features. Somehow, the younger woman appeared familiar. The sharp, natural angle of black eyebrows matched that of the high cheekbones. "Why do I feel like I know you? Have we met?"

"I modeled from the time I was thirteen," Natasha explained. "I've been on hundreds of magazine covers. When I got too old, I went into real estate and I have brokerages from Seattle to Bellingham."

"You're not that old," Liz said.

"Thirty-one and over the hill in my old business. No worries. I'm one of the top-ranked brokers in the Pacific Northwest. I love real estate and have a good reputation, but Zeb is making me nuts."

"He's a constant issue," Brazos continued. "He thinks we're just roommates and tries to introduce me to eligible men so he can be alone with Tasha. He thinks I'll leave her. Of course, in our careers, we must be discreet. I want to make partner and most of her clients would lose it if they knew we were gay."

"Weird." Heather frowned thoughtfully. "Zeb never was stupid. He didn't push where he wasn't wanted."

"He thinks he always knows best and says since he knew me when I was a kid, I can't be serious about Bree."

It still confused Heather, but she decided to go with it for now. She'd get straight answers from Zeb when they met. The least she owed him was help straightening out his affairs after the way she used him in Iraq. He never realized she wasn't as serious about him as he was about her, but she'd thought only kissing him occasionally and refusing to complicate matters with sex should have given him a clue. "How do you two want to play this?"

"I'll give you his phone numbers," Natasha said.

"We don't want to hurt your relationship with Durango," Brazos said. "We just want you to distract Zeb."

"You can't hurt what's between me and Durango. If he doesn't shape up and put me first, we're through. I've already told him. When I ran into Laredo today, he promised to have my back too."

Brazos nodded. "Okay. It worries me when Durango goes off to fight unsanctioned wars in other countries. Haven't you figured it out yet, Dauntless? He's been a mercenary for years even before he and our cousin, Denver, opened a branch of Nighthawke Security in Washington state."

"Isn't that illegal?" Liz paled, fear and concern apparent in her tensing body. "Won't the police arrest him?"

"Only if it becomes a tax issue or if he goes somewhere the US doesn't want independent military contractors," Brazos said. "He doesn't. Uncle Quentin sets high standards too and all the mercs who work for Nighthawke adhere to them. Amarillo and I watch out for Durango, but it's still dangerous."

*And they don't know the real truth, not that I'm going to share it.*

Heather stood. "Is there somewhere private where I can use my cell phone and call Zeb?"

"In my office." Brazos led the way to the door. "I'll show you."

Alone in the small room, Heather sat behind the desk that took up most of the space. Stacks of files and papers covered the metal surface. Little wonder Brazos referred to the tiny space as a cubicle.

*I usually don't call men, but I pay my debts, even the emotional ones.*

When Zeb came on the line, Heather asked, "What's happening, Major? I thought you'd be in the Army past forever."

"Well, I'll be damned. Captain Heather McElroy?"

"Who did you expect?" She laughed. "Brazos and Natasha think we should meet so I can keep you busy. Want to go to the nearest Army base, find the officers' club and watch a sunset while we talk about life?"

"Or else a sunrise or two or three," Zeb agreed. "I've missed you. Did you ever marry that jarhead?"

"No. He can't get his head out of the fourth-quarter position." Heather paused, then opted for the hurtful truth. "I still love him, but it's hard when he constantly rips my heart to pieces."

"Been that. Done there. Got the T-shirt." Zeb's tone was as somber as hers. "Where do you want to meet? When?"

She mentally debated the questions, then gave directions to Pop's Café in Baker City. "I'll meet you at eight. Sorry about the late notice, but I'm headed home to Nashville on Saturday afternoon."

"We'll bring each other up to speed. I can always visit you there if things work out for us this time."

"Sounds great." Heather hastily ended the call. She didn't want another man, especially one who made her feel emotions. When she and Jeff Ransom visited the lawyer on Tuesday, she'd encouraged Jeff to kiss her. His expertise tempted, but he admitted he loved someone else.

She buried her face in her hands. *What's wrong with me? Why does it have to be Durango Hawke, who stirs my soul? How long can I stay away from him when he's a walking heartache? And what will happen if I really do walk away for good this time?*

# CHAPTER NINE

After a long moment, Heather rose to her feet. No point in texting Kate, her B.F.F. and roomie who happily looked after the twins. A former Army nurse, Kate would only quote what she had before, that repeating the same mistakes with men and expecting different results was insanity.

Heather took a deep breath. She had forty-eight hours to work out things with Durango, if it was possible. How could it be? He wouldn't agree to stop looking for Waco. And if he didn't stay home, what kind of father, much less husband, could he commit to being? All questions, no answers.

She returned to the conference room. Natasha made her excuses and left, promising to meet Brazos at home before they left for a dinner engagement.

"We're meeting up with Dominique MacGillicudy, one of Natasha's sorority sisters who is another real-estate broker," Brazos said. "Be afraid, Heather. Be very afraid. Dominique wants to rehab your grandparents' house and she's not someone who takes *no* for an answer. She's been nagging Durango about it, and he keeps telling her to talk to you."

"I haven't seen it in years," Heather said. "She'd better not hold her breath."

"I'm just giving you a heads-up," Brazos said. "I was at Pop's Café yesterday to meet a client and Pop says if you don't get your skinny butt up there tonight, Heather, he'll drag you behind his old truck. He wants you to sing with Dick and his boys before you go home. Pop's already threatened George with permanent expulsion if he doesn't behave."

Heather laughed. "With conditions like that, how can I refuse?"

"Especially since you know if you're home with me, I'll make you play poker for hours."

"Yuck! No offense, Liz," Brazos said. "When you have a deck of cards, you do more damage than a grand jury. Isn't making *your kids* strip their minds and confess all their sins some form of child abuse?"

"You're the lawyer, Brazos. You tell me."

The lighter tone set the mood for the discussion that followed. Heather agreed to ask for child support from the time the twins were born until they finished college. In addition, Brazos wanted to request payment for medical costs, daycare, and education. Liz added conditions to help with Heather's daily living expenses.

"It'll be cheaper if he just marries me," Heather griped. "That's what he'll say."

"It's a lawyer's trick to always ask for more than we want, but we'll agree to child support. Okay, Heather?"

"Fine, since that's all I want." Heather didn't miss the look Liz and Brazos exchanged. "I mean it, you two."

"I hear you, but we have to get his attention," Brazos said. "I'll add private school tuition. Now, what about visitation?"

"A lot of men leave their kids with their parents and I can't stand yours, so I don't want them near my babies." Heather waited for Liz to speak, but her mother didn't disagree. That was interesting since she rarely criticized her next-door neighbors.

"It works for me." Brazos made a note. "I certainly wouldn't allow my kids to see my folks. That is, if I ever have any." She wrote another line. "Unfortunately, I don't believe Durango has come to terms with them. However, he won't want Tex or Eli using them as props in a political campaign so I'll push that idea, and it should help keep the twins safe from them and their agendas."

Heather nodded. "Glad we're on the same page."

"I think we're done here," Brazos agreed, passing her a sheet of paper. "If you'll sign this for me, I can serve Durango and George tonight. Do you want me to handle the details of your inheritance?"

"Can you help me arrange to stay in Tennessee as long as possible without jeopardizing the ranch?"

"Of course. I'll do whatever you want as long as it's legal."

"Great." Once they finished the paperwork, Heather led the way from the law firm to the elevator. It felt as if a giant load had been lifted off her shoulders. She could relax. Even though Brazos was Durango's sister, the lawyer acted as if her first loyalty was to Heather.

"I'll drive," Liz said when they reached the car. "You look as if you'll pass out any minute. It's nearly two hours to Lake Maynard at this time of day. Why don't you nap? I'll wake you up when we get home."

"I'm not that tired." Heather pretended she needed to focus on the parking lot and surrounding vehicles. "Sometimes, I have nightmares."

"I'll wake you up," Liz repeated. "I've never believed in letting a person suffer, especially not my daughter."

"I'll try to sleep." In the passenger seat, she tipped back her head and closed her eyes. She'd rest and perhaps, she'd doze a little.

It seemed like a matter of minutes when Liz spoke again. "Heather, we're here."

"That was a fast trip." Heather stretched in the car, amazed she'd slept. "I'm going to get ready for Pop's."

"It's barely seven. You could nap a bit longer and then go to Baker City."

"No, I'd sleep too long." That would be pure madness. She knew the memories that had tormented her for years would be waiting. She'd hear dying soldiers begging for help she couldn't give while they bled out in the midnight hours.

She hurried into the house and upstairs to her old room. Before she showered and changed clothes, she took the time to call Kate and the twins. The talk didn't last long since the girls were already in bed. Heather promised to phone the next day before lunch. Because her babies were fine, it was safe to go out for the evening.

She needed to *cowgirl up* for a night at Pop's Café. She opted for a green plaid western blouse, thigh-high navy tights so her light-blue denim, hurricane-style skirt with the button fly didn't look too short, although it ended six inches above her knees, and a matching denim vest. She pulled on high-heeled dress boots. More makeup to hide the circles under her eyes and she was ready for dinner with Zeb Steele.

Liz held out the receiver to the wall phone when Heather entered the kitchen. "It's Durango."

"Really?" Heather lifted her chin, determined to sound bored when she took the phone. "What do you want?"

"I'll pick you up in a half hour for dinner," Durango said. "I want to know all about the twins. What are their names?"

She debated. He deserved to know a little, especially since his sister planned to take him to the proverbial cleaners. Besides, it might make him act like their daddy.

"Answer me, Empress."

"I hate that nickname." She opted for her most disdainful tone. "All right, jarhead. They're tall for their age, have red-gold hair and your eyes. I named them Dallas Waco and Galveston Fenella since Fenian is a guy's name."

"My God." Durango's voice shook. "I don't deserve you."

"Got that right. It was for their uncles, moron, not for you. I call them Ally and Toney."

"Are they identical?"

Heather shook her head, then recalled he couldn't see her. "Most people say so. *I* can always tell them apart." She smiled suddenly. "They'll love confusing you. They think it's a game. I call it Mix and Match."

"Sounds as if they're just like you." He paused. "All right. I'll pick you up at eight. Bring pictures of them."

"In your dreams, Hawke. You've made it plain you have more important places to go and things to do. Besides, I'm taking applications for a new daddy for my girls." She heard him swear and grinned. She had him on the ropes now. Time for an imaginary punch to the gut. "I'm meeting Zeb Steele for dinner. You remember him, don't you?"

"I'll skin you alive and nail your hide to the barn wall."

She dismissed the threat. He wouldn't hurt her. "Oh and give your little sis, Amie a message for me. Tell her I auditioned Jeff Ransom the other day. He's a superb kisser, too good for her. I may opt for him if Zeb's gotten old, fat, and bald. So long, loser."

She hung up the phone and whirled to confront her mother. "What?"

"I think you may have overdone it, Heather Marie." Liz went to the refrigerator, opened it, and removed a plastic basket of produce, ready to make a salad. "Never surround a man or a horse on four sides. You have to leave them a way to go."

"I'm not afraid of him. Other than what happened twelve years ago, he's never laid a hand on me except when I wanted him."

"He could lose his temper." At the farmhouse sink, Liz washed the head of iceberg lettuce. "Doesn't that concern you?"

"Heavens, no." Heather started for the back door. "Durango pulls out his emotions, examines them, and then decides if he feels anything. He's a complete robot. Tonight will get his attention."

"If he overreacts, remember I warned you." Liz began to tear up lettuce. "Do you want me to tell him where to find you, Madam Arrogance?"

Heather giggled and swooped down to hug her mother. "Yes, please. You're the best."

Liz kissed her cheek. "Glad you think so. Now, give me your plane ticket. Your dad and I are flying back with you on Saturday. Laredo is going to stop in and take care of the cat and Flash for us. Sooner or later, you'll have to realize that you always come first with us, honey, and I don't know how to make you see that the kids in the 4-H club never took anything away from what we felt for you. Maybe, with the girls. We have a lot of time and spoiling in mind for them."

"They'll love it." Wondering if her mother had a point, Heather put the ticket on the counter before she headed to the back door.

———

"I wish you could hear me, Liz." Waco Hawke leaned against the doorframe to the living room and watched the older woman prepare supper. She hadn't changed much in the past eight years. Still petite, plump curves stuffed into jeans and a bright red sweater. Long black hair streaked with gray swung around her hips. If he'd shown up here back in the day, when she was cooking, she'd have insisted on feeding him a meal.

"I should have been nicer to you and Art instead of acting like a know-it-all brat. And I never was decent to Heather. I always put the moves on her, and she constantly slapped me down. She freaking decked me when I kissed her. You raised a decent woman."

Not for the first time he wanted one of the ice-cold beers Art kept in the fridge. "And she named her kid after me. I never expected that—not when I told Durango lies about her. I was pissed because she always made it plain, I was nothing compared to him. If I'd been him, I'd have kicked my butt down the street, but he's always been more ethical than any of the rest of us. Granted, he was raised by Uncle Quentin and Aunt Vicky who taught him to be a human being. We didn't have that luck."

No point standing here trying to carry on a conversation with a woman who couldn't hear or see him. He left her in the kitchen and headed for the recliner and the flatscreen. Time to watch the cable news and the ash-blonde reporter who'd read the day's headlines. He'd pretend the woman was talking directly to him, the way she had when they dated in high school.

---

It didn't take long to drive to Baker City. Heather parked outside Pop's and went into the large cedar-shake building. The door she chose opened into the restaurant and she glanced around the room. Zeb Steele hadn't arrived yet. Only couples and various families sat at the tables. She strolled into the lounge, waving at the three dark-haired men onstage and went to greet the old man behind the bar.

"You're late." Pop informed her, a grin taking over his wrinkled face.

Heather tried to swallow the lump rising in her throat. She went around the bar to hug him. "I've missed you too."

Pop snorted. "So, you make it big as a country singer yet?"

"I'm not that good." Heather grimaced. "Nothing like the competition, Pop. I try. I'm lucky to get three or four paid gigs a month and more unpaid ones. Good thing Mom and Dad insisted I get my nursing degree, so I'd have something to fall back on if music let me down."

"Buncha idiots." Pop smoothed her hair. "You've got more talent in your little finger than any of those half-naked cheesecake princesses I see on TV dancing around in their unmentionables."

"You're prejudiced." Heather hugged him again. "Anyhow, I'm thinking about coming home. The McElroy ranch is mine now."

"Well, if you do, I need a reliable girl singer." Pop patted her back. "Go knock 'em dead. Let me know if George's mouth overloads his common sense."

"Will do." Heather blinked back the tears and walked toward the stage. Bill O'Connell was the tallest of the trio, waiting for her. He had graying black hair and dark blue eyes. He'd been a good friend of her uncle's, but opted to follow his father into law enforcement rather than the military.

Dick O'Connell, the Baker City police chief, was only an inch or two shorter than his oldest son. Broad shoulders filled out his blue western shirt tucked neatly into dark blue slacks. He had short, black hair liberally sprinkled with white and blue eyes. He smiled and set aside the bass guitar he'd been tuning.

"Hey, girl." Bill came out from behind the drum set. "You look great. We've missed you, Rusty."

"He's got that right." Dick smiled at her. "You don't want to know how hard it is to keep a gal singing with the band when Bill's married and George only wants to flirt. He's not in it for the long haul since his divorce."

"Are you all going to sing or talk?" Pop called from behind the bar. "What am I paying you for?"

"I didn't know we got paid," George retorted, a mirror image of his father and brother. "I thought we did this for love and affection, not to mention fame in Baker City."

Heather giggled when Pop shook his fist at them. "George, Brazos will probably hit you with some papers for Durango tonight," she said.

"She already tried. She called and wanted to know my fax number when she couldn't email my office." George scowled, obviously thinking like a lawyer again. He had the most musical talent of the O'Connell men. If it had keys or strings, he could play it. In local opinion, that included lace-up logging boots. "This is Baker City, and we barely have cell service, and the Internet fails whenever the weather is wonky. What is she thinking?"

"That it's 2019?" Heather asked sweetly. "And we should get some cell towers and decent Internet service?"

"Then she tells me she's taking every cent Durango inherited for your kids," George went on. "Where's her family loyalty?"

"I think she's more into that sisterhood stuff where women stick together." Bill winked at Heather. "Besides, why would you expect her to be loyal to a slimeball like Tex Hawke?"

"I guess." George's attention returned to his organ.

"He's been upset since you let him make such an ass of himself on Tuesday," Bill explained. "Durango ripped him a new one when George said the kid undoubtedly wasn't his. His secretary called me to run interference because she thought my brother was going to get thrown through his plate-glass window, but Durango didn't need me for back-up."

Heather caught her breath and stared up at him. Hearing about the defense warmed her all the way to her toes. A smile trembled on her lips. "Thanks for keeping the peace, Bill."

"That's my job."

"I don't think much of a man who gets a woman pregnant, then abandons her," Dick said. "Want me to chuck Durango in my jail? It's empty. I hardly get any action on weeknights."

"Don't tempt me." Heather smiled at the police chief. "I didn't know I was pregnant when I left, and I didn't tell Durango until I came back on this visit."

"We still take care of our own and there's plenty of room," Dick told her.

"Go to work," Pop yelled. "Talk later."

The door to the lounge opened and Heather saw a small, blond man limp inside, leaning heavily on a carved wooden cane. Pity swelled. She swore softly. "I'll be back for the second set. I've got a dinner date."

Bill followed her gaze. "Who's the flatlander?"

"Zeb Steele. He was a major in the Army Rangers. We met in Iraq."

"Shoot-fire." Dick glanced around the bar that was slowly filling up with Baker City regulars. "I'll pass the word. I don't have time to take a bunch of injured loggers to the hospital in Lake Maynard on my night off when I want to play music with my boys and hear you sing."

"Thanks, Dick." Heather started across the room and stopped when Bill touched her shoulder. "What?"

"Just an FYI. George will be on his cell or the landline to Durango ASAP."

"Oh, I do hope so," Heather said, smiling. "Last time Zeb beat the hell out of Durango, I didn't get to sell tickets or popcorn."

Bill's jaw dropped. "That little pissant whipped Durango?"

"Yes. Zeb started it and finished it. It took a while for Durango to hit back because Zeb was on crutches at the time."

Heather walked across the room, regretting the heels that gave her three inches on him. Somehow, when she met his brown eyes, the difference in their heights didn't matter. "It's good to see you. Hope the place isn't too down-home for you, Zeb."

His rawboned features warmed pleasantly when he grinned back at her. "Looks like Hollister. Ever been there?"

"No. Is it a logging town too?" Heather slipped her fingers into the crook of his free arm. "Where is it?"

"It's over on the Olympic Peninsula. It's a company town started by Natasha Hollister's grandfather." Zeb glanced around the lounge. "Are we eating in here?"

"Let's go into the restaurant. Once the music starts, it gets too rowdy to have a conversation."

"Fair enough." He escorted her toward the doors on the other side of the lounge.

They chose a table, and the waitress brought menus. Zeb ordered a bottle of white wine. As the meal progressed, both relaxed. Stories of their time in Iraq naturally led to what they'd done afterward.

Before dessert, Zeb excused himself for a moment. He was barely out of sight when Durango sauntered over to the table.

"What are you doing here?" Heather hoped Zeb would be gone long enough for her to encourage Durango to leave. "You can't stay. You have to go."

"He's not coming back." Durango pulled out Zeb's chair and sat. "You've been ditched, Empress."

"I don't believe you. Did you do something to him?"

"Me?" Durango tried to look innocent. "I'm the guy sitting here."

Heather glared at him, then signaled Pop's grandson. "Dray, could you see if my friend's all right? He went to the restroom."

"The little guy with the cane?" Dray asked. When she nodded, he gaped at her. "No way, Rusty. He left. I saw him go through the lounge to the parking lot. Did he stiff you with the check? Shall I try to catch him?"

"No need." Durango took out his wallet. "I've got it covered."

Heather glared at him. "I know you had something to do with this, Durango Quentin Hawke. When I find out what, you'll pay."

"Go sing for Pop." Durango shrugged one wide shoulder. "I'll take you home after the next set."

"I have my own car and I'll drive myself."

"Don't push your luck." He stood, came around to pull out her chair. He picked up her left hand, pushed the emerald ring she'd left behind on her third finger. "I'm tired of the games. Stop flirting with other men and trying to piss me off. Behave yourself or we'll leave now."

"I do as I please." She gasped when he captured her chin in hard fingers.

He bent his head, kissed her, a quick fierce possession. "You've been away too long, babe, but tonight, you'll please me." He slid an arm around her waist. "Do you want to sing first or not?"

# CHAPTER TEN

Heather opened her eyes. She felt Durango's shoulder under her cheek. How did she know it was him, not some other man? Something about his scent, his feel. She'd always know him.

He must have felt her stir. "Soda in the cooler. Aspirin in the glovebox." His deep voice was calm, too calm.

It held a note she'd heard before but didn't quite recall where or when. She sat up, pushed away the thin blanket covering her. They were in his pickup. Headed where?

She didn't ask. Instead, she studied the terrain outside the windshield. What little she could see were trees and hills along a night-darkened highway. The headlights revealed the next stretch of pavement and a few other vehicles. She leaned down to open the container and remove an icy can of cola from the six-pack.

She yawned. She was still tired. Other than the nap on the way back from Everett to her parents' home, she hadn't slept in close to a week. "How did I get here?"

"I brought you." His tone was patient. "You fell asleep at the bar between the third and fourth sets. You run yourself ragged. You need to stop sometimes."

She grimaced, popped the top on the soda, and swallowed some. It didn't surprise her she'd drifted off at Pop's. The loud conversations, music from the jukebox, and other sounds in the cocktail lounge would have ensured it was safe to close her eyes, to doze for a short time. She wouldn't dream.

"Where are we? On the way to Lake Maynard to Mom and Dad's?"

"No." Durango's attention remained on the highway.

"Then, where are we?"

"Almost to Ellensburg."

"What? Why?" The town was close to central Washington state, located east of the Cascade Mountains at the junction of two interstate highways. "I didn't agree to go on a road trip with you."

"You sure didn't." His tone took on the edge she hated, too low, almost menacing in its intensity. "You've crossed way over the line, Heather Marie."

"What line?" She focused on washing down two of the pain relievers. "Why are you freaking out? What has your grundies in a knot?"

"What do you think?" He kept driving east, his attention on the road. "You staged a major hissy fit when you left me."

"I warned you ahead of time I was through providing system support. I told you I had a great job opportunity and a recording contract in Nashville and I was going there. Are you still pissed because I moved our furniture into a house for Amarillo? Or because I arranged for her and Maria to live with Gino Petrocelli? They needed his family's protection."

"It took a little while for me to realize it was the right thing to do."

"Then what else can it be?" She studied his set jaw. "You got in one fight after another at that biker bar where Brazos waitressed back then. Paying her tuition so she could focus on law school got her out of there."

"Again, you saved the day for her. Keep going and you may figure out your transgressions."

She eyed him warily. "Okay, I agree lending Laredo your truck after he wrapped his around a tree when he was wasted was tacky. I shouldn't have done that, but I was devastated when you didn't have time for me."

"That worked out for the best too. He's stayed clean and sober for almost five years, apprenticed successfully with Sean Killian in Liberty Valley, and is well on the way to having a shoeing book with four hundred clients."

"Then I don't have a clue why your tail-feathers are in a knot. If you had the brains God gave a rock, you'd be able to figure out I didn't know I was pregnant when I left. That came as a surprise to me too. I expected you to come after me and when you didn't—" She shrugged. "I reinvented my life."

"Still not it."

She heaved a sigh and tried to sound reasonable. "There are lights up ahead so we must be close to a town. Why don't we find a restaurant and talk?"

"We'll stop, but I'm done talking."

She stared at him while she finished the soda. The silence grew oppressive. "Durango, what's happening? This isn't like you."

"Really?" He switched on the turn indicator and moved into the exit lane. "Are you sure?"

She shifted on the bench seat and struggled to recall where she'd heard that strange sound in his deep voice before. It thudded like doom in her ears.

They'd been together most of her life. As much as she provoked him, he wasn't the one who lost his temper. He usually stood like a mountain and watched her, as if her rages were pure entertainment. When her anger subsided, he'd haul her off to bed and jump her bones except for those times when she jumped his.

Except once, she thought. When he found her in Iraq, the spanking had been the start of their most serious fight and she'd believed it'd be a permanent breach. She'd returned her engagement ring and the cloverleaf pendant before she and Zeb began dating.

After the brawl between the two men, Durango visited her. He'd ignored her stormy recriminations and ripped into her. The lecture culminated in a night of fierce lovemaking leading to their reconciliation. Zeb found them together the following morning. She'd ended their relationship while Durango lurked like a behemoth in the background. And he sounded the same way tonight, as if his legendary patience had come to an end.

She quivered when he drove into the empty rest area, choosing a spot at the far end in the shadows of pine trees. She knew he'd noticed the burned-out light at the top of the nearby pole, but he didn't mention it and neither did she. "Let's go into town and talk there."

He looked at her and switched off the engine, pausing to reach over his shoulder and turn off the interior dome light. He pocketed the keys. Without speaking, he opened the driver's door and climbed out, closing it behind him. He stalked around the front of the pickup to her side of the vehicle. He unlocked the passenger door and reached for her. The cab of the '57 Chevy was too small to evade him. She flung the empty pop can at him.

He smiled, but there was no humor in the sight. He snagged her arms and pulled her across the seat to him.

She tried to twist away, but he was too strong. He shifted, caught her wrists with one hand. He drew her closer until he stood between her legs, her right one pinned between him and the back of the truck seat. He pushed the short skirt up her thighs.

She could hardly move. She moistened dry lips, staring into his face, the dark blue eyes. "Please."

"I told you, Empress. Tonight, you're pleasing me and I'm definitely pleasing you. We've been apart too long." He adjusted their positions slightly, bringing her closer. He released her hands. "Put your arms around my neck."

Instead, she unsnapped the western shirt, revealing his broad chest and sliding her hands toward his shoulders. "I'm not ready for you, not when I haven't been with anyone else."

"I already knew that." He lifted her enough so he could finish pushing the hurricane-style skirt around her waist. "You will be."

She heard the shriek of her underwear tearing and felt cool night air on her skin. She gasped when he cupped her bottom in large hands, squeezing the cheeks softly before pressing her parted legs further apart. He hadn't removed his jeans, only unbuckling his belt, unfastening, and lowering them a couple of inches. The denim rubbed against the inside of her thighs.

"Not yet. I'm not ready."

He paused, looked at her, and nodded. "All right."

She moaned as one of his fingers found her, probed gently, and then slid inside, soon joined by a second. His thumb rocked against the tiny bud in the curls. "Oh, *God*. Please, Durango. Please."

His smile widened. "You did miss me, didn't you, baby?"

"Yes, you know it." She writhed on the seat, moving with him as he stroked her to a frenzy. She heard herself begging for more. He stopped before she climaxed.

"You're ready now." His hands shifted to her butt and he thrust into her. He was so big, and she felt every inch of him.

She should stop him while she could still think. She didn't. She met his movements, unable to resist. There was only the meeting of their bodies. He didn't try to kiss her, just this rapid taking as if she were only an object of his desire. His woman, she realized suddenly.

Like he'd said, she'd stepped out of line. He showed her who she belonged to as if she were a captive or spoils of war. He acted like she was his plaything, not a real person. She dug her fingers into his muscled forearms. "This isn't what I want."

"Yes, it is. It's what we both need after all this time." He increased his movements, deep thrusts mingling with shorter ones. His thumb found her clitoris and rubbed. "Beg me."

She came suddenly, shattering among the stars. When she returned to sanity, he'd paused. She stared into the cobalt depths of his gaze. "You didn't—"

"Finish? Not yet."

He started again, the steady, long slow strokes that would drive her to another climax. It was what he intended. He wanted to make her crazy.

She clawed at the back of his shirt. "Hurry."

He didn't. The deliberate motions continued. She groaned, bucking against him. Nothing she did altered the deep, even steadiness of his thrusts. She muffled her scream against his shoulder, biting him as she came a second time.

"You're supposed to be begging."

The taunt rasped on her mind, the way his jeans chafed her inner thighs.

"You—" She couldn't think of a name to call him. She moaned, clung to him as he began once more. Her hips met his. She knew she was too close to the edge. Would he ever end this?

He did, coming as she did a third time. She longed to collapse on the truck seat. She couldn't when he held her against him. How did he continue to manage to stand? One final squeeze of her bottom and then his hands slowly caressed her hips, working their way to the vest she still wore.

He opened it, then popped the snaps on the western blouse. He was still inside her, soft where he'd been hard moments before. She rested her head against his chest. "Not again."

"Payback, Empress." He chuckled into her hair. "You're barely begging."

She shuddered when he found the front clasp of her bra and unhooked it. Her breasts were freed to his touch. They spilled into his hands. His fingers teased her nipples. She trembled. "What are you paying me back for? Dinner with Zeb?"

"That's over." Durango bent his head, blew softly on a nipple. "You were out of bounds when you came onto Jeff. He's the only other person who knows what I do."

"I sent him to you." She arched her back, a silent plea for him to keep making love to her. "Anyway, he kisses better than you do."

"Really?" Durango laughed softly against her skin. "Remember that when I make you scream for me."

Was he serious? She met his gaze and read the truth in his eyes. He planned to take her again, here in the cab of his truck as if he had all night to claim her. "This is insane. Regardless of what your lawyer friend told you, I'm not some convenient slut you can buy."

"I'll say." He began to harden inside her. "I haven't had a woman, my woman since you left in '14. You're not the least bit convenient."

The blunt expression of his fidelity warmed her heart, but she was determined not to show it. "You could have chosen somewhere else to make love to me."

"I'll remember that when I have you tomorrow. I'm damned well going to try to make up for lost time." He arched a brow. "Ready to beg?"

The mockery infuriated her, and she raised her hand to slap him. He caught her wrists, pinned both behind her back, holding her so he could enjoy her breasts. She gasped, groaned, and then cried out in pleasure when he kissed, licked, and finally sucked her nipples.

She clenched around him as he hardened inside her, moaning his name. She knew this only added to his triumph. If he'd taken her and she hadn't enjoyed every moment of it, he'd be less of a man. No one else made her feel as much. Kissing Jeff had been sweet, but not earth-shattering. Dating Zeb was a way to anger Durango. How could she be so manipulative? Granted, both men chased her even when they knew how she felt about *her* man.

"Think about me." He gritted the words into her hair as he began to move. "Only me. And what I make you feel."

How did he know when her thoughts slipped away from him? She twisted against him, arching, rising, and falling. She kissed his neck, his ear, but couldn't reach his mouth. He wouldn't have it. All of this was orchestrated to his plan and part of her admired that.

She was seconds from her climax when he stopped. "What?" She gripped his arms, digging her nails into the sleeves of his shirt. "Come on. Move, damn you."

"Beg, baby." He laughed and trailed a line of kisses over her throat to her breast, toward her nipple. "Make it good."

"I hate you." She barely breathed. She lifted herself against him, trying to finish what he'd started. He remained perfectly still. Why did he have to be such a controlled bastard? "Do it. Finish it."

"Beg me." His tongue curled around a nipple. "Tell me how much you love me."

"I won't." She reared up, twining her fingers in his hair, yanked it. "I told you. Finish it, damn you."

He laughed harder. "Not until you beg." He nipped at her ear. "And promise to quit smoking. I don't like tasting tobacco when I want to taste you."

She hated him when he treated her like this, and she loved him too. She wouldn't give in to his demands. She wouldn't.

He tormented her with tiny movements of his hips, little strokes in and out until she was ready to scream. "You know you want me. Say the words."

She couldn't last. She needed more. He had to move, really move. She surrendered. "All right. You win."

"Do I get what I want?"

"Yes." She promised everything he asked and more in total capitulation.

Afterward, she lay beneath him on the truck seat, dimly aware he propped most of his weight on his elbows. She sighed, turning her lips against the strong column of his neck. "I bet you think you've won."

"Only because I have." He followed the gold chain that held the cloverleaf pendant with his tongue. "Want me to prove it?"

"No." She tipped back her head as he kissed the hollow of her throat. "Not here. We can't keep having the place to ourselves. Someone will see us."

"I can change your mind, can't I?"

She heard the victory in his bass tone and eyed him. "Yes, you already know it, don't you? Please, Durango."

"All right." He levered up and off her. He stood by the passenger door. "We'll go now, Heather."

She watched him tuck in his shirt, adjust his jeans. He didn't look like the man who just royally screwed her in the cab of an old pickup truck. Heat burned into her face. Her skirt was still rucked up around her waist. Her blouse was open and so was her bra. The remains of her panties were on the floor.

She sat up. She adjusted the lace cups and hooked her bra before she snapped her western shirt, buttoned her vest. She struggled to push down her skirt, still bunched around her hips. Muttering swear words, she glared at him. "You misbegotten, son of a—"

He leaned into the cab, close to her, too close. "Behave, Empress. As much as you rant, rage, and issue edicts, I can have you begging for me in seconds. You'll scream for me if I put my tongue on you."

"You wouldn't dare."

"And in you." He stroked her knee through the thigh-high stocking. "And I'd like to right now."

The fire in her face intensified. "You can't. I'll—"

"What?" He smiled, bending nearer. "Want me to show you?"

She caught her breath. Actually, she did, but she wouldn't say that. "Not yet."

"Fine. Tell me you love me." He ran his fingers up her thigh. "Say it like you mean it."

She scowled at him. When his hand continued the inevitable journey toward the curls between her legs, she yielded. "All right. I love you."

He found her, cupping her. "What was that?"

"I said it. What more do you want?"

"Sincerity." Two fingers eased inside her and he began to slide them in and out. His thumb sought the tiny bud and rubbed gently. "Say it again."

His hand moved, and she joined the pattern, met each motion. A husky moan erupted before she could stop it. "I love you. I love you. I love you."

Release swamped her, and she almost fell backward in the seat. She glared at him, aware his fingers were still inside her. Then, the movements began once more, sliding out and then deep into her.

Unable to resist, she rose to meet his hand and the rhythmic thrusts of those clever, large fingers. "I've said it again and again."

"I know, but I haven't heard it in years." His thumb rocked into the bud. "I decided I want to hear it a few more times before we hit the road. Say it now."

# CHAPTER ELEVEN

When he finished this time, she lifted her hips enough to smooth down her skirt. "I hope you realize I didn't mean a word of it."

"Now, don't make me prove you wrong. We've got miles to go. Say you're sorry for lying and we'll hit the highway."

"Okay, I'm sorry. You win. I lose." She didn't glance at him to see if the taunting apology was accepted. "Of course, I do love you so very, very much."

"Baby, you'll be lucky if we leave here before sunrise."

The promise shocked her. She didn't want to think about how stiff and sore she'd be from tonight's lovemaking, and she certainly wasn't ready for it to continue. Or was she? Annoyed by the smugness she saw on his features, she glowered at him. "All right, Hawke. You did win, but you never even kissed me, not really."

"Nope." He feathered a thumb over her lips.

She tasted herself and trembled. "Why don't you kiss me?"

"Not until we make love."

She lifted her chin. "Then what was all this?"

"You gave me a lesson in leaving damn near five years ago. And I just gave you one in manners. You deserved it."

She leaped toward him. She'd claw the arrogance off his face and make him pay.

He grabbed her wrists. She bit at his throat. She kicked him. "You filthy miscreant." She butted him with her head. "I hate you."

He shook against her. Had she scared him? Good.

"Get your freaking hands off me."

She tried to kick him again and found herself pinned under him on the truck seat.

"Isn't this where we started?" Amusement and passion mingled. "I'm ready to have you again."

"In your dreams." She bucked. "I don't want you."

"Really?" He released her and stepped back. "Okay, baby. Whatever you say."

She gaped at him. "I thought you said you were—"

"Ready?" He arched a brow. "You know I am, but I've never forced you. Have I? Admit it."

"Wow, you think you're all that, don't you?" She lifted her chin, knowing he'd wait to touch her. "You're right. I always want you as much as you want me."

"Good girl." He smiled down at her. "Glad we agree on something."

"What does that mean?"

"This." He reached for her, pulled her to him. "And now I can finish that lesson."

Before she could escape, her skirt was hiked around her waist again. He curved his hands around her bottom, lifted her.

She gasped, spreading her legs so he'd know she did want him, wanted the intimate kiss. His tongue slowly swept over her and she smothered a moan when he explored the folds of skin. He slowly worked his way into her, one long kiss after another. She cried out when his tongue teased, tormented, and drove deep. He knew exactly what she liked, what she craved. He lapped at the small bud of flesh, licked it, and settled in as though he intended to spend the rest of the night and all the next day with his mouth on her.

When he finally drew her clitoris into his mouth and sucked, she came apart, calling his name. He chuckled softly against her, his breath warm, and then he started all over again. His tongue explored, teasing, driving deep before he began tormenting the tiny bud once more.

It seemed like a lifetime later when he lifted his head. He was right. He'd made her howl for him as she came, one stormy climax after another. She'd tangled her fingers in his tawny-gold hair and begged whenever he paused. How could he do this to her? She'd abstained the entire time she was gone. She hadn't missed sex enough to sleep with anyone else, and two days after she arrived, she was with him.

She struggled to sit up, propping herself on an elbow. He stood by the passenger door, watching her. She shivered when she saw the look of possession on his face. What was wrong with her? He treated her as if he owned her. His woman. He hadn't been particularly gentle or tender, but he hadn't hurt her. And she liked what he'd done, loved it. That stunned her.

She took a deep breath, tried to change the subject while she wrestled her skirt back into place again. "Well, this should take care of a birthday or two."

He ran a finger down her nose. "This was your comeuppance. It has nothing to do with our birthday tradition."

"As if I'll let you touch me again."

"Careful, sweetheart." He smoothed her hair. "I never can resist your challenges. But we have people expecting us and miles to drive."

She blinked at him. "Where are we going?"

"Idaho."

"Why?" She twisted, pushed her torn panties into the garbage bag on the floor. "That doesn't make sense."

"Yes, it does." He took the bag she handed him, closed the passenger door of the truck, and walked around the rig, pausing to toss the sack into a nearby trash can.

She waited until they were on the highway, heading east. "Explain, Hawke. Why are you driving to Idaho?"

"To get married."

"No way. I've told you for years. It's either me or Waco. I won't marry you while you're in and out of CONUS, the continental United States."

"Right. I told you the games are over." The lazy menace deepened in his low tones. "I didn't get your suitcase, break up your date, haul you out of Pop's and take you until you screamed, to hurry up and wait one more time. We're getting hitched."

"What?" Rage blossomed. "Who do you think you are?"

"You're mine, baby. Always have been. Always will be." Eyes on the highway, he reached to pat her knee, squeezed it. "We both know you love me."

She jerked away, moving closer to the door, wishing she had a large mallet to club him over the head. "What did you do to Zeb?"

"Me? Nothing. I left him to Laredo and Ransom."

"What did they do to him?" When Durango didn't provide an immediate answer, she raised her voice. "Damn you. Answer me."

"Be nice." Faint humor lightened the bass rumble. "Start one of your snot-slinging, foot-stomping hissy fits and I'll end it. I don't mind pulling over and taking you on the side of the road. You're the one who doesn't want to be embarrassed if a highway patrol cop sees us, not me."

She glared at him in the dark cab. "What did they do to Zeb? They didn't hurt him, did they?"

"No. It's not his fault you were playing games with both of us. They locked him in the storage closet where the O'Connells keep their instruments. They'd have found him and let him go by now."

"And you arranged for Dray to lie to me? He'll pay too."

"No, he won't. You'll leave the boy's head on his shoulders. Laredo told Steele that his car had been hit in the parking lot. Worked as a distraction. Dray probably did see him leave through the lounge."

"But not what happened when Zeb was in the hallway." She eyed Durango, impressed by the strategy, although she wasn't about to admit it. "And you call me a manipulator."

"You are, but you needed to remember not to push me." He chuckled. "Are you going to sulk another four or five hours?" He patted the seat next to him. "Come over here."

"I won't encourage your nonsense. You can't force me to marry you."

"You want to bet on that?" He shrugged, flashed a quick grin. "You'll lose. Again."

"Freaking jarhead." She gave up the battle and slid over to sit next to him. "You're such a macho pig. You were even before you enlisted in the Marines."

"I know." He stroked her knee, his hand slipping under her skirt. "And you love it, don't you?"

"So what?" She pillowed her head on his shoulder. "You don't deserve me. One day, I'll stop loving you."

"Don't try. You'll make me mad." His fingers slid further up her thigh. "And we might not find a rest stop."

She gasped, caught his wrist when his hand found her. "Not when you're driving, you fool."

"Sure about that?"

"Positive." She bit back a moan when he stroked the curls before a finger eased into her. "And you didn't answer me about the wedding."

He kept driving, one hand on the wheel while the other cupped her, and he slid a second finger inside her. His thumb roved over the tiny bud in the nest of hair between her legs. "Keep thinking and you'll figure it out."

Before she could, she found herself moving back and forth with his fingers as they slipped in and out of her. Dimly, she knew this was a dangerous maneuver when he was behind the wheel, but they'd survived in so many warzones, three tours for her and countless ones for him. They'd taken so many risks that she didn't worry now. She convulsed around his hand, one long climax. "Oh, *God*. You—"

He chuckled before he started moving his fingers again, his thumb rocking into the bud once more. "How many times do you think I can make you come between here and Spokane?"

"Too many." She nipped his ear. "Can you keep the truck on the road if I return the favor?"

When she reached for his belt, he hastily captured her hand with his. "Okay, you win, baby. I'll stop teasing you for a while."

"Spoilsport." She giggled, pressing closer against him. "And the wedding? What's your scheme, jarhead?"

"It's easy. What day is it?"

"Thursday, May 2nd."

"Try again. It's Friday, May 3rd, and you're flying out tomorrow."

"And you'll keep me with you until I marry you." She yawned. "Is that it? If I don't, I'll miss the twins' birthday on Sunday."

"That's it."

She stretched lazily. "There's a flaw in your plan."

"Really?" He flicked a sideways glance at her before concentrating on the road. "What?"

"You're not that big a jerk." She sighed, turning her head to kiss the side of his neck. "But I can be a real bitch. You won't let both of us miss Ally's and Toney's party. Plus, my parents are going back with me, and you left out the three-day waiting period when we get a license in Washington state."

"Not in Coeur d'Alene, Idaho. No waiting period. No blood tests. We don't even need witnesses."

"You think you've won this round, don't you?"

"Only because I have."

"Well, if we go through with it, you can put me on a plane back to Seattle right after the ceremony."

"I don't think so." His deep voice held implacable calm. "You're not pulling one of your stunts and filing for an annulment because you claim the marriage wasn't consummated or telling everyone in Baker City I'm impotent. Not that they'll believe you because we have twins, but I don't need the hassle."

"Why, lover? Whatever put such ideas into *my*, I mean *your*, head?" Annoyed, she shifted slightly away from him, desisting when he squeezed her knee. She knew he'd use his hand on her again and she needed to think of ways to hijack his scheme prior to the ceremony. "I'll show you."

He chuckled. "You always do."

---

She'd fallen asleep. He pulled onto the shoulder of the road long enough to get the folded blanket off the floor of the truck and cover her with the red Washington State University throw. He put his arm around her, held her close while she slept. She rarely admitted she belonged to him. Of course, when she did, she used the fact to get whatever she wanted.

It didn't bother him, but George O'Connell, his friend and lawyer, never could see Heather's strengths. He took offense at her sharp tongue and quick wit. When she packed up, left, then hid the twins, George didn't understand how or why Durango didn't bear a grudge.

He'd get through the wedding tonight and deliver her to Seattle-Tacoma International Airport before he told Heather about the upcoming trip to Colombia. It'd infuriate her, but he'd talk to Denver and have his cousin arrange security for his wife and kids.

Dawn began to lighten the orchards, the freshly plowed hay, and wheat fields, brown dirt shining. He'd always liked the rolling hills and the vast open spaces stretching to the horizon. More than once, he'd tried to convince Heather to move here, but she refused to consider the idea. Now that she'd inherited the McElroy farm, she'd never leave Baker City, and he didn't blame her.

Coeur d'Alene wasn't far from Spokane, nestled in Idaho border country. He turned into the parking lot of the Longhorn Hotel, a sprawling three-story structure, and pulled into a vacant parking spot. He grinned when he spotted his cousin, Bendigo, a tall, dark-haired man in cowboy attire of jeans, a western shirt, and a denim jacket coming from the office. Good. It'd be more of a wedding with family. Besides, Bendigo had always treated Durango as if he were a younger brother when they were boys, rather than a school-year visitor.

He switched off the engine of the old pickup, removed the keys from the ignition. "Wake up, baby. We're here."

"No way in hell I'm marrying you, jarhead." She yawned and sat up, staring through the windshield. "I mean it."

"Be nice." He traced her pout with his finger. "Or I'll ask the preacher to put *obey* back in the ceremony just for you."

"Rot in hell." Her tone was pure sweetness.

He chuckled, tugged gently on the long copper mane. Then he gave into temptation. He wrapped his hand in the red length and kissed her, his tongue sweeping into her mouth and laying claim.

A rap on the driver's window interrupted. He stopped, glanced over his shoulder. "What?"

Bendigo opened the door. "Wait for the honeymoon, son."

Durango laughed. He released Heather and swung out of the rig to hug the older man. "So, you made it."

"Me and the folks. I flew into Paine Field in Everett to pick up Liz and Art." Bendigo smiled at Heather. "Come on out, honey. I'm glad you two settled your differences."

She slid out of the pickup. She stretched, yawned again, and then took a moment to straighten the short denim skirt. She smoothed her tumbled hair. "So, you two boys planned this farce?"

"I did." Durango frowned at the note of scorn. "I invited Bendigo, Uncle Quentin, and Aunt Vicky along with your folks. Where is everyone?"

"Dad and Art are in the restaurant swapping lies. The two moms went shopping." Bendigo studied Heather with knowing cobalt eyes. "They decided you needed the perfect dress."

"Moms?" Heather's tone grew spiteful, and far too sweet, obviously determined to protect herself from his cousin's criticism even if he hadn't shared it yet. "I thought your mother died when you were an infant, Benjy."

"Ouch." Bendigo cocked a brow. "Don't you remember Dad's advice, Durango? He's always told us not to mess with a cook, a mule, or a red-headed woman."

"I'm a slow learner." Durango reached for her, slid an arm around her waist, and pulled her close. "She's pissed because I hauled her out of Pop's Café when she was with another man."

"I see. What happened to the guy?"

"I had him locked in a storage closet for a few hours." Durango felt her quiver when he rested a hand on her hip. "We've been on the road ever since."

"Then I'll bet you could use something to eat. I'm proud of you. There was a time you'd have half-killed a man for trying to take your woman."

"I'm not his." Heather lifted her chin. "I'm not marrying him. If I must make a scene, I will."

The defiance didn't surprise Durango. He'd expected her pride to rally once she'd slept for a few hours. "We'll talk about it when we're alone, Heather Marie."

"Spit in the wind and call it a shower."

He chuckled, guided her toward the back of the truck, and unlocked the vintage canopy. "Where's our room, Bendigo?"

"Back there." Bendigo pointed to the individual cabins on the far side of the parking lot. "I thought you two would want privacy. Is everything okay?"

"It's fine. She was pregnant when she left me. We have twin daughters and we're getting married." Durango met Bendigo's gaze, a mirror of his own. "If something happens to me when I'm on a mission for Nighthawke, you look after them."

"No problemo." Bendigo reached in the back of the pickup and collected suitcases. "I've got your back now that I know what's happening. For a moment, I thought I was loco."

"You're his cousin." Heather jerked her head toward Durango. "It's close enough for government work."

"I told you before. Be nice." He patted her seat. "I like your ranting and raging." Durango pinched her tush quickly. "Not to mention your sweet tyranny."

"Honestly." Bendigo led the way toward one of the cabins. "Didn't I tell you to wait for the honeymoon?"

# CHAPTER TWELVE

Durango waited until they were in the cabin. A king-size bed was the centerpiece, a nightstand on either side. By the window overlooking the parking lot was a table and two chairs. A flat-screen television, which neither of them would bother to watch, was mounted on the wall above the dresser.

He gripped her shoulders and turned Heather to face him. Keeping his voice low so he didn't entertain his cousin, Durango said, "This is how it works. You marry me and everything will be slick as ice."

Indignation darkened the green eyes. "And if I don't? What then?"

"You explain to Art and Liz why you won't." He ignored the sudden hiss of her breath. "You also tell them you might be pregnant again. We never take any precautions, do we?"

She caught her breath. A blush brightened her face, then she managed to meet his gaze. "Was that why you did all this?"

He lowered his head so only she could hear his whisper. "And because we belong together. You'll be thirty-four this summer and I've turned thirty-eight. We're parents. It's long past time for us to act like grownups, instead of trying to constantly one-up each other. "

She didn't answer for a moment. She studied him with mingled respect and confusion. She moistened her lips. "I guess I have a wedding present for you then."

"Really?" He framed her face with his hands, leaned down to brush her mouth with his. "What?"

"I intended to give it to you before I left." Wariness crept into her gaze. "Will you be mad because I planned to hurt you with it?"

"Of course not." He dropped a kiss on her nose. "You'll do anything to win. All's fair in love and war, baby. Show me."

When he released her, she crossed to her suitcase and opened it, removing a layer of clothes. She piled them on the bed.

He went to look. His cousin already was. Durango's gaze fell on a framed studio photograph.

Two small strawberry-blond girls sat on Santa's lap. Both had the urchin grins he rarely saw on Heather's face anymore. When had she stopped smiling? Dark blue eyes, the color of his own, twinkled up at him. They wore ruffly navy dresses, obviously donned for the special occasion, white tights, and ballet-style shoes.

He put his arm around Heather's waist, his hand resting on her hip. "Which is which? Who is Dallas? Galveston?"

Silence and then Heather pointed to the child who appeared as if she'd leap in excitement. "That's Dallas, Ally for short. It took five tries before Galveston, Toney, would smile at the same time."

"Amateurs." Durango studied the picture of his daughters. "I'll have to take my own photos to get decent ones."

There were two other framed photographs. One showed the twins with the Easter bunny. The next was of the duo in fairy princess costumes for Halloween.

"This is my favorite." Heather took out the last picture, one of the twins in jeans, T-shirts, boots, and equestrian helmets riding actual ponies. "They always argue about who gets the pinto."

Durango chuckled at the child sitting on a small bay, a fierce scowl on her face as she glared at whoever took the photo. Her twin sister beamed from the back of a black and white Shetland. The girls looked like real children, not models. "This is the one I want. Who gets the others?"

Before she responded, Bendigo asked, "Are there enough for Mom and Dad to have one?" He grinned down at Heather. "Vicky's been a mother to me since she married Dad when I was eight years old. You won't give her any heartburn, will you?"

"Of course not. I love Vicky." Heather heaved a sigh. "The jarhead pisses me off most of the time, but he'd be a real mess if she hadn't raised him. It's up to Durango. I brought one for him, one for my folks, and one for Tex and Estelle, although I really can't stand them, so you can have it for your parents. I already gave Pop one to hang in his office."

Bendigo hugged her quickly. "You've always been a hell of a woman, Heather. Want to marry me instead of him? Like he says, he's a slow learner. His head is so hollow, he has to talk with his hands to keep away from the echo."

"We could spend the next fifty years insulting him." She giggled. "It might be fun."

Durango reached for her hand, drawing her close. "Come here, you." He shook his head. "When will I learn not to let you two join forces?"

He gestured to the photo of the twins with Santa. "Shall we give this one to Aunt Vicky and Uncle Quentin?"

"No, that one's for my cousin, Ann Barrett." Heather looked defensive. "Choose a different one, Bendigo."

He nodded, then selected one of the girls in the fairy princess costumes. "Mom will love it. She's always wanted little girls to spoil after raising six wild boys."

Heather passed him the framed photograph of the twins with the Easter bunny. "You'll have to give this one to Mom and Dad at the same time, or I'll hear about it all day. Even if they haven't said anything to you or your folks, they're still pissed at me for not telling them about the twins before."

"Deal." Bendigo started for the door, pictures in hand. "We're meeting for brunch at 1300 hours. I'll tell them to expect the two of you then."

Durango glanced at the clock radio on the nightstand. "One o'clock, civilian time. That gives us nearly five hours. Thanks."

When his cousin left the room, Durango pointed to the photo of the twins with Santa. "Why does Ann get this one, baby?"

"Because she made the dresses for the girls and sent them." Heather's gaze remained on her suitcase.

"So, she knew you were in Nashville the whole time and about them. Is that it?"

Heather nodded. "When I confided in her, I thought she'd betray me in a heartbeat. She didn't. Last time we talked, she said it was my secret to share, not hers. I'm sorry."

"For what?" He pulled her into his arms. "Your mom told me she knew where you were and lectured me constantly for making the wrong choices."

"I swore her to secrecy." Heather tipped her head, bewilderment on her face. "I made her promise not to give you my address or phone number, but I never really expected her to keep her word. She loves you so much. I didn't tell Mom about the twins. I wanted you to know first. Pop, my cousins, and everybody I talked to in Baker City didn't share either."

"Hoist on your own petard, Empress." Mentally, he tested the idea of people's allegiance to her. Liz's behavior wasn't new. She made no secret of the fact that her daughter came first, last, and always. As for the people who lived in Baker City, he had a certain number of friends there, but again, they were related to Heather. She was one of them and he wasn't. Like they'd told him repeatedly, she was family. He wasn't, at least not yet. He hoped that would change after the wedding.

"Laredo and my sisters told me to grow up more than once and to go after you." Durango kissed Heather, softly and quickly. "Amarillo read me from *The Book* time and again. She's always loved you and called you her 'real' sister."

"She's good to Maria."

"Yes, but it's not the same." He tried to think of a way to explain his youngest sister. "She's decent to the girl. It feels like Amie goes through the motions of being a mother as if she's an actress on TV."

"Maybe more counseling would help. Don't be mad at her. I told her it was your idea to help her get a place of her own, a job, and everything else. She didn't believe me."

"She's a smart kid, Empress, and she probably suspected I wouldn't have arranged to emancipate her from the folks. You did that. Do you want to get some sleep before brunch?"

"Not yet. I'm taking a shower and then calling the twins."

"I want you to bring them home, Heather Marie. ASAP."

"Remember what I always tell you. Want in one hand, crap in the other, and see which fills up first."

He entwined a hand in her hair and kissed her, silencing the protest. "I mean it, baby."

"Try saying, 'please' asshat. If you want me, you come back with me tomorrow." Her eyes sparked like an emerald fire. "Either I come before your brother, your parents, and your business, or I don't come at all."

"Damn, baby." He claimed her mouth with his for a long, slow kiss, then lifted his head. "I thought I made you come a dozen times in the truck. Guess I'll have to try again."

She kicked him in the ankle, and swore when she stubbed her toe on his boot. "Do you ever listen, Marine? Damn it! I'm important too."

"I know you are." He snagged her wrist and towed her to the nearest chair. He sat down, pulled her onto his lap. The short skirt almost hiked up enough on its own, but he pushed it up farther. He cupped the nest of fiery red curls between her legs. "Let's see how long it takes me to show you that this time."

---

When she woke, he was still sleeping beside her. He must be as worn out as she'd felt after all their sexual shenanigans. She propped up on an elbow and watched him. He was a tawny-haired giant of a man. The sheet fell enough that she saw the mat of brown hair on his wide chest, but not the narrow waist. Broad shoulders, muscled arms, long legs, and those clever fingers that drove her to insanity and beyond.

He was a hunk and a half. No wonder she always wanted to jump his bones. And apparently, the road ran two ways. He couldn't resist her either. It always made her feel like the sexiest woman alive when he hauled her off to bed. Wait a minute. Wasn't this their pattern? He distracted her with sex and then went off to play soldier.

No. He'd said the games were over, that he intended to marry her. He'd never done this before, never set up a *fait accompli* with her parents and the uncle and aunt who raised him. Before she walked out on him, he wanted her to arrange the ceremony, a big wedding in the Baker City church with Reverend Tommy presiding. She'd barely looked at dresses, much less at invitations, or set a date. This time felt different.

She glanced at the radio-alarm clock on the nightstand. It was almost eleven hundred, and they were supposed to meet her parents and his family in little more than two hours. She had time to call the twins. She reached for her purse, removed the cell phone, found the contact list on it, and waited for the call to go through. When Kate answered, Heather said, "Hey, how's it going?"

"Fine." Kate paused. "Did you have a chance to talk to your dad about the kittens he promised the girls?"

"What kittens?" Heather paused. "When did they talk to Dad?"

"It was breakfast time here, so it must have been around 0500 hours there. He and your mom had just landed at an airport in Idaho. Toney woke up from a bad dream and wanted you, but your phone wasn't working, so we tried hers. I was concerned because it was so early, but they couldn't have been nicer."

"It's their stock in trade," Heather said. "Let me talk to Toney first. Is she all right?"

"Terrific. She's all excited about the kitten and she's squabbling with Ally."

"Are you serious? Toney never disobeys Ally, who's the boss of their world."

"We never offered kittens before, Heather. Here's Toney."

"Hi sweetie." Heather softened her voice. "What's going on?"

"I gotta Gramma and Grampa and I getta have a kitty. I'm naming it myself."

"Okay, Toney." Heather saw Durango's eyes open, and he shifted to stare at her. "Your daddy's here, honey. Do you want to talk to him?"

"Does he know 'bout my new kitty?"

"Not yet. You can tell him." Heather handed her cell phone to Durango. "Toney wants to talk to you. Be gentle."

He nodded, then turned on the speaker so they both could hear. "Hi, Toney." Apparently, there wasn't an answer and he stared across the room. "I love you, Toney."

Heather eased closer so she could hear her daughter's response, but by the odd look on Durango's face, there wasn't one.

He repeated the words. "I love you."

Another silence. Then a tiny, childish voice asked, "And Ally?"

"Ally too," he said.

Something thumped in the distance and Heather reached for the phone, but he didn't give it to her. Instead, he waited.

After a few minutes, a little girl demanded. "Whobody has Mommy's phone?"

"It's me. Durango Hawke. Your daddy."

"Are you done being a so-jer yet? Are you goin' to come live with us?"

"I'd rather you come live with me, Toney."

"I'm not Toney. I'm me, Ally. Do you want just Toney?"

"No, I want both my little girls."

"And Mommy?"

"Oh yes. I definitely want your mommy."

"And Auntie Kate?"

"Just a second, Ally. Heather, who is Kate? Ally wants to know if Kate is coming home too."

"Of course," Heather spoke into the phone but left it in Durango's hand. "If we move here, she does too, Ally."

Another question followed. "Gramma Liz is comin' for our birthday. We get kitties. Does our daddy want them too?"

"Sweetheart, I want you, Toney, Mommy, and Aunt Kate," Durango drawled. "You can bring all the animals in the world with you."

"Even a 'berry pony? We want one like the one who taught Mommy to ride."

"A 'berry pony?" Durango frowned. "What's that? A toy horse?"

"No! Don't you know nothin'? Me and Toney want a 'berry pony for keeps, forever and ever. Mommy says it can't sleep in our room. It hasta have a room of its own."

"I see. What's a 'berry pony, Empress? The girls want one."

"Not right now." Heather spoke into the phone. "Dallas Waco, we've discussed this before. We can't keep a pony, especially a for real 'berry one in the house. That's final."

"Can we go pony-riding? We been super good. Auntie Kate said so."

"Yes. I'll take you and Toney on Sunday after church. Remember, you and Toney are coming to get me at the airport tomorrow. It will be after your nap, so be sure you take a nice, long one. Toney too."

"We gotta get Gramma Liz and Grampa Art too."

"That's right." Heather took a deep breath. "Now, Ally. I want you to be nice to Toney. She names her own kitty. You're not supposed to boss her around. That's my job and Aunt Kate's."

"It's not fair. She thinks and I talk. I've told you lots of times."

"I'm telling you what I want, honey." Heather bit back a smile. "Toney picks the name. You can tell me what she chooses."

"Okay. I love you, Mommy."

"I love you too. And Toney."

"Are you bringing our daddy home?"

"If he's done being a soldier." She heard her daughter drop the phone and knew Ally had raced to tell her twin the news. She took the phone from Durango and waited. In a moment, Kate was back on the line. "Hi again."

"Did you work out something with Ally? Will she stop picking on Toney?"

"Not in this life, Kate. We compromised. Toney names her kitten and Ally gets to tell me that name."

"Brilliant. It's why you get the big money. Then I'll ask Toney what the name is, and she can tell me."

"Sounds like a winner, Kate. Hug the girls for me. I'll see you tomorrow night." Heather ended the call and put her phone on the nightstand. She hesitated and then rolled over to face Durango. "Well, jarhead? Are you okay?"

"I'm not sure. It made it real, talking to them. I knew, but—"

"I know." She rested a hand on his jaw, felt the beginning beard stubble tease her palm. "They need a daddy. We need you."

"I know."

She kissed him quickly. "We both have to act like adults in this crazy world. Are you finally ready to make a home with me?"

"I've been ready ever since I came back almost five years ago and found you gone."

"Right answer, Hawke." She smiled down at him. "Now, prove it."

He chuckled, caught her hand, and pulled her on top of him. "Your turn, baby. Show me you still know how to ride a cowboy."

# PART 2

———————

BAKER CITY, WASHINGTON ~ JUNE 2019

# CHAPTER THIRTEEN

Heather pulled the rental car off the highway onto the paved shoulder. She switched off the engine, put the keys into her denim skirt pocket, and glanced over her shoulder at the twins sitting in their car seats in the back. "Wait here for me."

She slid out of her seat and shut the driver's door on Dallas' protests. The four-day trip from Nashville to western Washington state hadn't been easy with two four-year-olds and their kittens, but it was necessary. She eyed the large, garish sign in front of her grandparents' farm.

Winged purple and pink ponies with little cherubs wearing cowgirl gear riding them frolicked against a cloudy blue background. A golden sun smiled from one corner, rosy rays highlighting the top of the twelve-foot by eight-foot plywood boards. She gritted her teeth, offended by the blatant sentimentality before her gaze fell on the gold letters proclaiming the property was Hawke's Horse Heaven.

The next line said, "Training. Boarding. Sales." Then a website address and phone numbers were provided. She'd tried calling them and a perky receptionist answered, admitting it was an answering service and she could take messages about the potential horsy trainees.

Heather hadn't left any. When she looked up the website on the Internet, it was under construction.

She glared at the sign again before glancing down the road to the boundary fences. In her grandpa's day, they'd been a gleaming white. Now, the boards matched the sign, each section a different color. Purple, pink, blue, gold, rose, and then the pattern repeated.

Heather stalked to the wooden gates that blocked the driveway. It came as little surprise they were secured with padlocks and chains. Who did Durango Hawke think he was? This was her place, not his. It'd serve him right if she went to Baker City and bought a pair of bolt-cutters at the hardware store.

She studied the chain again. He knew her too well. It was reinforced steel, the type that was almost impossible to cut.

"You son of a—" She spun and marched back to the car. Did he believe the marriage ceremony six weeks ago was anything more than a farce? She'd show him. In the driver's seat, she started the engine, turned the car, and drove in the direction of Lake Maynard.

"Where we goin', Mommy?" Galveston asked.

Heather forced a smile when she glanced in the rearview mirror. "To your daddy's work, baby."

Dallas bounced up and down in her car seat. "Will he be there?"

"It's why we're going, sweetness."

"We're keeping the pretty sign, aren't we, Mommy?" Dallas asked, still excited. "We like it."

Heather grimaced. The damned thing looked like a child designed it. "We'll see, Ally. It makes me want to hurl."

"Auntie Kate says it's 'cause you had tummy flu," Dallas reminded her. "But you haven't upchucked since you started drinking tea at breakfast, not soda."

Kate had remained behind in Tennessee to finish selling the house and to ship their belongings. Heather sighed and hoped her best friend's prescription was correct. She'd received photos of the sign

three weeks before. The threat to the McElroy farm mobilized her into action. She quit her job, sang at a last few nightclubs, packed the kids and the kittens into the rental car, and headed for home.

Durango Hawke would pay! She'd see to it. He'd tricked her into marrying him. He said he was ready to be a husband and father. She thought it meant he'd come with her to Nashville for the twins' birthday, even if he hadn't point-blank said so.

Instead, she discovered he had plans to go to Colombia. Granted, he'd tried telling her that this was the last time, that he needed to lead the team, but after this, he'd make other arrangements.

Did he think she was stupid? Apparently so!

She'd told him to come to Nashville by the end of May. He hadn't. So, she mailed back her rings, something that should have him on the next plane. Once again, he didn't do what she expected. He sent pictures of that awful billboard. She muttered more swear words.

An hour later, she sat in the reception area of Hawke Construction. She'd driven across Idaho to Washington state today. She wasn't the only one who was tired. She studied the two small girls sitting in the chair next to hers. The twins looked as if they'd fall asleep any moment. It was past time for their naps.

Her gaze lingered on them. They'd provided her with a future, two incredibly special reasons to start a new life. What did Zeb Steele call it? Oh yeah, *Charlie Mike*—continue mission. Without her daughters, could she have survived this long? She'd learned the platitude was correct, war was hell. So was life. She closed her eyes and listened to the whir of the ceiling fan.

*The choppers came out of the sunset, headed toward the Evac Hospital. Chinooks. She knew by the rhythmic thumping that filled her ears, by the vibrations she felt in the air. She hurried across the compound, early for her shift. It didn't matter. With a mass cal underway, they'd be working round the clock in O.R. Even with a push on and lately, it seemed as if the troops were always pushing, she prayed Durango's unit wouldn't be in the thick of the fighting.*

"M-m-m-m-Mommy?"

The treble tone filtered through the din of incoming helicopters. Heather struggled to focus on the childish voice. It offered a rare peace.

"Mommy, no 'member. Mommy!"

Heather shook her head, sent her thoughts scattering. She turned, halfway across the office. When had she moved? She didn't know. She glanced down, saw the little girl in front of her. She dropped to her knees, gathered the child into her arms. "It's okay, Toney. I'm back."

"Me too, Mommy." Dallas joined them. "Hug me too."

Heather managed a smile, a reassuring one, she hoped. She drew both children against her, held them tight. She risked a swift look around the office. No one seemed to have spotted her temporary mental exit.

Phones continued to ring, dividing the receptionist's attention between them and her computer screen. Overhead, the fan turned, trying to circulate the air. That was it, Heather thought. The noise sounded so much like that of a distant chopper, she'd been thrown back to her last tour in a combat zone. She shuddered. She'd been a civilian for seven years. How long would it take to forget the dying soldiers who plagued her dreams?

Dallas pulled back, dark blue eyes wide. "I wanta see Daddy. Toney does too. Now!"

"Not yet, sweetie." Heather smoothed the strawberry blond hair. "Soon."

"I hate waitin'." Dallas heaved a dramatic sigh. "How come we gots to?"

"Because he's working." Heather repeated the excuse the receptionist had given, grateful for the opportunity to devise a plan.

How could she break in on him when he would act like the victor in their personal war? He'd ordered her to bring the girls home, and she had. Granted, he'd upped the ante when he threatened the ranch, her only security in an insecure world. He'd never understand she might have changed the battlefield. It didn't mean she'd surrender.

"You all better, Mommy?" Galveston inquired, concern on her small face.

"Sure." Heather released the girls from her embrace and allowed them to race around the office. It was rude, but it might irritate the receptionist enough to make her interrupt Durango.

Heather returned to the chair, sat down, and picked up a magazine. She flipped through it. Ten minutes passed.

Dallas charged back to stand in front of her. "Mommy, it's been forever. I want Daddy."

"Me too." Galveston came to a stop behind Dallas.

"All right, girls." Heather stood, taking a deep breath. She shook back her hair. She was out of patience too. "Like Grandpa Art says, 'Attack, always attack.' Let's do this!"

Heather tucked in Dallas' T-shirt and led the way toward the oak door, followed by the twins, ignoring the squawk of protest from the receptionist. For the first time, Heather noticed the framed photographs of structures the company built hanging on the office walls.

She'd overseen Hawke Construction when the strip mall in the nearest picture was underway. The same went for the department store in the next photo. Warmth eased into her.

Heather paused outside the conference room door, trying to prepare herself for the upcoming scene. She twisted the knob. The door opened.

A long table took up the center of the boardroom. A group of people in the chairs around it turned to stare at her and the twins. Most of them wore casual clothes, except Jeff Ransom in his usual dark suit, a fedora on the table in front of him. None were dressed like Durango. A sleeveless blue denim shirt was open, halfway down his chest, exposing tanned skin. Would he ever dress like a company president?

Durango didn't look up from the stack of blueprints in front of him. "What the hell is it now, Laurie?"

"Mommy, he said a bad word," Dallas informed Heather in a clear, carrying voice.

"He does that a lot, Ally. I guess you should share your teacher's time-out rule for those."

———

The words trickled into his brain like a spatter of spring rain drops. Had he gone crazy? Or did others hear that sexy taunt?

He slowly lifted his gaze, afraid he dreamed in the daytime. She stood at the far end of the room, the twins beside her like small bookends.

"This is real." He stood, shoving back his chair. He walked the length of the room and stopped in front of the trio. "It's about time, Heather Marie."

"Are you our daddy?" One of the children raised her chin and tipped back her head to look up at him. "Are you?"

"Yes, honey." He returned the steady look and marveled at the cobalt blue eyes that were the same color as his. He smiled, dropped to one knee. "Who is who? Which one of you is Dallas? Galveston?"

"I'm only Dallas when I'm naughty. The rest of the time, I'm Ally," the little girl on Heather's left told him. "She's Toney."

"Can I call you Galveston?" Durango asked the child on Heather's right.

"No," Dallas told him. "Her name is Toney."

"Can't Galveston decide?" Durango tried not to laugh.

"No, I already told you."

Heather frowned at Dallas. "We've discussed this. Toney says what she wants."

Fury filled the child's face, but before a tantrum started, Durango intervened. "Do I get a hug?"

Heather nodded, urging the girls forward. They moved hesitantly into Durango's arms.

"Are you really our daddy?" Galveston asked.

"I really am." His hold tightened around both of his children. "I'm glad you've come home to me. Did you bring your Auntie Kate and the kittens?"

"Just our kitties," Dallas answered. "Auntie Kate's comin' soon as she can. And we getta have ponies, 'berry ones.'"

"You promised," Galveston whispered. "For our birthday."

"Then it's for sure." Durango held them tight. He looked over their heads to wink at Heather. "Remember what your mom used to say? We'd have kids just like us. Sounds as if there will be a real zoo on the old homestead."

"I'll limit animals to the ones I want to clean behind." Heather's tone was sweet, too sweet. "You're not much use," she paused, then added with sugary spite, "in the barn."

"I missed you too, Empress." He chuckled. Then he glanced over his shoulder at Tia, a full five feet, nothing in her jeans and plaid shirt. Plump and grandmotherly, the construction site manager would take offense if he didn't choose her to look after the twins. He smiled at her. "Will you take the girls to the cafeteria for ice cream cones? Their mom and I will be in my office. We need to talk in private for a few minutes."

"Mommy's mad at you," Galveston warned him softly.

"I know." Durango ruffled her hair and reluctantly released his children before he stood. "Go have some ice cream. When you come back, your mommy will be all over her hissy fit. I promise."

Dallas eyed him, tilting her head to one side and then the other. "Fibbin' gets you a long time-out. And no cartoons till you say sorry."

"I'll remember that."

He waited until the girls and Tia left the room. He wanted to pull Heather into his arms and kiss her. He had to wait. He enjoyed the rage that sparked in her green eyes for a moment longer before he looked at Jeff. "Let's postpone this meeting until the day after tomorrow."

"Works for me." Jeff winked at Heather. "Good to see you and the kids, *Capitana*. They've sure grown since I saw them the first time. You and Katie let me think they were hers."

Heather shrugged. "Even in the Air Force, you should have learned what 'assume' means, Jeff."

"True enough." Jeff nodded.

Durango eyeballed his friend. "Thanks for oversharing, Ransom."

"No problem." Jeff grinned at him.

Durango laughed. He rested a hand on Heather's shoulder and urged her from the boardroom. She jerked away from him, so he followed. He admired the way the full skirt swung around her knees, her bare legs, and her sandals. She'd dressed for the early summer heat.

She stormed into his office and whirled to face him. "You son of a—! How dare you try to steal my property?"

"Got you home, didn't it, Mrs. Hawke?" He liked the way the name rolled off his tongue, and he grinned. He closed the door, locked it before he turned, and leaned against it. He folded his arms. He enjoyed the way her breasts heaved under the sleeveless western blouse. "Go ahead, Mrs. Hawke. Rant and rave."

"As if I need your permission." She glared at him. "And don't call me that. I'm Heather McElroy. You're not changing who and what I am."

"You're mine. I've got the marriage certificate to prove it, Mrs. Hawke."

She fumed for a moment before she cussed him up one side and down the other. He ignored the words, relished the sound of her husky, low voice that always made him think of wild sex. Was there time to make love to her now? Probably not.

"Are you even listening to me? Damn you, Durango Hawke. Answer me."

He shrugged. "I was thinking."

"Don't strain yourself."

"About where to have you first." He scanned the room. "I could clear off the desk. Or the chair. Then again, what about the floor? Hmm, or up against the door."

"No way." She planted her hands on her hips. "You're not touching me."

"Want to bet?" He sauntered to her, caught her pointed chin, and tipped it to read the strain on her finely boned features. He should yell at her about the pain she caused, but the idea was a fleeting one. The last six weeks had been stressful for her too. He measured the wear and tear in her eyes, old eyes in a young face. "You look like hell."

"F. off and die, Marine. It's all your fault."

"Everything is, according to you." He bent to brush her lips with his, careful not to deepen the kiss. Given half a chance, she'd bite him. "It's what makes you special, Empress."

"Yeah, right."

He grinned at the snotty tone. He caught her wrist, pulled her after him to his desk. He opened the center drawer, removed the rings she'd sent him. "Come here."

"I won't. You can't make me."

"Hell, I can't." He grasped her left wrist, placed the gold band on the third finger, and followed it with the emerald. "Rant, rave, and issue all the edicts you want. I can handle you and I enjoy making you beg."

"There's more to life than sex."

"Not when you've been gone." He kissed her again. He fitted his hands around her waist, lifted her to sit on the desk. "It's been too long since our road trip."

"I hate you."

"Only when you're angry with me." He pushed up the skirt. "Let's see how long it takes me to change your mind."

"You can't. The girls—"

"Are safe having ice cream." His hands slid up her smooth thighs to the panties, already damp. His kiss distracted her while he removed them, and then he eased two fingers inside her.

She squirmed on the desk. "What if they want us? Someone could come in here."

"I locked the door." He smiled into her face. "Move for me, baby."

"I don't believe you, Durango Hawke. There's more to a relationship than sex."

"Not when I've been missing you." He started a slow out, in, out again motion with his hand. His thumb rubbed gently against the small bit of flesh in the fiery red curls. "Now, tell me you love me."

"I won't until you say it first."

"Sounds like we have a proverbial *Catch-22*. I'm damned if I do and damned if I don't." He kept up the pattern while she rose and fell, meeting his thrusts. Wet, hot heat surrounded his fingers as he moved them. "I'll take whatever crap you dish out. You're worth it, but the twins don't need to be upset by your fits. Save the sniping for when we're alone. Now, say the words."

She shook her head, but he knew she was close. His thumb rocked into her. She came, but even when she gasped, cried out in release, she didn't surrender.

He hooked a foot around the chair and pulled it close so he could sit between her legs. "You're a stubborn tyrant."

"Why is that news to you?"

"It's not." He slipped his hands under her derriere, drew her near. "Let's see what happens now."

"Damn you, Durango."

"Not what I want to hear." His mouth claimed her, roving through the bright red curls. He licked, lapped, and finally dove deep inside, his tongue taking her the way he would later tonight when he really had his woman. She was right. They were running out of time and he had to end this soon. He drew the little bud into his mouth and sucked.

She came apart, hands twisting in his hair. "I love you. I love you. I love—"

# CHAPTER FOURTEEN

Afterward, she levered off the desk, legs trembling when she stood. He bent, picked up her panties, and she snatched them out of his hand. "You never listen. You just think that having sex with me is enough. I listened to the vows you made and stupid me, I believed those promises. I should have known you'd never change, jarhead."

"What does that mean?"

"We always do the same thing. Hump like rabbits and never talk to each other. It's just a lot of sick repetition and I'm tired of it."

Sudden silence while he stared at her as if she was a stranger and she took advantage of it. She moved her purse off the visitor's chair where she'd dropped it, sat down, and quickly put on her underwear. Then she rose and hurried to the door, unlocking it, and walking out into the reception area.

She saw the twins and Tia coming toward her. Grateful the ice cream adventure had lasted the forty-five minutes she and Durango spent in his office, she smiled at her daughters. "Come on, chickadees. Let's go home."

Galveston hurried toward her. "Mommy, are you still mad?"

"No, honey." Even if she didn't tell him, Durango had made his point about not fighting in front of the little girls. "It's okay. Your daddy promised to clean up behind all the animals we have."

"Payback, Empress?" Durango stood beside her and smiled at Tia. "I'll be in on Monday morning so we can finish the meeting about upcoming projects. After that, you, Jeff, and Amie will have to keep the company functioning for a week or so."

"That's fine." Tia beamed at Heather. "If you need him around longer, call us. We'll be fine and he can do whatever you want at the ranch."

"If the gates weren't padlocked, we'd have met him there."

"Didn't he tell you?" Tia looked baffled. "The state went upriver and filled in all the overflow channels with rock. The flooding last November washed out the bridge. You need four-wheel drive to get through Cedar Creek when it's low and you can't when it's high."

Heather glowered up at Durango. "Why didn't you share that?"

"Because I was distracted by how beautiful you are." He put an arm around her waist. "George is working on permits. Since it's considered a 'wild creek,' it changed course and makes a replacement bridge a new structure. The county director is giving us a hard time and so are Herman MacGillicudy and his developer friends who want the McElroy spread for the gravel."

"Really?" She narrowed her eyes. "Did you provide them with my definition of 'want,' or did you keep it a secret, Hawke?"

He chuckled, squeezed her gently, and kissed her hair. "I didn't think they had a need to know, Mrs. Hawke. Be careful with any bad words."

"I'll consider it." Heather focused on the identical twins. The same height, the same strawberry blond hair, the same cobalt blue eyes, so she'd chosen a blue shirt for Dallas and a yellow one for Galveston to make it easy for Durango to tell them apart. While they were away with Tia, they'd switched their T-shirts and a game of Mix and Match was obviously in progress. Heather wasn't going to tell him.

Galveston frowned up at him. "You and Mommy have the same last name?"

"That's right, Dallas. You and Galveston are Hawkes too."

"Toney," Galveston corrected, her voice fierce. "Not Galveston. Her name is Toney."

Dallas tilted her head speculatively, her tone soft and sweet. "He can say Galveston if he wants."

Heather heaved a sigh, shaking her head. "Girls, don't do this. Not now. Not on the first day."

"Easy." Durango smiled at their daughters. "You're the one who said Galveston could make up her own mind what she wanted to be called."

Heather folded her hands, eyeing the children, then the man. "All right. I'll let the three of you work this out, but I don't want to hear any pissing and moaning."

"You won't, Mommy," the twins chimed. "We never do."

"I won't either. Thanks for stepping back so we can get to know each other."

They ambled outside, the babble of conversation behind them fading as the glass doors to the office building closed. Heather took a deep breath of fresh air. June in western Washington was an odd month. The sun might shine one moment, and a rain squall erupt the next.

"I didn't want to interrupt you at work, Durango. Now, I'm grateful I didn't go into Baker City for bolt cutters."

"You'd have noticed the bridge was gone when you arrived at the creek."

She hesitated, wondering if she should stop the game of Mix and Match the twins were playing, or let it go. His bass rumble broke into her thoughts.

"I'll get the truck. I'll tell Jeff to return this rental. Start unloading it."

The orders irritated her. She lifted her chin. Let him learn the differences between their daughters on his own. It'd serve him right if the twins outwitted him for the next fifty years. She adopted her sweetest voice. "Whatever you say, Hawke."

When he was out of earshot, she eyed the girls. "Okay, you two. What brought on this behavior?"

Dallas wrinkled her nose. "He's way bossy."

"And he can't hear what we say," Galveston added.

"Sweetie, I don't understand." Heather smoothed Galveston's red-gold hair. "There's nothing wrong with your daddy's ears."

The four-year-old heaved a huge sigh. "Mommy, he doesn't listen to us. Ally told him to call me Toney, but he didn't."

Dallas clung to Heather for a moment. "Are you gonna tattle?"

"Nope." Heather hugged both girls. "Mix and Match doesn't hurt anyone."

That issue resolved, she unlocked the car. "Ally, get your and Toney's backpacks. Toney, grab the stuff out of the passenger seat. I'll get the kittens."

Before she and the twins finished unloading their belongings, Durango arrived in a late model, green, Ford F-150 Lariat four-wheel drive. He parked carefully beside the car and began to remove the suitcases and boxes from the trunk to put them in the back end of the truck. "I have a canopy on order, but it hasn't come yet."

"I never thought I'd see the day you got rid of your restored Chevy pickup." Heather brought over the carrier with the two fluffy gray kittens. "Why did you?"

"I didn't." Durango opened the back door to the extended cab. "This rig is for you."

Guilt trickled into her mind. Maybe she should stop the twins' game. "You bought me a brand-new truck? How did you know I'd be here to drive it?"

"Because you're predictable, Empress." He carefully placed the crate on the floor. "I've always been able to make you do what I want."

"Really?" She eyed him, then gestured to the child seats in the back of the car. She'd let him work out his own deal with their daughters. He tended to let his mouth run away with him, but it wasn't her fault.

Once he'd secured the seats in the pickup, she helped the girls into them while he took the keys to the rental into the office for Jeff. She checked the kittens once more.

When Durango returned, she climbed into the passenger seat. "I know you'll insist on driving, Hawke."

He gave her a solid once-over, leaned down to kiss her, a quick soft touch of his lips. "We'll have to take this rig on a road trip soon."

Heat scorched her face. "Son of a—" she muttered.

His low chuckle teased her. He squeezed her knee, fingers trailing under her skirt, resting on her bare thigh for an instant before he stepped back. "Watch that potty mouth, Mrs. Hawke."

"Payback is hell." She glared at him. "Stop hassling me."

"I'll think about it." He snagged the shoulder strap of the seatbelt, started to draw it across her, his hand lingering on her breast.

She took the seatbelt away from him, clicking it into place. "Obviously, you need constant reminders about what's appropriate and what isn't in front of the kids."

"I'll keep that in mind." He shut her door and walked around the front of the pickup.

It didn't take long for him to drive through Lake Maynard and turn onto the highway to Baker City. The narrow blacktop road wound through the foothills of the Cascades. Giant evergreens marched alongside the pavement, broken by occasional farms and places where the trees had been cleared.

Up ahead, she saw the familiar snow-capped peak of Mount Carmody and two other mountains beside it. She glanced over her shoulder and noticed the twins had fallen asleep.

She let her attention return to the road. For the first time, she glimpsed her neighbor's new pink and purple sign, Cedar Creek Guest Ranch. "Wow, I didn't realize the Williams were reopening the place."

"They're not. Cat O'Leary McTavish won the place in an essay contest and moved in last fall. I had Ransom rebuild the boundary fences between the McElroy spread and the dude ranch."

"Have you talked to her about—?" Heather stopped, unwilling to bring up her uncle and his brother when the twins might overhear. "She could tell us if we have company."

"I know we don't." He glanced quickly at her. "I haven't bought groceries this week. Do you want me to go to the mercantile in Baker City?"

"I'm sure the freezer and cupboards are full," Heather said. "I'm not ready to see everyone yet. Let's go home."

"Okay. I did get milk, eggs, and fresh vegetables. We'll survive."

"Always have," she agreed.

He turned in the drive, stopped the truck. "I'll get the gates. You bring in the rig."

"Is the word *please* part of your vocabulary? Or is it one Marines don't use?"

"I'll work on it." He laughed. "Please drive your truck, baby."

"All right, but you take it through the creek this time." She unfastened her seatbelt, slid across the bench seat to sit behind the wheel. She studied the control panel, grateful the Ford had an automatic transmission. She hated shifting gears.

She drove through the gate, waited for him to close and lock them. She'd have to see about getting a set of keys to them or she'd be locked on the ranch. The idea didn't terrify or intimidate her. It held an odd appeal. She'd be safe. When she saw him approaching, she returned to the passenger seat.

At the riverbank, he showed her how to adjust the four-wheel drive and put it into gear. Then he eased down the bank into the water. He drove in a slow arc to remain in the shallows and drove toward the opposite shore. He pointed downstream. "You have to stay above that set of ripples or you'll sink into a hole and have to wade out. Not a biggie, because I have a winch on the Chevy and larger ones on the tractor and bulldozer."

"I remember Dad and Uncle Fenn talking to Granddad about that." She wrinkled her nose. "We've stuck a few trucks over the years."

"Yup, and we've got them out of the creek again." Durango guided the truck up the inside bank and headed toward the river beach. He paused at the next set of gates. "These just have a snap on the chain. I haven't needed to worry about trespassers since the bridge washed out."

"My turn to get them." Heather looked over her shoulder at the twins. Both were awake now. "Ally, do you want to help me? Toney?"

"I'll stay with Daddy," Galveston decided. "You go, Toney."

Heather took a deep breath and decided not to bring up the name switch. She climbed out of the pickup, opened the rear door, and helped Dallas out of the safety seat. They strolled toward the gold-painted wooden gates. "You could give him a break. How fair is this when he only met you today?"

"I'll ask Toney." Dallas skipped alongside her. "But he hasta be good, Mommy."

"All right." Heather swung the gates wide. She didn't turn back to the pickup. Instead, she began to walk up the long, tree-lined track. Cottonwoods, alders, and huge maples shaded the dirt road. She kept her pace slow so her daughter could stay beside her.

"Did you live here when you were little, Mommy?"

"No, my grandparents and Uncle Fenn did. I used to visit a lot when I was your age. My grandma and grandpa went to heaven before you and Toney were born."

"What about Uncle Fenn, Mommy? Is he in heaven too?"

Heather stopped. Another gate, about thirty feet away, blocked the driveway in front of her, but this one led to a pasture. Off to the left, on a rise of ground, was the large, three-story Victorian house. She almost saw her grandfather sitting on the porch swing. Grandma would be coming through the screen door carrying a tray with a pitcher of homemade lemonade, ice tinkling. Fenn would lie on the porch, head pillowed on his old dog.

They were dead and gone, every one of them.

Dallas interrupted the memories. "Mommy, what about Uncle Fenn?"

"He was a soldier, and he hasn't come home yet." She couldn't discuss the wargames the government played, not with a four-year-old. "I'm not sure where he is, Ally."

"Then he could still come back, so don't cry 'bout him no more." That settled to her satisfaction, Dallas looked around. "Mommy, what is it?"

Heather looked in the direction where her daughter pointed. Down the hill to the right was a huge steel structure. "It's an indoor riding arena. What's it doing here? My grandparents didn't have one. Where did it come from?"

"I built it for you after George told me you inherited the McElroy spread." Durango stopped beside them. Galveston swung from one hand as if he were a new toy. "Figured you'd need it to train horses year-round."

"Horses?" Dallas repeated. "Mommy, can we ride horses?"

"But Mommy's a nurse," Galveston broke in.

"Not anymore." Durango bent and swung Galveston up to sit on one broad shoulder. "Your mom likes horses better than sick people. If she wants, she can work with horses all the time."

"We like horses better too." Dallas tipped her head back to eye her father. "Mommy read us your letter 'bout being sorry to miss our birthday."

"And how you was trying to find us 'berry ponies," Galveston added. "Did you?"

"I'm trying, honey, but they're not easy to locate. What if we go see the horses in the upper barn now?"

"I want to check out the arena first," Heather said. "And I choose what I train. You better not have found customers for me."

"I know better. You'd fry my gizzards."

"Got that right." She liked the layout. He'd left one side open so the horses could see outside. The ends were closed in to block the weather. She opened the gate and stepped into the ring. It was a hundred and twenty feet by sixty, more than big enough for her use. She only worked two or three horses at a time. The clear-span roof meant she could jump horses if she chose, but more likely, it'd keep her safe if one cut loose in a bucking spree.

She walked across to the far side and studied the row of box stalls. "How many horses can I train?"

"You've got eighteen stalls, plus one for grooming with cross-ties, a shower stall, a tackroom, and grain-room. In the middle, you have an office. The restroom is attached." He gestured to the loft. "It holds thirty tons of hay. You can't see it from here, but there's a shavings crib at the far end with a covered walkway."

"You do make it hard to stay angry with you." Heather mused. "I'll work on it."

"I have faith in you."

125

Dallas jumped up and down. "It's been forever. Now, can we see the horses?"

"Yes, let's go." Heather headed for the gate. She'd return and drool over her new arena later. "We'll visit Gramma Liz soon and talk to her about ones for me to train."

"Let me go." Galveston wriggled until Durango did. She raced after her twin. "Come on, Toney. We'll find the real horses."

Heather strolled beside Durango after the twins in the direction of the smaller barn. "I can't believe you built that for me."

He shrugged, put his arm around her waist, fingers splaying on her hip. "I had to find a hobby. Otherwise, damn near five years of celibacy would have driven me to join a monastery."

"I'd have liked to see that. You're the horniest man I know."

He drew her to a stop. He framed her face with calloused hands, lowering his head. His breath was warm on her lips. "Are you gonna make me stay in the doghouse tonight? Or do I get to carry you off to my bed where you belong?"

"No way, Hawke." She shivered, moistened suddenly dry lips. "I'm not sleeping with you."

"Then, don't torment me." He bent his head.

When his mouth touched hers, she melted against him. She threaded her fingers in his tawny hair and kissed him back. Their tongues met, clashed, and dueled. She tore her lips away, moaned softly when he cupped her rear end, squeezing her butt with those large hands that drove her nuts. "Oh my Gawd, Durango."

He smiled against her skin, mouth trailing down her neck to the pulse in the hollow of her throat. "Changing your mind?"

She shook her head, sighing when he kissed her ear. "Not yet. You want me, don't you?"

"*God*, yes!"

"Well, you know what I have to say." She wrenched away from him and hurried toward the stable. "Want in one hand—"

He groaned, and she heard him coming behind her. "I don't think I can wait until I find a sitter and we go on a road trip, baby. I'm going to have you a lot sooner than that."

# CHAPTER FIFTEEN

Things had to change whether he realized it or not. Like he'd said, they were parents now and it was time to behave like adults. They couldn't just hump like rabbits at every opportunity when he was home. She'd count the minutes when he left on another combat mission until he returned, charging into her life, and they'd jump back into the nearest bed. He had to "daddy-up," and talking about a babysitter when he'd only met their daughters a couple of hours ago simply didn't cut it.

Heather led the way into the ten-stall barn and spotted the twins already standing outside the stall of a huge sorrel Warmblood. She recognized the mare as being the one his uncle had given Durango when he was a teenager. The horse traveled back and forth from Texas with him, coming in June and returning to Quentin's in September, boarding at her parents' place over the summer. "Isn't that Cinnamon?"

"Yes." Durango opened the hay-room door, picking up a five-pound bag of carrots. "Here. You can give her a treat."

"Oh, thank you." She knew he caught her sarcastic inflection, but he didn't say anything. She pulled out three long, skinny carrots and headed toward the old mare. Breaking off a piece, Heather offered it to the Belgian Morgan. Cinnamon accepted it as if it were her due, crunching the carrot into oblivion before nuzzling for more.

Instead of feeding Cinnamon, Heather glanced into the next stall. A big bay gelding stood and glared at her, pinning his ears, and baring ugly yellow teeth.

"I don't believe it." She caught her breath. It was her horse, Satan. She'd spent years training him until he took top ribbons at any show they entered. "Hey, buddy. How are you?"

She offered him a chunk of carrot. He snapped at the treat, narrowly missing her fingers. "Monster," she crooned. She held out another section.

Topping seventeen hands, Satan was as tall as Cinnamon, but his Thoroughbred and Quarter Horse breeding made him rangier and thinner than the mare. His coat was a deep, brownish red, meaning he was called a blood bay. His black mane and tail flowed long. While he had the traditional black stockings, he also had four white ankle socks. Those and the narrow blaze that ran from his star to the snip on his muzzle provided added glamor.

"You're so pretty." Heather gave the twenty-year-old horse another carrot. She dismissed the way he got closer and closer to her hand. He wouldn't bite her. He knew better. He just wanted to intimidate her.

"He's mean, Mommy," Galveston announced. "I like the other horses better."

"Can I feed him?" Dallas demanded. "I think he's awesome."

"Here." Heather gave each girl a whole carrot. "Now, remember to hold it up like an extra finger. Let the horse suck it up like a vacuum cleaner. Remember, they don't see colors the way we do. Fingers and carrots are almost the same shade to horses." She looked at the next stall, recognizing the young chestnut gelding. "And feed Flash too, so he doesn't get jealous."

"Daddy, will you help me?"

"Sure." Durango stepped up beside her, covering her little hand with his big one.

Heather showed Dallas how to hold the carrot again and then allowed the child to feed Satan by herself. Contrary to his threatening behavior with Heather, the gelding took the carrot slowly and carefully from the little girl.

"He's nice to me, Mommy," Dallas said. "Why is he being nasty to you?"

"I think he's still mad at me for selling him." Heather fed Satan one more treat, then moved to give Flash his share. "I found him a new home before I went—"

"To the scary, icky place?"

"That's right."

The twins had several names for the different warzones where Heather had been, one of the most common being *the bad place*. It was also how they explained her flashbacks.

"I found him a real good home with a nice girl," Heather went on. "But when I got out of the Army, she wouldn't sell him back to me."

Dallas petted Satan's nose when he nudged her. "Why is he here, then?"

"I bought him for your mommy when the girl was going off to college and she didn't want Satan to be lonely." Durango winked at Heather. "I should have told you when you visited in May, but we ran out of time."

Heather broke the last carrot in thirds and gave a portion to Durango for Cinnamon. "You were afraid of the competition. I'd have spent every minute riding Satan if I knew he was here."

"I wanta feed him again." Dallas took the piece of carrot and gave it to the huge horse. "Can I ride him?"

"He's too big for you," Durango said. "You'd better stick to ponies for a while longer."

Dallas scowled up at him and planted her fists on small hips and shouted, "I'm gonna ride him!"

"Stop it, Dallas Waco." Heather dropped to one knee to make eye contact with her daughter. "You won't ride any horse if you yell at him. They have big ears and hear a lot better than people. You know they don't like loud noises, don't you?"

"I'm sorry." Dallas softened her voice. "Mommy, I really wanna ride your horse."

"We'll wait and see." Heather held up her hand to halt the next protest before it started. "I haven't ridden him in ages. I don't know how good he'll be. You can ride Daddy's horse. Cinnamon is always nice."

"After you check Satan, can I ride him?" Dallas demanded.

Heather nodded, rising swiftly to her feet. A wave of exhaustion swept over her and she swayed. "I need to rest."

"But we wanna ride," Dallas complained.

"On Cinnamon," Galveston added. "Please."

The barn floor started to rise to meet her, and Heather's knees buckled. Before she fell, Durango caught her. He swung her up in his arms. "Don't. I can walk."

"Right. Did you sleep at all on the way home?" He didn't wait for an answer. "Come on, twins. We'll take your mom in the house for a nap. After that, you can ride."

"We're twins, but it's not our names," Dallas pointed out.

Heather turned her face against his chest, breathing in his scent. "Sorry, babe. You've got two little buggers to look after, and I can't help."

"I'll handle it." His voice was low. "You sleep. We'll unpack the truck, do some horseback riding and fix dinner."

"Settle the kittens in the pantry. Their food, litter, and sandbox were in one of the boxes in the trunk. The girls' boots and equestrian helmets are in their suitcases."

"We'll be fine, baby. I've got to make up a room for the girls. Any suggestions?"

"One with two beds." Sleep claimed her.

Hours later, she woke to find herself on the big brass bed in the master suite. A homemade patchwork quilt had been draped over her. She yawned, turned her head to eye the radio clock on the nightstand. It was almost 2030 hours, eight-thirty at night civilian time. She'd slept nearly five hours, oddly enough without dreaming.

"Mommy, you awake?" Dallas demanded from the doorway. "Come tuck us in."

Heather tossed the blanket aside and rolled to her feet, glancing at the pajama-clad child. "Did you take a bath? Brush your teeth? Be good for your daddy?"

"He still can't tell us apart," Dallas reported. "We were sorta good."

"Okay." Heather stretched, twisting, and arching her sore back. She was stiff from the long day of driving. She headed across the room. "He may as well have a baptism of fire."

Dallas entered the bedroom directly across the hall. Durango sat on the edge of one twin bed, Galveston ignoring him, face buried in the pillow.

Dallas climbed into the other bed. When she was under the covers, Heather adjusted the blankets. Then she went to Galveston, putting her hand on the little girl's back. "Sweetie, what's wrong?"

"I want my *blankie*." Galveston turned a red face to Heather, tears streaming down her face. "*He* won't get it."

"She has two blankets and a bedspread, Heather. She'll be warm enough. She's fine."

"Not without her *blankie*." Heather dismissed the comment. He'd only been a dad for an afternoon. "You don't get it."

She flipped back the covers to look for the patchwork quilt she'd made for Galveston before the twins were born. "Where can it be? Is it still in your backpack?"

More tears fell. "No, Mommy. I looked and looked."

"Damn it." Heather eyed Dallas. The little girl had a thumb in her mouth and an arm clamped around Henry, her beloved stuffed purple toy pony. "Honey, have you seen your sister's blanket?"

"Nope," Dallas said, around her thumb. "I bet we forgot it in the car."

Heather went in search of the backpacks. Empty, they hung neatly from hooks in the closet. The two boxes of favorite toys she'd brought had been unpacked. The girls' clothes were in the dresser drawers. She went through the entire bureau, trying to recall the last time she'd seen the ragged blanket. She glanced at Dallas. "Is it on your bed by mistake?"

"No, Mommy. I keep telling her she has to watch her special stuff or bad people will take it."

"I do watch!" Galveston wailed. "I want my *blankie*."

"I'll find it," Heather promised. She returned to the bed and cuddled Galveston close. "Now, let's think about this, Toney. Did we forget it in the motel this morning? Or did you have it in the car?"

"In the car." Galveston sniffled. "Ally spilled juice on it, and you said you had to wash it 'fore I could have it back. And you made Henry ride in the front with you and Ally got mad."

"Okay." Heather remembered World War Three nearly erupting in the back seat and removing the stuffed toy had averted disaster. "So, we had your *blankie* then. I went through the car three times and I'm sure it was empty when we left Lake Maynard."

"I'll call Jeff and have him check the rental in the morning before he returns it," Durango said. "Like I told her and you, she'll be warm enough without it."

"She doesn't need it for warmth. She needs it for the same reason Ally needs Henry. If it's not in this house, you'll go back to Hawke Construction tonight and find it." Heather scanned the room. "What else is missing?"

"Mommy, he didn't put plastic on our beds," Dallas announced.

"What else can go wrong? Durango, find some plastic and make the beds again, placing it under the sheets to protect the mattresses. Old shower curtains will work if there isn't anything else."

Suddenly, she knew what else was absent. Her belongings. "Where is my Army duffel and suitcase?"

"In the closet in our room," Durango said.

"Thanks." Heather hustled to the master bedroom. She didn't know how she'd convince him that she wouldn't sleep with him, but one crisis at a time. She'd settle the twins first, then deal with their father.

Her hunch proved correct. As soon as she opened her duffel, she saw the faded blue background of Galveston's beloved quilt. Yes, it needed to be washed, but that could wait until tomorrow morning.

Twenty minutes later, the emergency was over. Galveston had her blankie. The beds had plastic between the sheets and mattress covers. Actually, Galveston was the only one who still wet the bed on rare occasions, but Heather knew better than to discriminate between the twins. They insisted on being treated the same.

"Mommy, you be here when we get up?" Galveston asked anxiously.

"I never go to work without telling you and Ally." Heather finished tucking in Galveston and sat down on the edge of the twin bed. She glimpsed Durango leaning against the door, but reminded herself to keep her attention on the girls. "I don't have a job here yet."

"I told you, Toney. Mommy's not goin' to the 'spital no more and she's not singing yet either." Dallas continued to suck her thumb. "She's staying home with us."

"Forever and ever?" Galveston demanded.

"Until you're a lot bigger, pumpkin." Heather bent and hugged the little girl. "Now, it's time to sleep."

"Tell us a story first," Dallas requested.

"About you when you was little," Galveston finished. "And ridin' your 'berry pony."

"Okay, but then it's time for sleep." Heather hugged Galveston again and stood to hug Dallas. She sat down on that bed and began a long story of a little girl on a ranch with the favorite strawberry roan pony who taught her to ride.

Partway through the story, Durango slipped out the door. When the twins drifted into slumber, Heather crept from the room, desperately craving a drink. The bad bout of stomach flu had its after-effects. Alcohol still nauseated her. A smoke would be great, but tobacco made her puke too.

She'd settle for a soda. She sauntered into the kitchen, where Durango was sitting at the table. "Sounds like you got a workout. Don't relax. It gets worse."

"I was afraid of that." He leaned back in the chair. "I don't recall little kids being so much work when I lived with Uncle Quentin and Aunt Vicky and my cousins."

Heather laughed and headed for the refrigerator, opting for a 7-Up since it wouldn't upset her still-rocky stomach. "What did you make them for dinner? Did they eat it?"

"Mac and cheese. They liked it, but Galveston read me a lecture for making it from scratch, and not using the boxed crap."

Toney wouldn't do that in a hundred years, but Heather didn't say so. She twisted the cap off the bottle, took a swallow on her way back to the table. Obviously, the twins were still in the middle of Mix and Match. "How did they do with Cinnamon?"

"Great. I caught more hell when I said it was time to put her away and feed her supper, but they'd ridden almost two hours." Durango caught her hand, drew her down to sit on his lap. "I don't know how you do it. They're a challenge."

"You'll learn." She shifted a little and leaned her head against his shoulder. "It takes practice."

"Okay. I'm glad you brought them home, so I'll have that opportunity." He turned his head until their lips met in a long, warm kiss.

She sighed, barely noticing when he took the half-full bottle of soda and put it on the table. His tongue teased hers and she enjoyed the moment, exploring his mouth and allowing him to explore hers. The kisses continued, one melting into the next.

He lifted his head for a moment before his mouth found her ear, the side of her neck. He slowly unsnapped her blouse, peeling back the cloth. He cupped her breasts, thumbs teasing her nipples through the scalloped lace of her bra.

She moaned, squirming on his lap. "I wasn't going to bed with you."

"We're not upstairs yet, Empress." He kissed her again. "We're still in the kitchen."

"I know that."

He adjusted her position so she straddled him, and she felt his hardness pushing against her panties. She was already wet, and she wanted him. "Damn you, Durango."

"Keep being snarky, babe. You know I enjoy it." He unfastened her bra, sucking first on one nipple, then the other. She arched up to meet his mouth, thrilled by him. Meantime, his hands were busy under her skirt, pushing her panties aside so his fingers could move in and out. Her hips rose and fell. His thumb rocked into the bit of flesh, joining the pattern he'd started.

She came all at once, burying her face in the hollow of his throat to muffle her cries. "I don't believe you."

"Wait until I really have you."

"I've already said it. I'm not going to bed with you."

He lifted her slightly, hands sliding over her hips under the skirt. "Who said we need a bed?"

She pulled back in time to see her panties fly onto the floor. Her skirt still covered them, but she was naked underneath it. She realized he'd unfastened his jeans, freed himself. "What are you doing?"

"Having my wife right here and right now."

She gasped, fingers biting into his shoulders, and stared into the deep blue eyes. When he thrust into her, she caught her breath. He was so big, filling her. She moaned, clenched around him.

His hand threaded into her hair and his mouth was so close to hers. "Time to ride, baby."

She yielded, her lips meeting his in a series of kisses. And she did ride, rising, falling, taking him along in a new dance until she exploded among the stars and he joined her.

Afterward, she rested her head on his chest, fingers toying with one of his nipples. "I didn't plan on this, but you did, didn't you?"

He kissed her forehead. "Always, Empress. I'll always want you."

She sighed. "I just wish I could stop wanting you."

"Not in this lifetime, sweetheart." He kissed her again, a quick touch of his lips. "Now, if we take a break, I'll fix you dinner."

"What are we having? Leftover mac and cheese?"

"I have steaks marinating and spuds in the oven. Cherry cheesecake from the new bakery in Baker City for dessert."

"Really? Those are my favorites."

"I know that. We can wait to go upstairs, Mrs. Hawke. It will just make you hotter."

"You'll wait until you promise me forever and mean it." She felt him harden inside her and he gripped her hips. "I mean it."

"And you know what your orders do to me, my pretty little tyrant."

She gasped, clutching his muscled arms when he moved under her, in her. "What are you doing?"

"My turn to guide the ride. Kiss me."

# CHAPTER SIXTEEN

Friday, she woke to sunlight streaming through the bedroom window. Home, she remembered. She was finally home, but how had she gotten to bed? She'd been watching an insipid late-night movie, interrupted by frequent bouts of commercials. She must have fallen asleep in the recliner, and Durango carried her upstairs.

Now, she was back in the big, brass bed in the main suite, snugly tucked under the covers. She saw her skirt, blouse, bra, and sandals on the far side of the room lying across an upholstered rocker near the closet. She sat up slowly. Her stomach didn't rebel at the motion.

Great. Maybe the long onslaught of stomach flu had finally ended. Did she want to try standing? She tried pushing aside the blankets, swung her feet to the floor. Okay, so far, so good. No nausea. She glanced at the clock. It was almost 1300 hours, one o'clock in the afternoon. No wonder she felt good.

She stood, frowning at the soft, sloppy gray T-shirt that hung past her hips. It had to be one of his. It definitely wasn't hers. He had a huge hang-up about privacy. He never looked in her purse, much less her suitcase or duffel. She'd unpack her own clothes later when she found a room of her own. Like she'd told him more than once, she wasn't sharing the main suite with him.

Granted, it was humongous. It had two walk-in closets and an adjoining en-suite bath on the other side of the sitting area with its couch, rocking chairs, bookcases, and even a TV. Her father had said that at one time, it'd been a nursery for the newest baby until the child was old enough to have a room of its own.

For all his toxic, macho posturing and hauling her off to bed whenever Durango had an itch he wanted scratched, there were personal spaces he wouldn't invade. In his own charming, arrogant way, he was a keeper. He just needed more training, and she was the woman to provide it.

She went across the hall to check on the twins. Their new room was empty, but their father must have helped them tidy it. Dirty clothes were in the hamper, toys picked up, and beds made. Normally, her daughters expected Heather to clean up behind them, and she enjoyed doing it. Yes, she spoiled them a little, but she'd been so thrilled to have them after two miscarriages. She'd thought she'd never be able to have kids. She was so lucky to have a future with them and after those three combat tours, she knew it better than most.

Wandering through the second story, she opened the doors to the two fully furnished guest rooms on either side of the twins' bedroom and decided she'd move into the larger one. There were four more bedrooms on the top floor, but she didn't want to climb another flight of stairs at the end of a long day.

She stopped in the bathroom at the end of the hall. The mirror revealed the remnants of yesterday's cosmetics. She grimaced and lingered long enough to scrub away the raccoon look of leftover mascara. Afterward, she continued the tour of the house. When she arrived in the kitchen, she spotted the note under a magnet on the fridge.

*Baby, the girls, and I went grocery shopping. You were asleep, and we didn't want to wake you. Back soon, Durango.*

Under the scrawled words, she saw several Os and Xs, the twins' symbols for hugs and kisses. Why would she complain about them being gone when she enjoyed the mere idea of being alone? Returning upstairs, she swung her suitcase on the bed, opened it, and found clean clothes. Then she headed for the shower.

She relished the hot water, luxuriating in the steady spray. She shampooed her hair. He must have replaced the tank. Back in the day, she always ended with a freezing cold shower because the hot water never lasted long enough. No one pounded on the door, demanding either entrance to the bathroom or attention. The phone didn't ring. Nobody came to the house, not a salesperson or a neighbor. It was quite different from Tennessee.

After the shower, she dried off, dressed, opting for an old pair of faded, loose jeans, and a green T-shirt that proclaimed when *God made man, She was only joking!* She braided her still-damp hair, not bothering with makeup. Then she pulled on socks and her riding boots. She went back downstairs, ready to find something to eat.

A caffeine-free cola and slab of cherry cheesecake made the perfect breakfast. Heather sat at the table, glancing around the large country-style kitchen. It looked the same as it had after her grandfather and Fenn remodeled it almost twenty years before as a surprise for her grandmother. Since Heather was the one who chose the quartz countertops, flooring, and new wooden cabinets, they all went together.

Grandma never liked an island, saying it took up too much space, and she only used the dining room for formal occasions. She wanted to be able to walk around the room. Besides, she needed room for the antique wood cook-stove in the corner. In the event of a bad winter storm, they often lost power. She still needed to cook meals and heat the house for the family.

Heather leaned back in the chair, focusing on the laundry and adjacent pantry rather than thinking about the night before. All Durango had to do was touch her, and she yielded. *Hell, and there are times when he only looks at me, and I have an orgasm.* She finished eating and put the plate and fork in the new dishwasher.

She heard a thump in the living room and went to investigate. The kittens were climbing up the river-rock apron, and as she watched, one already made it to the mantel, where he'd pushed off a picture. Laughing, Heather picked up the photograph of the twins, recognizing it as the one she'd given Durango. She put the picture back in its place. Luckily, the glass hadn't broken.

She plucked the kitten off the mantel and lowered him to the floor. "Behave yourself, Smokey." Then she removed the other one from the rock-wall climbing project. "You two are going to have to learn some manners, Ashes."

She debated the choices. She could stay inside and clean the house, but it so wasn't her thing. Wait a minute. There were horses in the barn. Satan and Cinnamon were trustworthy and if she wanted some excitement, there was Flash. She'd ride out and inspect the ranch. After all, it was hers now.

She grabbed a handful of carrots from the fridge and went to the back door. A wooden plaque in the shape of a key held an assortment of keys. She studied them. One ring attached to a wood four-leaf clover held five keys. She lifted it off the hook, turned it over, and saw her name etched into the shamrock. One of these must open the tackroom where she'd find Satan's gear.

Following the wrap-around porch, she walked down the stairs and moseyed in the direction of the stable, enjoying the sun's warmth. In the barn, Cinnamon nickered a welcome. Heather petted the mare, gave her a carrot, and then greeted Flash. After that, she moved on to Satan. The gelding pinned his ears and glared.

Heather fed him a treat. "I never beat or starved you. I rescued you from that." She picked up the halter and lead. "Let's go riding."

She stepped into the stall, fitted the nylon halter, and buckled it. Satan nuzzled her, and she hugged him. "Missed you too, bugaboo."

Leading him from the stall, she parked him outside the tackroom. It only took twenty minutes to groom him and clean his hooves. It was easy to find the saddle meant for her. Brand-new and custom made, it had a nameplate on the cantle. She laughed, shaking her head. "I'll *Empress* you, Hawke."

The saddle was lighter than she expected and fit Satan to perfection. She swapped out the halter and lead for his nylon bridle, a bright purple that matched the blankets and pads. Outside, she closed the barn door. She eased the reins up on either side of his neck, slid her left foot into the stirrup, and mounted, swinging onto Satan's back.

She rode toward the hill that rose behind the barn. As if he knew what she needed, Satan walked toward the trail that led up the ridge. She petted his brown neck. She wanted to see *her* land, all of it. Four hundred thirteen acres of woods, springs, meadows, and of course, Cedar Creek, large enough to be a small river, and it was all hers. With three rising terraces, the land eventually rolled down to the creek.

Her great-great-grandfather homesteaded the original hundred and sixty acres in 1893, adding more property to the ranch as it became available. Each terraced portion of the farm had its share of barns, storage sheds, and even a cabin or two for the help. There weren't any ranch hands now. The work was too hard for most people.

She didn't care about that. The developers could rot in hell. She'd save the McElroy spread for her children and grandchildren. She reined Satan to a stop at the top of the first hill. Left or right? The overgrown path to the right would take her to Fenn's A-frame cabin. Shrouded by giant cedars, pines, and hemlocks, only the family knew how to locate his sanctuary.

No stranger had ever found it. She doubted Durango knew where it was. The cabin was invisible from the trail or air. Built without permits, the county bureaucrats didn't know it existed. A ghost's house, Heather thought. The place haunted her the way Fenn did. He'd be thirty-eight now, the same age as Durango. Fenn hadn't come home after his Ranger patrol was captured in 2011. He was dead. He must be dead.

Sometimes, she pretended he wasn't. She'd dream he'd made it home. If she looked, she'd see him working stock or doing repairs on the ranch. He'd loved the place as much as she did. From the time he was a little boy, he wanted to be a soldier. He'd planned to have an Army career and then come back to the McElroy spread. He hadn't lived long enough to fulfill that goal.

She wiped away her tears. She swung Satan to the left and away from the barely visible track that led to Fenn's cabin. She wasn't ready to deal with a hard dose of reality. She longed for him to return home; might pretend he had, but she knew it was a fantasy. It was time to ride on, to *Charlie Mike* as Zeb Steele said. *Continue Mission*, she told herself. Put one of Satan's hooves in front of the other and check out the rest of the ranch.

---

Durango glanced at his daughters. At her insistence, Dallas helped him push the grocery cart. At least, he hoped it was Dallas. He'd called her that all day. She hadn't corrected him once. Galveston helped choose food. She had a predilection for cookies, soda, candy, chips, and sugary stuff. Her story that they didn't have to eat any veggies except broccoli amused him. He wondered what Heather would say about that.

Both girls wore identical blue T-shirts proclaiming Nashville to be the home of country music. Blue jeans and sneakers added to their resemblance. They'd badgered him for identical hairstyles, French braids. Luckily, he'd learned to do them when he showed Cinnamon. Otherwise, he'd have been in trouble this morning.

He smiled down at the girls. "Did we forget anything?"

"Mommy's cigarettes," Dallas said.

Galveston came back to stand next to her twin. "They still make her sick, so she's not smokin' no more."

"What do you mean?" Durango frowned, concern mounting. "She was tired yesterday. She needs to catch up on her sleep."

"She had tummy flu," Galveston said. "She threw up lots and lots. Auntie Kate told her, no more cigarettes."

"And no vodka either. It makes her really hurl." Dallas added. "And she couldn't have cola for breakfast either, not for a long time. She was mad."

This sounded serious, a lot worse than a mild case of stomach flu. "How long was your mom sick?"

Dallas considered the question. "Ages. Yesterday, she barfed when she smelled our egg muffins."

"You gots to leave the bathroom door open all the time," Galveston informed him. "Can we go now?"

"Sure." Durango pushed the almost full cart down the aisle of the supermarket. "Has your mom seen a doctor?"

"No way. Don't you know nothin'? Doctors are stupid idjits who cut folks open for fun," Dallas told him firmly. "Mommy and Auntie Kate said. They know everything."

"Great," Durango muttered.

Heather had already passed on her prejudices about the medical profession. It ought to make hauling her into Baker City to see Doc MacGillicudy a fun experience.

"Okay, girls." Durango turned the corner and pushed the cart up the next aisle. "Let's get more food for your kittens and more soda for your mom."

"I hope she feels better soon," Galveston said. "She 'members the bad place lots now. She goes there and Ton, I mean Ally hasta get her back."

"That's right," Dallas agreed. "Mommy gets mad easy when she can't forget."

Durango eyed the twins. How often did they mix up each other's nicknames? They'd done it at least six times today. Wouldn't it be easier if he continued to call them by their full names? He'd ask Heather when they got home. He followed their daughters. This time, he'd have to show her he was different, that he intended to put her and their children first.

He'd already told Denver to find a different team leader for the upcoming excursions to Colombia. His cousin argued Durango was the best choice, but Nighthawke had a policy against sending married soldiers into real hotspots. He'd be a piss-poor commander if he insisted rules didn't apply to him. Bendigo had offered to step up if Denver didn't find someone else in the next month.

"Can we get ice cream, Daddy?" Galveston asked.

"For your mom?" Durango teased. "Or for you?"

"For us."

"All right, but only if your mom and I get some too."

"Okay," Dallas agreed quickly.

The ranch was quiet when Durango parked the truck in front of the old Victorian house. He'd barely helped the girls out of their seats when they pelted inside to find their mother.

"Mommy's gone." One of them returned to the porch, tears bubbling in her eyes and streaking down her cheeks. "She said she wouldn't leave us to go to work no more."

"She didn't, Galveston." Durango patted her shoulder. "Let's see if she left a note."

Carrying two bags of groceries, he strode across the porch and through the front door. She wasn't in the living room. The door to the den was closed and locked. She wasn't in the downstairs half-bath or the fancy dining room. No sign of her in the kitchen and no note either. He put the bags on the counter and spun.

He hurried upstairs. Not in the guest rooms or in the twins' bedroom. He went into the master suite where he found his other daughter standing by one of the walk-in closets. "Any ideas where we can find your mom, Dallas?"

"I'm Toney." The four-year-old glared up at him before pointing to the green duffel and then to the open suitcase on the king-size brass bed. "Mommy didn't go to work. Her stuff's all here."

Durango didn't know how to respond. Before he decided, he heard a shout from downstairs.

"Here's Mommy! She's ridin' a horse. The mean one."

He relaxed and rested a hand on Galveston's shoulder. "You're right. I should have known she'd take Satan out for a ride."

"Not unless you asked her." The child pulled free and raced from the room.

Would they ever accept him? He followed. At least they were with him now. He had a better chance of being their father when they lived in the same house. Now, how long was it going to take him to tell them apart?

---

Riding toward the green pickup, Heather reined Satan to a stop and petted his sweaty neck. She waved to her daughter waiting on the steps. "Hi, Toney. How was the shopping?"

"Okay." Galveston came across the yard and stopped several feet away. "He's a mean horse, Mommy. He bited at Daddy today."

"Satan bluffs a lot." Heather smiled, trying to reassure the child. "Just pet him and pretend you're not scared."

"But I am." Galveston stuffed her hands in the pockets of her jeans.

"Chicken!" Dallas jeered as she joined her twin.

"You do it," Galveston snapped back.

"Girls, no fighting." Heather's tone held maternal warning. "Horses don't like it and neither do I."

"But Mommy," Galveston whined. "She started it."

"You always say that, you weenie." Dallas approached and petted Satan's face. "He's mostly nice. See."

"No, he's not."

"Enough." Durango came to join them, holding out two frozen treats. "Can you girls eat yours outside?"

"We have to sit down so we don't spill." Dallas took her Fudgsicle and headed for the porch steps. "Come on, Toney."

Galveston accepted the orange creamsicle with a sunny smile and trotted after her sister. "Wait for me, Ally."

"Ice cream at this hour?" Heather frowned after the twins. "Durango, if they eat junk food now, they won't want supper."

"Yes, they will." He rested one arm across Satan's neck in front of the saddle. "They chose the menu. Hot dogs, chili, and chips."

"Yuck." She wrinkled her nose in disgust. "Spicy food gives me heartburn. I'll find something else."

"Since when? You're the one who pours on the hot sauce. You used to buy it by the case. What's wrong?"

"I had a bad bout of stomach flu." The concern on his features warmed her heart. "For the past three weeks, I've tossed my cookies at practically everything. They had to transfer me out of surgery before I left the hospital because I couldn't assist with operations."

"Well, if you aren't better in a couple days, we'll go see Doc MacGillicudy in Baker City."

"You can dream, jarhead. I do as I please." She trembled when he stroked her knee. "What?"

"I like it when you please me too, the way you did last night." He winked at her. "Or the way I pleased you in my office."

"I told you yesterday." She narrowed her eyes and glowered at him. "We aren't sharing a bed for the duration."

"Yes, we will." His grin broadened. "You'll be hotter than hell. You'll beg for me before too much longer."

"Say again!" She sniffed. "Is this Fantasies-R-Us?"

He chuckled, trailed a hand over her knee toward her thigh. "Not yet, but I have lots of those after almost five years."

# CHAPTER SEVENTEEN

Heather nudged Satan with her boot and he side-stepped away from Durango. Two steps, but that was enough space.

"I need to do something about the caretaker," she said. "Most of the boundary and cross-fences are shot. The only good one is between the McElroy spread and the Williams place. Two hay barns have fallen on the upper terrace. Someone poached a dozen old-growth cedars worth major bucks. Three acres of alder and maple have been high-graded too. Thistles, blackberry bushes, and foxglove have taken over the hay fields."

"The place needs work," Durango agreed, following her. "It's why I moved in after I heard you inherited it last summer. See anything you like?"

The sun glinted off the roof of the indoor arena and the sight brought a smile. He'd tried to restore the farm, but years of neglect couldn't be overcome in a short time. She leaned down to kiss him. "Yeah, and I'm looking at it now, Hawke. Maybe I'll keep you as a toy-boy."

His amusement faded, replaced with a heated look that made her quiver. "Sounds like fun."

"I knew you'd like it." She straightened in the saddle. She glanced to where the twins finished their treats. "I'll let you unload the rig and take the twins for a while to give you some peace."

"Works for me." He stepped back. "Do they ever mix up their nicknames with you?"

"No. Why?"

"Just curious."

She hesitated, stared off into the distance. "They do it when they're playing 'Mix and Match' sometimes."

"Mix and Match? What's that?"

"You're pretty smart for a Marine." Heather signaled Satan to pick up a slow walk. "Figure it out, Hawke." She rode to the porch. "Come on, kids. Help me put away my horse and tell me about your day."

"Okay," the twins chimed, joining her.

Heather rode to the corral in front of the stable, dismounted, and began to unsaddle the old bay gelding. "What did you guys do today?"

"We went shopping at lots of stores," Galveston reported. "We gots new crayons, the big boxes. Daddy said he'd put my name on my box so Ally can't break them."

"I only do it so we gots two of each color," Dallas protested. "Else we have to use both boxes all the time."

"What about you, Ally?" Heather choked back an appreciative grin. "Did you have fun too?"

"Sure. We gots new jeans and new cowboy boots and no dresses, 'cause I told Daddy they're sappy and we don't like 'em."

"I do sometimes," Galveston said.

"I don't ever. And we went to see a real pretty lady 'cause Daddy said he had papers to give her 'bout us. He says her name is Auntie Bree and she's his little sister, only she's most as big as you, Mommy."

"She has candy at her desk, and we got some," Galveston said. "Then Auntie Bree told Daddy to take us to see Auntie Amie so she wouldn't have her feelers all hurt."

"And we had ice cream cones again at his work 'cause that's where she was."

Heather eyed the pair. "And you convinced your dad you needed more ice cream when you got home. Did you tell anybody I don't let you have that much sugar in one day?"

"You wasn't there," Dallas pointed out, "and nobody asked, so like you always say, they didn't have 'needs to know.' We got lots of junk food at the store too. Daddy never says no, like you and Auntie Kate do."

Galveston nodded.

"Well, when your daddy learns my rules, the fun is going to stop," Heather warned them. "I hope you got some of my favorite potato chips, not just yours."

"We did." Galveston beamed at her. "And that 'nana split ice cream you like."

"Good job." Heather hugged both girls. After she released them, she returned to fussing over the new saddle.

Durango arrived a few minutes later. "Let me carry that inside for you." He scooped the saddle and pads off Satan's back. "I'll put it in the tackroom."

"Okay." Heather caressed the nameplate once more. "It's a beaut, one of the most comfortable I've ever ridden. I've never had a brand-new saddle before. This is real special."

Embarrassment followed by pleasure flickered into the cobalt eyes. He started out of the corral, the saddle in his arms. "I'll think of a way you can thank me later, baby. Maybe you can quit calling me a jarhead because I was a Marine."

"Only if you stop calling me 'Empress.' That gets old in a hurry." She took a couple of steps after him. "Granted, it'd be a shame to waste that nameplate."

He laughed and opened the barn door. "Guess I'll just have to suffer."

"I reckon so, cowboy." She turned her head to eye the twins. "Why don't you two tell your daddy about the Mix and Match game?"

"It's no fair," Dallas protested. "He started it. He can't tell us apart."

"It's about time to share the rules, Dallas Waco." Heather headed back to Satan. "You go in the tackroom with your daddy while I put away my horse. Work it out. There's two of you girls and only one of him."

"Yeah, but he's big and we're little," Dallas complained.

"Come on, Ally." Galveston led the way. "We been winning two whole days."

"Okay." Dallas rapidly regained her good cheer. "Anyhow, we can still play and beat him."

"That's the spirit." Heather unhooked the reins from the fencepost and led Satan toward his stall. This was another way to show her gratitude for the efforts Durango made, but it was all she was willing to do. He'd think he'd won a real victory if she moved into the master suite with him. *So not going there! He can just hurry up and wait!*

---

"So, what's the deal with this game?" Durango cuddled the twins and studied their faces, trying to find differences between them. "Are you trying to confuse me?"

Dallas leaned back against the support of his arm. "You gotta learn to tell me and Toney apart."

"I see." His heart melted at the stubborn defiance on her small features. "You're so much like your mama." The other little girl snuggled close, her arms laced around his neck. "Did I ever get it right today? Or was I wrong from the get-go?"

"You knew in the house when we looked for Mommy," Dallas said.

"He knew at breakfast when you slurped your milk," Galveston said.

"You slurped louder," Dallas informed her sister.

"I had to. I was 'tending to be you."

Durango chuckled, holding his daughters tighter. "Do you play this game with everyone?"

"Not with Mommy or Auntie Kate. Mommy knows all the time and Auntie Kate's a good guesser," Dallas said. "Grampa Art was fun. He never knew."

Galveston heaved a huge sigh. "Gramma Liz made us stop."

"Yeah, 'cause she says fun isn't fun—"

" 'Less it's fun for everyone," Galveston finished. "We were having a good time."

"I'll bet." Durango kissed the top of each red-gold head. "Your Gramma Liz used to tell me and your mommy the same thing when we picked on my brother, Waco."

Dallas wrapped her arms around Durango's neck. "Can we have a brother? We wouldn't be mean to him, not ever, and we wouldn't play Mix and Match with him."

"Well, I don't know. You just got here." Durango looked over their heads as Heather walked in the tackroom with the bridle. "What do you think? A baby brother or two?"

"Nope, not yet. The girls are still learning to take care of their kittens and next comes 'berry ponies. Baby brothers take a lot more care and attention, so we'll hold off on those for a while."

"Mommy's the boss." Durango slowly released the twins. "What's next on the agenda?"

"I need help grooming Satan," Heather said. "Dallas, why don't you grab some brushes and help me?"

"Then can we brush Flash?" Dallas asked.

"I think that's a good idea," Heather said. "We want him to be as pretty as the others."

"Me and Daddy will brush Cinnamon." Galveston followed her sister over to the shelf of plastic totes that held currycombs and other equipment. "Okay, Daddy?"

"Sure, Galveston." His reward for the correct name came as a sunshine smile tossed over a small shoulder and it warmed his soul.

---

"They're a pair of cuties." Waco Hawke watched the two little princesses explore the containers of grooming paraphernalia, hunting for specific brushes while Heather guided them through the process. "You should have a houseful of kids by now, bro, but you've always been a day late and dollar short. What is your problem?"

No answer, of course. Durango couldn't hear him, and neither could Heather. He followed the family down the barn aisle. Weren't animals supposed to be sensitive? Well, these horses didn't prove it. They ignored him too, their attention on the carrots that his older brother provided.

Waco hung out a while longer, but boredom overtook him. He wandered into the house and happily spotted the large flatscreen on the wall. There was a recliner, but he bypassed it for old man McElroy's antique rocking chair in the corner. Two gray kittens shadow-boxed by the bookcase that ran the length of the end wall. He spotted the remote, turned on the TV, and found his favorite cable news channel where the ash-blonde news reporter read the latest headlines.

He'd have to remember to turn it off when they came inside. He didn't want them doing what Liz McElroy did and bring in the O'Leary to try and talk to him. *If I wanted to talk about my feelings, I'd see a chaplain.*

---

Later that evening, Heather leaned back in the old rocking chair in the living room. She liked the way Durango had remodeled the room, taking out the wall between it and the formal parlor that her grandmother used for guests. Now, the living room was almost as big as the kitchen. The focal point for most people was still the river-rock fireplace. It shared a chimney with the wood cook-stove in the kitchen.

A new couch was on the far side of the fireplace. Bookshelves stuffed with paperbacks and hardcovers lined two of the walls. The old grand piano stood in splendor in the opposite corner, and she wondered if her copies of country sheet music were still in the bench-style seat adjacent to it. She didn't ask. She'd look later.

Durango sat in the recliner next to her. Both of them preferred the rocker because it was in the corner, but she'd nabbed it first. She had a clear view of the room, or as he put it, a clear field of fire. "I'm sorry about the girls' behavior today. I thought after fooling you yesterday, the fun would have gone out of it."

He chuckled. "Be honest, Empress. If you had a twin, you'd make my life a living hell, wouldn't you? I know I couldn't resist the opportunity for mischief."

"You're right." She smiled at him. "I guess it's why I don't have the heart to get after them too much."

"You wouldn't, anyway." He pulled the lever to prop up his feet. "Your attitude has always been that people who get tricked are a waste of oxygen. You're like your mother. The two of you have never suffered fools gladly."

Heather considered his estimation for a few minutes. It didn't hurt her. He sounded as if it were a fact and not worth a fight. He accepted her for who and what she was. The knowledge eased some of the heartache she felt. He might not be around all day, every day, but he didn't want to change her.

Zeb had always lectured her about how to be a good Army officer. Jeff was too fragile. He couldn't believe she was a human being with her own flaws and foibles. He thought she was some sort of saint and whatever she did was perfect. It was difficult to live up to his worship. The new understanding of Durango brought a certain peace.

She rocked in silence for a little longer. Finally, she said, "They used to fool me when they were babies. Not when we first came home from the hospital, but later as they began to resemble each other more and more."

"What did you do?"

"Dressed them in different colors for a while." Heather giggled. "Then, I'd know who I'd fed. It was easy to know who needed her diaper changed."

"Well, that makes me feel better." He laughed. "How am I supposed to tell who is who? They're the same size. Their eyes and hair match. Even their voices are identical. So are their movements."

"You have to recognize their personalities," Heather said. "Soon, you'll be able to look at them and know."

"Some help you are."

"Try this. Dallas will argue with you, not just for herself, but also for Galveston. Dallas is the smart mouth. Galveston is more sensitive, quieter, and more easily hurt. She uses it to manipulate me. I feel terrible when I correct her."

"You feel guilty when you criticize anyone but me. You don't show it." After a moment, he stood, came over to her, and held out his hand. "What do you say we share?"

"Think it will hold both of us?"

"It always has before."

She slowly closed her fingers over his and let him pull her from the chair. He sat in the rocker, drew her down to sit on his lap. She sighed, relaxed, and pillowed her head on his shoulder. She ought to tell him tonight. She couldn't. She'd do it later. If he went to Colombia, all bets were off. He'd have to move out of her house. She not only wouldn't live with him, she wouldn't sleep with him either.

Hours later, the movie she'd been watching came to an end. The credits rolled, and she contemplated finding another insipid comedy. Why bother? She rose to her feet. Durango went to bed at midnight. She wouldn't join him in the master suite. She hadn't told him she usually didn't sleep at night. It was the reason why she opted for graveyard shifts at the different hospitals where she worked and sang at various nightclubs whenever she could. It allowed her to nap during the days and avoid the memories.

Nightmares had plagued her since she came home in 2012 from that last tour. Of course, most people didn't realize or acknowledge that military women died during wars too.

Rather than return to the safety of the rocking chair, she drifted across the room to the huge picture windows and stared across the quiet lawn.

Huge cedar trees marched along the short rise that sloped down to Cedar Creek. She'd played under their boughs as a child. Her daughters would do the same. Perhaps Shakespeare had been right about immortality. Her life continued in those of her children. Too serious an idea for this hour of the night when she didn't want to ponder anyone's mortality, particularly her own.

She headed for the front door and onto the wrap-around porch. She walked out into the night. Frogs croaked, an early summer chorus. Wind rustled through the evergreens. She couldn't even hear the hum of traffic on the highway, a half mile away. It was three in the morning. The world was asleep, all except her.

She sauntered in the direction of the barn, contemplating if she should take Satan on a moonlit ride. She looked up at the dark sky, suddenly aware that clouds started to cloak the stars. A storm brewed. She wouldn't risk the old horse's legs. She'd wait to ride him again. She swung to study the pines on the ridge behind the house. It felt as if someone or something lurked in the shadows.

She stretched, yawned. She felt as spooky as a green-broke colt. She needed to get some sleep. Otherwise, her mind would continue to play tricks on her. She was finally home where she was safe, not in the middle of a warzone. She yawned, turned back to the house. Inside, she locked the front door.

Upstairs, she checked on the twins. She fixed Galveston's covers. She picked up the stuffed purple pony and tucked it back into bed with Dallas. "I love both of you so much. Sleep tight, sweeties."

She left their bedroom door open so they could see the hall light and come find her if they were frightened. She went into the room next door. She'd unpacked her things earlier. She undressed, put on a favorite, long-sleeved, floor-length flannel nightgown. Okay, so it looked like something her grandmother would wear, but it was warm, and it got cold in the Cascade foothills even in the summer.

In the double bed, she curled under the covers. Dimly, she heard rain begin to tap-dance on the roof. Two hours later, the constant explosions of remembered shelling roused her. She didn't bother to totally wake up. No point to it. Taking the comforter with her, she rolled off the bed onto the floor. Safe on the carpet, she slipped under the bed and allowed slumber to claim her.

---

When he woke, he was alone in the main suite. Was Heather still downstairs? Had she fallen asleep in front of the television? Rain pounded on the roof and thunder rolled overhead. He propped up on an elbow. 0600 hours. He had to check the generator in case they had a power failure and bring in wood for the cook-stove in the kitchen. Where the hell was she?

An hour later, he still didn't know. He'd been through the entire house. The girls slept soundly in their room. The horses were safe in the barn and he'd fed the three of them. He stood by the corral, trying to get a signal on his cell phone. No such luck. The storm continued to build in intensity. The wind wailed and rain pounded his shoulders, making his back ache.

He'd go in the kitchen, use the land-line there and contact her parents. Perhaps one of them came to pick her up. Heather hadn't driven anywhere. The Ford 150 was here and so was his Chevy. Inside, he dialed the number he knew by heart. He waited through fourteen rings.

"Who the hell is this?" Liz demanded in sleepy tones. "It better be life or death, or I'll make it that way."

"It's me, Durango." He tried not to laugh. Liz wasn't a morning person, and neither was Heather. "I called because Heather came home with the girls."

"You phoned in the middle of the night to tell me that? Why didn't you wait until a civilized hour?" Her voice trailed away, but he heard more grumbling.

"What's going on, Durango?" Art took over the conversation. "Is Heather all right? The kids?"

"They're all fine. Heather's not here. I've looked all over the house and in the barn. Both trucks are in the yard. Did you or Liz—" Durango stopped, aware of the foolish question. He'd been the one to tell them their daughter was home. "I'm sorry."

"Don't be," Art said. "Look under the beds. We'll be up to visit in an hour or so. We have a cat and kittens for you."

# CHAPTER EIGHTEEN

"I can't believe I'm up and dressed before nine in the morning when nobody's sick, hurt, or dying." Liz refilled her coffee cup. She brought the pot over to the table and topped Art and Durango's mugs. "Where's Heather?"

"Asleep upstairs, under the bed in the guest room." Durango felt his face redden. "I was stupid."

"Concern isn't dumb, son." Art sipped black coffee. "It's okay."

"Speak for yourself." Liz sat down at the table and hid a yawn with the back of her hand. "Married couples sleep together. If you were, you'd know when she got up. What's wrong with you two?"

Art coughed and looked up at the ceiling as if it held all the answers in the universe. "It's not our business, Liz."

She snorted. "You're the one who does double-speak, Art. I want to know what Durango has done wrong this time. He should be able to tell the truth and shame the devil."

The patter of footsteps on the stairs saved him from having to respond. Durango smiled with relief when his daughters entered the room, both girls wearing green footie pajamas. "Hey there. Did we wake you?"

One of the girls held a purring gray kitten. "We heard you talking so we knew somebody was here."

"You don't talk to yourself like Mommy does." The other child spoke around the thumb she sucked.

"I see." Durango hoped he'd be able to tell the twins apart today. He didn't want to make a bigger fool of himself in front of Liz and Art.

The little girl stopped sucking her thumb. She pelted across the room to hug Art. "Hi, Grampa."

"Hello, sweetness." He scooped her onto his lap. "How's my girl?"

"Good." She snuggled close, popped in her thumb again. "You know who I am?"

"Of course he does, Toney." Liz gathered Dallas and the kitten into a warm embrace. "Wait until you see what we brought you. A momma cat with her babies. They're in a box in our truck."

"More kitties?" Dallas asked, her cheek against Liz's shirt. "Why?"

"Your Uncle Laredo brought me a whole fleet," Art said. "And your Gramma Liz likes me to share."

"It's part of being good." Galveston favored him with her sunshine smile. "Mommy says."

"That makes it right." Durango drank some coffee. "When did Laredo get into the animal rescue business?"

"It's a secret." Liz hugged Dallas. "He takes them away from bad people who'd hurt them and brings us injured dogs and cats. When Art has them healed up and ready to go, I find homes with folks I trust."

"So, what's the secret, Gramma?" Dallas asked.

"Who the bad people are. We don't want those meanies mad at Uncle Laredo."

"Okay," Galveston agreed. "We won't tell nobody our new kitties had a bad home. Right, Ally?"

"Right!"

"Good one." Durango decided he'd have to discuss the situation with Laredo and learn the rest of the story. Where did he find the animals who needed him? Had his long-time girlfriend, Jacinth Sweeney, the little waitress at Pop's Cafe convinced him to join one of her activist groups? What were the two of them doing?

---

Heather barely heard someone call her name. Maybe, if she stayed out of sight, she'd be allowed to sleep. She was exhausted. The last thing she wanted to do was drag her weary body across the compound to the O.R. or to do triage on the wounded soldiers who arrived.

"Heather, where are you? It's time to get up." The voice sounded like her mother's. What would happen next? Would she miss the war the way she'd missed the school bus when she was a teenager? Was her mother going to write a note because Heather was late for combat?

"Mommy, where are you?" Concern mounted in Galveston's voice.

"Under the bed, Toney. Mommy likes to sleep there."

Light filtered into Heather's face as someone moved the blanket hanging off the bed. She turned her head. "Good morning, Ally."

"We brought you coffee," Dallas announced. "And guess what?"

"What?" Her stomach felt queasy, and she wondered why. Would it take forever to recuperate from the flu? "Have you two been up to mischief?"

"Nope. We been real good," Dallas said. "Gramma Liz is here. We got to help make biscuits and sausage gravy for breakfast. Toney and me cut out the biscuits with cookie cutters. There was reindeers and Santas. It was fun."

"The stars burned," Galveston mourned.

"Only on the points and Daddy ate them anyhow. We saved some for you," Dallas said.

"And gravy too," Galveston added.

Just the idea of sausage breakfast gravy made Heather gag. She rolled out from under the bed. She leaped to her feet, raced to the bathroom at the end of the hall, grateful to reach the toilet in time. Afterward, she rinsed her mouth, scrubbed her teeth and washed her face. She combed her hair and tied it back in a ponytail. How much longer would this damned stomach flu last?

When she returned to the bedroom, she found the twins trying to make the double bed. "Where's your grandmother?"

Dallas dragged the yellow striped comforter across the mattress. "She went to make tea for you."

"Gramma says coffee will make you hurl again." Galveston propped up the pillows. "Gramma says we gots to put you back to bed again."

"Great idea." Heather's head spun. She grabbed for the bedpost, sank down on the covers. "What time is it?"

"Almost 'leven hundred," Dallas said. "It's why Gramma thought we should wake you up. Now, she says you gotta have more rest."

"Come on, Mommy." Galveston patted the quilted down cover. "We're ready to tuck you into bed. Gramma told us we gotta take good care of you."

Heather laughed and obeyed, sliding back into bed, letting them adjust the blankets while she leaned against the pillows. They were so excited, thrilled at the opportunity to look after her. "Come on up here too." When they did, one on either side of her, she wrapped an arm around each of them, snuggled the girls close. "I love you."

Galveston pressed her cheek against Heather's chest. "You'll be all better soon?"

"It's only the flu." She dropped a kiss on each strawberry blonde head. "I worked too hard at the hospital, but I'll rest now that we're at our new home."

"And be fine." Dallas eased closer to Heather's left side. "Gramma said."

"And Grandma's always right." Liz entered the room, carrying a package of saltine crackers and a cup of peppermint tea. "Did you girls make your beds today?"

"It's Mommy's job." Dallas continued to cuddle close.

"But Mommy's still sick." Galveston scrambled off the double bed. "Come on, Ally. You help me and I'll help you."

Dallas heaved a dramatic sigh, plonked another kiss on Heather's cheek before clambering off the bed to follow her sister. "I sure hope you're better soon."

"Me too." Heather suppressed a smile as she took the cup of tea. Oddly enough, the spicy mint aroma didn't nauseate her. "How did you know this would help?"

"Because I'm never wrong." Tearing open the end of the crackers, Liz passed over one. "Eat. And I'll tell you the proper way to raise your children."

"Don't, and we'll say you did." Heather ate the first saltine, washing it down with sips of tea. "They're barely four. They pick up their toys, put their dirty clothes in the hamper, their dishes on the counter. They usually mind me and except for the games of Mix and Match, which don't bother *me*, we're good."

"Fine, then shall we talk about safe sex?" Liz passed more crackers to Heather. "And the consequences when you don't have it?"

"I'm not pregnant. Not again. It was pure luck when I had the twins." Heather glowered at her mother. "I can't be. It's the stomach flu. That's all."

"As the saying goes, 'denial isn't just a river in Egypt.' " Liz sank on the edge of the bed. "Are you telling me that you and Durango use precautions all the time? Before and after the wedding?"

Her face felt as if it burst into flame. Heather took more crackers.

"Damn it. Let me think about this. All right? Don't say a word to him. He's barely grown up."

"At the wedding, Quentin said he doesn't allow married men to go on dangerous missions for Nighthawke." Liz ran a hand through her hair. "Does Durango accept that, or is he going to try to continue being a mercenary?"

"I haven't had the courage to ask." Heather stared into the remains of the green peppermint tea. "If he won't make a serious commitment, how can I live with him?"

"It's something the two of you will have to work out on your own." Liz put an arm around Heather's shoulders. "He'll think marrying you is enough."

"It's not." She leaned into her mother's embrace. "Men. You can't live with them and you can't just shoot them."

"It'd only piss him off." Liz smiled. "If you want me to take the girls home with us so you and Durango can talk, I will."

"Let me think about it," Heather repeated. She finished the tea and the next two crackers at the same time. "I'm going to try getting up again."

Liz nodded and rose to her feet, standing beside the bed. "I'll help if you need me."

"Thanks." Heather flung the blankets aside and cautiously sat up. Her head stayed on top of her neck and her stomach didn't twist into knots. Maybe she could handle mornings after all. She slowly stood, thrilled when she didn't lose control and race for the toilet at the end of the hall. "I might survive this time too and hopefully, it's just the stomach flu."

"Yeah, right."

Heather ignored her mother's comment and crossed to the window, pulling back the drapes. Lightning slashed the gray sky while thunder thumped regularly, and rain pounded the soggy earth. "Looks like we're having a spring monsoon season."

"I'll check on the girls and see if they're finished. We're going to make cookies."

Heather crossed to the dresser, collecting clean underwear, jeans, and a T-shirt. "I didn't know you baked. You always bought cookies at the grocery store."

"I started when we were in Hawaii. I found out I like to make desserts."

"Better late than never," Heather teased. "I'll take a quick shower and join you downstairs." *I didn't expect her to be so supportive, but I should have.*

In the bathroom, she put her clothes on the vanity, stripping out of her nightgown. She turned on the shower, adjusted the water temperature, and stepped under the spray. Picking up the bar of soap, thoughts raced through her mind. She hadn't told her mother about the desperate need to drink and how mornings started with the proverbial hair of the dog.

Vodka numbed the pain, the anguish of watching young boys die when they should be home enjoying teenage pleasures. She couldn't talk about the I.E.D.s or seeing children younger than the twins who'd had arms and legs blown off by explosives. *I failed so many times. Why did I live to come home?*

Other women died in combat. Why hadn't she? If she had, then she wouldn't be struggling to put her life in order now. It was so hard to take control, to make her days count for something when, in the grand scale of things, it really didn't matter. She shook her head, wondering why she felt so depressed. Was it the rhythm of the unceasing rain?

She turned off the shower, wishing she could switch off the memories as easily. She toweled dry, dressed. She combed her hair, tied it back. Heather hung the damp towels to dry on the shower rod. Later, she'd throw them in the laundry.

Returning to the guestroom, she tucked the nightie under the pillow. The twins must have made the bed for her. The sheets and blankets were tucked in with hospital corners, but the angles weren't as sharp as she liked. The bedspread was wrinkled, and she debated a do-over, then changed her mind. Her daughters had done their best and she wasn't going to let them think she didn't appreciate it or them.

She went to the dresser, added a spritz of her favorite vintage *Babe* cologne to her wrists, her neck. She picked up her mascara and darkened her lashes while she contemplated whether to apply the rest of her makeup. Banishing the idea, she swung around and started for the door, glimpsing the photo of Durango in combat fatigues on the nightstand. She wondered if she ought to put it in a drawer and decided against it. Besides, the twins would miss it. The picture went everywhere with her and it was how they'd first known their father.

Thunder still boomed, and the rain continued to beat on the roof. Enough was enough. She had to quit avoiding her parents and Durango. Downstairs, she heard voices in the living room. Instead of heading there, she went to the kitchen and made herself another cup of peppermint tea before joining the others.

Durango sat on the couch with the twins. Liz had his recliner and Art had pulled out cushions to sit comfortably on the carpet. Heather went to the rocking chair in the corner. Once she had her back to the wall, she was safe. She forced a smile. "Good morning."

"Gramma's showing us pictures of Hawaii," Dallas said. "She had lots of birds there and she saw wall-bies."

Heather relaxed, amused. "Really, Mom? Where did you keep them? The apartment or the garage?"

"The bedroom!" Liz shot back. "Your dad had to sleep on the couch."

"Honest?" Galveston asked, blue eyes wide.

"No, sweetie. Gramma and I are teasing."

"I want one of them wall-bies in my room," Dallas decided.

"And where would Toney sleep?" Heather sipped the tea while she waited for an answer. "She and Ashes like their bed."

"We won't mind," Galveston said.

"No wallabies or kangaroos," Durango drawled. "Kittens are enough work."

Before Dallas argued that point, Art intervened. "What about the new kittens? Won't they want to sleep upstairs too?"

"What new kittens?" Heather glanced around the room. "Where are they?"

"By the washing machine. They gots to get used to us. Daddy said we can't feed the momma from the table." Dallas heaved a sigh. "She didn't mind."

"She likes sausage." Galveston finished the story. "We don't, but we had to eat it, anyway."

Heather's shoulders shook with suppressed merriment, and she glanced at Durango. "The girls really don't like meat and I don't force it on them."

"They told me they only eat what they like." Durango frowned at her. "And I'll tell you what I told them. In this house, meat, veggies, fruit, and milk are on the menu every day."

"Wow, you do think you're large and in charge." Heather wrinkled her nose, then winked at the twins. "Your daddy goes out of town a lot on business. When he's gone, we'll hit the junk food train, but we won't overload on ice cream. Deal?"

"Deal," the twins chimed together.

"Don't bet on it, ladies."

Heather drank more of the tea. "We'll keep all of the cats in the house until they're used to living here. Durango, have you had any problems with coyotes?"

"What?"

"Coyotes," Art said. "You're just outside Baker City, son. If there's a bunch of coyotes around, they'll go for your cats and chickens. So will the hawks, owls, and eagles. Keep an eye out."

"There aren't any coyotes around here," Durango said.

"Strange." Heather finished her tea. "Dick O'Connell told me there was a lot of logging going on and usually that brings the coyotes in closer."

"Remember when Fenn used to hunt them?" Art smiled at the memory of his younger brother. "He frightened off more than the four-legged ones."

"He used to sneak up on us when we wanted to be alone and scare me half to death." Liz laughed. "He was an awful brat, but he was so quiet we never heard him in the woods."

Heather winced as Durango joined in on the reminiscences. He didn't seem upset by the subject. Instead, he talked about Fenn and the stunts they'd pulled together. If he'd lived to come home from Colombia, he'd be thirty-nine, but he didn't and he wasn't.

"I'm going for more tea." Heather stood, careful to keep her back to the wall. "Anybody else want something?"

"Not for me," Art said. "What about you, Liz?"

"I'm good."

Durango shook his head and Heather started for the kitchen.

Suddenly, she saw a flash of lightning in the yard. A loud boom followed.

Heather hurled herself forward, hitting the floor, the cup rolling away when she landed on top of her father. "Incoming!"

# CHAPTER NINETEEN

She felt her father pat her back, then shift her to one side as he rose to his feet. He walked across the room. Didn't he understand they were under attack? "Dad, get down. Don't be a target."

"Easy, honey. It's just an early summer mountain storm, thunder, and lightning. That's all."

Sobbing loudly, Dallas clung to Durango, while Galveston cried more quietly. Heather turned her attention to the girls. "I'm okay. Get down here with me."

"No, Heather." Art took calm control of the situation, crossing to the picture windows and opening the heavy drapes the rest of the way. "Durango will take care of the twins. Come look outside."

"No way." She remained prone. "I'm not exposing myself to whatever is out there."

"Then lift your head and look." Art gestured to the huge yard, more like a field surrounded by large trees. "That last bolt of lightning struck a maple. It may have sounded like a mortar round, but it wasn't."

Durango stood, carrying the twins over to join Art. "Your grandpa's right. Trees fall in storms and we just have to be careful, not afraid."

"It was only a tree." Dallas sounded astonished. "Mommy, come see."

"I'm still scared." Galveston wept.

"That's 'cause you're a weenie."

"Am not."

"Are so."

Liz stood. "Well, I was scared too, Toney. What if us *weenies* go make cookies before the power goes out and the oven doesn't work?"

"Sure." Dallas wriggled free of Durango's hold. "Let's do it. Come on, Toney."

Durango lowered Galveston to the floor and watched as the twins and Liz headed for the kitchen. "I wonder what kind of cookies they plan to make. I better get the chocolate chips for them. The generator's ready in case we lose electricity."

"There's always the cook-stove," Art added. "That's how my mom baked cookies during storms. Have you cleaned the chimney this year, son?"

"Last fall. Gotta go. I sure as hell don't want peanut butter cookies. They still make me gag so I'm on a chocolate chip mission."

Art laughed. "Pretty strong hint, son."

"Mom can handle it." Heather slowly rose to her feet and went to the windows, standing next to her father. Part of a huge maple tree lay on the lawn, luckily not striking the power line running to the house. Puffs of smoke still curled from the split half of what she supposed would be called the trunk, although it had to be at least thirty or forty feet high, towering in the air.

She glanced at Durango when he returned. "If you cut up the wood and let it season for a year, I'll be able to burn it in the woodstove and fireplace."

"No problem, but I'm not doing it in the rain. I'm a huge *weenie*. And keep your cotton-picking fingers off my chainsaw, Empress. It's too big for you to run."

"Want to bet? I've used it before and I will again." She was grateful for the distraction. Somehow, some way, she needed to regain control of herself. She couldn't break down like this in front of the girls.

Dallas stood in the doorway. "Mommy, Gramma wants to know what bowl we should use."

"The big blue one. It's large enough to quadruple the recipe."

"What's qua-ruple?"

"It's when you make enough cookies for the *real* Cookie Monster, not the one on TV. Otherwise, your daddy will eat all of them and not leave any for the rest of us."

Durango tugged gently on Heather's ponytail. "I do not."

"Do too. Why do you think there never were any in the cookie jar?"

"Because it's a stupid place to keep them."

"You're silly." Dallas giggled and headed for the kitchen. A moment later, she was back. "Mommy, where is the blue bowl?"

"On the top shelf of the cupboard by the sink."

Before Dallas could return to the kitchen, Galveston came into the living room. "Mommy, where is the brown sugar?"

"Honestly, can't your grandma find anything?" Heather left her father and Durango, taking the twins by their hands. "Come on, kids. Let's go help bake cookies. How on earth did that woman manage to make biscuits and gravy this morning?"

Durango gazed out the window. He owed Liz big-time. The woman knew how to distract and keeping Heather busy would do the trick.

"What's going on?" Art frowned at him. "I've never seen Heather fall apart like that."

"She's a little on edge, and these mountain storms are enough to rattle anybody."

"Not my daughter. Fenn always said that Rusty had nerves of steel. When she came home in 2012 and told us she'd resigned her commission, I asked how things really went. She said nothing happened she couldn't handle during the last tour, but she was tired of the never-ending war."

"She said she had a bad bout of stomach flu these past couple weeks, so she can't depend on cigarettes and vodka, her usual crutches," Durango said. "She'll be okay, Art."

"I hope you're right." Art bumped his arm. "Come on, son. Let's fill the wood-box and fire up the cook-stove. Then we won't have to worry about the electricity."

"Works for me."

The power went out shortly afterward. The generator provided sufficient light for the downstairs, so he didn't have to drag out the kerosene lamps. Baking cookies took longer in the antique cook-stove, but it entertained the girls. Heather started an old-fashioned stew for supper, setting meat and onions to simmer in a cast-iron pot. The aroma filled the kitchen. After lunch, they settled around the table to play *Go Fish* until naptime.

It'd been years since he played the card game with his cousins, but it didn't take long to recall the rules of asking for and matching up the numbers or face cards. Dallas won the first time and Galveston the second, at which point Heather took them in the living room to nap on the couch. Liz offered to remain there to watch them, claiming she needed a rest because Durango woke her up at the crack of dawn.

Before he argued the point, someone knocked on the back door and he went to answer it, surprised to see his younger brother waiting on the porch. "What's going on, Laredo?"

"Isn't that my question?" Laredo wiped his feet on the mat and stepped inside, shrugging out of a denim fleece-lined jacket. "Friday dinners are mandatory when the folks get home from the other Washington and you didn't show last night. Eli said your cell phone didn't work, and I offered to track you down because I knew you didn't want him here."

"And I wasn't going there," Heather said, coming into the room. "Want some coffee? Have you had lunch, or should I make you a sandwich?"

"I ate at Pop's on my way through town. Everybody was there. It's the only place with power." Laredo paused long enough to hang his coat and hat in the laundry room, then came into the kitchen, nodding a greeting to Art. "Wish I'd known you were home, Heather. When did you get here?"

"Thursday night." She headed to the stove, filled a mug from the battered coffee pot. "If the phone lines hadn't gone down with the power, you could have called."

"Yes, but then I wouldn't be able to visit." Laredo grinned at her. "You're going to have a houseful of folks if the creek rises anymore."

"Worse comes to worst, you can always drive out on the road through the guest ranch." Durango smiled at her when she topped his cup and then Art's. "Rob Hendrickson and I had a bulldozing good time in March when we put it in again."

"Boys and their toys." Heather shook her head, then gestured to the table. "Pull up a chair, Laredo. Mom and the girls made chocolate chip cookies. I'll get some for us."

They'd barely sat down when someone else tapped on the door. This time it was Jeff Ransom.

Durango nodded. "*Qué pasa?*"

"*Nada*, Angel," Jeff said, with a shrug. "I heard your folks asking about you last night and figured I needed to stop in and make sure you and *La Capitana* got a heads-up. Didn't realize your brother already had given you the word."

"I'm still glad you're here." Heather went after another mug. "Saves me the trouble of calling."

"Why would you?" Durango eyed her, and then measured Jeff slowly. As usual, the tall, brown-haired man wore his personal uniform of a dark three-piece suit, a white shirt, black tie, and highly polished dress shoes. In his right hand, he held a black fedora. There would be a pistol in Jeff's shoulder holster and a knife or two within easy reach. "Why do you want him, Empress?"

"Because you'll be going out of town in a week or two, Angel, and if I want this place fenced and cross-fenced, I need Jeff." She advanced on the other man, her green gaze narrowing on his face. "Damn it, I told you not to eat at that woman's house. You did it, anyway, didn't you?"

"I had worse in the prison where Angel found me."

"I don't want to hear your crap." Heather put the mug on the counter instead of filling it with strong coffee. "If you're going to hurl again, the bathroom is over there. Meantime, I'll fix you something to settle your stomach."

"Sounds like you two know more about each other than I thought."

Jeff's face didn't reveal emotion, but the coal-black eyes remained wary. "We talked a lot when I was in the hospital before she sent me to you. I did what she wanted. Watched your back, Angel, and kept you safe."

"You could have smacked him upside the head a time or two." Heather began mixing a concoction of herbs into a glass of ginger ale. "I wouldn't have objected."

"You didn't say that at the time."

"I will in the future, Jeff."

"Why do you and Jeff call Durango an angel, Heather?" Laredo interrupted. "It doesn't sound like either of you think he is one."

"Short for his nickname." Jeff didn't shift his attention from Durango. *El angél de la muerte,* the angel of death. Takes him sixty seconds to kill a man."

"On a bad day. Normally, I'm faster."

"I know. I was there."

Art deliberately stepped between the two of them. "If you boys are going to squabble, take it outside. I won't have blood on my mother's kitchen floor."

Jeff smiled. "I'd never fight with Angel."

Heather brought over the glass filled with ice and her favorite remedy for upset stomachs. "Drink this and I really wouldn't ask you to intervene, Jeff. I enjoy my battles with Durango too much to share them."

He rested his hands on her hips, pulling her back against him. She rarely admitted that, but must think the former pilot needed to hear it. "You and me both, baby. You and me both."

She nodded, her bright hair pressing against his chest. "Talk to me, Jeff. Why did you go there?"

"So Amarillo and Maria wouldn't."

Durango frowned over the top of Heather's head. "Do you mean they ditched you there?"

"They never arrived," Laredo said. "Neither did Brazos and her latest girlfriend. Jeff and I were the only ones who showed."

"And I didn't expect hot pepper sauce in the spaghetti," Jeff added with a wince. "Who does that when only a few people like it?"

"Durango's mother." Heather heaved a sigh. "She's the same woman who used to put it on their tongues if they swore, lied, or said anything she didn't like."

"Everybody has some kind of discipline, Heather." Laredo reached for a third cookie. "We weren't exactly the world's greatest kids."

"You didn't deserve to be tortured, either."

"That's enough, Heather." Durango saw the concern mount on Art's face. "We'll talk about it later."

"Fine, jarhead. Understand this. They are never alone with the twins."

"I already agreed when I gave your papers to Brazos." He dropped a kiss on top of Heather's head. "Any other kids we have are safe too. I don't want them going through what I did when I came home during the summers."

---

Thankfully, the storm subsided in the late afternoon, and everyone could leave after supper when electricity was restored. Heather and Jeff agreed they'd tour the ranch on Monday after lunch and plot out the new fences. That evening, after she'd bathed the twins, tucked them into their beds, and read two stories, she went downstairs.

She joined Durango in the living room, pleased he'd left the rocking chair for her. She paused in the doorway to admire his lean, good looks. Blue jeans and a plaid flannel shirt emphasized the cowboy image. Like her, he wore socks in the house, leaving his boots in the mudroom. She longed to run her fingers through the tawny gold hair, but she restrained herself.

He placed the newspaper he'd been reading on the coffee table. "Everything okay?"

"Fine." She measured the classic strength of his features. Why did he have to be the man she loved? Why couldn't she settle for less? Those dark blue eyes saw clear to her soul.

He shrugged. "Okay, baby. 'Fess up. You've got evil on your mind. What rotten stunt have you pulled now?"

"What are you talking about? I've done nothing."

"Well, you will." His attention returned to the newspaper.

She stalked across the room toward the rocker in the corner. "Freaking Marine." She pretended to ignore his deep chuckle as she passed him.

He caught her hand, pulled her down on his lap. "Spit it out, Empress."

"Let me go." She aimed a slap at him with her other hand, swore when he grabbed her wrist before she connected. "Who do you think you are?"

"The idiot who married you, wife." He lowered his head.

She turned her face, managed to avoid the kiss. "I don't want sex."

"Liar." His lips trailed down her neck. "Tell the truth. I dare you."

"All right." She lifted her chin. "It doesn't matter if I do want you. I'm not sleeping with you."

"You will." He released his hold on her wrists, wrapped his arms around her. "What's on your mind?"

She took a deep breath. It was difficult to argue with him when he held her like this. She felt the muscles of his legs underneath her, the warmth of his chest against her cheek. "It's over."

"What is?" He rested his chin on top of her head. "The ice queen treatment? Sleeping in a guest room? Didn't you say you weren't ready for sex a minute ago?"

She wriggled, desisted when she felt him harden against her. "I'm not trying to turn you on, but I'm finished playing house with you. It doesn't mean anything."

"Go on." His arms tightened around her. "What's the problem?"

"You're not going to be around much longer, are you?"

"You're my wife." His tone was even, too even. "You're with me where you belong, and I'm not letting you pull one of your crappy stunts."

She wished she could see his face, but his hold was impossible to break. She tipped back her head and glimpsed the fierce line of his jaw. "I want a man who provides safety, stability, and security for me and my daughters. We don't need a hero determined to commit suicide."

"Not again, Heather Marie. Quit your bitching."

"Give it up, Durango. They're dead. If they weren't, the Army would have them back by now."

"It's a moot point until I convince Uncle Quentin to let me go with the next team. I need Nighthawke's support and their mercs behind me. I'll keep the hunt alive, and you'll wait for me when I have to go there."

"Like hell." She saw a muscle twitch in his jaw. "You won't live with me when you're playing soldier of fortune."

"Want to bet? Kick and scream. It doesn't matter. We're married. I'll stick and stay. So will you."

She ignored the edge in the bass rumble. "You're going somewhere, aren't you? When?"

"Texas. Next Friday. It'll be a short training mission. I'll be back in less than two weeks." He turned his head, trapped her with the cobalt blue gaze. "Don't push your luck, Mrs. Hawke. I'll cloud up and rain all over your parade."

She forced herself to remain still when he traced her lips with his thumb. "You haven't seen anything yet. If you go, don't come back."

"Or what?" He captured her chin with calloused fingers. "You'll walk out on me again?"

"No. This is my place." She met him, glare for glare. "I'll file for divorce. I'll get a restraining order. You won't see the twins. I'll make sure of that and I'll take your company as well as every cent you got from your grandfather to support us."

"You're a vicious little tyrant, sweetheart." He bent his head, his breath warm on her lips. "And your snotty threats always make me horny."

She tried not to tremble when he tangled a hand in her hair. "I'll make your life hell."

"You always have." He grinned with sudden appreciation. "If you couldn't make me miserable, baby, you sure couldn't take me to heaven."

Before she could speak, his mouth claimed hers. The pressure of the kiss forced her lips apart. His tongue taunted hers into a passionate duel. What was she doing? She didn't want to make love, did she? She pushed on his shoulders, wrenched out of the kiss. "We can't."

"We are." He cupped her breast, his thumb tormenting one of her nipples. "You want me, and I want you." He paused long enough to pull off her T-shirt, tossing it to the floor. "Nothing's changed that."

She surrendered to the steamy kiss for a moment, dimly aware he'd unhooked the front closure of her bra. She dug her nails into his back when he lifted his mouth from hers. "Damn you."

"Say you love me, Missus Hawke." He blew softly on her nipples.

"I won't." She stifled a groan when he strung kisses over her breasts. He barely tasted her skin. Her nipples tightened under the teasing flicks of his tongue. Why was she so sensitive?

*Oh, my Gawd! Am I actually pregnant?*

She yanked on his hair. "I hate you."

"You're hot all right." He unfastened her jeans, slid two fingers inside her panties, and then inside her. "You'll beg a dozen times before morning."

"No way." She arched against his hand, shuddering when he started a slow in-and-out motion, his thumb rocking into her. "I really hate you."

"Remember that when I have you." He kissed her.

She yielded, unable to resist. How could she fight when she wanted him so much? She sighed when his lips left hers. Tender breasts, morning sickness, heartburn. Why had she kept denying the obvious? And he planned to return to Colombia sooner or later. But he intended to make love to her first.

"You son of a—" His mouth stopped the insult.

Afterward, they lay together on the couch. She pillowed her head on his shoulder. She shivered when his hand roved down her back, smoothing the waist-length curtain of her hair. "I do hate you sometimes, Hawke."

"Yeah, I know." He kissed her forehead, her eyebrows, her lashes in quick butterfly touches. "I'd feel bad if I believed you. I hear it whenever I don't bow and scrape."

She buried her face against him, struggling not to cry. She already had the twins. She was probably pregnant again. She'd get a test in town tomorrow and take it. And he was planning to return to Colombia to search for that worthless bum, Waco.

"Sex means nothing. I'll throw your sorry ass out of my house next week."

"These challenges make me hot." He drew her on top of him. "Let me change your mind. Time to ride a cowboy."

# CHAPTER TWENTY

Sunlight shone through the master suite windows when she woke in the middle of the big brass bed. She felt the warmth of his long body next to her, the weight of his arm on her hair. She opened her eyes and turned her head to look at him.

He sprawled across the king-size bed, taking up more than his half of it. She studied his relaxed, sleeping face. Slowly, she brushed a lock of tawny, gold hair from his forehead. No wonder he was tired. He'd made love to her three times in the living room before he carried her upstairs and they'd done it two more times in the bedroom.

She propped up on an elbow, tugging her hair out from under him. She glanced at the clock on the nightstand. Oh, 0600 hours. She sat up. Oops, too quick and she leaped to her feet to run to the en-suite and puke her guts out. She was rinsing her mouth when she saw him standing naked in the doorway. "In case you think I'm going to jump your bones this morning, get over it."

"I was worried when I heard you. What's wrong?"

She pushed by him, grabbed one of his T-shirts off the top of the dresser, and yanked it on, shoving her arms into the sleeves, the hem hitting at mid-thigh. "I'm guessing until I get a test, but I think you knocked me up again."

He gaped at her as if she'd sucker-punched him. "What?"

"We've been humping like rabbits whenever we're together. Even when

I try to talk to you, we end up in bed or having sex wherever we are." She stomped toward the hall door. "And we never take precautions when we're Stateside because we're freaking stupid. So, I'd say I'm pregnant. And if it's twins this time, I'm having Dad castrate you unless I do it myself."

She heard a muffled sound and swung around. "Now what?"

He was right behind her and pulled her into his arms, still chuckling. "You're amazing."

"Why? Because I may have a bun in the oven?"

He kissed her forehead. "Are you going to happily hate me for the next seven and a half months?"

"You know it."

The tenderness in his eyes and slow, gentle smile made her knees quiver. "Women have been having babies forever, Hawke. We already have twin girls."

"But this time I'll be here for it." He picked her up and carried her back to the bed.

"Should I believe you?"

"Definitely." And he kissed her.

Hours later, she woke still remembering how he'd made love to her, softly and oh so sweetly. Shadowy, butterfly kisses as if she'd break under the pressure of his lips. Slow caresses, his fingers brushing her skin and when he finally eased inside her, he rocked her world with little thrusts until she came, twice or was it three times before he did.

She turned her head, saw a can of ginger ale and a sleeve of crackers beside the bed. Okay, so he'd grown up when she was gone. He used to try to take care of her when she was sick, but she generally kicked him out of the bedroom and told him to leave her to die. *Not this time. I've grown up too.* It didn't take long to shower and dress in jeans, a T-shirt, and sloppy sweatshirt.

Downstairs, she found him making pancakes, frying bacon, and scrambling eggs for the twins. He glanced over his shoulder, smiling at her. "How do you feel? Want to go to church with us?"

She checked the clock on the wall. A little after 0900 hours. "Have you checked the creek? Can we even get off the place?"

"We'll have to take the road through the dude ranch." He flipped the hotcakes. "That will let me show you where it is if you want to go to town when I'm in Texas."

She nodded and glanced at the twins, who happily put plates and silverware on the table. They already wore the dark blue A-line casual skater dresses with the Peter Pan white collars her cousin, Ann had sent them. Obviously, Durango didn't understand the twins should change for church after breakfast. Then again, he'd only been an active daddy for a few days. "Come on, girls. I'll do your hair."

"Okay." Galveston placed the last fork on the table. "I want a French braid like Daddy makes."

"No worries. I'm the one who taught him that when he was showing Cinnamon."

"I want a ponytail," Dallas said.

"And you can have one. It'll make it easy for Reverend Tommy and the folks up town to tell you apart."

"It has to be the same." Dallas stormed toward her, ballet slipper shoes stamping on the tile floor. "We're twins."

"But I wanna braid." Tears filled Galveston's eyes and her voice. "I getta pick sometimes, Ally."

Heather rested a hand on her belly. *To think next year, I'll have even more drama. I don't know if I'm ready for it.* "Okay, girls. Here's the deal. Today, Toney chooses the hairstyle. Tomorrow, Ally does."

"No!" Rage swept into Dallas' face. "I want ponytails."

"Tomorrow, Ally."

"No! Now!" Dallas jumped up and down, skirt swinging around her knees. "No, no, no!"

"Enough." Durango put down the flapjack turner and strode toward their recalcitrant daughter. "One more word and you're standing in that corner."

Dallas stopped and glared up at him. "Toney too. She's bad too, Daddy."

"No, she's not. Just you, little miss." Durango pointed toward the bathroom. "Get your hair done and if I hear you being rude, I'll put you in that corner. By yourself."

She backed a step, obviously shocked at the idea of being separated from her sister. Then Dallas whirled and raced after her twin. Heather suppressed a smile as the girls hurried toward the bathroom. She flicked a glance at Durango, mouthing unspoken gratitude. Amused, he returned to the pancakes.

After the meal, she went upstairs and changed into a green floral dress with a slit, knee-length hem. Decorator buttons ran from the v-neck to mid-thigh. The skirt swirled around her knees, exposing bare, tanned lower legs. She opted for low-heeled sandals and shifted her belongings to a casual straw purse. Makeup and gold bangle earrings, and she was ready to make an appearance in Baker City.

Outside, the sun shone and there were only a few puffy clouds in the blue sky after yesterday's storm. She spotted Durango helping the girls into their seats and went to join the family. He glanced over his shoulder when he heard her, then opened the passenger door of the Ford 150 and waited to assist her.

"I haven't broken either arm or leg, Hawke."

"I'm being a gentleman, sweetheart. Be nice or I'll rat you out to your mom."

"She figured it out before I did." Heather watched red rise on his cheekbones. "You'd better worry more about my dad."

He started the truck, drove through the field bordering the indoor arena and into the woodlot. Evergreens lined the winding track, and she realized he'd brought in gravel for the new truck road. She hadn't spotted it when she rode Satan, opting to take the trail up the ridge to view all the acreage.

He kept driving and eventually, she saw cyclone fencing. "How high is it?"

"Four feet on the boundary because we wanted the deer to be able to jump it. Six feet where people might be, so it'd serve as a deterrent for trespassers."

"That makes sense."

He came to a stop at a chain-link gate, put the truck in park. "You'll find a key on that shamrock ring of keys I made for you, but drive through after I open up, will you?"

She nodded, unfastened her seatbelt, and slid across to sit behind the steering wheel. On the other side of the gate, she reversed the procedure so he could take over. He knew these people, and she didn't. A short time later, he pulled up in front of a three-story Victorian house like the one on the McElroy spread and she thought they must have had the same architect.

A tall, dark-haired guy with short thick black hair that was almost a military high and tight cut came down the front steps. He was in cowboy garb. He glanced their way and waved at Durango, sauntering toward the truck. "Morning. Thought we might see you come this way, since the creek is rising after yesterday's storm."

"Heather, this is Rob Hendrickson. Rob, this is my wife, Heather McElroy, and our daughters, Ally and Toney."

Something about the other man seemed oddly familiar, but Heather couldn't quite decide what. She was almost sure they hadn't met before. She nodded and smiled. "Hi, Rob. It's nice to meet you."

"Likewise." He gestured to the tall redhead with hip-length copper hair in a white maternity dress, ushering two young girls in their direction. "My wife, Cat O'Leary McTavish."

"O'Leary?" Heather stared at the other woman who appeared almost like a doppelganger. "Wow, we look a lot alike."

"That's what happens in Baker City when all the families are related. We have many redheaded women. A guy has to be careful when 'duck' isn't just a bird."

Heather laughed. "You don't sound too scared."

"I'm not. See you at church." He turned and headed toward his family.

She frowned after him, still wondering why she felt like she knew him when they hadn't been introduced before. She'd have to ask her parents if he'd been a member of their 4-H club back in the day. It seemed as if they'd joined a caravan after they crossed the bridge behind Rob's bright red Mustang and two other rigs joined them. "Who are they?"

"Your cousin, Ann Barrett, and her best friend, Margo Endicott. They're getting married this summer, not to each other. Ann's engaged to Dick's nephew, Harry Colter and Margo's fiancé is an Army Reserve officer. I've already been invited to both weddings and I'm sure Ann will want you to be an attendant."

"I'm barely home." Heather frowned thoughtfully. "We'll have to stop at the mercantile so I can see if my invitation was forwarded from Tennessee. Do you have a box at the post office there or do we need to open one?"

"I get my mail at Hawke Construction," Durango said, "but we can swing through after church. Family is family in Baker City, so I'm sure Maxine Garvey already has a mailbox for you."

"Thanks for the warning."

It might sound somewhat snarky, but she meant it. He drove through town, past the cedar-shingled buildings to the lot adjacent to the church. With the twins on either side of her, Heather walked beside Durango toward the oversized carved wooden doors where a silver-haired elderly man stood waiting. He didn't wear the traditional dark suit associated with most preachers, but a plaid flannel shirt tucked into faded jeans.

He beamed when he saw her. "Heather McElroy. It's so good to have you back."

"It's good to be here, Reverend Tommy." She suffered through his warm hug, then another when he called out to his wife, Virginia. More embraces followed along with several kisses as the Baker City inhabitants flocked around her. Why had she ever agreed to come and get the faith? She spotted the smirk Durango barely hid and wished she'd worn her cowboy boots so she could kick him in the shin. Next time, she promised herself.

The glad-handing ended when the service started inside. Ally and Toney happily went off with the other children downstairs to Sunday school. Ann's daughter, their new cousin, Devon, proudly announced she'd introduce them to everybody. The McTavish-Hendrickson twins offered help if it was needed.

What a day, Heather thought that evening. After church, they'd done the social hour in the reception hall and she'd done her best meet-and-greet routine, including being nice to Dominique MacGillicudy when the blonde fashion plate offered to redo the entire McElroy house. Heather had said she'd consider it, and figured she'd earned another star in her crown in heaven because she hadn't baldly recoiled.

They'd had lunch at Pop's Café, then Durango drove out to the Murphy place so they could pick up fresh organic vegetables, homegrown eggs, farm-raised meat, raw milk, and what he called "real" cheddar cheese made on the farm. More visiting and she met the newest addition to the family, Tate's wife, who was pregnant with twins. Sully had invited Heather to her house, saying she wanted to pick her brain about having two babies, but there was time. The younger woman wasn't due until September.

Heaving a sigh, Heather debated changing from her dress after she tucked the twins into bed. It seemed like too much trouble. She paused in the guest room to kick off her sandals. Quit stalling, she told herself sternly. Peace at any price wasn't her style. It was time to face the elephant in the living room. Okay, so it wasn't an elephant.

It was one giant-size Marine who'd found it utterly amusing when she was overwhelmed by one relative and family friend after another today. She glanced at him as she entered the room. He wasn't watching TV but reading the Sunday paper. Grateful he'd left the rocking chair for her, she bypassed the recliner where he sat, carefully remaining out of reach.

She rocked for a few minutes while she considered how to broach the subject. "It was past time for me to come home."

"Agreed." He leaned back in the recliner as if waiting for the proverbial other shoe to drop. "What else, Mrs. Hawke?"

"The twins need to know you before you get yourself killed, Angel."

"Thanks for the faith in me."

"Give it a rest, will you? Like I keep telling you, Fenn and Waco were Army Rangers. If they could have escaped, they would have. They're dead. You're going to die if you keep looking for them."

"The cartels trade prisoners all the time." He frowned. "Besides, Uncle Quentin is on his hobby-horse right now. He says I have to set an example for the other married mercs. If he won't let them go, I can't either."

"Then why are you leaving soon?"

"I need to go to Texas and train my possible replacements until I convince him and Bendigo that I can handle it."

"Right, and if I believe you're home to stay, you'll sell me a bridge in the desert." She rocked a while longer. "The ranch is mine."

"I won't take it away from you, baby. It's been in your family since 1893, shortly after Washington became a state. It should go to our children."

"It will eventually. Meantime, I intend to operate the place. It will provide me and the girls with a home, a stable environment." Her lips quivered at the unintentional pun.

"Is this when you try telling me to go?"

"There's no point in moving back to Lake Maynard." She kept her tone calm. "You're not going to be around that much this summer, are you? It will be sufficient if you stay in the bunkhouse. I'll tell people you're renting it while we work out the custody arrangements."

"You've never cared what anyone thought before."

"I never had children before, Durango. They learn by example. We're married, but we've never had a conventional relationship. They'll be going to school next year and Baker City is a small town. You saw that today when everyone was oohing and aahing over me and them."

"Nobody is going to think I live in the bunkhouse."

"I don't care about my relatives in town. They can think whatever they want," Heather retorted, her tone even. "I won't have your parents calling me a whore or a slut in front of my daughters."

"They only say those things to hurt you."

"And you. Do you think they're so stupid they can't see you've built a shrine here to worship me? They never did like the way you put me on a pedestal." She shook her head. "I don't know if they even realize what you've done here. The house is exactly the way I like it. You kept all my grandparents' furniture, and you expanded this room the way we talked about eons ago. The indoor arena is perfect for training and when Mom starts passing the word I'm back and ready to ride, I'll have a ton of clients. My horse is out in the barn along with yours. Hell, if they go into Baker City, they'll hear from everyone that you think I walk on water without stepping-stones."

"Is that what you think I've done?" He watched her, his gaze narrowing. "Built you a shrine?"

"Haven't you? You've felt guilty for as long as I can remember. Guilty for being their firstborn, guilty because your parents never loved you, and I always did. Guilty because you came back alive from Iraq and Afghanistan and all those missions as a mercenary. Guilty because I left you. You're so busy feeling guilty, there's no room for any other emotions, not love, or joy, or pain, or anger."

He pushed his hands in the pockets of his jeans, stretching the denim across his flat stomach. "You piss me off, Heather Marie. You had no business hiding my kids to get at me. You came back for a short visit six weeks ago, and the games started all over again. We're married, but you think that gives you license to play mudpies with my guts. It doesn't. I've had enough of your tricks. I'm not letting you treat me like crap anymore."

"Treat you?" Heather sputtered. "You arrogant, misbegotten jarhead! What about the way you treated me? You never cared about me. You used me! You lied to me! You made a fool of me for years! I was the only one who didn't know you had no intention of running Hawke Construction when your father foisted it on you. I was so gullible I thought you were serious about a future with me. Everyone else knew you were on the way to Colombia to look for Waco. Not me."

"Nobody else knew. You were the only one smart enough to figure it out. And you kept threatening to turn me over to the cops."

"No, I didn't. I said if they knew, you'd be in jail. I didn't say I'd send you there. I used to love you a lot."

Slowly, he stood, strode toward her. "Say again, babe."

She raised her chin and glared at him, spacing out the words. "I don't love you. Hell, most of the time, I don't even like you and I've got no respect for you or for myself when I let you treat me like a piece of tail."

"That isn't true, and you know it."

"No, I don't. You didn't even care enough to come after me or the girls when you knew where we were in Tennessee."

"You're not the only one who knows horses. I've trained enough of them to know they'll come to me when they're tired of running around the corral." He stopped in front of the rocker, his hands resting on the arms of the chair, and leaned close. "You're no different, Mrs. Hawke. You came back to me."

She caught her breath. He was close, too close. She smelled the spicy aftershave he used when he shaved. Her nipples tightened against her bra. "I'm not a horse, damn it. If you think I'll 'lick and chew' and act like you're the boss of me, get over it. I won't!"

"You're here, aren't you?" He bent his head, his lips near. "Pitch all the fits you want. I like it when you're hot and bothered."

She should push him away, keep fighting with him. Instead, she arched high enough that her lips touched his. "Want me?"

"Always." He chuckled. "Is this when you talk dirty and tell me where to crap?"

"Always," she mocked.

"I don't think so." He began to unfasten the buttons on her dress, opening it to reveal the lacy bra. His thumbs found her nipples, rubbed gently. "You ripped me apart when you said exactly what you thought of me. Now, we do make-up sex."

She nipped his ear, kissed his neck. "What if I don't want you?"

"Liar." He kissed the top of her breasts. "You'll always want me as much as I want you."

She gasped when he pushed up her skirt, slid his finger inside her panties. "Aren't you forgetting something? I'm kicking you out of my house."

"Not tonight. That happens tomorrow." A second finger joined the first and both slipped inside her. "Aren't you going to start issuing orders, my pretty little tyrant? Start by telling me what you like, what you want me to do."

# CHAPTER TWENTY-ONE

Monday afternoon, when she came downstairs after putting the twins down for their nap, she found two aerial maps on the kitchen table. "What are these?"

Durango continued loading the dishwasher. "Jeff called. He'll be here in thirty minutes, and you'll need the maps to show him where to lay out the new boundary fences you want."

"Makes sense to me." She picked up the first one, studying the view. To her amazement, she saw a clear trail along the back line. He must have run the bulldozer around the property at some point, and that made things easier for Jeff. They'd be able to drive across country instead of walking. "What's the plan for you and the girls?"

"They'll probably want to ride Cinnamon. After that, snacks, cartoons, and horsey chores. I'll put a roast in the slow cooker and then it won't matter how long it takes you and Ransom."

She nodded. "And you don't have issues with us going out alone?"

"I trust you, baby, just like you've always trusted me. We don't cheat on each other. We never did."

She eyed him while he did the domestic routine, finding the slow cooker, taking a roast out of the freezer. It'd take a little longer to cook if he didn't thaw it first, but it'd be done by early evening when all of them were ready for supper. "What did you call it when I dated other guys if it wasn't cheating?"

"You always had a curfew, and you never set anyone up to get his head busted."

She debated telling him that she'd kissed a few frogs over the years. None of those guys compared to him in or out of the sack, but he didn't need to hear how wonderful he was in bed. Besides, it wasn't like she'd have slept with anyone else, not even Zeb Steele. "You do realize the road runs two ways, don't you, Hawke?"

"Hearing you use the microphone to stop mid-song when you were onstage to tell some gal to keep her hands to herself cured any doubts I had."

"Just checking." She watched him put the roast in the pot, top it with onion soup mix, and crossed the room to find him a small cutting board. "Use this for the yellow onion you're going to chop, so I don't have to deal with the smell on the big one when I want to bake. Anything else?"

"The warnings were better than the alternatives." He followed directions. "Granted, Pop never complained when you did an entire set of Loretta Lynn songs."

"He likes classic country. I told him to hire a bouncer to keep out the slut contingent or have them arrested, but he and Dick O'Connell said there weren't any laws against being sleazy."

Durango grinned appreciatively, then went to answer the back door. While he was distracted, she topped the roast with mushroom soup, then refilled the can with a cup of strong coffee and added it to the pan. The addition drew his attention when he returned, followed by Jeff. "It tenderizes the meat, Hawke, and if you think your daughters gripe about sausage, you don't want to hear them if the roast beef requires too much chewing."

"I'm learning."

"Good to know." She glanced at Jeff, wondering what it'd take to have him change into casual clothes from the dark suit. "I hope you're planning to join us for supper, or we'll be eating leftovers for the next month."

"I'm here for that."

"All right. Let's hit the road. We're taking my truck."

"I told Ransom to bring one of the construction rigs from our fleet this morning when I was there for our meeting," Durango said. "It has a chainsaw, weed-eater, hedger, and all the hand tools you'll need to get across country."

"Plus, a front-mounted, industrial winch if we get stuck." A wooden cane in his hand, Jeff held the back door for her. "Want me to see about adding one to Heather's rig since she'll be off-roading around here?"

"No. I bought the super-cab for her to drive into town. I told Tia's boy, the head mechanic, to go through the fleet and detail one of the older four-by-fours for us to use at home. I want it here before I leave for Texas on Friday."

Jeff inclined his head, and Heather heaved a sigh. "Does it ever occur to the two of you that I make my own decisions? If I wanted to drive the new truck around here, I certainly could."

"No, Empress. You'll have a decent rig that can take a beating. See to it, Ransom."

"You got it, *jefe*."

Heather gave up the battle. She certainly wasn't going to win with either of them. She paused to look at the roast, kissed Durango quickly, and headed out the door, Jeff behind her. "Do you two get added points for making me crazy?"

"We enjoy it." He escorted her to the dark blue Ford 250 super-duty truck. "May as well get used to us, *La Capitana*, since Angel says you're home to stay."

"He's a macho pain in the butt. If I had any brains, I'd fall in love with you."

"He'd lose it and I like my life the way it is." Jeff held the passenger door for her. "Let's just be good friends. I'll take his sister."

"You're not Brazos's type, so I'll guess you're talking about Amarillo." While he slid behind the wheel and started the truck, Heather studied his once classically handsome features. There was only so much surgeons could do with olive-toned skin. Unfortunately, all the scars weren't hidden by his graying hair. The worst carved a line from below his left ear to the jaw line. A young woman could judge him by his looks and find him wanting. "Jeff, you can do better on a bad day. The Hawke bunch aren't easy to love."

"I know. Amarillo's it."

"What about Maria?"

"She likes me."

Questions crowded Heather's mind as she directed him to the road up the ridge that eventually led to the back boundary. "How did you two meet? When did she fall in love with you? What kind of relationship do you have with Maria? She's my goddaughter and I worry about the kid."

"I met Amarillo when I arrived." Jeff grinned appreciatively. "She stalked into Durango's office and tried to fire me. I told her I wasn't going anywhere. She's been trying to get rid of me ever since."

"That doesn't sound like love to me. How can you marry her? Neither one of you deserves or needs more heartbreak."

"I love her. She knows how prison feels. Hers was worse than mine."

"How do you figure? I saw your medical records. The surgeons had pretty well repaired you by the time you checked into the VA hospital where we met."

"It was only my body, not my soul. Besides, I was a grown man when I went through hell. She was just a child."

"Right." Heather gestured for him to take the track to the left, amazed the old roads she wanted to take were in such great shape. Durango must have had a bulldozing good time up here. "Kate and I are the ones who helped you regain a sense of self, Jeff. What about Maria? Do you blame her for anything that happened to her mom?"

"Of course not. What kind of man would blame a seven-year-old? None of this is Amarillo's or Maria's fault. I talked a karate instructor into giving Maria lessons when she was three. I paid for them, told Amarillo it was a birthday present. Once the girl has her black belt, we'll go for judo."

"Did you sign up Amarillo too? She needs to be able to protect herself."

"I couldn't get her to go for it. She's too wary of being touched or touching other people." Jeff guided the truck through a grove of evergreens. "I bought her a hot pink Glock, 9mm handgun and took her to the range to teach her how to use it a month after I met her. For Christmas that year, I gave her a pilot's survival knife and she carries it everywhere. She's deadly with it."

"It doesn't mean either of them will ever trust you." Heather struggled to keep her voice gentle. "I don't want you hurt. You've been through enough."

"You could help me again."

"How?"

"Maria's father. Who is he?"

"I can't tell you."

"But you know." The calm certainty in Jeff's voice made the words a statement, not a question. "It isn't Gino Petrocelli. He doesn't know either. He's connected. I told Amarillo to keep him and his relatives away from Hawke Construction."

"And she agreed?"

"When she argued with me, I reminded her that we didn't want law enforcement looking too closely at Angel's activities."

"That makes sense." Heather focused on the rolling pastures and evergreens outside the vehicle. She wasn't like him or Durango. She'd never been able to hide her emotions for long. She couldn't betray Amarillo or break the promise made to a traumatized fifteen-year-old back in 2014.

"Don't worry, *Capitana*. When I find him, I'll take care of him. I've promised Gino he can put the remains in a concrete bulkhead on one of his relatives' highway projects."

"The two of you fill me with confidence. Jeff, let it go. It's history."

"Not yet. When *he* is, Amarillo will know she and Maria are safe, that they can trust me."

The lethal words hung in Heather's mind for the rest of the afternoon while they inspected the boundaries and used red survey tape to lay out the replacement fence lines. She agreed to use cyclone fencing and chain-link gates, like what Hawke Construction did for Cedar Creek Guest Ranch next door.

Meantime, she had to keep what happened to Amarillo from coming to light. It hadn't been enough to hide the truth. If it weren't hidden, at least one man would die. Heather had to admit she wouldn't miss him. Anyone who'd rape a girl until she was pregnant at thirteen, giving birth shortly after she turned fourteen, deserved to die. However, Jeff and Durango shouldn't pay for destroying the molester.

She still didn't come up with a brilliant solution when they returned to the house, or during the evening when she sat alone in the rocking chair watching television. After everyone fussed over her in Baker City the previous day, she hadn't dared to buy a pregnancy test at the mercantile. She didn't want the entire town gossiping about her.

Since she probably was pregnant, she couldn't open the new bottle of vodka she kept in the pantry, and she wouldn't have a cigarette either. She wanted a healthy baby to add to the family. She rose to her feet on the next round of commercials. Okay, if alcohol, tobacco, and caffeine were temporarily off-limits, she'd dish up a bowl of ice cream and junk out in front of the flatscreen. She wasn't going to bed at midnight. She'd never sleep. She'd suffer through one nightmare after another.

She wasn't dealing with the onslaught of memories. She couldn't stand to watch soldiers die repeatedly or see huge wounds while she struggled to staunch the flowing blood. She didn't want to hear voices begging for help during triage or play God one more time sorting out those they expected to die from the ones they could save. Had there ever been a time when she wasn't plagued by ghoulish hallucinations even when she was awake?

No answers and she scooped more ice cream into the bowl, adding fudge sauce, chopped walnuts, and whipped cream to the giant sundae. She had to hurry back to her show. On the next round of advertisements, she'd mute the sound and call Kate. Perhaps they could share a few of the horrors without triggering remembered pain.

---

He woke at his usual time, 0500 hours, to another sunny summer day. Heather, he thought. He wanted to see her even if she wouldn't share the master suite with him on a regular basis. Tossing the blankets aside, he rolled out of bed. He pulled on a pair of jeans and patrolled the upstairs.

The twins still slept. He picked up the stuffed purple pony and tucked the toy back in with Dallas. He fixed Galveston's blankets, paused by the door to the larger guest room, and noticed the empty double bed. This time, he checked underneath it, but Heather wasn't on the floor.

He went downstairs. He saw lights in the living room and heard the morning talk-show hosts conversing. Heather slept in the rocking chair, a litter of empty dishes on the coffee table. He gathered her gently into his arms, swung around, and carried her toward the staircase.

"It was bad." She turned her face against his neck, and he barely heard the whisper. "Mass casualties. Thought we'd never finish."

"It's over now." He kissed her forehead. "It's safe. Sleep, baby. You're safe. I've got you."

That afternoon, he hummed along with the classic country song on the radio. He'd stopped for a load of grain and baled, plastic-wrapped shavings on the way home from Hawke Construction. He pulled off the highway, wondering how soon he could get Heather into bed tonight. The question distracted him the rest of the way down the drive, through the creek, and up to the house. He'd unload the truck after he saw her, kissed her.

The mountain of clothes in the front yard stunned him. He slammed on the brakes. What the hell? He parked, turned off the engine, and threw open the driver's door. Leaving the rig, he strode to the pile of jeans, shirts, jackets, boots. All his!

Anger shook him. Worry followed. Had the twins seen their mother's fit of rage? What did they think?

He headed for the house, swiftly climbing the steps to the porch. "Heather. Damn it. Heather Marie!"

She met him at the front door, a stack of camouflage fatigues in her arms. She flung the uniforms at him. "I told you Sunday night. You don't live here anymore."

He stepped over the military gear, grabbed her shoulders. "Where are the girls?"

"None of your business."

He lowered his voice, furious. "Where are they?"

"At my parents'." Fury glittered in the green eyes. "I'll bring them home when you're out of my house."

"What brought this on? You were fine yesterday."

"Fine, hell." She punched him in the ribs. "I'm pregnant, you son-of-a —! I took three damned tests at Mom's. You knocked me up. Get the hell off my land."

"In your dreams." He ignored the next blow, dragged her against him. "You never could hit worth a damn."

She was his. What would it take to make her admit it? His mouth claimed hers, his tongue dueling with hers. One fierce kiss followed another until she clung to him in wild surrender. He twisted his hand in the thick red mane of hair he always wanted to see spread across the pillows in their bed and lifted his head. "You're mine, aren't you?"

"Yes, you freaking jarhead, but it doesn't mean nothing."

He chuckled in grim acceptance, recognizing the saying they'd used in combat. Nothing had any meaning, not life or death, and everybody died. The only question was when. "Say you love me, or I'll have you right here and now, Mrs. Hawke."

"Rot in hell!"

He snagged the front of her T-shirt. "Want me to take this off you?"

"No." She shoved at him. "Stop it. You win. I'll say it."

"Make it sweet or it won't count."

"Fine. I love you." The husky, sexy tone continued, "You louse-ridden, worm-infested piece of jackass crap—"

His mouth closed over hers, stopping the flow of insults. She trembled in his hold. He slowly lifted his head. "Are you sure about this, Heather Marie?"

"About what?" She glowered up at him.

"Me out of the house?" He saw her chin quiver, then she nodded. "All right."

"You'll actually go?" Her eyes widened as if she'd never seen him before. "You'll leave me?"

He inclined his head, placed his hand on her belly although she didn't have a bump yet, but she was having his baby. Again. It was real and only she would take three tests to be certain before she confronted him. "Family tradition, Empress. The house belongs to the woman. I'm not leaving here. You'll have to ask me to move back inside."

"I won't, not in a million years."

"Yes, you will." He managed to laugh at the bewilderment on her lovely face. "You'll hate groveling, sweetheart, nearly as much as I'll enjoy it."

She backed away, glaring at him. He laughed when she slammed the door between them. It didn't sound as if she liked what she'd won. He bent, gathered up the pile of uniforms on the porch. He'd move into the bunkhouse for now. It wouldn't be for long. There was too much passion between them to remain apart when they lived on the same property.

He couldn't show her she'd cut him to the quick with this stunt. If he had the sense God gave a rock, he'd have found a different woman years ago, but it wasn't an option. He was hers, as much as she was his.

He walked into the cabin behind the house. He was grateful he'd had Linda MacGillicudy's crew clean the place and put fresh linens on the bed when she looked after the main house for him. At least, the bunkhouse had electricity and indoor plumbing, conveniences added by Heather's grandfather.

The back door opened into a kitchen with a laundry room off to the right. Directly adjacent to the kitchen was a living room. A narrow set of stairs led to the loft bedroom. On the other side of the staircase was the door to the bath. Durango carried his clothes to the couch. Once he had his belongings out of the yard, he'd put everything away.

It wasn't the first time he'd slept here. The summer after Heather graduated from high school, she moved up to the McElroy place to stay with her grandparents. Durango had taken a job building fence on the ranch. He studied the cabin again. There weren't any memories here. He'd slept alone in the double bed upstairs.

He grimaced. Old man McElroy had threatened to castrate him without anesthesia if Heather so much as stuck her toe in the cabin. But that had been years ago, Durango thought. They were adults now, married even. Her grandpa wouldn't so much as haunt the place if they were together.

It was past time to create some new history. Whistling, Durango headed out to collect his clothes. An hour later, he'd settled into what would be his temporary home. He walked back to the large Victorian main house, across the wrap-around porch and through the back door, leaving it open behind him. He found her in the kitchen, peeling potatoes.

She spun around, paring knife still in her hand. "What do you want?"

"My wife." He snagged her wrist, removed the knife, and dropped it on the counter. He picked her up, carried her out the door, pausing to close it behind them. "I have to make sure you know where to find me."

"I wasn't looking."

He lowered his head, brushed her mouth with his. "That's one more thing I have to change."

# CHAPTER TWENTY-TWO

Heather picked up the restaurant menu and studied the choices again. The last two days slipped by quickly on the ranch while Durango prepared for his trip to Texas. Tonight, he'd suggested dinner at Petrocelli's Pizza Palace in Lake Maynard, and she'd agreed. Other than packing her off to the bunkhouse on Tuesday afternoon for three hours of lovemaking, the two of them hadn't spent any time alone.

He didn't complain about sleeping out there. *Not that I'd have listened, but he's still in the house for meals and to interact with us.* She glanced up as he and the twins came to join her. "Did you find all the good songs on that old-time jukebox?"

"We stuck to country classics and golden oldies because I know what you think of the newer stuff." He boosted Galveston onto a chair and then lifted Dallas onto hers. "Did you decide what kind of pizza we want?"

"A veggie combo for you guys and I'm going with their chicken fettuccine alfredo and hoping the sauce doesn't give me heartburn."

"Sounds good." His gaze narrowed. "Jeff did the PMs on the bulldozer when he brought in that construction truck. Don't take the new one up in the boonies, Heather. It's a piece of crap."

"Daddy, teacher gives time-outs for that word too," Dallas warned him.

"Then it's good she isn't here." Heather propped her chin on a fist. "Why did you buy me a sissy, girly truck?"

"Because it matches your eyes. It's pretty and you can take it through the creek and around Baker City and down to Liberty Valley. It will melt like tissue paper if you hit a tree or slide in the mud. The construction rig Jeff brought has four-wheel drive, an industrial winch on the front end, new car seats for the girls, and a full tank of gas."

After they ordered their meal, she listened while he continued telling her what to do if she stuck the older Ford 250 in the back country on the ranch. Finally, she interrupted. "I get it. You're concerned. I'll be fine. I've been off-roading since I was ten years old when Grandpa and Fenn taught me to drive. My grandma said I had to be able to reach the pedals in their truck, or they'd have done it earlier. I'm not a city slicker, Hawke. Like you say all too often, quit yer bellyaching."

"I don't say that."

"I know. I'm being politically correct, so I don't get in trouble for using bad words in front of the girls. I don't want a time-out."

The comment earned giggles from the twins and silenced him until the food arrived and they'd started eating. Then he said, "I'll be back before the Fourth of July. Usually, my family visits the ranch for the holiday. Is that a problem?"

"The whole Hawke family? Does that include your parents?" Heather eyed the twins who happily munched away on the pizza slices he'd cut into chunks for them. "Do you want an honest answer?"

"Count your blessings. Since the bridge washed out, my folks can't do the big celebration this year for all my dad's closest political supporters. Now that you're home, you can decide how often you want them to visit. This year, it will only be them, Laredo, the girls, their significant others, Eli Roberts, and his staff. We can renege on any future invites."

"Got that right." Heather swirled more noodles around the fork. "I like your sibs and they're always welcome in my house. The extended Hawke clan from Texas is too, but your folks and I have never gotten along so this is the last time they come to the McElroy ranch. Deal?"

"Deal."

---

The next morning, he packed two suitcases and carried them over to the front porch of the house a few minutes before Jeff arrived. When he walked into the kitchen, he saw her spooning cookie dough onto a baking sheet. "Ransom will be here soon to take me to the airport. I'm leaving my truck too. Don't lend it to Laredo."

"You don't need to worry about him." She gestured to the key rack. "Hang the ring there. You already helped him get a decent rig for horseshoeing."

"Least I could do since I didn't want him driving mine." Durango strolled toward the sink so he could watch the twins playing in the backyard. "I'll be home in ten days. If you need anything, call Jeff. He knows how to bring in supplies, but I've already stocked up on hay, grain, and shavings."

"We'll be fine, jarhead. Stop fussing."

"It's what I do." He managed a smile, strode to her, and pulled her into his arms. "You're mine, baby. You have been since Liz and Art brought you home from the hospital when you were two days old."

"Yeah, right. You've said that several times before. This is when you tell me you love me, Hawke. I've heard you say it to the girls."

He held her closer. He couldn't say those words to her. She didn't understand why, and he didn't know if he'd ever be able to tell her. She already had plenty of issues when it came to his family. He wasn't going to validate those. Instead, he repeated his claim. "You're mine."

"I know." She pulled back and forced a smile. "Be careful. It isn't combat, but if I recall, Nighthawke uses live ammo for training."

"I'll try." He kissed the coppery red hair. "You stay safe too and protect our little ones, even those who aren't here yet."

She caught her breath. "I can't bear it when you leave me." She clung tighter. "I'm so scared I'll lose you too."

"You won't lose me. You'll never lose me." He brushed a kiss over her forehead, then kissed away the tears on her eyelashes. "When I get home, you'll still make me sleep in the bunkhouse, right? I bet you won't even save some of those cookies for me."

"With your daughters?" Heather managed a weak laugh. "No way!"

Two gentle kisses later, he released her. She turned and picked up a plastic container off the counter along with a thermos of coffee. "Here. Share these with Jeff on the way to the airport. Hug Vicky, Quentin, and the rest of the crew for me."

"I will." He snagged her chin, bent his head, and kissed her again. "See ya in ten days, babe." He started for the back door.

"Durango, don't forget to kiss the girls and tell them goodbye."

---

The farm seemed empty the next day, with him gone. She found herself roaming from room to room in the house. She vacuumed and dusted the downstairs. She found a key to the den on the shamrock ring Durango made for her. When she opened the door, she spotted the locked gun safe in the corner. After her grandfather died, his weapons went to her father, so Durango must have his rifles, handguns, and collection of knives safely stored inside the cabinet.

She opened the chest with several sliding drawers and found maps of Colombia. She didn't turn on the computer or look in the electronic records, much less the hard copies in the big wooden file cabinets. This was his business, not hers. She left the room, locking the door behind her.

At some point, she would tell him to get this crap out of her home. For now, it could wait. She returned to housework, stripped the beds, made them with fresh linens, and did three loads of laundry. She was in the middle of scrubbing the kitchen floor on her hands and knees when Galveston raced in the back door.

"Mommy, come quick! Satan was rolling in his stall, and he's stuck against the wall."

Heather leaped to her feet, following her daughter out the door. "Where's Ally?"

"In the barn."

Heather ran for the stable. A cast horse could injure himself internally. He might also bruise his legs and scrape his body. She raced down the barn aisle, coming to a stop outside the stall. Satan was on his feet and Dallas stood by the door, soothing him with baby talk and stern lectures.

"What happened? You said he was cast, Toney. How did he get up?"

"You gotta ask me, Mommy. I was here. Toney went to get you. This man helped."

"What man?" Heather whirled around, scanning the stable. She and the girls were the only ones in the barn beside the three horses. "I don't see anyone."

"He went 'way. He was fishin' and he heard me yelling at Toney to hurry. He fixed Satan."

"Where is he now?"

"I told you, Mommy. He's gone." Dallas reached up and petted Satan's nose. "He went to find his friend Bill. They was still fishin'. I told him to come back soon. Okay, Mommy?"

"Sure." Heather looked up and down the aisle again. No strangers. Apprehension crept through her. She didn't see anyone, but the twins rarely lied to her. Not about anything major. "Come on. It's time for a snack. Let's go have cookies and milk."

She followed her cheering daughters out of the stable. She stopped when she saw the footprints in the mud by the water trough. The fisherman wasn't heading for the creek or his supposed friends. The tracks pointed to the ridge behind the buildings.

Later that afternoon, she was still on edge when she saw an older truck pull up in front of the house. She walked out on the porch wondering about the visitors, then recognized her distant cousin, Dray MacGillicudy, in the passenger seat. A bearded young man in jeans, a Huskies T-shirt, and boots climbed out from behind the wheel, giving her a friendly wave. He reached in the back, pulled out a toolbox, and started toward her.

Heather waited until both guys drew closer. "What's happening? Why are you here?"

"Hi, Heather." Dray bounded up the steps to kiss her cheek. "Durango stopped by on his way out of town yesterday and gave me a key to the front gate. I'm supposed to take care of the horses every day."

"Say what? I don't get it. You don't know as much about horses as I do, and I can look after them myself."

"Not according to your hubby." Dray grinned at her, mischief in the electric blue eyes, black hair curling down to his shoulders. "He says you're expecting a baby and I'm to turn out the stock, muck the stalls, bed them, feed the night hay and grain for you. If you need firewood or have any chores, I'm supposed to do that too. And before I leave, I'm to bring the horses back into the barn."

"Really?" She looked him up and down, all teen guy in jeans and a plaid flannel shirt. "How are you at digging holes?"

"Sure, I can do that. Did you need a fence repaired?"

"No, I need a big hole, six foot deep, seven foot long, three foot wide. I'm putting Durango in it when he gets back and if he's lucky, I'll shoot him first." Heather ignored Dray's hoot of laughter and turned to the other man. "You're Ted Fenwick, aren't you? We met last week at church."

"That's right. Please don't make Dray dig another hole. I work for the local phone company and I'm supposed to wire in a bunch of extensions for you. Durango says when he calls to check on you, he doesn't want a bunch of crap that you didn't hear the one in the kitchen ring. And you've been around Baker City long enough to know what lousy cell reception we have."

"I do, and I'm still killing Durango." She spun and stalked back into the house. "That doesn't mean I want everyone and their brother having the number, Fenwick. If his parents call me even once, you're a dead man walking."

"Got it. Nobody in town likes Tex, but he has a lot of clout back East. If we could get someone decent to run against him, it'd be a different story in the next election."

"Well, I'm busy," Heather said, "but we'll keep a good thought."

Dray headed off to the barn to take the horses out to the large pasture so they could graze. Heather and Ted walked through the house, discussing where to put the extensions. When he started laying out tools, she went into the kitchen and picked up the phone, dialing Quentin and Vicky's number outside of Houston.

A deep male voice answered. "Hawke Mortuary. You plug 'em, we plant 'em."

"Ha, ha. Who is this? Bendigo?"

"Nope, it's Gus. You want my big brother?"

"This is Heather. Where's Durango?"

"Training. He'll be back tonight because Momma says church is mandatory tomorrow. Want him to call?"

"Not needful. You tell him Ted Fenwick and Dray are here. I don't want any more surprises. Got it?"

"You bet." Gus laughed. "Want to know what he said when Dad and Mom asked how you were?"

"Am I going to like it?"

"Probably not. He said, pregnant."

Heather glared at the receiver in her hand. "Anything else?"

"That's about it, but he promised you wouldn't name the baby Augustus after me."

"F.Y.I., I'm having Dray dig a grave. Your cousin is toast when he gets home."

"Okay, honey. He said that you promised the door was open for all of us and Dad says we're coming for Christmas because he doesn't think you should be flying down here in December."

"You're always welcome, but tell Durango to keep his big mouth shut. He doesn't need to share our business with the entire state of Texas."

"We'll try."

She replaced the receiver and headed into the living room, not sure how she felt about him announcing their news to his relatives. On the one hand, they'd have a new addition to the family in February. On the other, she wasn't comfortable sharing the news during her first trimester. After three months, she wouldn't worry so much about a miscarriage.

Her irritation mounted during the social hour after church the next day when Dray's mother brought over her calendar to set up appointments to clean the house. When Heather protested, Linda said Durango paid in advance for her crew to wash windows, scrub walls, clean carpets, and do other things a pregnant woman shouldn't be doing.

By the time Heather resolved that issue and set up dates with her cousin, the Murphy teens arrived to discuss their duties with her. They explained that Durango had hired them to restore the rose garden to its former glory when he moved onto the McElroy place. Heather eyed the pair. Like most of the other troubled teens who'd lived on the Murphy farm, these two opted to use their foster parents' last name.

The girls wore fashionably torn jeans, floral, ribbed, shrunken T-shirts, enough makeup for an entire cheerleading squad, plus plenty of earrings in their actual ears. Heather was amazed Bronwyn Murphy, the family matriarch had allowed them to dress like that for church, but then decided the older woman had been doing foster care for years and knew how to choose her battles.

Naveah, a gorgeous Black girl, pulled out a chair. "We need to continue the liquid feeding schedule for the bushes and check for pests and rust."

"We've got to remove the damaged leaves and blooms again." Chantrea, a slender teen with long, dark hair, sat down too. Concern grew in the Asian-American's dark, almond-shaped eyes. "Have you been watching for slugs? They're really bad this year. We should come early to wash off the leaves. Does tomorrow work for you?"

"What about school? It's Monday. Don't you—"

"It's finally out for the summer," Naveah interrupted. "Dray can bring us two or three times a week. Lock always tells us to monitor the irrigation time when we water, so we don't flood the garden."

"If you pay him, Dray can pick up more mulch at the big hardware store in Lake Maynard. It's cheaper than buying it at the mercantile in town," Chantrea added. "Durango taught us to use the aged horse manure for fertilizer, so it doesn't burn the plants and there's plenty of that on your place."

"All very good points." Heather glanced across the room where her daughters sat at a table with their cousin, Devon, and the two McTavish-Hendrickson twins. "I'll see you in the morning. Bring equestrian helmets if you want to go in with the horses."

"Durango gave me one to use when I groom them," Chantrea said. "I keep it in the tackroom."

"Sounds good. You can help the girls with Cinnamon while Naveah teaches me about the roses. I haven't done anything with them since I helped my grandmother back in the day, and that was a long time ago."

"Works for us." Naveah stood. "Mom said to tell you we'll bring your eggs, milk, fruit and veggies in the morning too."

"Don't forget the carrots." Heather watched the two head across the room to join their family. Before she could rise to her feet and collect her daughters, her cousins Ann Barrett and Jacinth Sweeney arrived, accompanied by Sullivan Murphy, Margo Endicott, and Cat McTavish. "What is this? A coffee klatsch?"

"I wish," Sully said, "but I'm off coffee until September when my twins come."

"Longer than that if you plan to breastfeed," Margo informed her. "I'm starting a veterans group for women, and Ann suggested inviting you, Heather. We've all served, and our issues are different from the guys. Cat gets to come because she deals with her share of vets."

"Mostly dead ones," Cat said cheerfully. "Your great-aunt looks a lot like you, Heather, and she always has a lot to say. I'm bringing Jassy along to babysit since she doesn't freak out when my girls do their version of the O'Leary walk or talk. And heaven knows what this baby will be like."

Heather looked around the table at the other women. They varied in heights and sizes, but all of them had different shades of red hair. Amused, she wondered if it was a requirement to live in Baker City. "I'll think about it. My best friend, Kate Flanagan, is coming to live here soon. We met in Iraq and I contacted her when I moved to Tennessee."

"She's welcome too," Margo said immediately. "When and where do we want to meet?"

"Since you and Ann already live at the guest ranch and Jassy works there part-time, I recommend my place," Cat said. "Shall we start next Wednesday morning?"

After more discussion, they agreed on a time. Sully said she'd bring cheesecake and the new owner of the bakery, Twila Garvey. She'd recently lost her husband in an ambush in Afghanistan and could use support from others who'd been there.

Later that afternoon, a cable news show played on the television when Heather and the twins entered the house after an early supper at Pop's Café. She picked up the remote and turned off the flatscreen. She didn't ask the girls if they'd left on the TV. If they had, it'd be a cartoon channel, not the news. And it certainly wasn't the cat. They'd found Cop-Car, the black and white momma, sleeping on the porch in the summer sunshine. All the kittens had been locked in the laundry, so they'd remember to use their litter box, not disgrace themselves in the rest of the house.

Heather put the cherry cheesecake in the refrigerator, wondering if she should arrange for Cat McTavish to visit and see if there was someone haunting the old house. It wouldn't be her grandparents. They'd felt the same way she did about the "talking heads" blathering nonstop about nothing at all.

She eyed the twins. "Let's go change your clothes and we'll ride before supper."

"I want Satan," Dallas said instantly. "Okay, Mommy?"

Heather nodded. "And you can have Cinnamon, Toney. Does that work?"

"Yes! Come on, Ally." Toney raced for the stairs, followed by her sister.

# CHAPTER TWENTY-THREE

For the next week, she kept a close eye on the twins despite the frequent guests. Dray helped Chantrea groom the horses, neither of the teens complaining when the little girls helped and took turns riding. Chantrea stuck with the older horses, but Dray enjoyed exercising Flash. Naveah taught Heather all about the roses and other flowers. Linda MacGillicudy and her crew came twice and cleaned the house from top to bottom. She even did the bunkhouse.

Heather didn't see any sign of the stranger who'd saved Satan, but she certainly wasn't willing to risk the twins' safety and drive the construction rig around the ranch looking for the man. When Durango returned, things would be different. She'd search every inch of the McElroy spread and discover who was trespassing.

The first meeting with the other women broke up the week. To her amazement, she found the old strawberry roan pony who'd taught her to ride out in the barn along with his best buddy. Cat explained they'd basically retired to the guest ranch, but she didn't own them. They were loaners from a friend of hers who had a stable in Liberty Valley. At some point, they might return there, but meantime they'd teach her twins to ride and of course, her new baby too.

Durango wasn't available when she called his aunt's and uncle's home. Heather didn't know if he was avoiding her, but Quentin swore up and down that his nephew wasn't leaving CONUS now that he was a husband and father. During one of her discussions with the older man, she said, "I wanted peace and quiet when he was gone, Quentin. I didn't know he'd arranged for the entire town to visit me. What's up with that?"

"System support, sweetheart. He wanted you to have back-up until he returned."

"I'll remember that and try to be grateful, but I'd really like to have the place to myself and the twins once in a while."

As if somebody, somewhere, heard the wish, it came true the next Saturday. The Murphy girls were off with friends. Dray popped in to take care of the horses, then went to a demolition derby in Liberty Valley. The weather warmed, and it was hot enough to take the twins to wade and splash in the creek.

Heather sat on a blanket. Beneath her, she felt the ground vibrate. A loud explosion rocked the afternoon. The ground shook even more. *Incoming artillery.* They were under attack.

Galveston ran toward her. "Mommy, what's that?"

*Bombs*, Heather thought, but didn't say so. "Come here, now!"

"We wanta play some more," Dallas protested.

"Move it. With me. This instant!" Heather bolted for the creek and the twins. A loud boom. She hit the dirt. A moment later, she stood. Ran to the twins. Grabbed each girl by the hand. She propelled them toward the tree line.

Another faint whistle. A change in pitch. She felt more than heard it. Without thinking, she threw herself on the ground, covering the children with her body. An explosion. At the pause between bombs, she was on her feet again. She pushed the girls forward. Halfway to the rows of cedars and maples. Fifty feet to go.

It seemed to take forever to cross the stretch of ground where they were open targets. "Crawl," Heather ordered, determined to keep moving.

A soft sob escaped from Galveston as she obeyed. Dallas was silent and stoic. When they were safe in the sheltering evergreens, they rested. She reached in her shorts, pulled the cell phone from her pocket. No signal. Damn it! When would Baker City have enough towers for regular access to the outside world? She had to get to the house, call for help. Who?

"Mommy, are we in the bad place?" Dallas asked.

"Yes, honey." Heather listened intently for the next shell. "We sure are."

They hid in the trees until the explosions faded. She didn't know what was being bombed or why. Did Baker City still exist or was it the target? When the shelling ended, she headed for the house with the twins. The horses stood at the paddock gate, Flash pawing and snorting, his unease apparent.

She urged the girls into the tackroom, then opened the barn door on her way to the pasture. The horses cantered inside, slowing to a trot in the aisle. They were smarter than most people, she thought, as they went into their individual stalls. They had plenty of water and she gave them extra flakes of grass hay. Now, if she couldn't get to them in the morning, they'd be safe.

In the house, she decided the most secure place would be the basement. She went upstairs to the twins' room, followed by her silent daughters. They helped her move the mattresses down to the cellar. She brought down sheets, blankets, and pillows. After she made up the temporary beds, she loaded up on food and water plus kerosene lanterns for light, preparing for a siege. At least this attack was real, not a figment of her imagination or memories.

"I think we're ready, girls."

"Are we going to sleep down here?" Dallas asked.

"Yes, sweetie."

"For how long?"

"Until the loud noises go 'way, Ally," Galveston said.

"That's right." Heather hugged both girls and led the way back to the kitchen. "Do you two want to watch TV while I check the horses one more time?"

"Sure." Dallas dashed toward the living room, shouting over her shoulder. "Come on, Toney. Let's find some 'toons."

"Mommy, can we bring down the kitties?" Galveston lingered a moment longer.

"Of course, we will." Heather waited until both girls were in the front room before she hustled out to the barn. The horses were fine, happily munching on their hay. She hurried to the house and checked on the twins, still distracted by their cartoons. She went upstairs to the guest room and the lockbox secured on a top shelf of the closet.

She opened it, removed the .45 automatic Colt pistol and the small magazine that only held five rounds. She had extra ammo, but she might not need it. If they were careful to remain out of sight, they shouldn't be overrun, but she didn't want to take any chances. There must be some way to learn who was attacking what, but she wasn't sure how since she didn't want to leave the ranch.

In the kitchen, she cleaned and oiled the handgun. She loaded it, then replaced it in the lockbox. She hadn't fired the pistol in more than five years, but she still remembered how. Would she ever forget?

The sound of footsteps overhead brought her fully aware later that night. She rolled to her feet, opened the box, and removed the .45. Her hand closed over the butt of the pistol and she softly crept up the basement stairs. Moonlight filtered through the windows and she saw a tall silhouette near the back door.

He must have heard her somehow because he turned in her direction. "Don't even think about it, Heather Marie. Shoot me and you won't sit down for a month."

Relief swept through her. "You're home."

"That's right." He strode toward her. "We finished up training this afternoon and Bendigo brought me, so I didn't have to try to get a commercial flight."

"What happened out there? Who fired off those rounds? Is *The World* still safe?"

"What rounds?" He pulled her against him, taking the pistol, checking it before sliding it into the waistband of his jeans. "What are you talking about, baby?"

"They started shelling us this afternoon. It sounded like World War Three. Nothing landed on this side of the creek, but there's been mortar and rocket attacks."

"Are you sure? Everything looked peaceful when Jeff dropped me off."

"It was real. The girls heard it too." For a moment, she pressed close and let the comfort he offered steal into her soul. "I didn't imagine it, Hawke."

"I believe you, Empress." He stroked her hair. "It wasn't blasting, was it? The loggers use dynamite to blow stumps out of the way. The state traded off some of the old-growth up here while you were gone. They've been clear-cutting part of the foothills."

"It didn't sound like dynamite." She pressed her ear against his broad chest and listened to the reassuring rhythm of his heartbeat. "Mortars, mostly. Besides, it's been warm and dry while you were gone. Blasting can set off a forest fire and wildfire season is approaching."

"I'll make some calls in the morning and see if I can learn what happened." He tipped up her chin, kissed her quickly. "Where are the girls?"

"Asleep in the basement. We don't have a bunker."

"Let's put them to bed."

"Where? I brought down their mattresses for us to use."

"They can have the guest room, or I'll bring those mattresses back upstairs."

"I'm not sleeping in the master suite with you." She met his gaze.

"I want to be close to you and the twins. You're the sexiest woman in *The World*, baby, but I'm too tired to do you justice. Now, I'm putting our girls to bed and then I'm headed for a shower. You can do as you please."

"Fine." Heather considered the options. "I'll sleep in the basement until the shelling stops for good. I know it wasn't logging."

When he released her, she led the way to the basement, and he followed. "Are you okay?"

"Of course." Heather dropped to her knees beside Dallas and shifted the little girl into a snug embrace. "Let's do this."

"Mommy, what's the matter?" Dallas murmured sleepily.

"Nothing, honey. Your dad's home and we're taking you and Toney upstairs."

"Daddy?" Dallas called.

"Right here, Ally." Durango bent and gathered up Galveston. "It's late and all of us are going to bed."

"And Henry too?"

"I have Henry." Heather picked up the toy pony. "Durango, be sure you have Toney's blankie."

"Got it."

Tucking the girls into bed in the guest room she used didn't take long. She returned downstairs, aware he was right behind her. She stopped halfway into the kitchen and glanced over her shoulder. "Are you hungry? Shall I fix you a meal?"

"Sounds good."

She switched on the overhead lights and went to the freezer, removing a package of steaks. She gestured to the clock. "It's 0200 hours. Breakfast or dinner?"

"Dinner."

"All right. No whining while I nuke a spud for you, since it would take an hour to bake in the conventional oven."

"I can handle that. Where's the box for your pistol?"

"In the basement."

"Be right back."

"Okay."

She had a salad on the table when he returned. He sat, added dressing, and ate while she fried the steak. The buzzer dinged on the microwave. She tested the giant potato and decided it was finished. She forked it onto a plate, flipped the T-bone, and let it cook a little longer. He always preferred his meat rare, so she served it that way.

He never had been in the mood to talk or listen when he arrived home from a trip and she figured the same rule applied for training. She put the plate on the table along with the trimmings for the baked spud and a few slices of homemade bread from the loaf Twila Garvey gave her. While he ate, Heather sat across from him, sipping a cup of decaf peppermint tea.

After a while, he said, "Thanks, baby." He pushed back his chair and eyed her. "How are you feeling? You don't look as washed out as you did before I left."

"I'm better." She swirled the tea in her cup and drank. "I haven't hurled in the morning for three days. Until the shelling started, I was able to sleep more."

"Good." His gaze narrowed on her. "What happened to us? Sometimes, I don't feel like I know you, Heather Marie. Maybe I never did, not as a person."

She stared at him. "What's going on, Hawke? Were you reading women's magazines on the plane or did your uncle give you a lesson in sensitivity?"

"I'm serious. We've known each other since we were kids, but when did we stop talking to each other? I was thinking about what you said when I was in Texas, that we hump like rabbits when we're together. I never thought of it like that."

"What did you think it was? You're pure sex on the hoof, Durango Hawke, and we spend a lot of time screwing."

"It has to be more than that. You didn't trust me enough to tell me we had kids. I don't want to argue. I just want a straight answer."

She heaved a sigh and finished her tea. "I'd say it was Colombia and Waco. We came home and discovered he'd been captured. I didn't matter to you anymore. All you cared about was finding him and pleasing your parents."

"You weren't the same when you came back, either. The two of us used to enjoy being together. You couldn't bear to be alone—"

"You're right," Heather interrupted. "I was scared of the dark, terrified of thunderstorms. I spent more nights sleeping on the floor unless you were home and in bed with me. I partied all the time and tried to drown the memories in booze unless I was singing. And when we were together, all you wanted was sex."

"I never felt like it was only sex. Didn't we make love?"

"I felt like a piece of meat. You were never there, Durango. You didn't care how I felt about anything. All you wanted to do was listen to your parents complain about me and share those criticisms with me." She rose to her feet. The dishes could wait until later. "And then you constantly harangued me about wonderful Waco. You put him ahead of me even when I told you I had a dream job and a recording contract in Nashville."

"He's my brother."

"Yes, and he freaking tried to assault me when he was home on leave." She planted her hands on her hips, glared at him. "I know you'll be like my mother and say I asked for it since he showed up at a bar where I was working. He drank too much and needed a ride to your parents' place. I was stupid enough to trust him, so I agreed to drive him home when we finished packing up the instruments that night. He's your damned brother, and he's no good."

He gaped at her, holding up a hand as if to ward off the truth. "I can't believe that. He couldn't."

"He did, Durango. I've never lied to you, not once, not since I started talking." She started for the basement and the sanctuary it promised. "You should consider the fact your parents hate me because I love you. They'd do anything to split us up, and Waco always wanted what you had. Luckily, Zeb Steele thought it was fun to teach me self-defense tactics when we were dating, and I kicked your little bro's ass."

---

Her words stabbed into his heart. She'd never been so blunt before. Wasn't it past time they shared their feelings if they wanted a real future together? And his younger brother dared to put his hands on Heather? Durango didn't doubt her for a moment. It made so much sense, explained why Waco had been so wary the last time they'd seen each other. He must have expected Durango to kick his sorry ass all the way to Texas and back.

*And I didn't because I didn't know. Why did Liz betray Heather like that?*

*Rape is all about power, not sex. I know that much, even if Heather constantly calls me a jarhead and mocks me for being a Marine.*

She always laughed at his parents, acted as if their barbs didn't cut to the soul. Durango stared across the kitchen at the closed basement door. *She treated me like she loved me once.* He'd never forget the special way she smiled at him as if he were the center of her world. Now, she closed the door between them.

He stood. He started for the stairs to the master suite. He'd go to bed. Tomorrow would be a better day. Before he was halfway across the kitchen, he recalled Jeff's words on the way home from the airport. Life didn't come with guarantees.

Durango swung around. He'd spent almost five years alone.

Those empty days and nights taught him a lesson. He strode to the basement door and opened it. "Heather?"

No answer. He didn't hesitate. He went down the stairs, spotting her asleep on the mattress, surrounded by the cat and six kittens of varying sizes. He could carry her upstairs, but it was too late for that. Instead, he sat down and removed his boots. Lying down behind her, he gently drew her against him, careful not to disturb the felines.

"Durango?"

"It's me, baby." He tightened his hold, kissed her forehead. "Sleep. You're safe. I have you and you're safe."

"About time you got here," she muttered.

"Sorry it took so long."

---

He looked at the sleeping couple in the basement, amazed it'd taken so many years for Heather to share what he'd done. *Unforgivable*, Waco thought. *God, I'm a rat bastard.*

Heather hadn't realized he'd set her up six ways from Sunday, determined to have what his brother did. She'd never love him, but if he took her the way he had so many other women, then it'd destroy her relationship with Durango. And she might let Waco clean up that mess, might let him have her for the duration.

*I am a son of a bitch, but at least I come by it honestly. The old man is one too. As for my mother, she's evil to the bone. The woman is a total viper, and I can't believe Uncle Quentin actually slept with her. What was he thinking?*

The only decent thing his parents ever did was send Durango to Texas and Quentin. Unfortunately, his older brother didn't know how lucky he was. Waco drifted into the living room to turn on the television to watch his favorite newscaster. This time, he muted the sound. He couldn't hear her voice but seeing the ash-blonde beauty in a print blouse and navy jacket was enough.

# CHAPTER TWENTY-FOUR

"Mommy, lunch is ready. Are you getting up?"

The question slowly penetrated her mind, and Heather nodded without opening her eyes. "Sure, I am, Toney. I'll be right there."

She hesitated, wondering if her stomach would remain settled or if there would be another onslaught of so-called morning sickness. She lifted her head cautiously and waited. Nothing happened. She rubbed her eyes and carefully sat up, pushing the blanket aside. She still felt okay.

Time to try standing. When she looked around, she noticed she was the only inhabitant of the basement. She rose to her feet and sauntered toward the staircase.

In the kitchen, she saw Durango standing at the counter and she caught a whiff of grilled cheese sandwiches. Still no nausea. All right, she thought. *I can eat!* She glanced quickly at the girls, looking neat and tidy in shorts and sun-tops, their hair in neat French braids.

"Hey, sleepyhead." Durango smiled at her. "Glad you decided to join us."

"What about the rest of you? Don't tell me you were up at the crack of dawn."

"Not quite," he agreed.

"We all slept late," Dallas said. "Daddy called the police 'bout the banging."

"Really?" Heather took the cup of peppermint tea he offered. "What did Dick say?"

"That it was fireworks, not blasting." Durango returned to the stove. He eased the first sandwich onto a plate, put a second one on the griddle. "I'd forgotten to tell you we're outside the city limits and in the unincorporated part of the county."

"So what?" Heather demanded. "I don't get it."

"There's no limit on fireworks out here. They can legally be fired from June 28th through July 6th."

"Those things didn't sound like fireworks, Durango. They sounded—"

"Real loud," Galveston interrupted, looking up at him as he brought over her plate, the half sandwich cut into quarters. "They made the ground shake, Daddy."

"Honest," Dallas added. "We're not lying, Daddy."

"I know, and I believe all of you." He slid a second plate in front of Dallas. "A lot of people buy their fireworks at the reservations and then bring them out into the boonies to shoot them off."

"And those are the illegal ones that the other stands don't sell." Heather sipped her tea. "I'd forgotten about that."

"You're home now, baby. We have to deal with *what is*, not *what could be*. Dick's going to drive around and write citations when he finds anybody with M-80s. He said he'd pass the word to Reverend Tommy at church today and have him remind folks that fireworks are banned in Baker City." Durango put a whole sandwich on a plate, cut it, and served it to her. "Eat up. I made a fruit salad with your grandma's honey dressing because the girls told me they don't like tomato soup."

"Wow, you're easy." She picked up the first half of the sandwich. "Did you tell your dad not to put tomatoes on these the way I do?"

"We don't like them," Dallas reminded her. "And he sorta listens to us."

"'Specially if you're asleep," Galveston added.

"I think I'd better start making some notes for your dad." Heather picked up the sandwich and smiled at him when he carried over a large bowl containing sliced fruit, strawberries, pineapple, mandarin oranges, kiwi, and bananas. He'd added red grapes and blueberries for color. "This looks amazing."

"Hope it tastes that way." He joined them at the table.

After they ate, the four of them cleaned the kitchen together. Then Durango went to the bunkhouse and returned with brightly wrapped gift bags. "Souvenirs from Texas."

Dallas tore into the first bag, pulling out a brilliant floral swimsuit. "Mommy, can we go swimming?"

"Of course." Heather glanced at Galveston. "What did you get, Toney?"

"A swimsuit too." She opened the second bag and removed a doll in traditional fiesta garb. "Oh Daddy, she's beautiful."

Heather laughed when both girls clambered onto Durango's lap, covering his face with kisses. She opened the bag with her gifts. He'd brought her a box of her favorite chocolate-covered macadamia nuts. She eyed the small jewelry box and carefully lifted the lid. Emerald earrings sparkled.

She headed for the bathroom to replace the gold studs she currently wore. The new emeralds glowed with the same green fire as her engagement ring. She took time to brush her hair into a ponytail to flaunt the gift. When she returned to the kitchen, she found him lingering over a cup of coffee. "Where are the girls?"

"Upstairs, putting on their swimsuits. I promised we'd spend the rest of the afternoon at the creek."

"That will be fun." She made herself another cup of herbal tea. She touched the emerald in her left ear. "Thanks, babe. They're lovely."

"You'd have gotten them a long time ago if you stuck around instead of leaving in a tiff nearly five years ago."

Heather drank the peppermint tea while she contemplated pitching a fit. If she wasn't angry enough for an instant, furious response, what was she?

*I'm hurt. And I know how to deal with that. It's time to get even.*

"The proper response when someone thanks you, Durango, is to acknowledge it by saying, 'You're welcome.' I think you and the girls will have a wonderful time together. I'm going to take a shower and enjoy having you here to look after them."

"I assumed we'd spend the day together. We're a family now and I've been gone."

"It was your choice to go, not mine." She headed for the staircase. "Even in the Marines, I'm sure you learned what 'assume' means."

Upstairs, she went to the twins' room to see if they needed help to change, to make appropriate noises about their new swimwear, and to share her plans. They were thrilled at the opportunity to spend time with their father.

A short while later, the afternoon sun filtered through the maples and evergreens. Heather urged Satan up the narrow trail. He moved willingly into a slow jog. She adjusted her weight in the saddle, so her seat and legs moved with the older gelding, but her back and shoulders remained still. He flicked an ear and she leaned forward to pet his neck. "Steady, son."

The woods opened into a small clearing, an A-frame log cabin before her. Smoke rose from the chimney and she reined Satan to a stop. Who dared to trespass on her land? This was her place now. More than that, it belonged to Fenn. It was special, a home she pretended still belonged to him. It was okay if she visited, communed with his spirit, but nobody else had any business here.

She hesitated. Normally, she'd have dismounted, walked up, and pounded on the front door. She was alone and unarmed. Who'd take her seriously? Not a person who'd moved into an old cabin on her property without permission. She paused a moment longer, thoughts rattling through her mind.

The cabin had been built from evergreen trees on the McElroy property. No permits had been filed so the county authorities didn't have records it existed. Because of the surrounding cedars, the small house was invisible from the air and was a half mile from the back boundary. No vandals, drug traffickers, or other scum were taking over Fenn's home.

Even if the McElroys were the only ones who knew how to find the cabin, she might not be able to keep the secret any longer. She might have to share the location with Durango to enlist his help in removing the unwanted guest. Fenn's home would remain his, although it could stay empty forever. She swung Satan toward the trail.

"Hold it!"

Who—? Heather spun the bay around and rode toward the porch where the man stood. She studied his tall, thin figure when he limped toward her. Why did she think she knew him? He wore faded jeans, a laced-up suede shirt, and moccasins on otherwise bare feet.

She jerked Satan to a stop when she glimpsed his face. His features were brown, weathered, and wrinkled. His red and gray hair hung halfway down his back, tied with a leather thong.

*Fenn!*

"Fenn." Heather vaulted from the saddle.

She ran across the grass to throw herself into his waiting arms, leaving the horse to wait. "Fenn. *Oh, God.* Fenn, when did you get home?" She hugged him as hard as she could. He was real. And he was home. "Oh, Fenn."

"Stop being mushy." His tone was gruff, gravelly. "Women!"

Despite his apparent disgust, he held her as tightly as she held him. She touched his bearded cheek, feeling the scars beneath the hair. She framed his face with her hands. His green eyes looked as though he'd been to hell and barely come back alive. Hadn't he? "When did you get here?"

"About two years ago." Fenn's bony shoulders hunched as if he expected a blow. "I couldn't stay down there, Rusty. I couldn't."

Tears ran down her cheeks at the sound of the nickname he'd given her as a child because of the color of her hair. "I know. It's okay, Fenn. Believe me, it's okay."

He smoothed her hair awkwardly. "I wanted to stay, to talk to you when I saved that old stinker Satan, but I was scared. Your kids are so good. They're what? Six years old?"

"They turned four last month. Galveston Fenella and Dallas Waco, but their daddy isn't a small man."

"No, he's not. I should have stayed, but I was scared."

Heather felt sobs shake her body. Fenn had always seemed so strong, tougher than anyone, even Durango. She clung to her uncle. "It's all right, Fenn. I promise. It's all right."

She spent the afternoon cleaning the cabin. Neither of them were much for speeches, more for 'show, don't tell'. How were they supposed to bridge the distance between them, a distance made up of his eight-year absence? Even if he'd been home for two of those years, he hadn't shared that info.

Words couldn't begin to convey all her turbulent emotions. A thousand questions crowded her lips as she scrubbed the counters and table until the wood gleamed. She'd taken out the rag rugs so she could do a decent job on the plank floors of the three-room cabin. She'd packed up his dirty clothes and promised to wash them when Durango was at work. She made the bed with clean sheets and chewed out Fenn for not using them in the first place.

He seemed more amused by her activities than anything else. Of course, he helped by keeping the fire going in the woodstove, so she had hot water from the boiler. She walked out onto the porch in time to see him saddling Satan. It was still light but when she looked at her watch, she realized it was after 1900 hours, seven at night.

"I've got to get back in time to bathe the twins and put them to bed." She picked up the bag of laundry and headed for the corral. "I'll visit."

"Just you and your kids," Fenn said. "Nobody else."

"Who knows you're home besides me?"

"Nobody. As far as *The World's* concerned, Fenian McElroy died in Colombia. I'm Ben Cross. If anyone says different, I'm dead."

"Fenn, you're home. The cartel won't come after you here."

"They don't frighten me, but I'm not letting the US government or the Army finish what they started when they left me to die."

The words seemed to stab into her. "I don't understand." She studied his careworn face again, old before its time. "What do you mean?"

"I'm not a hero. Nobody official came to bring us home. They left us to rot and die."

Heather reeled, caught the corral rail to steady herself. He'd obviously survived years of torture, but lost his mind when he was captured in Colombia. "Nobody knows you're home?"

"Bill O'Connell suspects. I've seen him snooping around the place, but he hasn't found me. I figure even if he does, he probably won't say anything, not after I pulled him out of the creek when we were kids."

"Okay." She put her arms around her uncle. "I won't tell anyone who you are." It was the least she could do for him. He'd suffered enough.

---

It was nearly time to close the office for the holiday week. He and Amarillo had come in to catch up the last of the month-end paperwork. Jeff Ransom glanced toward the main doors when they opened, and a petite woman entered. Short black hair dusted with gray, her sturdy frame in faded jeans, and a silver T-shirt that proclaimed, *Do not meddle in the affairs of dragons for you are crunchy and good with ketchup!*

Her battered running shoes were silent on the tile floor. She scanned him slowly, then a smile lit her face and the dark brown eyes. She hurried across the lobby to greet him with a warm hug and a quick kiss. "Hey, how's my favorite chopper pilot?"

"Katie, it's good to see you. I'm not flying too much lately. How about you?"

Out of the corner of his eye, he saw Amarillo lurking in the passageway that went from the main office to the accounting department. Deliberately, he lowered his head to kiss Kate, but not as quickly as she'd done.

"Nice," Kate pronounced, her smile widening. "Very nice." She stepped back and swept a professional gaze over him. "You're looking good, Ransom. How's the leg holding up?"

"It works so I can't complain." He hugged her again. "And I still have it, so again, no complaints."

"That's something all right." Kate beamed up at him. "Where's Heather hanging her hat? Is she back with the jerk? How are my girls?"

"Your girls?" Jeff eyed her, amused. "I heard the twins belonged to Heather and Durango. When are you going to settle down, Katie? Have kids of your own?"

"When I find a man who kisses as good as you do to keep me warm at night," Kate teased. "Got any brothers?"

"Not anymore. They died while I was in Colombia."

"Oops. Sorry. I didn't know I was trespassing."

"Let's go to my office. I'll draw you a map to Baker City and call Durango. He can meet you at the creek and show you where to ford it. Do you have a four-wheel drive?"

"I traded in our cars to get one. Heather came ahead and I stayed behind to pack up, put the house up for sale and work out my notice. We both couldn't leave the hospital right away. They'd have been too short-handed. She wasn't much good once the morning sickness started, but she kept saying it was the flu."

"So that's why she really came back. I didn't know how to force Durango to go after her."

"If you had to force him, it wouldn't have worked."

"He's a good guy, Katie." Jeff held open the door to his office for her. "His emotions are frozen from years of abuse when he was a kid. He told me once that combat was the first place he ever got to shoot back."

"He's going to have to grow up," Kate said. "Heather may have come home, but she's not going to settle for less this time around. He'll have to show her that he loves her. She was devastated when he didn't join her in Tennessee, so it won't be easy."

———

It was almost 2100 hours, nine o'clock at night, civilian time, when Heather reached the stable. She swung off Satan and paused when she saw a blue four-by-four pickup in the yard. She didn't recognize the visitor's rig. Well, she'd play detective after she took care of her horse. She led him to his stall and unsaddled the big bay gelding. He immediately attacked the supper hay as if he hadn't spent hours stuffing himself on the grass up at Fenn's cabin.

She put the saddle in the tackroom and hid her uncle's laundry bag under a stack of pads and blankets. She turned off the barn lights and headed for the house, still wondering about the truck parked near hers and Durango's. She solved the mystery as soon as she walked in the front door.

"Mommy. Mommy!" Dallas dashed to greet her. "Auntie Kate is here."

"She's finally home." Galveston chased her twin down the hall.

"That is good news." Heather dropped to her knees and hugged the twin angels in their long flannel nightgowns. "Where is she?"

"Here." Kate came toward her from the kitchen. "Where have you been?"

"I'll tell you later." Heather rose to her feet and went to hug her best friend. "What did you do with Durango?"

"He's unloading the dishwasher and trying to convince me he gets to stay in the house for the duration."

"Okay. We'll kick him out later so we can have a girls' night."

Kate laughed. "This is the first time we've been off at the same time in forever. What's on the agenda?"

"Putting these two young ladies to bed and getting you settled." Heather took a deep breath. "Let me tell Durango I'm back and I'll meet you upstairs. Did you girls brush your teeth?"

"I'll take them." Kate ushered the twins in the direction of the stairs. "Hustle up, woman."

"No worries." Heather flashed a smile over her shoulder. She sauntered into the kitchen in time to see Durango sorting the clean silverware into the drawer. "That's what I like to see, a guy doing K.P."

He chuckled, but the amusement didn't reach the cobalt blue eyes. "You were gone a long time. Kind of rough on Satan, wasn't it? He's not accustomed to all day or all afternoon rides."

"He didn't work too hard." She bit her lip, struggling for control. "We were at Fenn's place. Satan grazed in the corral."

"I'm sorry." Durango left the dishes and crossed to her, drawing her into his arms. "I'm so sorry, baby."

"Me too." She couldn't tell him that her uncle was home and crazier than hell. She couldn't break her word to Fenn. She wanted him back the way he used to be, not the man she'd met at his cabin. "I miss him so much."

"So, do I, baby. So do I."

# PART 3

——————

BAKER CITY, WASHINGTON ~ JULY 2019

# CHAPTER TWENTY-FIVE

After midnight, Durango went to the bunkhouse. Before he'd left, they'd carried Kate's suitcases up to the third floor of the Victorian house, leaving the door open to the stairs in case the twins needed them. The two of them had always been night owls, leaving sleep for other people, primarily civilians.

"Tell me about this apartment," Kate said. "Did the maid live up here?"

"No, I did." Heather glanced around the L-shaped attic loft. "My grandfather converted these two rooms into a studio for me." She gestured to the short end with the kitchenette and bath. "I took most of my meals with him and Grandma, but I could always eat up here if I didn't want to socialize or came in late."

"Oooh, tell me more, party girl."

Heather laughed. "Because of the way my birthday falls in August, I was only seventeen when I graduated from high school. I really wanted to be a country star and Pop at the local nightspot agreed to hire me after one audition. My mom went berserk at the idea."

Kate moved onto dusting the dresser. "So, what happened?"

"My dad didn't want to listen to any more of our arguments. He said it brought back too many memories of his kid sister who married out of high school instead of following her dreams. Aunt Lucy was the one who taught me to play the piano. She left Baker City when I was six, almost seven."

"Where is she now?"

"Nobody knows." Heather shook out the bottom sheet, laid it on the double bed. "Her husband filed for divorce when she didn't return and subsequently moved in his girlfriend. My dad and grandparents wanted the cops to look for my aunt, but it didn't happen. They backed down when my uncle threatened to keep them from seeing Lucy's daughters. You'll meet Ann this Wednesday."

"But your folks let you come here." Kate opened the top drawer of the bureau. "Somebody has been cleaning up here. This already has fresh paper and is ready for my clothes."

"Linda MacGillicudy works part-time at Pop's Café around running a housekeeping service, and Durango arranged for her to come in once a week to do the heavy cleaning."

"That's unexpected." Kate carried over a duffel bag, opened it, and began to unpack it. "Most guys would think a woman could do it herself."

"He's different." Heather spread out the top sheet. "Frustrating, arrogant, macho, and with the libido of a teenager, but he doesn't hesitate to spend the money he inherited from his grandfather. I swear Durango hired half the town to come here."

Kate smiled. "So speaks the ice queen. You turned down every doctor who asked you out along with any other guys in Nashville. You said they didn't float your boat. I knew you weren't a nun, or you wouldn't have the twins."

"It's always been him." As usual, Heather had chosen two flat sheets for the bed, leaving the fitted ones in the linen closet. She took the time to create hospital corners, so the sheets wouldn't slip on the bed. "Unfortunately, he knows it."

"What did he think when you came here? You told me you started dating him when you were in college."

"He lived in the bunkhouse and built fence for my grandfather. We both had to follow the rules. I couldn't go there, and he couldn't come up here. I worked for Pop three nights a week and took nursing classes at the community college in the daytime. Basically, Grandpa and Grandma ran interference for me."

"Nursing was a fluke for you, not your heartfelt desire?" Kate finished emptying the duffel bag and opened a suitcase. "Why didn't you stick to singing in Nashville?"

"Too much competition. I'm good, but I'm not great." Heather picked up a blanket and put it on the double bed. "When I called you three years ago, I was almost out of money. I had infant daughters, and it was pure luck when you wanted a roommate and didn't blink at having three of them. Luckily, my parents had the foresight to insist I have a nursing degree to support myself if I didn't become a country star. Thousands of singers don't make it, especially the ones like me who just sing other people's songs."

"Having you and the twins saved me too," Kate said calmly. "I would have lost the house after my divorce. I had to buy my ex's share. That made the mortgage and taxes damn near insurmountable."

Heather shook out the comforter. "It helped we'd served together in Iraq. You didn't freak at my insecurities or lose it when I left on all the lights or drank Coca-Cola for breakfast."

"Likewise."

"So, we've talked enough about me. Share your dreams, Kate. You never told me before. Did you always want to be a nurse?"

"I used to read all the Cherry Ames books when I was a girl. I remember bandaging my brothers and forcing them to play hospital with me. When I couldn't catch *them*, I practiced on the dog and cat."

Imagining a young, determined, dark-haired Kate chasing down someone to be a patient made Heather laugh. "Well, let's leave Durango to babysit the girls one night and we'll go to Pop's. Even if I'll never be a star, I'm a damned good singer, Kate."

"I believe you. What's more, I believe in you. Don't keep putting your life on hold, Heather. We've got to live each day not just for us, but for those who didn't come home with us. We don't have expiration dates, and we don't know when our numbers will come up."

---

Natasha Hollister twirled the straw in her strawberry margarita and scanned the lounge at Petrocelli's Pizza Palace again. Brazos was late, not her usual practice. Something must have come up, Natasha thought. She hoped it wasn't too urgent, that it could wait for Brazos to take care of the legal emergency until they returned from Mexico.

Glancing across the crowded room, Natasha frowned at the sight of two men in the doorway. Zeb Steele stood by her twin brother, Nathan. She focused on the icy glass in front of her and hoped they wouldn't see her.

That hope died when Nathan strolled over and sat down in one of the empty chairs at her table. "How's it going?"

"Fine." Natasha stirred her drink with the straw again. "How are you?"

"Okay." Nathan glanced at Zeb as he joined them. "Zeb says you're talking about turning the Ballard brokerage over to him. Is it to make amends for jilting him when he was in Iraq?"

She allowed the silence to build a moment too long while she scanned the pair, one blond, the other dark-haired. Then she focused on Zeb. "Do you have the slightest clue why I avoid going to Hollister as much as possible? Everyone in town thinks I committed a capital offense because we split up when you were in combat."

"I could try telling them it was my decision." Zeb signaled the waitress. "Do you think it'd help?"

"It wouldn't matter if you took out another ad in the local paper." Natasha eyed her twin. Like her, Nathan had black hair and gray eyes. However, he was a few inches taller than she was, topping six feet. He was the male equivalent of her when it came to beauty, but she didn't like him. It was the first time she'd ever admitted that, even to herself.

"Is this a private party or can I crash it?" Brazos Hawke drew out the chair next to Natasha's, setting a briefcase beside her. "How was your day, lover?"

"Terrible." Natasha leaned over to kiss Brazos. "Better now that you're finally here. I showed three houses. All the families were home and either the kids or the pets had trashed the places. I don't know how many times I've advised sellers that properties must be clean to impress potential buyers."

"Sounds like my day." Brazos rested an arm on Natasha's chair. Private conversation ceased as the waitress arrived to take drink orders. When she headed for the bar, Brazos continued. "I was leaving the office when the secretary gave me a message from my parents. Attendance is mandatory at Heather and Durango's on the Fourth."

"That means Natasha will join us in Hollister for the day." Nathan glared at Brazos. "We don't appreciate you keeping her away from us."

"You never listen, do you, Nate?" Natasha heaved a dramatic sigh. "It's my choice where I go and what I do. I'll be with Bree. She'll need me. If you ever fall in love, Nate, instead of making tally marks on your bedposts, you'll learn how important it is to be there for a partner."

"Spare me the hearts and flowers lecture. Tell her how sick Dad is, Zeb. He'd like to see her."

"I can't." Zeb smiled at Brazos. "Is the captain there? I tried calling her in Nashville, but the number was disconnected."

"Of course, it was. She moved home when she finally married

Durango. It's why my parents are having heartburn. They like to give my brother a hard time for coming back alive from the Middle East, and Heather is his staunchest ally." Brazos shuddered and clutched Natasha's hand. "It's going to be worse than usual with Heather bringing her girls—"

"And Durango's," Natasha added.

"It's part of their bullcrap. According to my parents, they're not his kids."

Natasha tightened her grip, offering what reassurance she could. "We know that's a lie."

"I've got to be there, Tasha. They're barely four and *he* likes them young."

"I know. We'll both go." Natasha leaned close, kissed Brazos' cheek. "Can you imagine what Heather will do if *he* touches one of her daughters?"

"It'd be justifiable homicide as far as I'm concerned, even if Washington state doesn't recognize that defense." Brazos took a deep breath. "They're so stupid they think Durango won't protect children, whether they're his or not."

"They are." Zeb pulled out his wallet and placed a credit card on the table to pay for the drinks when the waitress came toward them. "If I couldn't convince the captain to choose me over that jarhead brother of yours, no other man did. And she was called the ice queen for a reason."

After the waitress left, Nathan picked up his beer. "Is this captain the woman you met after Natasha dumped you?"

"No, the captain was the reason I dumped her. Heather McElroy is all woman and what she does to a set of camos and combat boots." Zeb shook his head, admiration filling his deep voice. "She was my nurse when I was in the hospital. She kept me on my toes. She's all piss and vinegar."

Nathan set the beer glass on the table with a little too much force. "And my sister?"

"Sugar sets my teeth on edge even now. Back then, I didn't realize how boring it was until I met Heather. She never deferred to me or acted like I hung the moon and stars."

"Leaving the sugar for those of us who do like it," Brazos said. "I love Heather to pieces, but I'd never want to live with her. When she cuts loose, wise people run for cover."

"That's about right," Zeb agreed. "I want to come with you on Thursday and see the captain and meet the kids who could have been mine."

Anger replaced shock and Nathan demanded, "You're saying my sister was only a convenience?"

Zeb shook his head, picking up his beer. "No, not really. I never got to first base with her either. She was innocent and wanted to wait until our wedding night. After she was raped—" He shrugged. "You're a cop. How many men do you know that want used goods?"

Nathan leaped to his feet. "You son of a bitch." He grabbed Zeb's tie and yanked him out of his chair to his feet. "It wasn't her fault."

"You can't hit him or fight with him, Nate," Natasha intervened. "He's a cripple. Do you think he uses that cane for fun? Now, why don't you leave? He isn't saying anything you, Dad, and the rest of the family haven't told me time and again."

Nathan turned his glare on her before storming from the cocktail lounge. Natasha propped her chin on her fist and eyed Zeb. "What the hell are you doing?"

"Defending you." Zeb sat down again and took a lazy swallow of his beer. "Actually, I'm rectifying past mistakes. I'll force the Hollister family to make amends to you or die trying."

"They'll think you're a bastard," Brazos pointed out.

"That's the difference between me and Natasha. She worries about what they think of her. I know better than to let it rule me."

"Why do you want to see Heather?" Natasha asked.

Silence while Zeb stared into the distance, but didn't seem to see the lounge or its occupants. "I've got to come to terms with the past before I think about the future."

———

Late Monday afternoon, Jeff Ransom headed down the hallway to the accounting offices. He'd caught Amarillo glaring at him and muttering under her breath after she saw him with Kate yesterday, but that was nothing new. Amarillo had issues with him since he arrived three years ago. He'd told her more than once that he wasn't going anywhere. Occasionally, he managed to take her and Maria out for dinner at Petrocelli's, but that was the extent of their dates.

When he checked in with Durango today, the other man mentioned in passing that Amarillo was up to her usual tricks of trying to get rid of Jeff. He'd been ordered to smooth things over with the little witch again.

He opened the door, saw her doing data entry. Payroll, he thought. It was that time of the month and she'd be shorting his check once more.

"No rest for the wicked?"

She spun her chair around to face him, then jumped to her feet. "What are you doing here? Durango promised to consider sending you to Spokane for that new job."

"Sorry, *cara mia*. It's not happening." He headed toward her. "I don't trust you and you're not sending me away."

She reached for a letter opener on her desk, held the blade low instead of going for her knife. He admired her ability to improvise. She'd been taught by an expert. No matter what he did, she intended to cut him. "I'll get rid of you. One way or another."

"What will you do with my body?" He took four more steps, moving ever closer to her. "Have Gino and his nasty friends throw it in that bridge they're building on the new highway? I've told you before. Keep him and the rest of his outfit away from Hawke Construction, or I'll tell Durango everything and I have proof."

Her voice lowered, filled with rage. "You have nothing."

Jeff deliberately gazed at the computer. "Want to bet, *cara*? Would you like to risk it? What if I'm not bluffing?"

Both of them knew the truth was the first casualty when it came to survival. She eyed him, the blade between them. She backed toward the rear exit. They were alone in the building. She flicked a glance behind her, ready to open the door and run.

He caught up with her, snagged her wrist, and twisted until she dropped the letter opener. He pulled her to the chair, sat down, and drew her onto his lap. "So, you're having an affair with me, Amarillo Hawke?" He lowered his head, touched her lips in the briefest of kisses. "You're crazy about me and I've broken your treacherous little heart? Only Durango would believe that line of crap whether you're the one telling it or I am. Shall I mend it?"

She struggled to break free, but he continued to hold her. "If you hurt me, Gino will kill—"

"That's interesting." Jeff kissed her again, a mere whisper over her mouth. She liked it, but he still read fear in her dark chocolate eyes, felt the tension in the small, voluptuous body. "Gino Petrocelli, not Durango? You don't trust your brother even now, do you?"

"Trust him?" Amarillo's voice rose in anger. "He's the same as our father. Durango only helped me because Heather set him up. I knew it at the time, but I didn't care. She found me a place to live, got me this job, filled the cupboards with food from theirs, furnished my new house with their leftovers because she was leaving town—"

"Heather's a wonderful person and she's the only one who believed you when you told her the truth about Maria." Jeff held Amarillo tighter as she fought him, trying to wrestle away from him. "Look at me. Stop fighting and listen. Just tell me one thing. Do you want me to kill Maria's father?"

"You don't know who he is. Only Heather knows."

"I know."

She froze in his arms, stared at him, dread filling her face. "You know?"

He didn't say the name, but he knew for sure then, was certain then, and the idea sickened him. "None of it was your fault. Not yours or Maria's. I knew as soon as I saw her."

Amarillo began to cry, ugly wrenching sobs that shook her entire body.

Jeff cuddled her close. "You didn't let Gino take care of him. I can do it and not get caught."

"Gino." Amarillo sobbed out the words. "He'd—be blamed. People— would—know. So would—Maria."

"Okay." Jeff held her until the tears stopped. Then, he kissed her again, not gently and not briefly. He kissed her the way he'd wanted to the first time he saw her, a soldier home from war, as if it were only a pause before they went to bed. She liked it, enjoyed it, tangled her fingers in his hair, and met his passion with her own.

Slowly, he lifted his head. He studied the stunned bewilderment on her face. "Now, we both know."

He longed to touch her again, to caress her, to make love to her, but he couldn't, not yet. He had to give her more time and space, not only to heal, but also to grow up. "Like I said before, don't push me. No more games, *cara*."

"I hate—"

"Don't lie, not to me and not to yourself." He eased her from his lap, letting her stand on her own. "I already told you. I'm going to marry you, but you're just a little girl, barely out of your teens. I'll wait until next year. When you're twenty-one, you can tell me if you're ready or not."

She scowled at him, planted her hands on her hips. "I won't live with you, but I'm ready now."

"What does that mean?"

"Marry me now. *He* wants Maria and me at Heather and Durango's on the Fourth. If we don't show, *he's* going to have his lawyer come after me to try to prove I'm an unfit mother. *He* has enough influential friends to make the mud stick. I won't stand a chance. And if *he* gets custody—"

"The same thing will happen to her that happened to you." Jeff nodded. "All right. Finish the payroll, and we'll leave for Idaho tonight."

# CHAPTER TWENTY-SIX

Wednesday after lunch, Durango took off for a big grocery run in Lake Maynard, so they'd be ready for his family's visit the next day. Heather loaded up her girly pickup with the twins and Kate. They took the one-lane track through the woods to the dude ranch next door for the veterans' meeting. When they arrived, carrots in hand, Dallas and Galveston abandoned them to go to the barn with Rob and Jassy to see the ponies.

Amused, Heather led the way to the wrap-around porch where she saw Cat McTavish waiting for them. "Hey, just the woman I want to see."

"Should I be concerned?" Cat rested a hand on her baby belly. "What's going on?"

"I have company in my house, and I need you to come and tell me who."

"I don't understand why you're telling her you imagined somebody there," Kate said.

"Because I didn't imagine anything, and she's the O'Leary. It's her job to run interference between the living and the dead." Heather held up her hand. "Okay, so you're not a believer in the seen and unseen, Katie, but you're new to Baker City, and this is the way we do business."

"What happened?" Cat asked, obviously curious. "What did you see?"

"I didn't see anyone. I heard someone in the kitchen banging pots and pans when I came downstairs to fix lunch. I thought it was Kate or

Durango, but they were outside. He was giving Kate and the twins a riding lesson in the corral."

"Then what happened, Heather?"

"I told whoever it was to leave. My unwanted, invisible guest did, slamming the back door."

"Is that all?"

"Durango forgot to turn off the TV last night when he went to bed, and Heather's still miffed about it."

"It wasn't him, Katie." Heather folded her arms. "We don't watch the news, Cat. It's all the same old endless tripe about the morons in the other Washington when Congress is in session and the crap they pull when it's not. If it'd been Durango, he'd have had *Walker, Texas Ranger*, or a war movie on so he could laugh at the Hollywood soldiers."

"Sounds like Rob and his John Wayne addiction." Cat turned, gesturing toward the front door. "Let's go inside. The meeting will start soon. I've already promised our girls we'll go to the parade, carnival, and barbecue in town on the Fourth, so we'll come on Friday. Does that work for you?"

"That works," Heather said. "Durango's family and some of his father's political staff are visiting the ranch tomorrow. They're not particularly sensitive so I'm sure they won't realize the house is being haunted by someone or something."

"I still think you're being paranoid. Heather, there's no such thing as ghosts."

"Wait until you've lived here a month before you say that." Cat opened the door and led the way inside. "In Baker City, the ghosts are real."

Heather and Kate were in the middle of a final clean-up the next morning when the first of the visitors arrived. Dallas and Galveston dashed into the kitchen, the back door banging behind them.

"Mommy, somebody's here," Dallas announced.

"We saw them in a truck," Galveston added. "Whobody are they?"

"I don't know." Heather looked in the mirror to check her appearance. She'd opted for new blue jeans, a sleeveless print western blouse, and her lace-up Ropers. She'd tied her hair back in a ponytail and applied makeup for the first time this week, wanting to make an appropriate impression on Durango's parents on their last visit to her home. She escorted the twins past the dining room to the hallway. She paused when she saw Kate staring at the locked study door. "I thought you were vacuuming."

"I was. Look." Kate twisted the knob again. "I can't get in there to clean. Do you think it's your imaginary friend wanting privacy?"

"No, it's Durango. He doesn't like anyone to mess with his computer or blueprints from work," Heather said, remembering the evidence she'd found of his quest in Colombia. "So, we leave it, Katie. He can G.I. the den. Right now, we have company."

"Okay, I like that story a lot better than what you told Cat yesterday."

Heather nodded, increasing her pace when she heard someone knock on the door. She opened it, smiling at Brazos and Natasha. "Hello. It's good to see you. You're the first to arrive. This is my friend, Kate. And this is Durango's sister, Bree, and her partner, Natasha."

Kate smiled at the other two women. "Hi, it's nice to meet you."

Heather ignored the exchange of greetings, looking beyond the two younger women to the blond man climbing awkwardly out of the pickup parked next to hers. "Oh no. You didn't bring—"

"We couldn't get out of it." A blush crept along Natasha's cheekbones. "I'm sorry we didn't call and warn you Zeb was coming too."

"It doesn't matter." Heather shrugged. "Durango may have a freaking fit."

Concern filled Brazos' face and landed in sky-blue eyes. "Do you want us to try and send Zeb away?"

"No reason to. Durango's been royally pissed for days because he's sleeping in the bunkhouse. That's something I sure as hell don't plan to change."

"Mommy, you keep saying bad words," Dallas scolded.

"I'm working on it, Ally." Heather grimaced. "I'm just not perfect yet. Do you remember your auntie Bree? This is her friend, Natasha." Once she finished the introductions, Heather eyed her daughters. "Ally, would you and Toney go find your dad? Tell him we have company."

"Okay." Dallas led the way, Galveston right behind her.

Brazos ran a hand through sunshine-golden hair. "Is there coffee? I could use some before my parents arrive and raise a ruckus."

"Why would they?" Kate asked. "It's a holiday lunch."

"I'll leave you to bring Kate up to speed, Brazos." Heather started across the porch. "I've got to talk to Zeb before Durango turns up."

She didn't wait for a response, but strolled onto the deck, down the steps, and across the yard. On her way, she scanned Zeb. Yes, they'd seen each other in Pop's Café two months ago, but she had a better view of him in the daylight. Silver streaked his blond hair, lines of age were carved into his features. He leaned heavily on the wooden cane he used for support.

"What happened to you, Major?"

"Tasha's brother and I had a go-round a couple of days ago and I wrenched my hip." He shrugged. "I'll see my therapist after the holiday. The doctors told me I wouldn't walk again after the jeep accident I told you about, and some days are better than others."

"Isn't that the truth?" Heather put her arms around his waist and hugged him. "So, shall we grab a couple of drinks, sit on the porch and piss off a certain Marine?"

Zeb propped his cane against the truck and held her instead. "Was that all it was, Captain McElroy? Or did I mean something more than a way to hurt him?"

"Are you serious?" She linked her hands behind his neck and met his gaze with her own. "Come off it, Ranger. Why do you think he was so angry? He knew you were the only other man I'd ever really wanted, even if it never went further with us than a few kisses. He didn't have any serious competition before."

"Why didn't you share that back then?" Zeb slowly kissed her. "I never would have left you."

"That's why." She brushed her mouth over his. "I was young and dumb. I'd loved Durango from the time I was a child. It didn't matter how many times he broke my heart. I kept forgiving and taking him back. Then you came along and thought I was wonderful."

"You were. You are."

"I'm human," she said gently. "Durango knows all my faults and wants me, anyway. You thought I was perfect, and I couldn't live up to your expectations. Remember how upset you got when I'd lose my temper and start pitching a fit?"

"No."

"Liar." She kissed him again, then stepped back. "Don't worry. You'll see the past come alive when Durango's parents arrive and insult me. You'll realize all over again why it'd never have worked for us."

Zeb reached for his cane. "You could grow up."

"No way. It's vastly overrated." She glanced over her shoulder and saw Durango stalking toward them, the twins clinging to his hands. "Look who came for a visit."

"I see." Durango gritted the words, his voice a fierce rumble. "Steele."

"Stop being such a grump." Heather wrinkled her nose in disgust. She tucked her hand under Zeb's elbow and walked beside him to meet Durango halfway to the house. "Girls, this is an old friend of mine, Zeb Steele. Zeb, these are my daughters, Dallas and Galveston."

"*Our* daughters," Durango said.

Heather frowned at him. "Girls, why don't you take Zeb into the house and let me talk to your dad?"

"Good idea." Durango clamped an arm around her waist and guided her away from the trio, not speaking again until they were out of earshot. "What stunt are you trying to—"

"Stunt?" Heather repeated as her temper rose. "You're the one who's behaving like a jealous two-year-old." She glared up into the cobalt eyes, darkening with rage. "I married you, remember? "

"You threw me out of the house."

"You're lucky I haven't piled up your stuff and had a bonfire. This is my ranch, not yours. I know you feel obligated to have your folks here because you'd invited them before I came back, but don't push your luck."

"Baby, you're home with me now. Let's not fight."

"Then, don't start a war unless you're ready to pick the hill you want to die on, jarhead. I'm not living with you unless you agree to stay with me full-time, not say it's temporary until your uncle agrees you can go to Colombia. I'm opening the best training stable in the county as soon as the fences are rebuilt."

"Are you asking or telling me?"

"That was strictly a sit-rep." She looked him up and down derisively. "And don't piss me off any more than you already have. I'm willing to try to be polite to your parents today, but don't expect a miracle."

"Behave yourself." He gripped her shoulders. "Don't embarrass me in front of them."

"Screw you." She aimed a kick at his shin, protected by a leather boot. "Let go."

"In a minute." He lowered his head, his breath warm on her lips. "I'm tired of sleeping alone. They're not here yet and the girls have plenty of supervision. Give me a reason not to take you to the bunkhouse."

She trembled when he stroked her neck. *Damn it. Why do I melt when he touches me?* "I'm a McElroy and I do as I damned well, please."

He nipped her ear, trailed a line of kisses down her neck to the hollow of her throat and the cloverleaf pendant. "Wrong, baby. You're Heather Marie McElroy-Hawke, my wife. Keep up the crap-fest and you'll spend hours pleasing me tonight."

An hour later, she still ached for him, but she wasn't about to say as much. Instead, she sat on the porch watching as Tex Hawke's pickup came to a stop in the front yard, next to the collection of other four-wheel-drive vehicles. Durango's parents weren't the last to arrive. That honor was reserved for Amarillo and Jeff, who hadn't appeared yet.

Heather sipped her lemonade and leaned back in the porch swing, waiting until Tex and Estelle reached the front steps. "Hello. Welcome to my home."

"Why are you on the porch?" Estelle asked in her sweetest voice. She looked like the typical political wife in her tailored light blue dress and heels. "Are you waiting for us?"

"Not really." Heather inclined her head in salute. "I'm enjoying the peace and quiet out here. Durango's entertaining the rest of your clan inside. Tex, your cronies haven't shown up yet."

The front door opened, and the twins came outside, followed by Brazos. Dallas beamed at Heather. "Mommy, can we show Auntie Bree our horses?"

"Sure, sweetheart." Heather wondered when Satan and Cinnamon had become her daughters' personal mounts. "Girls, these are your dad's parents, your other—"

"Heather, I don't think it's a good idea to lie to them," Tex interrupted.

"You bastard." She leaped to her feet.

"Mommy, that's a bad word!"

Heather ignored the interjection from Galveston. "Apologize. How dare you say Durango isn't their—"

"Everybody knows he isn't," Estelle chirped in honeyed tones. "If he were, you never would have left him. We all know what kind of a slut you are."

Heather hurled the lemonade at the older woman, the liquid splashing her and Tex while the glass rolled across the deck. Both twins shrieked.

The next moment, Heather whirled to grab the twins' hands and hurried them down the steps. "Come on. We're leaving."

"Where we goin'?" Dallas asked.

Heather swore as she remembered her keys were in the house. Kate had the set to the blue truck and Durango undoubtedly had his. Well, there were the horses. "We're going for a ride. By the time we get back, your daddy's parents will be gone. And they're never coming here again."

The comment reminded her of Brazos and Heather glanced over her shoulder, but the younger woman was nowhere in sight. *It doesn't matter. I'll get the girls to safety and the hell away from Durango's parents.*

"How come we're goin' 'way, Mommy?" Dallas asked.

Heather opened the tackroom door. She handed Satan's bridle to Dallas and Cinnamon's to Galveston. "Because your daddy is going to have a big fight with his family and we're not sticking around to hear it."

"Whobody was them meanies?" Galveston finally questioned. "They don't like me and Ally."

"Oh, darling baby." Heather knelt and gathered both girls close. "Sweeties, it's not your fault. Those people don't like anybody, not your daddy, or Auntie Brazos, or Auntie Amarillo or Uncle Laredo, either."

"How come?" A tear slipped down Dallas' cheek. "They're nice. Unca Laredo says he's gonna give us puppies."

"Great, but he better remember to ask me first." Heather cuddled her daughters. "Those meanies, as Toney calls them, are your daddy's mom and dad, your other grandparents. On holidays like this one, they miss their favorite little boy more than ever and Waco isn't here."

"You've told us lots of times that mommies can't have favorites," Dallas argued. "You love me and Toney 'zactly the same."

"That's my rule," Heather said. "My momma, Gramma Liz, taught me love adds and multiplies. It doesn't subtract and divide. But your daddy's parents are different. They only had enough love for one child, not all five of them."

"They're sad meanies," Galveston decided.

"Yes, they are," Heather agreed, "but it's not your fault or Ally's or mine."

"It's not Daddy's fault either," Dallas said.

"Nope, it's all theirs." Galveston kissed Heather's cheek. "Where we goin', Mommy?"

"For a ride up to where Ben lives. He's the man who saved Satan. Ally, do you want to ride Cinnamon by yourself? Toney, do you want to ride with me on Satan?"

"It'll be fun," Dallas said. "I like that man."

"You won't let the mean horse bite me, will you, Mommy?"

"I'll never let anyone hurt either of you."

"Not ever?" Galveston asked.

"You got it, sweetie." Heather picked up Cinnamon's saddle and carried it toward the stall, followed by her daughters. She'd finished tacking the mare and started on her gelding when the barn door opened, and Kate entered the stable. "What's going on, Katie?"

"Brazos said for me to go with you and the twins." Kate held up two sets of bulging saddle bags. "She packed us a lunch and said she's going to let us get clear before she tells Durango what happened. Are you girls okay? Ally? Toney? Heather?"

"Them people are mean," Dallas said.

"We don't like 'em," Galveston finished.

"Join the club." Heather swung Satan's saddle onto the bay's back. "Thanks, Katie."

"Hey, we're all singing the same song." Kate ruffled each of the twins' hair. "So, let's bug out, ladies."

# CHAPTER TWENTY-SEVEN

Durango left Zeb Steele sitting on the porch swing. The two of them had shaken hands and called quits to their long-running feud. Zeb had offered his best wishes and congratulations on Durango and Heather's marriage. He'd even been decent about the intervention at Pop's Café two months ago, when he was locked in a storage closet for hours. *He's a better man than I am. I'll never give her up, not while I'm still breathing. Thank God, she married me, not him.*

When he entered the kitchen, he saw Brazos and Natasha sitting at the kitchen table, chatting in low tones. Laredo stood in the opposite corner of the room talking to their parents. Neither had dressed for a farm visit. His father wore a dark suit and tie. His mother was in an expensive dress and heels.

Durango glanced around again. "Where are Heather and Kate? Putting the twins down for a nap? Heather said they didn't need one today. They could go to bed after we watch the fireworks displays. We have a front porch view of the ones in Baker City and Lake Maynard."

Brazos shifted to eye him. "Heather took the twins and left after Mom and Dad told them you aren't their father."

"What?" Durango froze, then stalked across the room toward his father. The man barely topped six feet and wouldn't make a grease spot on the floor. "You dared to say that to *my daughters*?"

Concern slid across Tex's face. "Now, son—"

"It upset Heather more when Mom called her a whore who didn't know her children's father in front of the kids."

"Brazos, your mother didn't use that term. Tell the truth."

"I'm a lawyer, Dad. I always tell my truth, not yours or hers, and you stood by when Mom insulted my sister-in-law in front of me. I think Durango should know you called his wife terrible things after she headed for the barn with the girls."

Laredo stared at their parents as if he'd never seen them before. "What's wrong with you people? How could you do that to two little kids? How would you feel if one of Dad's hangers-on did that to us?"

"Be specific," Brazos said. "You should ask what if someone did it to Waco. He's the only one they ever cared about."

"That's not true." Estelle stepped around her husband and sons to make eye contact with her daughter. "You know we love all our children."

"You bet you do." Brazos rose to her feet, advanced a step. "It's why you stood by when he and Eli beat us. It's why you didn't feed us and pitched a fit when we went next door to Liz and Art's house, because they would. No wonder Amarillo called me when she eloped with Jeff Ransom. She said she wasn't spending time with you people, that she was through with your brand of love. You never protected us from his pedophile ring of perverts, but Amarillo isn't making that mistake. She's keeping Maria away from you."

"She didn't say that." Estelle paled. "She said her new husband refused to let her or Maria visit us. He even threatened to get a restraining order if we contacted them."

"Enough." Durango pulled out his cell phone. For once, he had a signal, and he saw a text from Jeff announcing his marriage. "I've got to tell Ransom again to call me on the landline here. Otherwise, I have to wait until I'm on the road to talk to him."

"I like Jeff." Natasha rose. "Since this is turning into a farce, Bree and I are leaving. We have reservations to fly to Cancun tonight and if we leave early, we can go to Petrocelli's for the lunch buffet."

"Don't be strangers." Durango despised the pleading note he heard in his voice. "Come visit. Heather—"

"Don't worry." Brazos hurried across the room to hug him. "What they did to us was child abuse, Durango. Beating, starving, locking us up, depriving us of friends, and worse. I'm serious about him and Eli. They have so much political influence that nobody ever goes after them. You got away during the school years because Uncle Quentin raised holy hell if you weren't back in Texas by Labor Day. We weren't that fortunate."

"I didn't know."

"No, the threats and punishments increased when we told. Help me out."

"How?" Durango asked. "What do you want me to do? Tell me and I will."

"Get Denver to provide security for Amarillo, Maria, and Jeff. Otherwise, they'll go to Gino's family and you don't want that."

"I'll call him today. Anything else?"

Brazos shook her head. "I promised to take your kids to the movies this summer. Kate, Tasha, and I are going to make jam next week. You'll see a lot of us."

"And Zeb," Natasha added. "I don't think he's recovered from his crush yet. He still suffers from the delusion that Heather's an angel, complete with wings and a halo."

The two women started for the hallway and front door. Then Brazos turned back. "Oh, I forgot to tell you. I sent anything that could go in saddlebags with Kate and Heather. There's still some fried chicken and salad left in the fridge for you."

Durango nodded, waited until they left before he confronted his parents. "Get out."

"Durango, you can't be serious." Estelle took a step forward, rested a hand on his arm. "Honey, don't you see? This is what Heather does. She keeps you away from your family. We love you and she isn't good for you."

"The hell she isn't." Laredo stepped between his mother and brother. "Bree and Amie are right about what the two of you call *love*. It's all power and control. You think you own us. If you really cared, you'd want Durango to be happy."

"Have you been drinking?" Tex demanded. "Because we want Durango to have a decent woman doesn't mean we hate him. We've always wanted what's best for him. We love him."

Durango stared at them, thoughts racing through his mind. How could they insult his children? He'd been a punching bag whenever he visited, but he assumed he was bad, like they constantly claimed. If he'd been good enough, he'd have been able to please them. Sure, they mouthed the right words today, but it was all lies. Why had it taken him so long to see that?

"I'm not a child. My daughters are. This is their home. I don't want

Heather taking them away whenever you're here." He gestured toward the front door. "Leave. Now. Don't come back. Call your sycophants. Tell them the invite's rescinded. None of you are welcome here again."

In moments, they were gone. Durango slumped into a chair at the table, burying his head in his hands. Where had she gone? When would she be back? Last time, it was almost five years. How long would it be this time?

"Get off your butt." Laredo stood in the doorway. "Let's take the construction rig and go find them before they eat the whole picnic lunch."

---

*Way to go, guys! You've had tough rows to hoe, and you made it. You've got more guts than I ever had.* Waco Hawke leaned against the kitchen counter and wished his brothers could hear him. *The girls are tougher than I expected they'd grow up to be after catching the old man with Bree. She didn't detail half the abuse she and Amie suffered, and Laredo isn't talking either. Of course, how could they tell Durango about being the "fresh meat" our father traded for political favors?*

Waco waited until he was alone before he headed into the living room to watch the news. He'd always wondered why investigative reporters didn't go after his father and expose the down and dirty facts about the man. Granted, when he listened to his favorite newscaster recapping the same stories repeatedly out of Washington D.C., it didn't come as a surprise. Most of his friends and compatriots were just like Tex Hawke, and Waco would bet more than one of the politicos pimped out their wives and kids.

---

The afternoon sun shone through the maples and alders, making sunlit patterns on the narrow, winding dirt path. Heather urged Satan into a slow jog and Galveston squealed in excitement. Heather hugged the little girl closer and leaned forward to pet the gelding's brown neck. "Easy, son."

"This is fun, Mommy."

"It sure is." Heather glanced over her shoulder to check on Kate and Dallas. "How are you two doing?"

"Great!" Dallas yelled. "Did you see us, Mommy? We went fast."

Heather smiled. Her daughters loved horses as much as she did. It was difficult to remember they'd just begun riding on a regular basis. The woods opened into the clearing and she saw the tiny cabin and corral in front of her. Smoke rose from the chimney. So Fenn was home. She'd started to worry about that on the way here.

"Whose place is this?" Kate asked.

"It belonged to my uncle. A friend of his lives here now, Ben Cross." Heather squeezed her legs and rode into the small meadow.

Fenn came out to stand on the front porch, a rifle cradled in his arms. When he recognized the visitors, he leaned the rifle against the rail. "Wasn't expecting company on a holiday."

"Some meanies came to our house," Galveston told him.

"And we came to visit you after Mommy threw her lem-ade at them," Dallas added.

"Rusty, what kind of behavior do you call that?" Fenn frowned at her. "You're too old to have tantrums."

"It was Durango's parents and they started it." Heather gestured to Kate. "This is Ben Cross. He's an old friend of the McElroy family. This is Kate Flanagan. We met in Iraq."

"Well, get down and come in," Fenn said. "I don't have much, but you're welcome to it."

"We have a picnic." Kate eased out from behind Dallas, passing the reins to the little girl, then dismounting. She untied the strings holding on the saddlebags. "Fried chicken, potato salad, chips, homemade bread, the works."

Heather slid out of the saddle. "Come on, girls. Time to socialize."

"We're riding our horses now," Dallas said. "We don't have to share no more."

"Just like Waco." Fenn limped to the corral and opened the gate wide enough for the twins to guide Satan and Cinnamon inside. "Never could get him to shut up about the damned horses. He nearly drove all of us nuts. Okay, kids. Tell those cayuses to go."

"Hang on a second." Heather unfastened the set of saddlebags on Satan and unhooked the laundry bag with clean clothes. "All right, Toney. He's all yours."

"Get up, Satan," Galveston ordered, shaking the reins.

The old gelding obediently ambled in the direction of the corral, and Cinnamon followed her stablemate. Heather struggled not to laugh at the twins' cries of encouragement. However, her control slipped when she saw the amusement on Kate's and Fenn's faces.

Heather handed the laundry bag to Fenn and carried the saddlebags toward the porch. "We've got apples and cheese."

"Chewing tobacco? Candy? Beer?"

Kate laughed. "I'll share my smokes. Heather's pregnant, so she's on the wagon."

"What the hell are you doing on a horse, Rusty?" Fenn measured her with a steady, green gaze. "Besides being stupid?"

"Shove it," Heather recommended. "I brought you a fifth of Durango's whisky. Give me any crap and I'll dump it out right here."

"Watch your mouth." Fenn scowled at her. "I oughta see him, that's what I oughta do. You ride a horse up here again, and I'm telling him to take better care of you."

"I'm not scared of you or him." Heather grinned. "Flap your gums all you want."

"What's wrong with Heather riding?" Kate asked. "She's going to start training horses next spring. She showed me all around the indoor arena Durango built for her."

"First off, she could fall or be thrown," Fenn said. "The horse might spook. Even an old duffer like Satan could get scared."

"He won't dump me," Heather retorted. "I'm a damned good rider."

"And that's a problem too. You'll be pushing to keep your weight down in your seat, legs, and heels."

Heather frowned thoughtfully. "I wonder if that's why I miscarried before the twins. I was still training back then."

"I'll do some research," Kate said. "Light exercise shouldn't hurt you."

"Thanks, Kate." Heather glanced at the girls riding in the corral. "So far, so good."

"What are you looking for?" Kate stood next to her. "Educate me."

"I'll put this away while she tells you." Fenn picked up his rifle with his free hand and carried it inside.

"I want the girls to keep the horses at least ten feet apart so they don't bite or kick each other." Heather pointed to Dallas. "See how she uses her legs to squeeze, not thump Cinnamon. It's the same way Toney is riding. They're not hitting or kicking."

"Got it." Kate sat down on the porch steps. "I'll watch them if you want to talk to Ben and put out the food."

"All right." Heather patted her friend's shoulder. "I really appreciate you coming up here with us, Katie. I couldn't stay down there."

"You wouldn't be any kind of mother at all if you hadn't protected your kids. That woman is lucky I didn't hear her. The least I'd have done is throw lemonade at her. I'd have rearranged her face."

Tears stung, and Heather blinked them away. She struggled to control her emotions, undoubtedly askew because of the pregnancy. "I guess I'd better clear things up with Ben, or he'll think I ride around on a broom."

"I'm sure he knows better," Kate said.

All in all, they'd had a nice holiday, Heather thought as she led the way back to her house hours later, a dozing Galveston in her arms. Granted, it was the Fourth of July, but that didn't mean she and Fenn weren't held hostage by their memories. She reined Satan to a stop in front of the house, lit up like the proverbial church.

She checked her watch. Almost 2200 hours, ten at night. Surely, Durango's relatives had left by now. Heather swung out of the saddle and lifted her daughter down into her arms. "Come on, sweetie. It's past your bedtime."

"I've got another exhausted munchkin here." Kate dismounted and helped Dallas slide off the mare. "I'll help you take them upstairs and then come take care of the horses."

"As soon as I tuck them into bed, I'll be out." Heather carried Galveston toward the porch.

The front door opened, and light spilled from the hallway onto the deck. "Where the hell have you been?" Laredo strode toward them. "We've been looking everywhere for you."

"Then why didn't you find us?" Carrying Dallas, Kate followed Heather. "We didn't go into town."

"The McElroy place is more than four hundred acres," Heather explained. "It's surrounded by another four thousand that belongs to logging companies."

"Thanks for sharing." Laredo glowered at them before his gaze fell on the two old horses cropping grass in the front yard. "I'll take care of the stock. You better tell your husband you're safe, Heather. He's in the kitchen."

"That's definitely your job." Kate bumped the door closed behind them. "I'm single for a reason."

"At least you admit it." Heather headed down the hall, pausing at the staircase. Summoning her courage, she headed into the kitchen. She saw him sitting at the table, blueprints scattered in front of him. "We're back."

"I see that." He studied her with a narrowed gaze. "Where were you?"

"At Fenn's." She cradled Galveston closer, grateful her daughter slept. "I lost it when your folks…"

"We'll discuss it later, Heather Marie. Put the kids to bed. They've had a long day."

She hesitated. It was stupid, but she had to know. "Did you really look for me? For us?"

He sat perfectly still, his eyes almost blank. His face revealed nothing. "After three tours in the *sandbox*, you certainly can watch out for yourself, Heather McElroy-Hawke. You've told me that often enough. I searched for my daughters. Now, put them to bed."

# CHAPTER TWENTY-EIGHT

Hurt remained even after she'd undressed Galveston, put a nightgown on the sleeping little girl, and tucked her into bed. Across the room, Kate did the same for Dallas, not speaking. When the twins were soundly tucked into their beds, Kate left the room, taking her silent sympathy along.

Heather sat on the edge of the bed, watching her daughters sleep. Why did their father's insensitivity hurt so much after all this time? Shouldn't she be accustomed to it by now? He refused to admit he loved her. At the wedding, he'd said "I do" during their vows when the minister asked, refusing to repeat the promises to love, honor, or cherish her for the rest of his life.

*Am I a fool for wanting more than he has to give? He didn't even look for me today. If I hadn't come back, would he have let me and the girls go? How many times am I going to let him trample on my heart?*

Durango stood in the doorway. "I thought you were putting them to bed."

She glanced at him from under her lashes. He leaned against the doorframe. "I like to watch them sleep."

"Another time. Now, you can come downstairs with me." There was an edge in his deep voice. "Now, Heather Marie." He took a step toward her. "Not when you get around to it."

She lifted her chin. She might be down, but she wasn't defeated, not yet. "Don't tell me what to do. I won't take it."

"You heard me." He straightened, strode to her, caught her elbow, and pulled her to her feet. "I already told you. We don't fight in front of the twins. I heard enough of that crap from Tex, Estelle, and Eli when I was a kid."

She glared at him. He was right, damn it. They couldn't argue with their children as an audience. Deliberately, she yanked out of his grip, adjusted blankets, and kissed each girl before she left the room.

She waited in the hall while he switched on the unicorn-shaped nightlight and switched off the overhead light. Like her, he kissed them good night and then followed her.

In the living room, she swung to face him. "Did Laredo have any problem with the horses?"

"No. He's gone. He's furious with me. Was that a bonus for you?"

She shrugged. "How am I supposed to answer that? Your parents have always treated me like dirt, but Laredo and Brazos were amazing today. I'm glad Bree felt comfortable enough to bring Natasha with her. They were good to the girls too."

"It didn't keep you here." Durango closed the hall door behind them. "You didn't have to disappear with the twins like we were monsters. You could have trusted me to look after them."

"Why? Was I supposed to think that ceremony two months ago changed anything?" She stood on firm ground now. "No, Hawke. I wasn't going to hope you did the right thing for once. The girls only turned four. They're not old enough to deal with your parents. They were crying when we got to the barn."

He leaned against the door, his hands knotting into fists. "They're my daughters too."

"It's our job to protect them." She met his dark blue gaze and hoped she'd manage to keep her emotions under control. "My folks made mistakes. They weren't perfect but they tried to do what they were supposed to do most of the time. You were the only one who said they sheltered me too much."

"I was jealous and stupid."

"What?" She gaped at him. "I don't understand."

"Liz and Art love you so much and I wanted my parents to treat me the way yours treated you." Durango folded his arms. "Today, when I heard what they'd done, I knew they couldn't. They wouldn't. I told them they're not welcome here ever again. I won't have my kids abused, not by them or anyone."

"And what about me?" She searched his face, trying to read his emotions, but like always, he did the robot routine that frustrated her. "Do you protect me from them?"

He shook his head. "You're an adult. You can take care of yourself."

"I can, but why the hell should I? If you love me, you 'watch my six' like I do yours."

"And you? Do you honestly protect me all the time and cover my back when I can't see behind me?"

"Why are you even asking when you already know the answer? I've always been there for you, Hawke. It's not supposed to be a one-way street. You ought to care about my feelings and look out for me too. We aren't supposed to frag each other."

"I'm no hero. I can't be here every minute to hold your hand. You've got to stand on your own without whining at me and, more important, without taking stupid risks. I know you'd die to protect the girls and our baby, but accidents happen behind the lines."

Tears burned behind her eyes, but she wouldn't let them fall. Instead, she struggled to swallow the huge, aching lump in her throat. Wasn't that the whole problem? She didn't know how to stand on her own two feet. When she was growing up, she depended on her parents. Her grandparents looked out for her when she was in college. The Army had babysat her too.

"I don't know what more I can do, Hawke. You're right. I shouldn't depend on you to take care of my needs. I have to survive, keep looking out for myself so I can look out for my babies, but I never wanted to be a single parent. I always hoped you'd step up, be a partner to me—"

"Damn you, Heather Marie." He strode to her. His hands closed over her shoulders and he pulled her against him. "I'm tired of your crap. You've spent years tearing up my sanity. I wind up saying things the wrong way. Whenever you're scared, you run away. It rips me apart. Never again."

"What are you saying now?"

"No more running away. Not for you or the girls. You stand and fight. You trust me to have your six."

"Really?" She trembled, tears clogging her throat. "Are you sure? I can't be *Wonder Woman* for you. I'm not so strong that I never make demands."

"I'm not being fair, am I?" He held her tighter. "I'll do better, I promise. You're right. We're married and we're in this together."

"What about your parents? Are you going to let them insult me in front of our kids?"

"No. Never again. This is your place, Heather. It's not mine or my family's. Nobody will ever badmouth you again. I won't tolerate it."

She heaved a sigh of relief, pressed her cheek against his broad chest. "That's all I wanted, Hawke."

"Do me one more favor."

"What?"

"Don't run off and leave my sister to tell me what drove you away."

"Okay, you've got a deal."

"Good." He lowered his head. His calloused hands slipped around her neck and he lifted her chin higher. His lips touched hers for an instant, then burned a path to the pulsebeat in the hollow of her throat.

She felt his soft chuckle against her skin and shivered in response before sliding her hands up his chest toward his shoulders. "Don't stop."

"I won't." His mouth trailed along her neck.

She moaned when his thumbs teased her nipples through her bra and felt them tighten. What was she doing? How could she send him to the bunkhouse if she allowed him to seduce her tonight? She pulled free, backed toward the door.

He didn't move. He stood like a statue in the center of the room, watching her as if she were prey and he was the hunter. "Come here, Empress."

She moistened dry lips and reached behind her for the doorknob. She shook her head. If he touched her again, she'd melt in his arms. "I can't."

He narrowed those incredible cobalt eyes, folded his arms across that impressive wide chest, and waited. "You heard me, Heather Marie."

Her knees quivered at the sound of her name drawled in his deep voice. Why did he have to be the only man who stirred her soul? She grabbed for the knob. "Not tonight."

"Scared?" A faint smile tugged at his mouth.

"Of you?" She shook her head. "Of course not!"

"Really?"

She released her hold on the doorknob, planted her fists on her hips. "Jackass."

"Just remember this jackass can have you begging for more in what? Two minutes if I have my hand on you, in you? And less if it's my mouth."

She lifted her chin, trying to ignore the way her panties dampened at the mere idea. He was halfway across the room, nowhere close to her. "The hell you say."

He crooked a finger. "Come here and let me show you."

"In your dreams." Pride dictated the response. She couldn't flee now. He'd know he was more than a hundred percent correct. Damn, she hated it when he challenged her. She strolled toward the rocking chair in the corner, careful to remain out of his reach. She sat down, picked up the remote, and turned on the television.

He laughed, strode to her, and pulled her up into his arms. He carried her over to the couch, sat down with her on his lap. "Where were we?"

"I was going to watch a movie."

"Later, much later." His mouth claimed hers.

She gasped, then surrendered, enjoying the fierce kiss. Her lips parted beneath his and his tongue coaxed hers into a passionate duel. Threading her hands in his tawny gold hair, she brought him nearer. It'd been forever since they were together, okay, slightly more than a week. How could she fight him when she came alive in his arms?

He lifted his head, his lips a breath away from hers. "Give me one good reason not to take you to bed."

"I will when I think of one." She moaned when he unsnapped her blouse, pressing his mouth to her breasts. She squirmed on his lap, pressing closer.

He unbuttoned her jeans, oh so slowly, and she sighed. "What's taking so long?"

"I want you begging for more." He chuckled and unhooked the closure on her bra.

Her nipples tightened even before he drew one into his mouth and sucked gently. "How did you know they'd be so sensitive?"

He stopped for a moment, flicking the other nipple with his tongue. "Research about pregnant women. I had to do something on the flight to Texas and then on the one home."

"You macho jack—" Her voice faded when he cupped her with one hand, rubbing the silk panties against her before pushing them out of the way. "Oh, my Gawd!"

"No, just your husband."

She gasped when he slid one large finger inside her, followed by a second. She arched against his hand, shuddering when he started a slow in and out motion, his thumb tormenting her. She caught his mouth with her own, kissing him while she moved with the pattern he set, rising and falling.

It didn't surprise her when their clothes ended up on the floor. More kisses and caresses while they pleased each other. Finally, he was on top of her, most of his weight on his elbows. He parted her legs, sliding inside her. She dug her nails into his back. "Do it. Do it now."

"Say please," he mocked. He pulled out slightly, then rocked back. "Beg me, baby."

"Make me." She rose against him, her hips meeting his. Little thrusts led to longer, deeper ones. She matched his movements. He always knew how to drive her beyond the stars, and she never could refuse him. He lowered his head, and his mouth took hers, one kiss following another. He continued the steady strokes at the same time, some shallow, others deep, until she came, clinging desperately.

She stared into his face, feeling him still hard and thick inside her. "You haven't—"

"Finished? Not yet." He shifted slightly and began moving again, faster this time. "Come with me, baby."

She did, her hips meeting his thrusts as they ascended further and further. They achieved fulfillment together, in an explosive moment. Afterward, he eased off her, holding her beside him on the couch while he stroked her hair. "Are you sending me to the bunkhouse?"

"Yes, but not yet." She sighed, turning her mouth into the hollow of his shoulder, tasting the saltiness of his skin. "Didn't your research warn you that pregnant women get horny?"

"Hmm, maybe I need to do more reading. Where's my phone?" He kissed her forehead, hands roaming down her back.

She returned the favor, exploring his chest. She caught her breath when he squeezed her butt, then his hand curved over her hip, slowly trailing toward the place she longed to have him touch. She nipped his ear. "Do it."

"What?" He barely touched the curls between her legs. "Say again, baby."

"Damn it, Hawke. You know what I want."

His hand cupped her. "Was it this?"

"Not quite." She arched against him, kissing the strong neck. "Do it now."

"Nothing but orders, Empress?" Two fingers slid inside her. "Time to dance, baby."

An hour later, she was almost asleep in his arms when he roused. "Move, sweetheart. We've got company."

"Is it one of the girls?" She'd barely sat up when he was off the couch.

"No, somebody else." He reached for his boot and the knife he kept inside. "Stay here."

She fumbled on the floor for her shirt, hastily yanked it on, shoving her arms in the sleeves. "I need my bra, my pants."

From the corner of her eye, she glimpsed a male silhouette by the door.

Without warning, Durango threw the knife. The visitor closed the door, barely in time. The blade landed in the center panel with a solid thud.

"Damn it, Durango!" The door opened a bare inch. "You almost killed me."

"Well, next time call on the phone when you're coming to visit, Laredo." Durango relaxed slightly. "You better wait in the hall."

"Are you crazy?"

"Yes, we are." Heather picked up her panties. "And he's right. Wait there."

"I don't think I'm old enough to know why."

"It's called make-up sex, Laredo." Heather tossed Durango's underwear and jeans at him. "Married people do it all the time. Get dressed, jarhead."

Laughing, he obeyed. When she had on her clothes, she crossed to the door, pulled out the K-bar. He came and took the blade from her, tucking it back into his boot. When he nodded, she opened the door to the hallway. "Come in and quit sniveling, Laredo. Man up!"

Her brother-in-law's jeans were drenched to mid-thigh and his boots leaked water on the hardwood floor. "I hit a hole in the river. I've been trying to get out forever, and I finally gave up. I need a tow."

"Looks like you also need some dry clothes," Heather said. "I'll find some."

"That'd be great." Laredo beamed at her with genuine affection. "Thanks, Heather."

"Make some coffee too, baby," Durango said. "And get out the whisky for me."

"Sorry, no can do." Heather kept the words flippant. She wasn't telling him she'd given away his favorite Canadian liquor to her uncle. "I poured out all the booze so you couldn't drive me to drink."

He eyed her and then nodded approvingly. "Good job, baby. I forgot. That was in my research too."

"Don't say it, Hawke, or I'll have Dad geld you."

"Say what?" Laredo asked, looking baffled.

"Heather's pregnant."

She aimed a punch at Durango, and he quickly stepped away. "I told you—"

"I didn't listen."

This time, she kicked him in the ankle. "Anyway, you shouldn't drink and go in the creek. It's from the snowpack on Mount Carmody."

"Bitch, bitch, bitch!" He sounded more amused than upset by her concern.

"Don't call me your family names." Heather tucked in her blouse. "If you get hypothermia, I don't want to hear any whining."

"Is that what you consider sympathy?"

"If you want sympathy, look it up in the dictionary between sex and syphilis."

He chuckled. "Give me a minute, Laredo."

"Why?" She gestured toward the front door. "Don't let it hit you in the backside."

Durango turned. He snagged her arm, bent his head. "When I get done with Laredo's truck, shall I find out what the latest edicts are, Empress?"

Before she answered, his mouth captured hers. She rose on tiptoe, tangling her fingers in his hair, and kissed him back, her tongue teasing his. Then she stepped back. "You should have listened more to my parents. First rule, I'm always right. Rule number two, if I happen to be wrong, the first rule applies."

# CHAPTER TWENTY-NINE

The men left for the creek and she went into the kitchen. She poured milk into a saucepan, setting it on low heat. Then she headed into the laundry room to find dry clothes. Both guys would need them after wading in the icy water. Sure, Durango acted like he was super strong, but she'd been an emergency room nurse long enough to know the effects of cold-water shock. Sudden immersion in freezing water could lead to heart attacks, even in young and healthy people.

Hot chocolate, grilled cheese sandwiches, and Bronwyn Murphy's homemade tomato soup were ready when the back door opened and both men entered a short time later. She turned to face them, noticing that Durango's jeans and shirt were as soaked as his brother's. "Did you get it out?"

"No, Laredo stuck it, all right," Durango said. "It's not going anywhere until daylight when I can hook up the dozer and yank it out."

"It was bound to happen sooner or later, especially since he was driving through the creek after dark. It's hard enough seeing the deeper holes in daylight." She handed each of them a pair of jeans, underwear, socks, and shirts. "Go change and then come eat something to raise your blood pressure."

"Thanks, Heather." Laredo kissed her cheek on the way to the bathroom. "I appreciate you respecting my sobriety. I haven't fallen off the wagon since the two of you put me in rehab, four years, eleven months, two weeks, and four days ago. I'm staying with it."

"Good for you. You're awesome. If I weren't pregnant, I don't think I'd be able to leave the booze alone."

"As the saying goes, you do it a day at a time." Durango took the clothes she offered. "Just keep it up."

"No way." Heather tossed her head. "I'm counting the days until I start drinking again. I need vodka to ward off the demons."

"Sounds like we're going to keep adding to the family if you avoid alcohol when you're expecting."

"In your dreams, Hawke. You may be a sexy devil, but you're not keeping me barefoot and knocked up." When he left to change, Heather opened the cupboard and removed the box of saltines. She arranged some on a saucer, then went to the fridge for lunch meat and cheese. When Durango returned, she eyed him. "Do you need a reminder that if we we have another set of twins next spring, I'm having Dad geld you?"

"I thought Art retired from his veterinary practice." Laredo laughed as he rejoined them. "Heather, do you want my clothes in the washing machine?"

"Please. I'll do them in the morning." Hopefully, the crackers and cheese would prevent the cocoa from giving her heartburn. She took the cup Durango offered. "Dad may be retired, but I know he'd step up if I asked."

"Isn't that a case of locking the barn after the horse has been stolen?" Laredo asked.

She ignored Durango's snicker. "I'll leave you to do the male bonding routine. I'm watching TV. You can sleep on the couch in the bunkhouse, Laredo."

She started toward the living room, then paused to look over her shoulder. "In case you missed the ad in the paper, your brother and I aren't living together even if we do have make-up sex when we fight. This is one barn door that's staying locked."

———

Durango sat down and picked up a grilled cheese sandwich off the platter in the middle of the table. "Eat something. She always fusses if we leave food."

Nodding, Laredo joined him. "Do you want some advice?"

"Yeah. I'm so desperate I'll even listen to you."

"Ask her what she wants. What will it take to be back in the house full-time? What do you have to do to have a real marriage?"

Durango didn't answer. His brother and sisters didn't know about the search for Waco. It wasn't something to be shared. "She's not ready to be my wife. She says it's not why she brought the girls home."

"Why is she here?"

Finishing the sandwich, Durango reached for the cup of soup. "She inherited this place, and she plans to open a training stable in the spring after the baby's born."

"I've got a news flash for you, big brother. She could have sold the property and bought acreage out of state. She'd never have to see you again."

"I hadn't thought of that." Durango felt a smile coming to life, not just on his face, but inside him. "What a little witch."

"You oughta know. How long have you loved her?"

"Since the first time I met her when Liz and Art brought her home from the hospital." Durango traded the soup for the hot chocolate. "She was two years old when I went to live with Uncle Quentin, and I missed her so much. I came back for a visit when I was eight. I raced next door to see Liz and Art and ran smack-dab into Heather. At four, she was a spoiled little princess who expected me to wait on her hand and foot."

"And you had nothing to do with that?"

"Hell, yes." Durango raised his mug in a toast. "Those big, green eyes snared me back then too. I'll do whatever she wants. She's always been mine."

---

*She heard the choppers coming in and knew they faced another mass casualty situation. She wasn't ready. They still had patients waiting in the wards that needed to be evac'd to the hospital ships off-shore. The Air Force planes hadn't arrived yet. She started to run toward triage, stumbling in the mud. She'd thought rain wouldn't bother her, not after growing up in western Washington, but she was wrong.*

*The rainy season and mud made everything worse. A rocket attack began as she reached the first patient. A kid in camos, no legs, only one arm—the left. Brain injury. Give him morphine and move on to the next injured soldier.*

*Between explosions, she heard voices. The wounded begging for help seemed to drown out the shouted commands of medical staff.*

"Cap, find my buddy. He's bad. Take him first."

"Cap, how about a kiss for luck?"

"Cap, how's my Gunny? He got hit."

"Cap? Cap? Cap!"

Shaking her head, she forced open her eyes. She heard a soft rumble and realized the sound came from the black and white cat draped across her chest, purring. She stroked the fur and met the knowing gold eyes of the mother feline.

"That was a bad one," Heather murmured.

"Mrrow," the cat agreed.

The voices weren't gone, Heather thought. Sometimes, they were quieter than others. She longed for a drink to drown them for once and for all. She clutched the cat instead, glimpsing her watch. 0500 hours.

Still holding the cat, Heather rose from the rocking chair. She went to the windows and opened the drapes. The clouds had rolled in, covering the sky in gray clumps. It rained, a steady downpour that reminded her of the rainy seasons in Iraq and Afghanistan.

"No!" She wouldn't remember the tours, not today, not now. She closed the curtains again, shutting out the rain. Durango would be up soon. Laredo was here. She'd fix breakfast for the two of them. They'd have to get an early start if they planned to haul that truck out of the creek before it rose. Still carrying the cat, Heather headed for the kitchen. Cooking always made her feel better, more in control.

---

As soon as Durango opened the back door, he heard classic country music and Heather singing along. He walked into the kitchen and found her setting the table. A pitcher of orange juice sat in the middle of the table. He spotted a platter of golden-brown biscuits, heat rising off them, and wondered if there'd be cream gravy for them. He smelled ham and bacon.

"Morning." He glanced at the three plates, glasses, and silverware. "Laredo will be in shortly. He stayed in the barn to check the horses' hooves."

"Their shoes are fine." She poured a cup of coffee and handed it to him. "I was about to shout out the back door for you guys." She forked rashers of bacon and slices of ham onto a plate and cracked eggs into the grease. "How do you want them?"

"Cook's choice." Durango sipped the strong, black coffee. "If I kiss you, will I be in trouble?"

"What was your first clue?"

"Does this mean no gravy?" He watched her closely.

"I want to eat too. It's why you're not getting sausage for at least another two months until the nausea ends." She kept her attention on the eggs. "I'll open a can of breakfast gravy and nuke it for you."

He put the mug on the counter. "If I have to eat canned gravy, I'm definitely risking a kiss."

When he reached for her, she raised the spatula in warning. "Behave yourself, Hawke. These eggs will never survive."

That slowed him down for a moment. He grabbed the potholder on the counter, lifted the skillet off the heat. He turned off the burner and pulled her into his arms.

"Let go of me. I'm making breakfast, not enduring your inept passes."

He smiled, lowered his head. His mouth closed over hers, staking a passionate claim. He tangled a hand in the coppery red hair, and the kiss deepened. A lifetime later, he lifted his lips from hers. "Do you have something to tell me, Heather McElroy-Hawke?"

"What the hell would I tell you?"

"For starters, you could say you're over the snit and I can move back into the house. Say you came home because you love me and you're here to stay with me."

She sniffed derisively. "Sounds like you're fantasizing, Marine. I'm here because this is my ranch. If you want me to take you back, you know what you have to say. And this time, you have to mean it."

"You're a stubborn, ornery woman."

"Nobody else would put up with your crap."

---

It cleared off early that afternoon and she turned the horses out to enjoy the sunshine. Dray must be off with friends because the teen hadn't shown up, and it meant she could muck her own barn. Hurray! The twins were supposedly helping her while Kate cleaned the house.

"It stinks in here," Dallas said. "Can we play in the yard?"

"Watch for your dad's truck." Heather smiled when the twins dashed into the sunlit area beyond the stable. How many times had she finagled Durango and Fenn into cleaning stalls for her? Still amused, she grabbed the plastic pitchfork and scooped manure into the wheelbarrow.

She'd finished Flash's stall and was moving onto Satan's when she heard the girls squeal and shout. The noise required investigation, although she couldn't hear the actual words.

She leaned the pitchfork against the stall wall and hurried from the barn. She skidded to a stop when she saw the twins, safe. They played with a small black and gray puppy who couldn't decide which child to chase. Durango watched from a few feet away.

"Where did you get that?" Heather went to join him and pointed to the dog. "What is it?"

"He's a gift from Laredo." Durango smiled down at her, wrapping an arm around her shoulders. "It's your fault. You're the one who arranged for him to apprentice with Sean Killian, and the guy breeds Australian cattle dogs and border collies. This is a blue heeler with papers that go on forever."

"Who is going to housebreak him? Who's going to train him? He's supposed to be a stock dog, isn't he? Who will keep him from chasing the horses?"

"That's our job. The girls are too little for the responsibility."

Dallas raced up to them, followed by the steel-gray and black furball. "Mommy, did you see my puppy? I named him Booey after the cartoon dog."

"You and Galveston have to agree on the name," Durango said calmly. "He belongs to both of you."

"He's mine!" Dallas planted both fists on small hips and glared up at her father. "You gave him to me first."

"Durango, we have two daughters." Heather bent and petted the puppy, who sniffed her fingers curiously, before trotting back to Dallas. "One puppy isn't enough. You should have brought home two."

"They can share."

"No, they can't. Laredo told me all about these dogs. They only pick one person as their owner. Booey belongs to Ally."

"Told you." Dallas sat on the grass and pulled the wriggling pup onto her lap. He tried to lick her face, and she giggled. "He's mine, all mine."

Tears filled Galveston's eyes and trickled down her cheeks. "I wanta puppy too."

"Don't cry, sweetie." Heather picked up her daughter. "Daddy's gonna go get you one right now. He's still learning about you girls, so we have to teach him too."

"Really?" Galveston sniffled and wiped her face on Heather's shirt. "Daddy's gotta learn?"

"Yes, I do." Durango frowned, then obviously surrendered to the tears. He lifted Galveston away from Heather. "Let's go see your uncle right now and get you a puppy of your own. I'm sorry. I goofed up. I didn't know we had to have two of them."

"It's okay, Daddy." A sunshine grin broke through the tears. "You're gonna fix it."

"You bet."

"I'm coming too." Dallas stood and scooped up Booey.

"No, you're staying home with your mom and Booey."

"I'm goin'. So is Booey," Dallas said firmly. "Toney don't talk much. You won't know what puppy to get. It hasta look like mine."

"No, Toney will choose by herself this time." Carrying Galveston, Durango strode toward his pickup. "Will you tell me which one you want?"

"I'll tell you."

"She won't talk, Mommy." Dallas eyed her mother anxiously as the old Chevy left the yard. "I talk for us."

"Maybe she won't have to say much." Heather bent down to hug Dallas and her puppy. "Remember when Auntie Kate and I tried to teach Toney to ask for her own cookie? Sometimes, you won't be there, Ally. Toney has to be able to do things for herself."

"We're twins," Dallas said. "We'll always be together, but she can pick her own puppy this time."

One step at a time. Heather hugged Dallas again. "Come on. Let's show Auntie Kate your puppy. Then you and Booey can help me clean the barn."

"Okay." Dallas' smile was almost a mirror image of her sister's.

They'd just reached the wraparound porch when someone drove a truck into the yard. Heather recognized her parents' red Chevy. "Wow, Ally. Now, you can show Grandma and Grandpa your puppy too."

When the pickup came to a stop and the driver shut off the engine, Dallas dashed to meet her grandparents, followed by the puppy. Heather hurried into the house to call Kate. "We've got company. My folks this time."

"This place is like Grand Central Station, Heather. I thought you said nobody could get in because there isn't a bridge over the river."

"Wait until October." Heather patted her best friend's back. "Cedar Creek will rise so high, nobody will be able to drive through it, and most people won't know there's a back road from the dude ranch."

"Promises, promises." Kate followed Heather to the front door. "What on earth does Ally have?"

"A puppy, thanks to her Uncle Laredo. Toney and Durango went after a second one."

"This place is turning into a menagerie." Kate stared at the cage in Liz McElroy's arms. "Oh, no. What is that?"

"We'll find out." Heather headed toward her mother. "Mom, what have you got there? A squirrel?"

"Tex live-trapped it and was going to give it to one of his friends to use for bait to train his hunting dogs. Don't get me started on that man. I'll probably take a page from Brazos' book and help his opponent in the next election." Liz heaved a sigh before holding out her hand to Kate. "Hi, glad you made it safe and sound from Tennessee."

"My trip was probably easier than Heather's. I drove by myself. She had the twins and the first two kittens you and Art gave her." Kate studied the squirrel with a professional eye. "What's wrong with his foot?"

"It's the one he was caught by," Liz said. "Art gave him a big dose of antibiotics and doctored the cut. We're turning him loose up here to fend for himself. I wish Tex and Estelle were better neighbors, but thankfully they spend much of their time back East. How are the kittens?"

"They're fine." Heather paused. "No wonder Brazos locked the entire bunch of flea-lions in the basement yesterday. Well, let's take your little friend to the backyard and set him free. I hope Cop-Car doesn't decide he's lunch."

"Cop-Car?" Liz asked. "Who is that?"

"The momma cat," Kate said. "Heather says she's the same color as the county sheriff's vehicles."

"She's just as lethal. So far, we're down eight mice, three rats, and two rabbits."

"Have you set out bait for the rats?" Liz asked. "If you find one, you know there's more."

"Durango took care of it." Heather glanced across the yard and watched her father play with Dallas and Booey. "Are you and Dad going to stick around a while and see Toney's puppy?"

"You bet." Liz walked beside Heather around the house to the area between it and the bunkhouse. "Sorry we couldn't make it yesterday, but I promised Darla Connors that your dad and I'd attend the Lake Maynard parade and the picnic afterwards. She took over the 4-H club after we retired."

"You didn't miss a thing." Heather silently counted her blessings. If her folks had been here, there wasn't any way she could have kept Fenn's return a secret. Her father would have known exactly where to find her and undoubtedly would have followed them to the cabin. "Kate and I took the girls for a picnic while Durango kicked his parents' tails."

"Were they rude to you?"

"Always. They were worse to the twins, so Durango gave them their walking papers."

# CHAPTER THIRTY

They left the squirrel in the crate in the back yard, the door open so it could leave when it was ready. Heading back to the front yard, Heather heard a truck. "That was a quick trip. I hope Toney got her puppy."

Parked next to Art's pickup, she saw Jeff's. He was accompanied by a petite, shapely woman with wildly curly black hair who stood talking to a young girl climbing out of the rear seat. "Who on earth is that? He married Amarillo a few days ago."

She headed toward Jeff in his usual black suit, hat in hand. As she approached, the younger woman turned, and Heather recognized her. "Well, I'll be—" She sped up and called a greeting. "Amarillo, what on earth have you done to your hair? I love it."

"It was Jeff's idea." Amarillo blushed. "He thought I should return to my natural color, and Gino's sister is a hairdresser, so we dyed it yesterday. Does it really look all right? I was afraid it was too dark."

"It's beautiful." Heather hugged Amarillo quickly and then turned to greet Maria, a small, dark-haired girl in shorts and a sun-top. "Now, I know where you got your lovely hair, honey. Wow, you're so tall. I couldn't tell when we chatted on the computer."

Maria wriggled in pleasure, clinging to Jeff's hand. "Do you know my new daddy?"

"I certainly do." Heather kissed Jeff's scarred cheek. "Looks like you got what you kept telling me you wanted. Amarillo and a daughter of your own. Congratulations." She winked at him. "I didn't know who was with you and I was going to give you a hard time for cheating on your new wife."

"He better not. You taught me not to share, Heather." Amarillo's gaze narrowed on Kate. "We weren't coming yesterday. Maria and I spend our holidays with the Petrocellis. We took Jeff with us."

"So, did Amie's real family approve of you?" Heather smiled at Jeff. "Or are you going to end up in a concrete bulkhead somewhere?"

"Heather Marie!" Liz gasped. "What a rude, insulting thing to say. Apologize."

"You've never met Gino. He's worse than I am." Heather tilted her head to one side. "Come on, Ransom. Spill your guts."

"Yeah." Kate slid her arm through Heather's and stepped up beside her. "Just because you survived everything we know you did doesn't mean you made it through your in-laws unscathed. Let's hear the dirt, rotor-head."

"What are you two talking about?" Amarillo demanded, looking at them and then at Jeff. "I don't understand."

Heather deliberately eyed Maria before answering. "Honey, go find my daughter and her new puppy."

Maria nodded, hugged Jeff once more. "You'll be nice to my daddy, right?"

"Always," Heather promised, and waited until the girl left. "She'll learn soon enough about the crap prisoners endure. We don't need to tell her, but you should know, Amie. Jeff went through hell before Durango busted heads and tails to rescue him back in the day."

"If you'd been stuck in those kinds of accommodations, you'd have seized all possible chances of escape too." Jeff removed his hat to run a hand through silver-streaked dark hair. A wide band of scar tissue encircled his wrist. "Anyway, the Petrocellis loved me. The women all want to feed me and gave 'Rilla,' as they call her, a hard time for me being so thin. Gino threatened to knock my teeth down my throat if I hurt her."

"I'll tell him he can't do that, not since you lost yours to an AK-47." Heather saw the incomprehension on Amarillo's and her mother's faces, and added, "A rifle butt. Ransom has a habit of talking when he ought to listen."

"And don't swallow those implants, Ransom," Kate finished. "We'll tell this wise guy what a hero you are."

"Not me, ladies." Jeff chuckled. "That honor is all Durango's. If he hadn't found me, I'd never have made it home in one piece."

"Even if he wants to watch over me, Gino likes Jeff." Amarillo glanced over her shoulder to Maria playing with the puppy and Ally. "Where's—"

"Toney and Durango went to get a second puppy." Heather smiled. "Laredo and Durango thought the girls could share, but that wasn't in the scheme of things."

"You let Durango take her away alone? To our brother's?"

Heather placed a hand on Amarillo's shoulder. "I trust him. And Laredo. If the day comes that I find I'm wrong, I'll get Gino to hide the body. Amie, most men don't rape little girls. Most aren't perverts."

"All men are like that." Amarillo's tone was flat and calm, certain. "You've got to protect your daughters." Another quick glance to check on Maria and then panic when she was out of sight. "I have to find mine."

Concern etched on his face, Jeff lingered after Amarillo hustled away. "Thanks for trying, Heather. It'll take more time for Rilla to regain her trust."

"How do you handle it?" Kate asked.

"I'm careful. I never spend a moment alone with Maria. I count my blessings. I thought it'd be years before Rilla agreed to marry me. I guess I should be grateful that her father's political organization threatened to sue for custody, but I'm not."

Liz frowned at the three of them. "Amarillo's always exaggerated everything that happens. She's a little drama diva. You don't believe her wild tales, do you?"

Heather caught a glimpse of orange coming up the track from the creek and was grateful for the excuse it provided. "I want to see Toney's new puppy. Jeff, come with me. Kate, will you help Mom keep the other kiddoes safe?"

"You know it," Kate said.

They walked across the yard toward the road. "What are you doing about Tex?"

"I spoke to the Petrocelli family attorney and he's going to contact him and Eli Roberts to explain that a restraining order isn't a good look for a politician who contemplates running for more than Congress, especially one that accuses him of everything he's done to my wife, and her sister and brother."

Heather shook her head, tightening her hands into fists. "Whatever else you decide to do, I'd opt for confidentiality, Jeff."

He nodded. "Gino and I have an appointment with his father's consigliere next week. We've agreed it's always better to seek permission first than forgiveness in this case."

She blinked. "Is Gino's family seriously connected to organized crime? I always thought it was a joke."

"Not a joke. I asked the lawyer if he'd also investigate what's holding up the permits for the replacement bridge to your place. George O'Connell is a fairly good lawyer, but he has limitations."

"I'll say. He was utterly incompetent as a trustee for my grandfather when I inherited this place."

Durango carefully parked his old Chevy next to the other trucks. Dallas ran to meet her twin, followed by Maria and Booey.

Heather opened the passenger door. "Take it easy, you guys. Wait a minute."

"What kinda puppy did you get, Toney?" Dallas demanded.

Durango helped Galveston out of her car seat, before lifting a pale reddish-brown puppy with a bluish cast to its coat out of the rig.

"She's pu-po," Galveston announced while the new addition squatted and piddled on the grass.

"She doesn't look very pu-po to me," Dallas said.

"Does too. You're being dumb, Ally."

Heather froze and looked at Durango. Was this what it would take to cause Galveston to stand up to her twin without bringing in parental reinforcements? It'd happened with the kittens. Would it occur again with a puppy? "How on earth do you get a pu-po puppy, Toney?"

"Not pu-po, Mommy. Pu-po. Her mommy was a red heeler, and her daddy was a blue one, so Unca Laredo says she's a pu-po one. It's her name, and my best new color 'cause he didn't have no green puppies."

"She's a registered purple heeler," Durango translated.

"I see." Heather bent to pet the puppy. "Welcome to the family, Purple."

The little dog sniffed her fingers, licked them cautiously, and then bounced off to jump on Booey. Heather laughed. "Toney, this is Maria, one of your cousins, your Aunt Amie's little girl. There's only one of her so this time you're really going to have to share."

As the three girls headed off to play with the puppies, she glanced up at Durango. "Be sure you say something nice about Amarillo's hair. It's back to her natural color. My parents seem to think she had a Beaver Cleaver childhood because she was the youngest in the Hawke clan, so help me run interference."

He framed her face with his hands. "Cut them some slack, baby. Liz and Art have done a lot of good over the years, but people are like horses."

"How do you figure?"

"Blind spots. You're the best horse-trainer in the area when you're working. You never get directly in front or behind a horse, so it can't bite or kick you or let one step on your feet. You stay where it can see you. Right?"

"Absolutely. Then I don't get hurt."

She flicked a glance at her mother, standing near her father and Kate. "Blind spots," Heather murmured. She'd never thought of that, never realized people had areas they didn't, couldn't, or wouldn't see. Perhaps they didn't want to see them.

What were Durango's? More important, what were hers?

***

Durango was grilling burgers, hot dogs, and chicken on the back deck when Dray arrived to clean the barn accompanied by the Murphy girls, who headed off to the rose garden. This time, Kate was the one who went to help with the flowers. Meantime, Heather and Liz created salads in the kitchen. Those would be accompanied by the lasagna baking in the oven and the assortment of desserts Amarillo brought. His younger sister hovered over the twins and Maria.

He heard puppy woofs and glanced toward the front of the house in time to see Rob Hendrickson guiding his heavily pregnant wife, Cat, up the steps. "Hi there. You arrived just in time. We'll be eating soon."

"Sounds great. I can always eat." Cat smiled at him. "Where do we find Heather? We brought Jassy along to watch the kids. She headed for the barn with yours, their cousin, Maria, and ours to see the horses."

"I thought I saw you." Heather came out the back door, wiping her hands on a dish towel. "Everything has been fairly quiet and calm today, so we may not have company."

"What are you talking about?" Durango asked. "My sister and brother-in-law are here. So are your parents. That doesn't count you, me, Kate, or the twins."

"I don't know if he's a believer or not." Heather cocked her head to one side, studying him. "I'm talking about a ghost, babe. I invited Cat here as the O'Leary to talk to whoever is living with us."

"Try nobody. If there's a stranger hanging around, I'd know."

That earned him a long look from those magical green eyes before his wife shook her head. "Not if you're doing the macho thing, Hawke."

"So, we'll do a walk-through," Cat said, her tone even. "Rob sees spirits too. If I miss something, he'll catch it."

"Interesting." Heather slowly measured him with her gaze. "I was talking to my mom, and she told me a story about a church picnic at the dude ranch when I was a kid—"

"Before my time." Cat ran a hand through her hair. "What about it?"

"Déjà vu when I met Rob," Heather went on. "It felt like we'd met before, but I didn't think we had. Mom said my cousin Ann and I got lost during a hide and seek game that was supposedly being supervised by her older sisters at the picnic. When we were finally found the next morning, I told my mother we weren't scared because a soldier stayed with us all night and guarded us from the bogeyman."

"I don't remember a picnic back then," Durango said. "If there had been, I'd be the one taking care of you, baby."

"By then, you were living with your uncle during the school year." Impatience filled Heather's voice. "And I was fine. So was Ann. And the soldier—"

"When you come for the women's veterans' meeting next Wednesday, I'll tell you the rest of the story." Cat squeezed Rob's hand. "I shared it with Ann, but it sounds like she kept it to herself."

"Works for me." Rob nodded, before winking at Heather. "Then we'll both know and you were a spunky little squirt back then."

"Always!" She grinned at him and the pair went into the house behind Heather.

Still wondering what that conversation meant, Durango spotted Art and Jeff standing in the yard and waved at them. When they joined him, he handed the meat fork to his father-in-law. "Heather's asked the local ghostbusters to inspect the place. She thinks we're being haunted. I'll be back in a few minutes."

Jeff followed him into the kitchen and Durango glanced swiftly at him. "What is this?"

"I've always got your back, Angel."

"There's no such thing as ghosts, Ransom. Heather's hormones are out of whack because she's pregnant and Liz was telling her some silly ghost story."

"I'll let you tell Heather that," Jeff said, barely hiding his smirk. "But you're not going to be able to sleep on my couch when she throws you off the ranch. I'm a married man now."

They found Cat, Rob, and Heather in the living room, where she'd apparently just turned off the television. "Again, we don't watch the news. Why would I have the TV on when there's a houseful of guests?"

Obviously looking for another solution, Rob asked, "Could it have been the kids?"

"When there are puppies and playmates?" Heather shook her head. "No, that's not it. And if it was them, why a talking head who is reviewing current politics? Shouldn't it have been cartoons?"

"Then, what is it?" Durango stopped in the center of the room, eyeing the three of them. "I told you nobody was here. Any real suggestions?"

"You could try asking the hotshot guy smirking from the rocking chair." Jeff folded his arms, stepped around Durango to stand guard in front of the women. "Talk, ass-hat! Why are you here and what do you want?"

"Have you lost it, Ransom?" Durango glanced at the vacant chair. "Nobody's there."

"Hold on." Cat held up her hand. "Last fall, when I moved to Baker City, Jeff was the only other person who talked to Rob."

"I don't get it. You were by yourself at the dude ranch until your husband came back and the whole town met him when we were fixing up the Haunted Halloween celebration."

Cat and Rob exchanged a meaningful look before she said, "You wouldn't believe me if I explained it, especially since you're not hearing what Heather said a few minutes ago. Trust me. Jeff has a different sort of gift than Rob or I do. We talk to dead people. Jeff told me he was captured in Colombia when his helicopter went down. He and what remained of his crew were captured."

"I know that." Durango hoped he didn't sound as impatient as he felt. "What's it got to do with anything?"

"They stayed with me," Jeff said. "The cartel separated us, but I saw them when they were dying." He looked at the empty chair again. "They came to see me in my cell, encouraged me to survive. They didn't travel as far as you have. So, who are you? Where are you?"

The rest of them waited in silence while Jeff listened intently to someone nobody else saw. After a moment, he nodded. "Are there others with you in the prison?"

Quiet from the audience before Jeff spoke again. "Is one of them a pilot? You need to fly out of there to the U.S. Don't wait for *El angél de la muerte,* the angel of death, to rescue you."

More time passed before Jeff stepped back and turned. "He's gone for now."

"Who is?" Heather demanded.

"Waco Hawke." Jeff jerked his head toward Durango. "Your brother. He's not dead yet, but he will be soon. It's why he can travel outside his body right now and why I can see him when he's dream-walking."

"What else? If he was here, he had more to say than that."

"I'll tell you in private. Let's go to your office."

Durango nodded, feeling as if he'd been sucker-punched. "I don't know what to believe."

"Join the club," Heather said, her voice even. "How long has Waco been in my house?"

"Off and on for the past few weeks," Jeff said. "He told me he left whenever the two of you started what he called 'making whoopie.' He said it was embarrassing to watch you two jump each other."

"Not near as embarrassing as it's going to be if he shows up here again." Heather eyed Cat and Rob. "Come in the kitchen with me. I need to help Mom and you two can advise me on what to do the next time I have company. There must be a way to tell him to turn off the television when he's done watching it."

Durango waited until the three of them left before leading the way to his den. "Why do we need to talk in private?"

"Because your father has been receiving ransom demands for Waco. The cartel knows who he is and that your family has plenty of money and political influence. When one bunch doesn't get the money, they ask again and again. Then they trade him off to a different bunch of cutthroats and the whole cycle repeats itself."

The words stabbed into him as sharp as the knife he kept in his boot. "My dad always claimed Waco was his favorite son."

"Doesn't sound like he meant it."

# CHAPTER THIRTY-ONE

The next day, Heather turned when the back door slammed open, banging against the wall. Her daughters ran inside. "What's up, ladies?"

"We wanta have a picnic with our puppies," Dallas announced. "Can we?"

"Sure." Heather smiled at the pair. "What kind of sandwiches do you want?"

"Peanut butter and jelly," Dallas said.

"What about you, Toney? What do you want?"

"Mommy, she always wants the same as me. Why are you asking her?"

"You know I want Toney to talk for herself." Heather waited.

"Peanut butter and honey," Galveston finally whispered.

"Me too, Mommy," Dallas instantly decided. "Make mine the same as Toney's."

"Okay." Heather went to the cupboard and found the staple of her existence. Peanut butter. What would she do without it? "Go wash up, girls. I'll fix your lunches."

"What are they having?" Durango looked at the clock as he came into the room. "Don't fix anything for me, baby. Jeff called and there's an emergency at the office, so I need to run into Lake Maynard. Do you want anything while I'm there?"

"I called Bronwyn for milk, eggs, cheese, and veggies. She's sending them with the girls and Dray." Heather opened the jar of peanut butter. It was almost empty. "I'll make a list for you."

"Okay." He glanced around. "Where's Kate?"

"She went for a walk. She says the ranch is the closest to a park she's ever seen." Heather didn't add that Kate's final destination would undoubtedly be Fenn's cabin. "She took her sketch pad. I don't expect her back until supper."

"Sounds good. I'll be home too. What are we having?"

Heather gestured to the slow cooker. "Old-fashioned spaghetti and meatballs. It will be ready when we are. Don't let the puppies follow you. They're waiting on the porch for the girls."

---

An hour later, Durango walked into his construction company headquarters. He nodded to Laurie, who was on the telephone. "Let Ransom know I'm here and ask him to come to my office."

Laurie hastily put the caller on hold. "Your father's waiting for you. So is your—"

Grimacing, Durango interrupted. "Tell Jeff to come in as soon as he gets here."

Without waiting for her response, Durango went into his large, private office. Tex Hawke wasn't alone. A sturdy boy with shaggy golden-brown hair, defiance on his youthful features, stood by the window. "Hello, I'm Durango Hawke. And you're—"

"He says he's your son," Tex interrupted. "Does Heather know about your bastard? Or that you have more than her two you've decided to claim?"

Durango's hands knotted into fists. Not for the first time, he wished his uncle hadn't taught him not to pound on men smaller than he was. He'd have loved to hurl Tex Hawke through the wall and create a new window.

Instead, Durango stepped between his father and the boy. "What do you want, old man? I threw you out of our house when you called my wife a whore. Are you pushing me for a reason?" He jerked his head toward the door. "Get out. Let me talk to the boy."

"We need to discuss the problems you're having with the family."

"They've been around longer than I have. They'll wait." He watched red creep along Tex's cheekbones before the older man turned and stomped out the door.

Alone with the kid, Durango went behind his desk and sat down. Looking at the silent boy was like staring in a mirror from years ago. "How old are you?"

"Almost twelve."

Durango nodded, studying the face and cobalt eyes again. The bone structure was identical to his own. So was the hair. "What's your name?"

"Luchenbach, but everyone calls me Luke." A flush edged the boy's high cheekbones, "Except my mom. She calls me Lucky because she says she's lucky to have me."

"Well, pull up a seat, Luke. Let's talk."

"You are my father, right?" Luke perched on the edge of a chair. "I found my birth certificate in our house, and it has your name on it. If I'd known I was coming here when I was visiting my aunt, I'd have brought it with me."

"It might say my name, but I'm not your dad." Durango wouldn't lie to the boy. "Don't be pissed off. If I were, I'd be proud to admit it and your mom and I would have a serious talk about child support and visitation."

"How do you know?" Luke demanded.

"Because I've only been with one woman in my entire life, Luke. We were getting ready to ship out to Iraq twelve, almost thirteen years ago, not preparing to have a baby." Durango snapped his fingers. "Wait, that's it. What's your mom's name?"

Luke glared at him. "If you're not my father, why do you care?"

"Because I'll bet you're my nephew, not my son." Durango rested his hands on the desk, leaned forward, willing the boy to believe and trust him. "Did your mom ever tell you his name?"

"She said everyone called him crazy, but not her."

"Not crazy," Durango said in measured tones. "Wacko."

"Wacko. Crazy. What does it matter? They both mean nuts."

"If he makes it home, I'll let you tell him that." Durango grinned. "My brother's name is Waco. When he was in high school, he was the star quarterback and everybody on the football team called him Wacko Hawke."

Luke's eyes widened with sudden hope. "Then where is he?"

"He's an Army Ranger. His patrol was wiped out in South America during a covert operation."

"He's dead, isn't he?"

"I hope not." Durango thought about what Jeff had told him a few days ago, and the information relayed to his cousin Bendigo, at Nighthawke

277

Security. Uncle Quentin was trying to arrange to pay a ransom, but heaven knew what would work or when or if anything they did would be in time.

"Two years ago, the sergeant leading the patrol escaped and made it back to the States. People have been looking for your dad ever since. Now, what's your mom's name?"

"No way. She'll freak. I'm supposed to be staying with my aunt, but I split when she decided to send me to stay with my grandparents. He pounds on me whenever he's pissed, and he's always pissed."

"Where is your mom?"

"She's in Hawaii on assignment. She'll be back in three days."

"What's her name?" Durango repeated, and waited for the answer.

"Tiffany Roberts."

"One of Eli's daughters? Well, that confirms it." Durango contemplated telling the boy the truth. Waco hadn't loved the girl. He used her. *No, not my business. If Waco comes home, he'll have to establish some sort of relationship with his son. And if he does his typical slide-step routine, I'll take care of the kid and his mom.*

"Waco and your mom dated off and on for years, but he had a lot of girlfriends. He wasn't nice, Luke."

"I know. Mom said he could be a dirtbag, but he always kept her safe from her dad, my grandfather and from that guy who was in here. I recognized him. I've seen him on TV."

Durango nodded. He never had liked his father's campaign manager and factotum, Eli Roberts. It wasn't a surprise the guy abused his own daughters and grandchildren. "We still have a problem, Luke. That guy is your other grandfather. He thinks Waco walked on water and if he discovers the truth, both my parents will try to take you away from your mom."

"No!" Luke leaped to his feet. "I only wanted to meet you because Mom claims you're my dad. I don't want to live with him. My mom is the best."

"That's what I thought. No worries." Durango waved to the chair. "Sit down, son. We'll lie to Tex and Estelle Hawke."

"You'll do that?"

"Definitely. You heard what he said about my daughters, and they've just turned four. If I won't let him near them, I certainly won't let him near you."

The door opened and Jeff limped inside. Durango met the other man's gaze. "Thanks for calling. Close the door."

When Jeff did, Durango gestured to a chair. "This is Luke Roberts. He came to visit because he thought he was my son. As far as my folks go, we let them believe it. Actually, he's my nephew."

Jeff leaned back, studying Luke. "Waco's or Laredo's boy?"

"Waco's. Do you want to tell Amarillo? If my parents discover the truth, they'll push for custody. They won't back off like they did with Maria when you threatened them with a restraining order."

"Not a threat. That comes later. More people who know a secret, less likely it is to remain one. Besides, if Rilla thinks you're the kind of guy who'd cheat on his wife, she might think better of me." Jeff winked at Luke. "After hearing how Durango saved my life during the war, my wife decided he's better than Superman."

"First I've heard of it." Durango laughed. "Usually, she chews me out for how I spend money. Will you try and reach Luke's mom and let her know he's staying with us until she's home? His aunt was going to turn him over to Eli Roberts and I wouldn't let that man near a dog."

"I included him in the restraining order so Luke will be safe with us in Lake Maynard." Jeff rose to his feet. "Come on, son. We'll go find some lunch in the cafeteria. I'll call your mom and make sure you can come home with Rilla and me."

"If she refuses, then ask if he can stay with Heather and me."

"Will that be a problem?"

"Not once she hears the name of Luke's mom." Durango ran a hand through his hair. "Of course, considering Heather's opinion of Waco, she'll decide he's lower than pond scum."

"Won't she be happier because I agree with her?" Luke asked.

Durango shook his head. "Not when I disagree with both of you. It takes a lot of guts to make it through Army Ranger training and I'm sure Waco is redeemable."

"There you go." Jeff crossed to the door and held it for Luke. "We'll send in your dad when we see him."

"Thanks." Durango stood. "Luke, where does your mom work?"

"At Coastal News in Olympia near the Washington State courthouse."

"Great. We'll find her." In the reception area, Durango headed for the secretary's desk. He could almost feel the young woman's disillusionment. It'd be better if her crush on him ended because he was unworthy and he didn't trust anyone but Heather and Jeff with the truth about Luke.

Jeff glanced at the tall boy walking beside him, gratified to have the mystery cleared up with such a simple explanation. Durango had his faults, but betraying *La Capitana* with another woman wasn't one of them. Opening the door to the cafeteria, Jeff ushered Luke inside.

The room wasn't empty. Three women sat at one table and he recognized them as part of Amarillo's accounting team. It must be afternoon break time. Jeff's gaze narrowed on her. She sat with her father at a smaller table, not far from her co-workers.

"Go tell the cooks what you'd like, Luke. I'll send Durango's father upstairs and meet you at the cashier."

Without waiting for an answer, he limped quickly across the room, barely using his cane for support. He wasn't sure whether he imagined a grateful expression in his wife's eyes or if he just wanted to see it. "Mr. Hawke, Durango is ready to see you now."

"What did he do with his bastard son?" Tex asked.

Jeff rested a hand on Amarillo's shoulder. "I brought the boy down here to eat while we locate his mother."

"I don't believe it. Durango would never cheat on Heather." Amarillo turned a fierce, dark glare on her father, then on Jeff. "How can you say such a thing?"

"Luke and Durango both tell the same story." Jeff tightened his grip, squeezing gently in a warning. "I think we'd better respect them."

A sneer twisted Amarillo's mouth as she focused on Tex again. "Considering the fact that you've never respected anyone, it's too late for you to start now."

Rage simmered in his silver-gray eyes. "I'm not the one who refused to join her family on a holiday and lied to a lawyer to get a restraining order."

"No lies," Amarillo shot back. "You're not using my daughter like you used me to gain political allies or favors. We're done with you."

Tex rose to his feet, his anger turning on Jeff. "You're not welcome at our house anymore."

"I only came to protect Rilla and Maria from you and your hangers-on. I'm a bigger S.O.B. than Durango ever thought of being. Stay away from my wife and daughter or I'll send copies of that restraining order to the press."

"She isn't your daughter yet," Tex snarled.

"She will be as soon as the adoption goes through and the Petrocelli lawyers promised to expedite the legalities," Jeff said. "They don't like child molesters either and your high-powered friends won't be able to protect you forever."

After her father stormed from the room, Amarillo turned in her seat to check out the boy at the counter. "Durango only dated when Art insisted Heather couldn't go out with him before her sixteenth birthday. There's no way my brother would have gotten another woman pregnant, regardless of what he says. He's protecting someone."

"All I know is what he told me," Jeff repeated. It might be stupid, but Durango would always be a hero to him.

Amarillo switched to rapid Italian, the language they always used for confidentiality. "Don't lie to me. That's Waco's boy, isn't it? And Durango's covering for him, isn't he?"

"He could be Laredo's."

"No way." Amarillo laughed. "Years of drinking and drugs make him look older than he is, but Laredo is only twenty-three. How old is that boy?"

"Almost twelve." Jeff headed to the cashier to pay for the boy's meal.

When they joined Amarillo at her table, she smiled at Luke. "I'm your Aunt Rilla and you already met my husband, Jeff. And your Uncle Durango, obviously."

Luke almost dropped the tray holding his burger, fries, soda, and a large slab of apple pie. "How did you know? Durango says he's my father."

"He's lying." Amarillo sipped her coffee. "You've got your father's eyes, hair, build, and facial features. Who is your mom?"

Luke carefully placed the tray of food on the table. "Tiffany Roberts."

"I've seen her reporting the news on TV. She's fantastic. I'd think she'd have more sense than to be with Waco even as a girl."

Pulling out a chair, Luke sat down and smiled at her with sudden charm. "She never says a nasty word about my dad. She called him Wacko Hawke and I came here because it was Hawke Construction, and I figured my dad owned it, especially since Uncle Durango's name is on my birth certificate."

---

Durango worked his way through a stack of correspondence by the time the office door opened, and his father entered.

"This is the first time you've been here since you ran the place into bankruptcy seven years ago." Durango leaned back in his chair. "Why did you come now?"

"I have a lot to discuss with you." Tex sat down. "First, what do you plan to do about your mother and Heather?"

"Nothing." Durango signed another letter finalizing a construction bid. "They've never gotten along, and I'm siding with Heather. She makes the rules and as we said in combat, I have her six. In civilian terms, that means I've got her back and nobody hurts her."

"How long will you two be together? She'll lose it when she hears about your son. She's always been unstable."

"Keep insulting my wife and I'll forget what Uncle Quentin taught me about not being a bully. I won't mind kicking the crap out of you when I remember how many times you beat me when I was a kid."

Tex straightened in his chair. "That's another thing. Who told you about the ransom demands? Which of my people came to see you?"

"That's for me to know." Durango lowered the pen and slowly swept a gaze over his father's face, noticing the muscle twitching in his jaw. "It is true, isn't it? They demanded money. You left my brother to rot, didn't you?"

"I'm not supporting extortion. We don't pay off terrorists. It's the principle of the thing."

"Even if it's your son?" His stomach knotted at the idea. "What kind of man are you?"

"I won't be threatened." Tex stood, rested his hands on the desk. "You had no business going to Quentin. He raised holy hell with me."

"Good for him." Durango rose, towering over the shorter man. "He's always been there for me and I knew I could rely on him to come through for Waco. None of your other kids ever could count on you. But I thought at least you loved him."

"I do, but I'm not giving up my honor for him."

"*Honor?* You don't have a clue what that means. Uncle Quentin does. He listens to whatever I need or want."

"He should. He's your sire."

"What?" Durango reeled, feeling the knowledge slice into his gut like a knife. "Quentin Hawke is my father?"

"I'm your legal father, you ungrateful monster, but Quentin sired you. It's why he wanted to raise you when he found out the truth. Victoria insisted on you coming to live with them when you were six. They agreed to let you visit us during the summer, but they refused to allow you to live with us full-time. Quentin said we weren't good enough to have you."

The words slowly sank into Durango's brain. He had a father, a real one who loved him, and a fabulous stepmother. They hadn't shared the facts with him. Confidentiality must have been part of the deal made with Tex and Estelle. *How much did Quentin pay to have me? There's no way Tex gave me up for free.*

"Jesus, it probably cut my real folks to the quick when I insisted on returning to Washington state after I graduated from high school and going to college here. I wasted damn near twenty years trying to get you and Estelle to love me. No wonder Heather calls me a jackass."

# CHAPTER THIRTY-TWO

Alone in his office, Durango removed the sealed bottle of Canadian whisky from the bottom desk drawer and opened it. The alcohol burned a path to his stomach. He took another swallow. If he had the guts, he'd call his aunt and uncle, tell them the truth he'd just learned. How could he? Quentin and Vicky always welcomed him, loved him, but they hadn't shared what they knew.

Durango thought of the big, gentle man who constantly hugged him and the other five boys who ran amok in the house. Quentin lectured and assigned extra chores for misbehavior. He never struck any of them. His strong moral code kept him from even raising his voice around the boys or Aunt Vicky. Unaccustomed tears burned the back of Durango's eyes. He lifted the bottle of whisky to his lips, letting the booze provide the comfort he desperately craved.

He was still drinking when he drove through the creek and up to the house hours later. He saw lights in the living room and decided he wasn't spending another night alone in the bunkhouse. She was his wife, damn it. She belonged to him and by God, tonight he'd show her that. He stalked in the front door, slamming it behind him, and stormed into the living room.

She sat in the rocking chair, complete with the cat and two of the kittens. The rest slept in the recliner. Heather didn't speak, just watched him with the cool green gaze that haunted his dreams and nightmares.

He strode across the room to stand in front of her, blocking the view of the flatscreen TV. "I need a woman tonight."

"Then go back to the bar and find her."

He glared down at her, spacing his words carefully. "I don't care what my father, I mean Tex Hawke, says. I never cheated on you. I went out with other girls because Art refused to let you date before your sixteenth birthday, but I never even kissed them. Or anything else."

"Only because you didn't want me to throw a fit and rip you into little tiny pieces." She eased Cop-Car off her lap and let the cat have the rocker. Heather stood, took the whisky bottle, and put it on the end table. She wrapped her arms around him. "What's wrong, lover? You only drink when you're wounded."

"It's not physical tonight." He clutched her close. "Nobody shot or stabbed me."

She drew his head to her breast and stroked his hair. "Oh, babe. Don't you know yet that emotional and mental anguish hurt more than physical pain?"

He buried his face in her shirt, feeling as if he were the same age as the twins, and his shoulders shook with barely suppressed sobs. "He hurt me."

"I'm sorry, lover. I'm sorry. Who did? Who do you want me to kill?"

"It's not your fault."

"I still don't want you hurting." She guided him to the couch and drew him down beside her. "I've got you, babe. Tell me about it later."

---

Crap, Waco thought, eyeing the two of them. Someone had kicked his big bro in the balls, and he wished he knew who. Durango was a giant of a man with no back-up. Hard-charging, stubborn, and proud, with a sense of honor that commanded respect. Hell, even when Waco pitied him for being such a stickler to his moral code, he always admired the man. *Yeah, you comfort him, Heather. He adores you even if he won't share it yet. He will someday. Meantime, I'm planning how to get home. Don't worry about me anymore.*

---

"What time is it?"

"0200 hours, two in the morning, civilian time." Heather stroked his tawny gold hair. "You've been asleep three hours. Are you ready to talk? What happened, babe?"

"A lot." He brought her down to lie next to him. "First, I met Waco's son. Then Tex freaked because he learned the Hawke family is bringing home Waco. Tex tried to say he didn't pay the ransom—"

"Because he's a cheap, money-grubbing bastard—"

"No, because it's apparently against his principles to pay for a prisoner, even his son."

"I'm going with my opinion. I really don't like him." Heather propped her elbows on Durango's chest, rested her chin on her folded hands, and stared deep into his eyes. "What else?"

"He's not my father. Uncle Quentin is."

"Awesome." She shifted to brush her lips across Durango's. "Did we get rid of Estelle too?"

"She's my mother. Be respectful."

"As the twins say, I don't wanna." Heather adjusted her position, rocking against him, and felt his response when he hardened, pressing into her. "Oh yeah, babe. Now, tell me we can dump that foul-mouthed bitch and replace her with Aunt Vicky. I love her."

Durango chuckled, feathered his thumb over her lips. "I should have known you'd be a happy camper. Do you want to take the twins and visit Texas before you're too far along?"

"Only if I can teach them to call Quentin 'Grandpa' and Vicky 'Grandma.' " Heather turned her head to kiss the side of his neck. "Between them and my folks, we'll have spoiled little princesses."

"Indubitably."

She shivered when he trailed a line of kisses to the hollow of her throat. "Later, babe. Tell me about Waco's kid. What's he like?"

"A charmer, but he's got a strong core of decency. Luke flat-out told me he wasn't interested in a share of Hawke Construction and his mom didn't need any money from me. I'll talk to her about it when she's home from her business trip. F.Y.I., she put my name on Luke's birth certificate and claimed I was his father. "

"Who is she?"

"Who do you think?"

"I have no idea. Waco won the football pool his junior and senior years in high school and he slept with a bunch of Ranger groupies after he enlisted."

"What was the pool?"

"The one the players started for the guy who got the most cheerleaders in the sack. Waco scored all the girls on the squad and half the junior varsity. Face facts. Your half-bro was a little scumbag. I don't know why you love him so much you're willing to die to bring him home."

"I don't."

"What?" Heather stared at Durango, studying his face, giving him a solid once-over. "I don't get it. I was sure you loved him. I always knew he meant more to you than I did."

"No, baby. Nobody has ever meant more to me than you do. I never even liked Waco. I looked after him because he's my brother. It's a habit."

"Are you sure?"

"Positive. You don't know how it felt to be passed over for your younger brother. I was six when Waco was born, and I stopped getting Christmas or birthday presents. My mother even quit buying me clothes. When we went shopping because the reporters took pictures of me in outgrown raggedy shirts and pants, we went to thrift stores. She said no point in buying new for a 'bigger is dumber' boy who'd outgrow them in a couple weeks."

"What a charmer. I didn't know."

"How could you, baby? You were barely two years old. It lasted six or seven months. When I was sent to live in Texas with Uncle Quentin and Aunt Vicky, I thought it was temporary. I didn't have so much as a suitcase or backpack. Estelle and Tex told me I was going for a short visit."

She saw pain etched on his features, and Heather wound her arms around his neck. "Why haven't you shared any of this before? Didn't you think I'd understand?"

"We haven't talked a lot since you came home, and I only found out what he tried to do to you a couple of weeks ago. How could I possibly love Waco when he assaulted the woman, I love more than life itself?"

"Whoa, jarhead." She gaped at him, measuring his sincerity. "Hold up there. You love me?"

"I've always loved you since the day Liz brought you home to me. You were their baby, but you were mine too. Didn't you ever figure out that's why I call you 'baby'?"

Her lips trembled into a smile and she blinked hard to keep from crying. "You were a four-year-old little perv, weren't you? Why haven't you said it before?"

"Because love and abuse went together in Tex and Estelle's house. Whenever they punished me, they said they loved me. I've never felt that way about you. I never wanted to hurt you and I didn't want anyone else to either. Hearing you say what Waco did was a turning point for me. I may have a hard time admitting or even acknowledging that he's like them."

"It's okay." She hid her face against Durango's broad shoulder. "I should have told you when it happened, but I was too embarrassed, especially after Mom said it was my fault for trying to help him."

"Oh no, baby." Durango covered the back of her head with his hand. "It wasn't. Never own that. Blind spots. Everybody has them. I sure have one where Waco's concerned. I hate him and because I hate him so much, I have to make sure he comes home."

"I don't understand." She pressed her ear to Durango's chest and listened to the comforting beat of his heart. "Why you, lover? Why can't we just leave him to Nighthawke Security and their teams?"

"I've got to be able to live with myself. How can I leave my brother in hell? I'm willing to risk my life for strangers like Jeff and other men. If I'll do it for them, why not Waco? If I can't live with myself, how can I expect you to live with me?"

"Because I love you and I want you alive and home with me and our kids." She pressed against him, trying to hold him so tightly he'd never feel rejected again. "Believe me, I can live with you if you never go back again. Trust me."

He rested his chin on her hair. "Knowing how I feel about him and the strong evidence we have that he's still alive, I have to be able to live with myself and my conscience. If I left him to rot there, I'd carry the guilt around for the rest of my life. I can't, baby."

She clutched him, longing to sink inside him. "I'm going to have a fit and fall in it if you leave me again. You know that, don't you?"

"I know." He kissed her forehead. "And I'll take you to bed and rock your world."

"Promises, promises." She sighed softly when he unsnapped the top buttons of her shirt. "What's the plan, Hawke?"

His thumbs teased her nipples, and she felt them tighten against her bra. "I know you have something in mind."

He kissed her ear. "Remember the last time we showered together?"

"Nearly a month ago, right after I got home."

"I thought it was forever ago." He sat up, pulling her across his lap. "There's a great big shower stall waiting for us. How about it?"

She giggled and looped her arms around his neck. "What are we waiting for? Take me to bed. I've already told you. I get horny when I'm pregnant."

It was natural to reach for her if only to prove to himself she was home where she belonged. He had to explore the empty side of the king-size bed several times before he realized she was gone. He switched on the lamp beside the bed. "Heather?"

A scrap of blanket caught his eye. He rolled over to her side of the bed and saw her sleeping on the carpet. "What are you doing? Why are you on the floor?"

"People die in bed, Durango." She yawned, not opening her eyes, and pulled the blanket closer. "I heard rockets."

"Fireworks, baby. They've been going off for the past ten days. They'll stop soon." Of course, they'd also start up with the various summer festivals and local fairs, but he wouldn't mention that. "Baby, we're not being shelled. Come back to bed."

A long silence before she asked. "Are you sure it's fireworks?"

"Yes, baby. I'm positive. Come here."

A few moments later, she joined him. She stretched out beside him, her body tense. "I keep having nightmares, Durango. I see and smell the blood, feel it on my hands, hear the wounded screaming. I'm going downstairs and watch TV."

"No, baby." He wrapped his arms around her and pulled her next to him. "I'm here. I'll take care of you. Hush, baby. Let's try to sleep."

At least she listened to him. She remained on the bed next to him and he held her tight, murmuring reassurances. "It's okay, baby."

He dropped butterfly kisses on her hair, her forehead, her lashes, her cheek, her jaw. "I'm here. I'll always be here, baby."

When she woke, the bed felt empty. Opening her eyes, she looked at the radio clock. 0900. No wonder he was gone. It seemed strange to be awake at this hour. When was the last time she'd gone to bed in the middle of the night? Only when she slept with him, she thought. Normally, she'd stay up and sleep at dawn. It made working graveyard shifts an easy choice.

Where was he? What did he think now? He'd been in so much pain last night that she couldn't send him away. Would he expect her to fall into his arms every night? *So, not happening, jarhead, not until you're home for the duration!* She tossed the blankets to one side and eased out of bed. When she stood up, her stomach didn't revolt. She remembered reading somewhere that if she suffered through morning sickness, she'd be less likely to miscarry.

She hoped the scientific study proved true. Losing a baby was pure hell. She walked cautiously toward the bathroom. A hot shower would wake her up totally and give her time to consider her marriage to a certain arrogant former Marine. Gathering her robe from the foot of the bed, she left the main suite.

She'd use the bathroom down the hall, not the one in the en-suite, the site of her downfall. Only a hard-hearted shrew would have refused to comfort the man she loved, and she wasn't that, even if his insistence on finding that scumbag Waco continued to piss her off. She'd keep her distance until Durango 'walked the talk', he gave her last night and was honestly home for good.

She checked the twins on the way. Both girls still slept. Heather covered Galveston with her blankie, picked up Henry, the stuffed toy pony, off the floor, and tucked him in with Dallas. Let them wake up on their own. They'd be much more cheerful, and the past few days had been hectic ones.

They played non-stop with the puppies, rode Cinnamon and Satan every day, and barely demanded to watch cartoons. They'd save those for rainy days, Heather thought. For now, she preferred they run around like real kids, the way she had when she was a child.

After a shower, she dressed in jeans, a T-shirt, heavy socks, and lace-up riding boots since she intended to visit Fenn today. How could she continue keeping his presence a secret from Durango? Jeff had said Waco was still alive. It should have surprised her that he saw the "nearly" dead, but somehow it didn't. Granted, she'd grown up in Baker City, where they lived side by side with the departed. It made it even stranger that there wasn't a trace of Aunt Lucy.

Fenn made it home. If he survived, so could Waco. Much as Heather hated him, she'd never leave him to die after years of torture and imprisonment.

Downstairs, she found Kate in the kitchen. "What's going on?"

"Not much. Durango went into Hawke Construction for a few hours and then he's going to the grocery. He said he didn't make it yesterday."

"No, he had to deal with Tex." Heather turned on the teakettle. "After that visit at his office, Durango was hurting, and I didn't have the heart to send him to the bunkhouse."

"Well, don't expect me to chew you out for not sticking to your rules, Ice Queen." Kate poured another cup of coffee. "I'm the one who let Ben in the window of my room."

"You're on the third floor." Heather stared at her friend. "I knew you visited him a lot at his place, but I didn't realize how serious the two of you were getting. How'd he get up there?"

"He climbed up the ladder from the balcony. And when I asked what ladder, he showed me these little blocks of wood nailed to the house."

"Wow, I never knew those were there." Heather opened a canister and fished out a peppermint teabag. "Good thing, or I'd have had Durango in the apartment back in the day and Grandpa would have kicked both our teenage horny butts. I've got to check out those."

"Me too. It's bound to look more secure in the daylight."

"Don't count on it." While her tea brewed, Heather headed for the phone. "I'm calling Quentin and Vicky. Tex told Durango that Quentin is his father and that makes Vicky his stepmom, so I've got to give them a heads-up about my expectations for grandparents."

"Wow." Kate's eyes widened. "What else did I miss 'cause I went to bed early?"

"That's about it. Durango's got some adjusting to do, but like he says, I'm a happy camper because I never liked Tex or Estelle."

"Yeah, but you didn't ask the question I would have."

"What's that?"

"If she slutted around on him once, who did the rest of Tex's light work?"

Heather hung up the receiver before the call went through, gaping at her best friend in total admiration. "You bitch! I never thought of that. You're absolutely right. No way he has four natural kids. How are we going to find out who did the deeds for him?"

"Next question. Why would he want his wife sleeping with other guys? Most men would throw a raging fit."

"Why wouldn't he send her to do it first?" Heather removed the teabag, wringing it into the cup before sipping the hot tea. "When Amarillo begged me to help her get away five years ago, she told me Tex pimped her out to various scumbags whenever he wanted political favors. She didn't know which one fathered her daughter, but she didn't want Maria to suffer the same fate."

"Jeff is a smart guy. He'll go on a rampage to protect her and Maria."

"I don't blame him, but he always quotes that line about revenge being best when it's cold. He told me he has plans for Tex and Eli, but we're not sharing that outside of this room. " Heather headed for the phone again. "Okay, so I'm calling Vicky first. I'll bet she knows who Estelle slept with when she was in Texas. And now that I'm Vicky's daughter-in-law, I'm hunting dirt."

Kate blinked, obviously confused. "But Estelle is Durango's mother."

"I know, but we don't like her, so I've disowned her. I'm claiming Vicky as my kids' paternal grandma."

"Can you do that?"

"I'm the momma here and I make the rules."

"Good to know!"

# CHAPTER THIRTY-THREE

As she was teaching the girls to ride that afternoon, Heather saw Fenn hiking down the ridge and coming toward her. The puppies promptly barked at him, then charged toward him. He smiled and bent to pet the duo. Heather waved at him. "What's going on?"

"I noticed Durango stockpiled rolls of fence wire over by the toolroom and I can use some. Will he miss it?"

"Nope. Jeff's bringing in a crew to rebuild the back boundary and I want him to replace the pasture fences too." She sauntered to the side of the corral and rested a boot on the bottom rail. "The keys to the construction rig are in the glove box or Kate has the ones to our four-by-four. When did you put those boards on the house, and why?"

"I didn't. Art did." Fenn laughed. "What? Did you and Durango think you invented messing around? Your dad used to hit the party scene when he was a teenager and he had to sneak out, so your grandpa didn't know. Poor Lucy and I slept on the second floor near their room because he was sure Art always behaved himself and we didn't say otherwise."

"Hard to believe Dad partied." Heather shook her head. "I never knew that. No wonder Durango says people have blind spots like horses."

"He always was the smart one in his family."

"I don't know." She glanced swiftly over her shoulder to check on the twins. They were carefully keeping space between the horses, and Heather turned back to her uncle. "Yesterday, Tex shared that Quentin is actually

Durango's bio-dad, so we're cutting Tex and Estelle out of our family herd."

Fenn whistled softly. "No loss, Rusty. Try not to do too much of a happy dance when your folks are here. They did a lot for Durango's sibs back in the day but didn't realize how much abuse those kids suffered."

"Thanks for the heads-up. I'll be careful."

Fenn and Kate had barely left the yard in the dark blue construction pickup when Heather spotted Durango's rig at the beach. She waited until he parked his classic truck in the yard before she called a halt to the lesson and helped the girls dismount. They left the old horses to graze. Then she and the twins went to meet him, followed by the two heeler pups. The back of the Chevy held assorted sizes of peeled logs.

Heather gestured to them. "What's this, Hawke?"

"A log playground. I found it at that big hardware store in Lake Maynard." Durango propped one boot on the bumper. "It has a swing set, a slide, a fort, a bridge, and a bunch of other stuff."

"It's for us." Dallas stared at him, awestruck. "When can we play on it, Daddy?"

"Let me build it first."

"When?" Galveston asked. "When are you building it, Daddy?"

"Today and tomorrow after work. On Saturday until it's done. If you ladies put away the horses, I'll let you help."

"We'll be right back." Dallas tugged on Heather's hand. "Come on, Mommy."

Heather smiled at him. "Oh, so I get to help too?"

"A little bit. I'll do the heavy lifting and you can't say any bad words."

"You've got a deal." She hurried toward the corral with the twins darting alongside.

"I like it better here than anywheres we've lived," Galveston said, utter satisfaction in her tone. "We've gots puppies and kitties and our own horsies—"

"Satan's mine," Heather protested.

"You gots to learn to share like you always tell us, Mommy," Dallas told her. "We'll let you play on our swings and slide. Toney, I bet our daddy can push us way high."

"Yeah," Galveston agreed.

When Dray arrived with the Murphy girls, the teens jumped in to help with the elaborate log playground. However, in a couple of hours, it was time for the twins' nap. When Heather came downstairs, she found Chantrea filling glasses with ice-cold lemonade.

Naveah passed Heather one. "Is now a good time for another piano lesson?"

"What about the playground? We have holes to dig and posts to set."

"Yeah, well Durango suggested we let him and Dray do that while I have my lesson and Chantrea does barn duty."

Heather sighed, then sipped the tart, refreshing drink. "Why do I think he's got more on his mind?"

"Because you're smart." Chantrea carried two glasses toward the back door. "Sully always freaks when Tate does his Dr. Internet thing. He's researched for months and tells her what she can and can't do because she's pregnant. Mom rats her out if she thinks Sully is doing too much and Tate hightails it here from the Army base."

"Now, Sully says it's kind of cute," Naveah went on, "but when they were first married, she used to yell at him a lot. It didn't do any good."

"I understand perfectly. You can get them out of uniform, but they still act like soldiers." Heather led the way to the living room and closed the door so the music wouldn't disturb the twins. "Okay, what song first?"

Neveah lifted the top of the piano bench. "When you go shopping, you've got to get some newer sheet music. All this stuff is at least twenty years old."

"Older than that." Heather watched the girl sort through the music. "My aunt taught me to play, and she was the last one to pick up her favorite country songbooks. She disappeared twenty-seven years ago. Which song?"

"This one by Deborah Allen." Naveah held up a folder. "What's a signature song, Heather?"

"Some singers have songs that made them famous. For Helen Reddy, it was *I Am Woman*. For Lynn Anderson, it was *I Never Promised You a Rose Garden*. And for Deborah Allen, it's *Baby, I Lied*."

"Wow, that's awesome." Naveah closed the bench and sat on it. "I told Mom I liked the music we played here better than the classical stuff I learned at my other lessons or the hymns I play at church. She was good with it."

Heather nodded. "I need to talk to Bronwyn about hiring Chantrea to help me when I start training horses."

"No, you don't. One of Bronwyn's nephews was killed by a pony and she freaks whenever Chantrea brings up riding. Dad signed the waiver

Durango gave him, and we don't mention horses when we're home." Naveah turned a dark gaze on Heather. "So, you ask about having her look after the twins and the new baby when you're working, and Mom will go with that. It's the same thing my older, foster sister, Quinn, does when her stepdaughter rides at Mindy MacGillicudy's place. Like Dad says, 'what the eye doesn't see, the heart doesn't grieve over.'"

"Or like Durango says, 'blind spots.' Horses aren't the only ones who have them." She scanned the African-American girl, hair in beaded cornrows, wearing a tank top, ragged denim shorts, and battered tennies. She must be a lot cooler than Heather felt in her jeans and T-shirt. "Okay, let's get started."

That evening, she leaned back in the rocker and contemplated turning on the flatscreen. A sudden wave of exhaustion swept over her and she closed her eyes for a moment.

"How's your back?" Durango came into the room. "Sore? Do you want one of my famous back rubs?"

"No way." She opened her eyes. "Those always excite me, and I'm not interested in sex."

"Liar." He crossed the room and rested his hands on the arms of her chair. "Prove it, Empress. If you weren't interested, I never could have gotten you in bed last night."

"I only slept with you because—"

"Come on, baby. Make it good. Tell me you felt sorry for me because of Tex's behavior yesterday."

"Sorry for you?" She stiffened when she saw the taunting smirk. "Don't make me laugh."

He traced a line down her cheek. "Watch your mouth, or I'll see how long it takes to make you beg for me." He straightened, drew her out of the rocker. "Like it or not, you're getting a back rub. I can't stand seeing that much pain on your face."

She hesitated, then let him guide her to the couch. "I'm not sleeping with you tonight."

"Fine. Take off your shirt while I get the liniment."

She stared after him when he left the room. Did he think he'd change her mind? Not happening, she told herself firmly. She removed her blouse, then laid down on the couch on her stomach. "You're not using the stinky peppermint horse stuff, are you? I hate it."

"Too bad, too sad. It works better than the crap they make for people." He popped the top on it. "Your virtue is safe. At least for tonight."

"Promises, promises."

She gasped when the icy liquid hit her skin. It seemed to heat almost instantly when he stroked her back. The movement eased into a light, kneading motion that loosened the ache in her muscles. She moaned softly, sighed, and began taking deeper breaths. He always knew exactly what she needed.

---

During the next half hour, Durango worked his way to her shoulders, along her ribs toward her spine. She'd totally relaxed under his touch. He unhooked her bra, pushing the straps aside so he could reach beneath them. She didn't protest. The remaining tension eased from her body.

"Did you change your mind? Are we going to bed together or are you sending me out to the bunkhouse?"

No answer.

He looked to see why. She was sound asleep. So much for his great romancing ability. He took time to put away the liniment in the vet supply cupboard and wash his hands. She hadn't awakened when he returned. He gathered her into his arms and headed for the staircase, turning off the lights on the way. They'd have one more night together before she sent him off to limbo or the bunkhouse by himself.

---

On Friday afternoon, Heather left Kate with the twins while Durango and Dray worked on the new log playset. She headed for the hills on Satan. Fenn would either be at the cabin or on the new fence for one of the pastures, and she'd find him. She'd awakened in Durango's arms this morning and she wasn't ready to share a bed with him again.

When Fenn wasn't at the cabin, she rode on through the woods. Peace seeped into her soul. Pine-scented air filled her nostrils. She was home on McElroy land and she was safe.

She spotted him digging a posthole and sang out his name so she wouldn't surprise him.

"Thought I told you to stop riding." He stopped work, turned to face her. "You're being stupid and reckless, Rusty."

"Stuff it." Heather swung out of the saddle. "I'm being careful, and so is Satan." She unwrapped the lead-line from around the horn and tied the old gelding to a tree where he could graze, lingering to remove the bridle. "If I weren't, I'd ride Flash. He's a lot peppier and more fun."

"What does Durango think about you being on a horse? He's got to have more sense than you do."

"He irritates me, Fenn."

"What else is new, Rusty? You've been complaining about him for as long as I can remember. If he ignores you, then you chase after him until you have his undivided attention."

"I thought if I married him, he'd stay home with me." Heather walked over to the fence line and sat on a convenient stump to watch Fenn finish digging the hole. "When he took me to the airport after the wedding, he told me he was going on an assignment for Nighthawke. I told him if he didn't come to Tennessee, I was done."

"You know full well ultimatums don't work with him. Why are you here, not in Tennessee?"

"Because I inherited this place—" She stopped, narrowing her gaze. "Under false pretenses. Grandpa wanted you to have it. I was the contingency."

"It's big enough for two of us McElroys. Even when you're being pigheaded. We both know you came back to Durango, 'cause storming out on him in one of your foot-stomping, snot-slinging hissy fits didn't work. I could have told you it wouldn't."

"Yeah, well, if you'd been here, maybe he wouldn't be such a noble jackass. Did you ever think of that?"

"Nope. If he weren't a noble jackass, you wouldn't be in love with him. And you wouldn't have been such a nuisance to Tex and Estelle. He never had any value to them, especially since they couldn't touch his inheritance. You put him on a pedestal to worship. Of course, he does the same with you. No wonder the two of you irritate them so much just by breathing."

She shook her head, refusing to admit how touched she was by his assessment. "Is it why Tex told Durango the truth, that he's Quentin's son? When did you find out?"

"Probably. And Kate told me last night that Quentin and Vicky are thrilled you want them in your kids' lives, that they get to be their grandparents."

"Well, they deserve the honor after raising Durango. They'll spoil the girls rotten."

"They aren't the only ones. Laredo already gave them puppies. Brazos will take them to malls and buy them whatever they want. Kate says

Amarillo has already started helping our cousin Ann make clothes for them. When you came home, Tex didn't lose one son. He lost all four of his kids and when they inherit the Hawke money, he won't get a cent because they won't share a penny with him or his sleazeball friends."

"I didn't take them away. He lost them when he favored Waco over them."

"And Waco wasn't a decent person. He always figured he could do no wrong. When his brothers and sisters got any positive attention, Waco made trouble. He tried to break up you and Durango any chance he had. He was bounced off a couple of Ranger teams before he landed on mine."

"You straightened him out, didn't you?"

"Had to." Fenn finished digging, picked up the split cedar post, and put it in the hole. "Wasn't going into combat with someone who'd get all of us killed."

Heather nodded, stood, and held the post while Fenn dumped in dirt and rocks, then tamped the soil. More dirt and rocks, more tamping. "You kicked the crap out of him, didn't you?"

"Had to." Fenn tried shifting the post, satisfied when it didn't move. "Boy lied more than a politician. He needed to learn Rangers don't lie to each other. We hold to our code."

"And Waco learned?"

"He's not stupid, Rusty. He wanted to be an Army Ranger, and he made it through the training, was a top student, but he didn't take some of the teachings seriously. It took four trips to the latrine, but he learned better." Fenn moved up the fence line and started digging the next posthole. "When we were captured in Colombia, it wasn't his fault. We looked out for each other."

"That makes sense." She glanced at Satan. The old bay contentedly munched on the knee-high grass. "I should forgive him. He enlisted when he was eighteen and he'd be thirty-two now. He's changed. I know I'm not the same girl I was in high school."

"We all grow up, some faster than others." Fenn dumped the dirt out of the digger, then shoved it back into the hole. "Don't ever leave your kids with Tex or Eli Roberts. Doesn't matter if it's girls or boys, Rusty."

Heather gasped. "How did you know?"

"Waco told me. Right before he enlisted, he walked in on his dad messing with Brazos. Tex swore it was a one-time thing, but Waco threatened to kill him if it happened again."

"Are you going to do it for Waco? They raped Amarillo and even gave her to their disgusting friends back in Washington D.C. Durango and I discovered she was pregnant when we got home from Iraq, right after you and Waco were captured. She was thirteen."

"You tell Durango what they did?" Fenn kept digging. "Never mind, Rusty. If you had, they'd be dead, and he'd be in prison."

"All I could do was get her out of there and emancipated when she was fifteen, so it didn't happen to her baby." Heather heaved a sigh as she watched him work. "It's why Brazos ran interference on the Fourth of July and helped me get the twins away."

"Right. Waco suspected it wasn't over. He said he wasn't giving his dad a dime of Hawke money."

"Oh, my Lord! I'll bet that's why Tex won't pay the ransom. He probably intends to inherit Waco's Army insurance and the Hawke oil money."

"Won't do him any good," Fenn said. "You had to make arrangements to settle your affairs when you shipped out, and so did we. Waco told me he left everything to a bunch of charities to make amends for what his old man did and appointed Tiffy Roberts as his executor."

"She's tough. She'll do what he wants." Heather hesitated, then decided to wait before she mentioned Waco had a son with the younger woman. "Was he in love with her?"

"Not that he ever said. He felt guilty because he didn't realize earlier what was going on with her. They used her like they did his sisters, and he took advantage of her when she asked for help. He made them promise to leave her alone because he was sleeping with her and didn't want to share."

"I see." Heather waited while he finished the hole, then stood and helped set the next post. When he moved farther up the line, she did too. "Fenn, how did you get home? The last Dad heard was the Army had no clue how to find you and we should declare you dead after seven years."

"I escaped. I came home."

"Have any help?"

He scanned her with a sharp green gaze. "Wouldn't tell you if I did."

"Is blood still thicker than water?" At his nod, she continued. "Durango goes to Colombia to look for the cartel's prisoners. It's why I left him."

"Dangerous job."

"He did it two years before I walked out, and he did more missions with Nighthawke Security while I was gone."

"He's still going, isn't he?" Fenn stopped digging and met her gaze. "I never knew you to run short in the guts department, Rusty."

"He's done enough, damn it!" Tears stung at the criticism. "So have I."

"No, Rusty. It's not enough until we all come home."

"I don't want to lose him." Tears slid down her cheeks. "I want him to stay home with me and help raise his kids."

Fenn put the posthole digger aside, coming to her. He drew her into a warm embrace. "Rusty, oh Rusty, girl. Don't you get it? Nobody but Durango and Nighthawke's teams are doing anything to get us home. You've got to be strong for him. You're providing system support and that's damn tough."

"Quentin said he wouldn't send him." She struggled to control the tears, not let the sobs control her body. "Durango wants to go. He won't stay behind, will he?"

"You know the truth better than anyone, Rusty. He can't."

# CHAPTER THIRTY-FOUR

That evening while she loaded the dishwasher, she wondered again how Fenn made it home. He hadn't admitted that Durango or Nighthawke Security rescued him, but she wouldn't be surprised. Did the Army know Fenn was here? She suspected he was AWOL. He'd been left to rot in one of the cartel's prisons, and bureaucrats didn't like people who didn't remain where the paperwork placed them.

She finished cleaning up the kitchen and went into the dining room. Durango sat at the long table, blueprints spread all over. As always, he'd closed the hallway door and had his back to the wall. "What happens when you find someone in Colombia? Do you turn them over to the U.S. Consulate? Do you bring them home? Do you call the military?"

"Not my job, Empress." Durango turned a cobalt blue gaze on her. "Why do you want to know?"

"I'm curious." She stood in the doorway, watching him. "Answer me. Who handles the details?"

"Uncle Quentin and Bendigo. Probably should say my dad and older brother. Jeff told me they checked him into a private hospital when he got to CONUS. Because he'd been tortured, he needed reconstructive surgery and dental implants. He gained weight. His hair grew out. He saw a therapist. He was debriefed by the Air Force before he went home."

"I heard a rumor the government wants those soldiers from covert missions dead."

"Same I've heard over the years. It's why Nighthawke takes care of it when we bring them back. They're okay, baby. Mostly, the government is interested in bones and skeletal remains. They can have them."

"Since they don't look for live soldiers, mercenaries like you do, and I'm sure Quentin—your dad—charges the government a fortune whenever he can."

"I do the job he hired me to do and I'm damned good at it."

"I don't want you to do it anymore." She glared at him, advanced into the room. "We have kids. You need to *daddy-up*."

He chuckled, pushed back the chair. He stood, closed the kitchen door behind her before he caught her hand and pulled her onto his lap when he sat down again. "Come lecture me some more, baby."

"I hate you." A tear slid down her cheek before she stopped it. She swiped it away. "Damn pregnancy hormones. I really do hate you."

"I know." He tipped up her chin. "I haven't had you in the dining room yet."

"You're not going to." She nipped at his thumb when he feathered it over her lips. "I'm serious, Hawke. Are you listening?"

"Be easier if you weren't wearing jeans, but I can make it work."

"You're such a horndog." She surrendered to his kiss. She hadn't come in the room for this, but why refuse when it was what both of them wanted? She wouldn't be missed. Kate was busy upstairs, bathing the twins and putting them to bed.

Heather moaned when he pushed up her T-shirt. It landed on the floor and he unfastened her bra. She threaded her fingers in the tawny-gold hair when he teased her nipples with gentle flicks of his tongue, squirming on his lap. His hardness pushed into her. "Please, Durango. Please."

He unzipped her jeans, opened them, sliding one big hand inside them to torment her, rubbing her panties against her. "Keep begging, Empress. You know I love it."

"You're supposed to be working."

"You're my favorite distraction. I can always work, but I can't always have you." He boosted her enough to push down her jeans, then her underwear before he helped her adjust her position, so she straddled him.

Turnabout was fair play, and she unbuttoned his fly. Before she could go further, one finger slipped inside her, followed by a second before his thumb found her. She managed to unbutton his shirt and kiss his neck. She moved with his hand as he began the pattern that always drove her crazy.

An hour later, she scrambled to find her clothes and dress. Western shirt still unbuttoned, exposing his amazing chest, he leaned back in the chair, lazily watching her. "I don't know why I bother trying to talk to you."

"Neither do I when you're so sexy." He eyed the pile of work in front of him. "After you're done pitching a fit, be a good girl and make me a pot of coffee. I'll be at this most of the night."

"Make it yourself." She pulled on her T-shirt, and stomped toward the hallway door, careful to stay out of reach. If he touched her again, they'd be screwing all over his damned work and her grandmother's antique oak table. Heather shook her head. "You haven't broken either arm."

Before she went to the living room to watch TV, she heard footsteps on the staircase and saw Kate descending them. "How are the girls?"

"Out like twin lightbulbs. The puppies are sacked out in their crate in the pantry. What's on the agenda for a wild and crazy Friday night when neither of us has duty at the hospital?"

Heather paused for reflection. The rule in the Army was always, *Don't get mad, get even.*

"We have a built-in daddy-sitter. Durango has a ton of paperwork and would enjoy peace and quiet to do it."

"Does he know that?"

"He will after we get cleaned up to go to Pop's Café. It's the closest to an officers' club around here."

"Works for me. Will you lend me something to wear? I don't want to go all the way upstairs to the attic apartment."

Heather eyed her best friend. "Ben there?"

"Not yet, but he'll probably arrive before much longer."

"Right. What's going on with you two?" Heather led the way into the guest room where she kept most of her clothes. "Want to share that news?"

"He thinks sleeping together means we'll get married and live happily ever after. I don't do long-term commitments."

"Really?" Heather opened the closet, removed her white dress jeans, a gold suede chamois shirt, and fancy ivory dress boots. "Then why rock his world?"

"Damned if I know." Kate scanned the contents of the closet. "Okay if I borrow your L.B.D.?"

"Sure." Heather took the black, long-sleeve knit mini dress off the hanger. She always looked super-sexy in it. The scoop neck, bodycon silhouette, and mini length totally drove Durango nuts in the best possible way. If he saw her wearing it to perform on stage, she barely made it in the front door when they returned home. "I have fishnet stockings and black pumps to go with it."

"Thanks, Heather."

On her way to the shower, she checked in on the twins. Galveston still had her blankie and Dallas had her stuffed toy pony. Smiling, Heather hurried to the en-suite, leaving the bathroom down the hall for Kate. The girls wouldn't miss her tonight.

They met in the guest room at the same time after their respective showers. Heather pulled on the gold top. "This may sound dumb, Kate. Are you doing what you did with Jeff? You slept with him, built up his ego, and gently sent him on his way when he thought he was another Casanova. He decided leaving you was his idea."

"So what? After what he'd been through, it was the least I could do, and it wasn't a hardship for me." Kate sat on the double bed, drawing on one of the thigh-high fishnet stockings. "I didn't love him."

"You didn't love any of the guys you dated in Tennessee after you split up with your ex."

"Didn't love him either, although I tried. You can go ahead and call me a slut. I heard it from the Army lifers in Iraq and later in Afghanistan. I never could disappoint a pilot, especially when so many of them were on one-way trips."

"What about the one you loved? What happened to him?"

"He died, Heather." Kate reached for the second stocking. "Ambushed. So I started dating a doctor. A *separated* one. Know what I mean?"

"Yeah. He was separated from his wife, all right. Until his unit went back to *The World*."

"He broke up with me the week before he left." Kate reached for the mini-dress. "From then on, I thought, *what the hell?* I didn't drink, and sex was just as good for putting me to sleep. A cheap ticket to oblivion."

"And my—" Heather paused, rephrased the question. "Ben? How do you feel about him?"

Kate unzipped the dress, pulled it over her head, and snugged it into place. "Go ahead and say he's your uncle. I already knew."

"How? He didn't tell you. He thinks the government will kill him if they learn he's home."

"Your hair, eye color, and bone structure." Kate slid her arms in the long sleeves. "His first name is close to your uncle's. Plus, his nickname for you, the way he orders you around. Of course, the way you act like he walks on water was another clue."

"I haven't told Durango that Fenn's living here." Heather stepped behind her friend to zip up the dress. "It looks better on you than it does on me."

"I've got another ten pounds to fill it out." Kate scanned Heather's figure. "And you'd better start putting on some weight, girl. You're eating for at least two."

"There's plenty of time. I'm only two and a half months along." Heather picked up the white jeans and slipped into them. Normally, the pants clung to every curve and she'd struggled to snap them in the past. Tonight, they fastened easily. "Damn, I hate when you're right. I've lost the five pounds I've been griping about forever."

"Told you."

"Shut up." Heather sank on the double bed and pulled on her knee-high fashion boots. "I'll eat more."

"I'll remind you." Kate added the black stack heels. "If you're meddling in my love life, the least I can do is return the favor."

"I'm sure." Heather went to the bureau to find the silver concho belt that fancied up the V-neck top. "Consider cutting my uncle some slack. He's real lovable."

"I know." Kate brushed her short dark hair. "It's a heavy-duty risk. I haven't been in love for a long time, but he's the kind of guy who might change my mind."

"My turn." Heather unfastened the band holding her ponytail and ran the hairbrush through the waist-length red hair, leaving it to hang free. "I'll keep nagging you. Let's get out of here. We can discuss men while we drink beer."

At Kate's disapproving look, Heather added, "Okay, you drink beer. I'll stick to something non-alcoholic and decaf."

She led the way downstairs after another quick check on the twins. Durango came out of the dining room at the sound of her high-heeled boots on the kitchen tile. She enjoyed the way his eyes widened. "We're going to Pop's. You've got the kid watch."

"Say again, baby. I don't think I got that."

"You heard me." She moistened suddenly dry lips and tipped back her head. "We're partying. You're not. Walk the puppies a couple of times so they don't piddle in their crate."

"Lots of orders." He chuckled, bent his head, and brushed his mouth over hers. "Run along, little girl. Just remember who you belong to and who's waiting at home."

"And remember you sleep in the bunkhouse, Hawke. Alone."

He grinned down at her, caught her chin in calloused fingers, and kissed her again. "I'll stay inside until you're back. Don't forget what your decrees do to me."

When they walked into the cocktail lounge a short time later, Heather gazed around the room. The O'Connells weren't on stage yet, but that didn't mean much on a Friday night. They either hadn't started yet or they were on break. She nodded to a few people she recognized and ushered Kate over to the bar.

"Kate, this is Pop MacGillicudy." Heather smiled at the old man. "Pop, this is my best friend, Kate. He used to let me sing here before I was any good."

"You were always good, Rusty." Pop winked at her. "Granted, sometimes I don't admit it when you won't sing Patsy Cline."

"Will I never hear the end of it?" Heather demanded with a grin. "Yell at Durango when he hauls me out of here early, not at me."

"Then stop pissing him off," Pop told her. "Where is he? Parking the truck?"

"We left him home to babysit," Kate said. "You don't have to worry about him."

Pop laughed and gestured to two empty stools. "What do you want to drink?"

"I'll have a beer, whatever's on tap." Kate perched on one of the stools. "Heather, what about you?"

"Ice water with a slice of lemon."

Pop drew the beer first, putting the pint jar in front of Kate. "What's going on, Rusty? Usually, you have at least one drink before you go onstage."

"Can't I just have a glass of water without answering a million questions? Maybe I decided to go straight and stay on the wagon. Did you ever think of that?"

"Nope, 'cause it ain't true. When you were here in May, you had four wine coolers. You wanted a fifth one, but Durango put his foot down before I could. Like I told him more than once, you can't drown your troubles in alcohol. You've got to face them."

"Okay, I'm pregnant." Heather heaved a sigh when Pop put the glass in front of her. "I'd take out an ad in the paper, but Baker City doesn't have one."

"Sooner or later, we will. My nephew's talking about starting one when he gets here." Pop turned his attention on Kate. "Let me know when you're holding a reception for Heather and Durango. I'll bring the food."

"What's going on, Pop?" Dick sauntered to the bar, followed by Bill and George. "Where's the party and when?"

"Have to figure all that out," Pop said. "Rusty and Durango got hitched without us back in May, but we're having a hootenanny soon for them."

"Want to bet?" Heather caught the interest in Kate's gaze and turned to introduce the O'Connell men to her. Concern grew when Kate began flirting with George.

Heather slid off the stool, gripped Bill's hand, and pulled him toward the stage. "You've got to keep George from asking her out."

"Why? He's been divorced for years and his ex-wife won't be a problem since she remarried."

"Kate's involved with—" Heather stopped and stared into Bill's blue eyes. "Can't you just take my word for it?"

"Who is he? Some guy from Tennessee where you lived?"

"No, he's from here." Heather's voice faded at the sudden certainty on Bill's face. "He's scared to death and hiding from everyone. Kate hasn't been in a serious relationship since her fiancé died in Iraq."

"So, they're both terrified of what comes next." Pity filled Bill's tone. "Don't worry, Rusty. I have your six and theirs. I'll help get things squared away."

At the bar, Pop looked them up and down. "I want the band to promise to behave themselves when Durango's folks turn up."

"What happens?" Kate glanced at Heather. "What do you do?"

"We start singing the old Sonny and Cher hit *Gypsies, Tramps, and Thieves*. It annoys Pop big-time." Heather sipped her water. "Anyway, Pop. I'm not doing that anymore. We found out a couple of days ago that Quentin Hawke is Durango's father and since I can't stomach Estelle, I disowned her in favor of Durango's stepmom. Vicky's a doll and she's promised to spoil the twins rotten."

"What are we going to do to them?" George asked, gesturing to the group of people who'd just walked in the door. "There's Tex and his entourage. We can't make them feel welcome."

"You could do something that shows how much you adore Durango, Heather." Kate finished her beer. "What about that song you were teaching Naveah yesterday?"

"I need a couple of gals to do back-up." Heather waved at her cousin

Jassy Sweeney waiting tables, and the young waitress approached them. "Are you up for it, Kate?"

"If I get another beer afterward." Kate pulled out her phone. "Come over here, Jassy and I'll show you what we're going to do."

"Is it evil?" Jassy eyed Kate and then Heather. "Do we get to do something dirty to Tex and his crew?"

"You know it," Heather said. "Are you in?"

"Always."

"Oh, that's another good one." Heather faked her sweetest smile as she considered melodies. "We'll add it to the repertoire of Patsy Cline songs. We'll start and finish with the Deborah Allen song on each of the next three sets."

Dick looked up from where he huddled with the others over Kate's smartphone and the video she showed them. "Do you think they'll stay that long?"

"Who knows? We'll find out." Heather drained the last of the ice water. "Let's go, girls! I'm taking your organ for this song, George."

"It's okay. I'll play guitar."

Heather led the way onstage and sat down behind the organ. She'd worked for two hours with Naveah and they'd played the song repeatedly on the grand piano while the young girl learned it. After she left, Heather played her old favorite several more times. She'd fallen in love with it years ago, since it expressed her emotions about Durango perfectly.

She hit the starting chords on the organ, heard the low drumbeat as Bill joined in, and then the guitars. She sang the first lines of *Baby I Lied*, Kate and Jassy chiming in beautifully at the appropriate time. The ensemble rocked through the old pop song as if they'd worked together for years, as if this wasn't the first time.

Loud applause when they finished and Heather traded places with George, taking his guitar. She launched into a fast-paced version of Gretchen Wilson's *Redneck Woman* that had people hitting the dance floor and shouting "Hell, yeah!" with her. The band alternated fast and slow songs that kept the place hopping. By the middle of the set, they'd had several requests for the Deborah Allen song, so Heather called Kate and Jassy back to the stage and they did *Baby, I Lied* again.

Tex Hawke, his wife, Estelle, and Eli Roberts lasted longer than Heather thought they would, but on the fourth rendition of the song, they got up and left. Laredo met Heather at the bar at the end of the second set. "Are you going to do that whenever they show up?"

"Indubitably," Heather said sweetly. "Since Durango isn't Tex's son, I don't have to be nice or polite anymore."

"Say what?" Laredo gaped at her, hazel eyes wary. "Are you serious?"

"Yup. Tex shared the good news a couple of days ago. Your uncle Quentin is Durango's dad, and he's thrilled about being a grandpa. That makes Vicky, Durango's stepmom, my kids' other grandma. I'm cutting Estelle out of my family herd." Heather paused, then kissed his cheek. "When I learn who your bio-dad is, I'll tell you, because I'm pretty sure Tex Hawke isn't it. Meantime, why don't you and your sisters do those D.N.A. tests?"

# CHAPTER THIRTY-FIVE

Baker City rolled up the sidewalks shortly after midnight, even on weekends, so it wasn't late when they drove into the front yard and parked the pickup. Once in the house, Kate headed upstairs to the attic apartment and Heather went into the living room. She saw Durango sleeping on the couch. She lingered by the door, allowing her gaze to sweep over his long, lean body. When had silver started to infiltrate the tawny gold hair?

"What's wrong, Heather Marie?"

"Nothing. How did you know I was here?"

He continued to lie unmoving on the sofa, his eyes still closed. "The Marines taught me a lot. So did being in Iraq and Afghanistan. Looking for Waco and the others, I learned more. I know better than to let anyone sneak up on me when I'm sleeping. I don't plan to die in combat, baby."

"I thought the war was over for you."

"Has it ended for you, baby?"

"No, I don't think it will. I've never forgotten the blood, the wounded, the sand." She paused, continued when he didn't speak. "The mud during the rainy season, the heat, the insects, the rain on the metal roof of my CHU or the fits from senior officers when we forgot and called them 'trailers' instead of 'containerized housing units.' "

"I know." He opened his eyes, held out one hand. "Come here, Heather Marie. Let's help each other through what remains of the night."

"Only if you understand it doesn't mean anything, Angel."

"I know." Faint amusement trickled through his deep voice. "Trust me, baby. I know."

She turned off the lamp on her way to the couch to curl up next to him. She smoothed his hair, put her hands on his shoulders, and pressed her cheek against his chest. "I get so scared sometimes. I hear the voices of the wounded. I smell the blood. I see them."

"Hey, baby. Remember what we learned there. It doesn't matter. It doesn't mean anything."

She relaxed against him, her body melting into his. "You're right."

"Only one thing is important. I always want you in my bed and with me every day, too."

"You're just a horny old man, lover."

"Just with you, Empress, just with you."

Saturday morning, she made herself another cup of peppermint tea and sat at the kitchen table reading yesterday's news in the Lake Maynard paper. If she looked out the glass-paned back door, she would see the twins playing in the side yard and Durango working on the log playground. Kate hadn't come downstairs yet. It was her turn to sleep late.

She heard footsteps on the porch and glanced up from the paper to see Durango coming inside. "Hi, how's the latest project?"

"Almost finished." He headed for the coffeepot. "Anything exciting happen in town last night?"

She debated telling him about the conspiracy to drive Tex and Estelle Hawke out of Pop's Café and decided against it. Durango might say he was done with them, but she wasn't going to push her luck or make him feel like he had to defend them from the inhabitants of Baker City.

"Pop wants us to have a big reception as soon as we decide on a place. We still don't have a bridge, so I was thinking we should do it at the dude ranch. What do you think?"

"I like it. I already rent the party barn to provide security there, so it will work for an event. Do you want to have it before or after Cat McTavish has her baby? She's due in August."

"I'll talk to her at our veterans' meeting next Wednesday." Heather turned to the next page. "Pop wants us to do something about his grandson, Dray."

"He's a good kid." Durango filled a cup with coffee and took a lazy swallow. "He wants me to hire him to work at Hawke Construction."

"He graduated from high school last month. He was accepted at four universities in Washington state and several others in CONUS, plus one in

Alaska. He still hasn't chosen one. He says he's not going to college in the fall. Pop and Linda think he should, since he's not talking about a gap year."

"And what do you think?"

"Pop and Linda have always been wonderful to me." Heather reached for her tea. "I owe them. I'll bet even you can't make Dray go to college, let alone stay for a degree."

"What's the bet? It's got to be something I want."

Heather sipped her tea and hoped she looked innocent. "What if the bet was whether you moved into the house?"

"I'm already here more than you thought I'd be." He leaned against the counter, eyeing her over the coffee cup. "It'd have to include you and I sharing the same bed for the duration, Empress, not just when you're—" He arched a brow. "Horny."

Heat warmed her cheeks, and she struggled to ignore it when amusement darkened his cobalt blue eyes. "Beast. All right. We have a bet. If you win, you're back in the house and my bed. If I win," she hid a smile. "If I win, you expand the kitchen in the bunkhouse and cook your meals there."

"You know those edicts of yours make me hot." He put the cup on the counter, crossed to her, and his mouth claimed hers.

Before she surrendered to the kiss, the back door banged open. She pushed him away, turning her head.

Dallas charged into the kitchen, followed by the blue heeler puppy. "Daddy, you're s'posed to be buildin' our fort, not huggin' and kissin' Mommy. You're not workin' no more."

"Maybe she should supervise the crew on the new boundary fence," Heather teased. "Guess you better get back to work, Daddy."

"Soon." He kissed her again before looking at their daughter. "It's not ready yet, Dallas. I'm taking a break, but you and Galveston will be able to play on it by lunchtime."

Eyes shining with pleasure, a broad smile on her tiny face, Dallas whirled to run from the room, Booey right behind her. "Toney, we getta play on it after lunch and 'fore naptime."

The slamming of the door prevented Heather from hearing her other daughter's response. "Sounds like you've got your work cut out for you, Hawke."

"Maybe so. Maybe no. Dray will be along to help soon."

Three days later, Heather knelt to hug the twins once more. "You two be good and mind Auntie Kate. I'll be home this afternoon."

"After naptime," Galveston said. "Right, Mommy?"

"Right." Heather glanced at Kate. "What's the plan for today?"

"Making cookies and cupcakes for the veterans' meeting tomorrow." Kate ruffled Dallas' strawberry-blonde hair. "I've got the two best helpers here."

"Wonderful." Heather kissed her daughters. "I'll see you later."

"Where are you going?" Dallas asked, for the hundredth time. "What are you and Gramma Liz gonna do?"

"Find us presents, Ally. Mommy already said so."

"But I wanna know what."

"It's a surprise." Heather repeated the same answer she'd been giving since Saturday. "And if you're bratty, you earn a time-out, Ally."

"And Toney too," Dallas announced with satisfaction.

Heather bit her lip. Punishments were something else the twins insisted on sharing, and she hadn't found a permanent fix for that yet. *But I will.* Keys in hand, she headed for the front door.

Painted Pony Park, a local horse-breeding facility, was on the west side of Lake Maynard. Heather couldn't quite believe her mother wanted to start a search for ponies there. Darla Connors specialized in purebred, registered, show Paints and Appaloosas, and priced them accordingly. Granted, she and Durango weren't short of money, but that didn't mean they wanted to spend a small fortune on riding ponies.

She parked the truck next to her mother's sedan and saw her waiting on the back porch of the one-story country rambler. Liz came down the steps, waving as she approached.

"How are you? How do you feel? Have you seen Doc MacGillicudy yet?"

"I'm fine. I feel great and no, I don't need him." Heather hugged Liz. "I've missed you and Dad."

"Whose fault is that? We haven't moved now that we're home in Lake Maynard. You should bring the twins to see us more often."

"The road runs both ways, Mother. If the creek's down, you and Dad should pop in occasionally."

"Then we will. When you get tired of us, say so. Now, how are you and Durango getting along?"

"Pretty good, all things considered." Heather walked toward the house where the office was apparently located. "We're adjusting. He knows how I feel about his mercenary activities and so far, he's sticking around instead of flying off to Colombia."

"Your dad and I want a good relationship with the twins. I'd have appreciated knowing about them before they turned four."

"I'll bet. And you'd have shared the information with their father. Did it ever occur to you that if I wasn't important enough for him to come after me, then it'd have broken my heart to have him only show up because I was the mother of his children?"

"Yes."

Her mother's quiet reply shocked Heather. Before she demanded answers, a petite, dark-haired woman in western garb approached. She nodded, a professional smile, not a friendly one on her pretty face.

"Darla, this is my daughter, Heather McElroy. Like I told you on the phone, we're looking for two ponies for my grandkids."

"What exactly do you want?" Darla asked.

"Gentle, well-trained, and old, at least twenty, but I'll go down to fifteen if they're smart," Heather said. "I want ponies with sense, not the kind that trot and gallop because my daughters give the wrong cues. Childproof, no spooking, no biting, or kicking."

Darla's smile warmed and became genuine. "That's different. Most people who come here want ponies with transmissions installed by the local mechanics. Do your daughters know how to ride?"

"Somewhat," Heather said honestly. "They're still learning. Their dad's taught them more than I have, because he has more patience."

"What are they riding now?"

"My old horse and their dad's." Heather met the other woman's blue gaze. "It worries me. If they fall, the girls could get seriously hurt."

"Satan and Cinnamon have a lot of sense," Liz said.

"He tops sixteen hands and Cinnamon's closer to eighteen. One goof-up and the girls could be injured or dead." Heather deliberately kept her tone even. "I'll never forget that Fourth of July parade in Everett when a horse spooked from the fireworks. The kid fell and smashed her skull on the pavement like an overripe watermelon."

"Heather Marie!" Consternation spread across Liz's features. "You were only six. How could you even remember that?"

"It'd be more reasonable to ask how I could ever forget?" Heather eyed the other horsewoman. "My kids won't be riding anywhere but on the McElroy farm."

"Okay." Darla took a deep breath and ushered them in the direction of the indoor arena. "Let's go look at ponies."

As they walked down the wide concrete aisle, she pointed out the attributes of each possibility. She knew their breeds, training, and temperaments. At the far end of the stalls, Heather saw two small paint ponies. One was a brown and white tobiano. The other was black and white. Both had gentle eyes and good manners when they accepted the carrots that Heather offered, neatly avoiding her fingers.

"They're so cute." Heather scratched the black mare's forehead. "How old are they?"

"A little young for you. That's Flicka and she's twelve. Velvet is her best buddy and she's thirteen."

"They're too little," Liz said. "The twins are going to be big girls."

"Tall, like their dad. And I'm pregnant. The baby can ride these after the twins outgrow them."

Darla ran a hand through her black curls. "Did Liz tell you I have a buy-back clause? If you ever want to sell my ponies, they come back here. They don't go to strangers. My husband is a lawyer, and he wrote our ironclad sales contract."

"It won't happen with us." Heather gave out more carrots. "Satan was my horse back in the day and Cinnamon was Durango's. They have a forever home with us. What kind of training do these two have?"

"English and Western. They can game and jump up to three feet." Darla caught the frown Heather shot her way and hastily added, "I don't believe in jumping ponies, but their previous owner did. They were born and raised here, but I sold them once and bought them back when the kids outgrew them."

"Who did they belong to?"

"Sally Winthrup. I'll be happy to provide the number or email address for you."

"I have it. Sally and I went to school together," Heather said, turning her attention back to the ponies. "I want to look at their legs, have my shoer come and check their hooves, and have Dad inspect them. Is it possible to see someone ride them?"

Darla nodded. "I'll call the house and have my daughter join us while I saddle. She's comfortable with both ponies."

Flicka and Velvet seemed to be exactly what she wanted, Heather thought as she entered her house later that afternoon. She glanced in the empty living room, then headed down the hall toward the kitchen, stopping when she saw Galveston sitting on the floor near the doorway. "What are you doing, honey?"

"Waiting." Tears filled Galveston's dark blue eyes.

"For what?"

"For Ally."

"Where is she?" Heather flicked a sideways glance toward the bathroom, then at the staircase. No Dallas. "Where's your sister?"

"Doin' time-out." A tear streaked down her cheek and Galveston sniffled. "I want her."

"Why aren't you with her?"

"I wasn't bad, and Daddy said I couldn't do time-out."

"I see." Heather scooped the child into her arms and carried her into the living room. "Come tell me what Ally did."

"She got mad." Galveston turned her face into Heather's shirt. "We was making cupcakes. Auntie Kate said it was my turn to do sparkles."

Heather nodded and kissed the red-gold curls. "And Ally didn't want to stop doing them?"

"No, and she 'frew the bottle of sparkles at me, but she didn't mean it."

"I know." Heather snuggled the little girl closer. "Is that when your dad gave her a time-out?"

"He wasn't home yet. The sparkles fell on the floor and Auntie Kate said Ally had to help clean them up 'fore she frosted cupcakes. And then Ally dumped the frosting on the floor too. And she jumped in it and 'fore Auntie Kate could do anything, Daddy got home."

"And then Ally had a time-out?" Heather was privately amazed Durango had that much control after enduring so much abuse as a child. "Wow, that doesn't sound too bad."

"Daddy said to mind Auntie Kate and Ally yelled at him and 'frew frosting on the floor."

"Wait a minute. I thought the frosting was on the floor before your dad got home."

"First, Ally 'frew the blue frostin', then red, then yellow. And she kept yelling at our daddy. And he picked her up and put her in a chair and said she had to do time-out till dinner."

"That's a real long one," Heather said. "No wonder you're worried. But why aren't you sharing her time-out?"

"Daddy won't let me. I asked and asked. Ally told him we do everythin' together, 'cause we're twins. He said, 'Not this time' and Auntie Kate said something 'bout a hill and went upstairs."

Heather held her daughter tight while Galveston cried, more upset about the separation from her twin than Dallas' punishment. Murmuring soft endearments, Heather hugged the four-year-old. At the sound of footsteps, she looked at the doorway as Durango entered, concern on his rugged features.

"Is she all right?"

Heather nodded. "Where's Ally? Still doing time-out?"

Worry increased on his face. "I told her if she helped clean up the mess, she could go play, but she won't."

"Of course not. It wouldn't be fair." Heather smoothed Galveston's hair. "Okay, sweetie. No more crying. I need to talk to your dad, and you need to wash your face. Can you do it by yourself?"

"Then can I be with Ally?"

"Yes." Heather waited until Galveston left the room. "Sounds like you had a real workout."

Bewilderment mixed with the concern on Durango's face. "What do I do now?"

"Cut yourself some slack, Hawke." Heather sighed, rose to her feet, and hugged him. "Did you lose your temper and smack the kid?"

"Of course not. She's too little. I could hurt her, and I'd never do that. Quentin—I mean my dad—used to say that being bigger than most guys meant I had to be more careful because I was stronger than them. And it goes triple for not putting my hands on kids."

"There you go." Heather tipped back her head and eyed him. "If I got the story straight, you gave her a time-out and separated her from the other half of her soul."

"That pretty much covers it." Durango wrapped his arms around her, tension seeping from his huge body. "Dallas was making so much racket, nobody could hear me when I talked, so I raised my voice. I didn't think it was a big deal giving her a time-out and letting Galveston play when she hadn't done anything wrong, although Kate told me I'd picked the wrong hill to die on."

Heather laughed and hugged him again. "You actually did a good job, Hawke. Now, go tell Ally she's off the hook if she apologizes to Toney for throwing cupcake decorations at her. Otherwise, it's time-out until supper."

A faint smile tugged at his mouth. "And I save face."

"So does she. Be sure you hug her and tell her that you love her, even if you don't like the mess she made."

"And the two of us are going to clean it up?" Durango asked.

"Afraid so, lover." Heather nodded, wrinkling her nose in disgust. "Next time, don't give Ally a time-out until *after* she's cleaned up her mess. And I write down that Toney has a credit toward her next tantrum so she can share Ally's punishment."

"How many credits does Galveston have?"

Heather paused to calculate the amount. "Five."

"Is that all?" Durango seemed impressed. "She acts calm, like nothing rattles her."

"She's four. You haven't realized she's a lot like you." Heather kissed him quickly. "She has a temper, but most people don't know it because it simmers for a long time. When she reaches the boiling point, all hell breaks loose. And everybody hears it."

# CHAPTER THIRTY-SIX

Heather gave Durango a head start before she followed him to the kitchen. She found him hugging Dallas. She scanned the area, unfavorably impressed by the globs of blue, red, and yellow frosting on the floor and the scattered candy sprinkles. "What a mess."

"It's my fault," Dallas announced, snug in Durango's arms. "I got mad when Auntie Kate said I had to share."

Heather nodded, sinking her teeth into her bottom lip to bite back the amusement. "I'm proud of you for taking responsibility for what you did, Dallas Waco."

"But you still don't like the crap on your clean floor." Dallas heaved a huge sigh. "I guess I better help scrub."

"If you and Toney want to help, you can," Heather said. "It's not part of your time-out, Ally. And we both should stop saying crap."

"Is it a bad word, Mommy?" Galveston asked.

"It's not a very nice one." Durango gave Dallas one more quick hug and lowered her to the floor. "I reckon you don't like my time-outs."

"No! They're mean, Daddy. And I'm not being bad no more if Toney can't share 'em."

Durango chuckled. "If I give a time-out, the girl who earned it does it by herself and I don't give credit slips."

Wide-eyed, the twins stared up at him, then looked at Heather. She shrugged. "Credit slips work for me, but so does no dessert, standing in corners and the occasional smack on bottoms. Make good choices and then none of those consequences happen."

Dallas nodded soberly. "I'll get the broom."

Galveston waited until Dallas was sweeping up the candy and then asked. "Mommy, do we still get our presents?"

"Sure." Heather dampened three rags and passed one to Durango, another to Galveston, and kept a third for herself to wipe up the frosting. "Not today. I didn't find the right ones yet."

"Are you going shopping again?" Dallas asked.

"Yes. On Thursday with your daddy and I'd better not come home to a mess like this again, girls."

"You won't!" Dallas and Galveston chorused.

That evening, after the twins were in bed, Heather settled in the rocking chair in the corner of the living room, the Lake Maynard newspaper in hand. She opened it to the classified section.

"How did you and Liz do today?" Durango crossed to the recliner. "Did you find any suitable ponies?"

"Maybe." Heather kept her attention on the advertisements. "We went to three different farms. The owner of one up north said all their ponies are trained with the hit and kick method. If a child kicks, the pony goes and if it's hit, the pony gallops. I'd prefer the twins not learn to abuse animals."

"Good horsemanship doesn't require it. What about the others?"

"The one near Everett didn't have anything appropriate. The horses were smaller than Satan and Cinnamon, but not nearly as reliable. The best were at Painted Pony Park, Darla Connors' place. But her prices are astronomical. Still, the ponies are as trustworthy, responsive, and child-proof as if I trained them. Darla's daughter rode them for us. She could crawl under their bellies, run at them, make loud noises, and they never flinched."

"They sound perfect. What's the catch?"

"Like I said, Darla wants too much for them. She has a buy-back clause in her contracts. I called Sally Winthrup. She owned the ponies I wanted at one time, but they went back to Darla when Sally's kids outgrew them. She told me that Darla is a real witch, but Sally spelled it with a 'b.' "

"Why? What did Darla do?"

"She's a super control freak. She showed up at odd times every month to inspect the stalls where the ponies lived to be sure they were clean, insisted on seeing their hay and grain whenever it was delivered although

Sally only buys from Jones Hay and Feed, one of the best suppliers in Liberty Valley. Darla demanded to approve the shoer and veterinarian, wanted copies of their records when they visited. If Sally protested, Darla sent her lawyer husband, who works as a deputy county prosecutor, to do a walk-through. If he was busy, then it was one of their cop friends who worked the animal abuse cases."

"On the books or off? Does he pay them to harass people?"

Heather glared at him. "Of course not. But who wants the cops going through their barns when they're trying to make a living? Sally said that back in the day, the strictest county animal control officer was an Army vet, Beth Chambers, and she had the broom she rode in on. Most stable owners in Liberty Valley were terrified of her and celebrated when she was promoted to homicide."

"Wow. Sounds like the Connors would prefer not to be in the sales business at all." Durango picked up the remote and turned on the TV, but kept the sound muted. "Will I get thrown out of the house if I remind you that you had the same conditions when you sold Satan before we shipped out? When you came back from Iraq and Afghanistan, you visited him more often than you did your folks."

Heather read the next ad. "Maybe I did, but I had some damned good reasons. And we provide a great home for our critters."

"Darla doesn't know that. Shall we send Laredo to look at the ponies? I can ask Summer O'Neill to contact Darla about the feed. Dick O'Connell will be happy to tell her that we don't abuse our stock and he's never had an animal control complaint about us."

"We can't afford her prices even if the stock is purebred and registered."

"Sweetheart, we can't afford not to pay what she asks. We're trusting our kids to those ponies. I don't want anything less than the best."

"I'll think about it." Heather marked a third ad. "When you talk to Dick, be sure it fits into his schedule. He's investigating my aunt's disappearance. He told Mom and Dad, it's looking stranger than ever. Lucy hasn't used her credit cards or paid taxes for almost twenty-eight years. None of her daughters have heard from her, and neither has anyone else in town."

"What about Cat McTavish? You said she talks to dead people."

"True, but she's been in Baker City for less than a year. She says she hasn't met everyone yet and there are more ghosts to go. I told Mom I'd ask her tomorrow at the veterans' meeting." Heather glanced up from the newspaper. "By the way, you're not staying in here tonight."

"Why not? Because you're in a snit?"

"Nope. Because you think me being here and sleeping with you makes everything okay in our relationship."

"I didn't know we had one of those. I thought we were married." He pretended to wince at the glare she shot in his direction. "Still can't take a joke, huh?"

"You should have listened to your dad when he told you not to argue with a drunk, a skunk, or a redheaded woman. You still haven't learned that yet."

"Do I get a kiss good night before you throw me out?"

"No." She pointed to the door. "Don't let it hit you in the backside."

He stood, put the remote on the table beside her. He placed his hands on the arms of the rocking chair and bent closer. "If you change your mind, you know where I am."

"Ha, ha. Remember, if Dray doesn't go to college, you're converting the bunkhouse into a permanent residence."

Durango chuckled, brushed his lips over hers. "Want to bet?"

The sound of rhythmic thumping woke her. She was sitting in the rocking chair in her own living room, but she still heard helicopters. *Incoming wounded!* She shook her head, tried to force away the smell of blood, the sound of someone calling her name. Stumbling to her feet, she went to the window. She tore open the drapes. She stared into the pre-dawn sky.

Army choppers, two of them flying over the ranch. Maneuvers, she told herself. It had to be the Army Reserve from Paine Field in Everett doing early morning training flights. The war was over. She was home. She was safe. She repeated the silent litany over and over.

*Captain McElroy. We need you in triage, stat.*

*"I'm coming," Heather called. Where was her flak jacket? Her boots? Her—She ran from her CHU out across the compound, slipping in the damp grass. Odd, she hadn't seen grass for so long. She had to get to the hospital, to where they brought in the wounded.*

*"Cap, did you find my brother? He's bad!"*

*The question penetrated through the cloud of shouted commands from nurses, doctors, and staff. She paused by the injured boy. Shrapnel wounds in his leg and hip. "Your brother? What's he doing here?"*

*"We signed up together, made them promise to keep us in the same unit, Cap. He was hurt worse than me. Find him, Cap."*

*"I will." She started toward the next soldier. "When I do, I'll tell you."*

*"Thanks, Cap."*

*Blood soaked her clothes, her hands seemed to be everywhere. Nowhere to run, nowhere to hide—the words pounded in her brain. They beat with the same meter as the choppers bringing in more wounded. Another mass cas situation. They never ended, never got better.*

*Suddenly, she found herself in the ward, ignored by the nurses and doctors hurrying by. She walked slowly toward the back of the room, her gaze fixed on the curtain screening off the expectant patients. She needed to check the heavily drugged soldiers, waiting to die.*

*"Cap, find my brother."*

*"Cap, my brother."*

*"Cap!"*

Rain misted her face. Moisture from the damp grass soaked the knees of her jeans. She felt the vibrations of the departing helicopters rather than hearing the whir of their blades. Slowly, she looked around the front yard. What was she doing outside? Vaguely, she remembered the voices crying for help and the blood.

She shook her head. That way lay madness. She wouldn't remember, couldn't allow herself to remember. She rose to her feet, padded toward the front porch, changing her mind halfway there. She went around the house, past the log playground to the long, low cabin where Durango slept.

She opened the door, stepped inside, shutting it behind her. She climbed the stairs to the loft bedroom. He was asleep, the blanket barely covering his lean hips. His muscled back caught her gaze. Then she sat down on the top stair and removed her boots. Her socks followed.

He rolled over, propped up on an elbow, and watched her. "What's going on?"

"Shut up." She stood, unsnapped her jeans, stripped them off, and her panties. She unsnapped her blouse and shrugged out of it, dropping it on the other clothes. Unhooking her bra, she tossed it on the floor. She stalked toward the double bed, barely realizing he held up the blanket for her so she could join him. She pounced on him, pinning him beneath her, and captured his mouth with hers.

He tangled his hand in her hair, pulled her lips away from his. "What's going on, baby?"

"Be quiet. I didn't come to talk. Make me forget everything but you."

"All right." He brushed a trail of kisses along her throat. "Easy, sweetheart."

"I don't want it easy. I said I want you." She pushed him down, hands on his shoulders, sliding down so she felt his hardness between her legs, right where she wanted him.

Before she adjusted her position to take him inside her, he rolled so she was beneath him. He claimed her mouth at the same moment his body took hers. The fast, furious rhythm of his thrusts took them to the edge of the universe.

"Don't stop." She shuddered against him, their hips meeting one last time as they rose and fell together. He stopped before either of them reached their climax. She drew a ragged breath, dug her nails into his back. "More. I need more."

"Tell me why." He paused to kiss her forehead, her eyebrows. "Are you madly in love with me?"

Yes, but she wasn't admitting it. She rocked upward. "Make me forget, damn you."

He began to move again, little teasing thrusts this time. "You've got to face the horrors, not run from them. You're using me to stop your pain."

"You deal with the memories your way and I'll deal with them my way. Now, do what I want." She kissed him. "Take me, damn it, and stop bitching about it."

"I'm not complaining." He shifted, going deeper in a series of long, leisurely strokes. He kissed her as he began a new pattern of thrusts. Some movements were deep, others shallow, and then his pace increased. "You won't be able to think of anything but how much you love me."

"Promises, promises."

That afternoon, when she and Kate returned from the veterans' meeting, she led the way into the house. She stopped in the hall when she saw the door open to the study. Durango sat behind the desk, Jeff in the visitor's chair, and surprise of surprise, Fenn leaned against the opposite wall, a bottle of beer in his hand.

Heather eyed her uncle. "What's going on?"

"Got tired of hiding." Fenn shrugged. "Thought I'd come read Hawke the riot act about you riding Satan. It's not good for you or the baby, Rusty."

"Stuff it." Heather walked over to hug him. "I do as I please. Welcome home."

"Women. Too danged mushy." Fenn wrapped an arm around her shoulders and held her close. "How was your meeting?"

330

"Good." She eyed Durango and the stack of maps on the table. "Have you walked the puppies lately?"

"Actually, they're outside in the doggie pen that Jeff brought. Are the girls ready to play with them?"

"After their nap. We had lunch at the dude ranch." She gestured to the papers in front of him. "Do you have something to tell me, jarhead?"

"We'll talk about it later, Heather Marie."

"You bet we will." She hugged Fenn once more, then spun around. "Come on, girls. Naptime."

"But we're not tired," Dallas whined, struggling not to yawn. "We're too big for naps, Mommy."

Galveston nodded, but Heather ignored the protests, pointing to the stairs. "I used the landline at Cat's to order pizza and pasta from Petrocelli's in Lake Maynard, Hawke. When you get done with your superhero crap, go get dinner."

She didn't wait for an answer. Instead, she followed her pouting daughters toward the stairs. Behind her, she heard Kate's voice.

"Margo Endicott's arranged for Mindy MacGillicudy to start attending our meetings next week. She's a retired high school counselor who will offer head-shrinking advice for the next month or so until she goes on a cruise to Alaska."

"Doesn't sound like *La Capitana's* too thrilled about the idea," Jeff said. "Had my share of therapy since I got home. It helped."

"I'm glad for you," Heather muttered, climbing the stairs behind the twins. She had enough people dancing in her skull. She didn't need one more person telling her what to think and what to do.

Hours later, she sat in the rocking chair in the corner of the living room. She tried to watch the insipid comedy on the flatscreen, but she was too angry. He hadn't said anything. He just sat in the recliner and waited. Finally, she muted the sound on the TV. "You're going again, aren't you?"

"I don't have a choice, baby."

"You have all the choices in *The World*, Hawke, but you're choosing him, not us."

"We have more intel. I've passed what Jeff heard from Waco and what Fenn told us to Denver. He's in charge of organizing the team."

"Then let him do it."

"He did, but he didn't count on the new team leader being in a car accident and breaking his leg. This is the last time, Heather."

"I've heard that too many times before. When are you leaving?"

"Saturday morning. I'll fly to Texas and go from there. Bendigo's trying to negotiate the ransom, so he can't lead the team."

"Change your flight and go tomorrow."

"What are you saying?" Durango narrowed dark blue eyes and stared at her. "I don't understand. We're shopping for ponies tomorrow."

"No, we aren't." She clicked off the television. "I'm done, Hawke. Go pack your crap. Go to Texas. Go to Colombia. Go to hell. Just don't come here when or if you make it back to CONUS."

"I get it." He stood. "You're scared. This isn't the answer, Heather Marie."

"It is for me. I want a husband, a real one. I want a father for my kids." She rested a hand where she'd have a baby bump sooner rather than later. "You want to be a soldier for hire. Time for me to grow up and realize I'm on my own. Just like always."

# PART 4

———————

BAKER CITY, WASHINGTON ~ AUGUST 2019

# CHAPTER THIRTY-SEVEN

She was upset last night so he'd gone to the bunkhouse. He'd give her time to simmer down, to understand this was best not only for them but also for Waco. He had two days to soothe hurt feelings, play with the girls and hopefully have make-up sex with their mother, Durango thought.

When he walked into the kitchen, he smelled freshly brewed coffee and saw Fenn sitting at the table. "Where is she?"

"Gone." Fenn gestured to the pot on the warmer. "She and Kate packed up the kids and left. Heather said for me to look after the puppies, cats, and horses. They'll be back Sunday night."

"I'm leaving Saturday morning."

"Guess that's why she woke us at 0200 hours and gave Kate a sit-rep."

"You could have come out to the bunkhouse and told me."

"I could, but she's my niece and if she's not willing to provide system support yet, I can't make her." Fenn drank more coffee. "You're going to have to make a decision about what you want most, Durango."

"Her. It's always been her."

"Then it's time to fish or cut bait. Call your dad and arrange for somebody else to lead the team."

"It's too late for that."

"Then you don't get to bitch. Time to deal, Angel."

"I will, and we'll work it out when I get back."

"Good luck with that. You'll have to do some fancy talking to win her back."

"And I will."

---

The twins loved the trip to the huge water park at the resort near the state capital, although they complained about not having their critters. However, there were plenty of kid-centric activities to amuse them, and they asked more about the puppies and kittens than they did their dad. They arrived in Baker City on Sunday in time to attend church, pick up picnic goodies at the mercantile, and then headed for the ranch.

Monday before Linda MacGillicudy arrived with her crew to clean, Heather went to the bunkhouse and packed the rest of Durango's clothes in the three canvas Army duffels she'd bought at the military surplus store on the way home. She loaded the bags in her pickup. She told Linda to scrub the place from top to bottom and change out all the linens, curtains, and towels because the place needed to be ready for a handyman. Heather suspected the older woman thought Durango would be back in the house after his business trip, but there wasn't any point in confirming or denying it.

While she watched TV that night, she contemplated calling Denver and telling him to get Durango's belongings out of her grandfather's study. She decided against it. Okay, she was majorly pissed, but it didn't mean she wanted to risk his life. She certainly didn't want all and sundry knowing exactly where to find him in Colombia. Tears stung, and she wiped them away. Damned pregnancy hormones!

Tuesday afternoon, she drove over to the dude ranch to drop off his clothes at the party barn he'd rented for the Nighthawke Security crew. Her anger almost melted when she spotted the tall, tawny-haired hunk in the office. It took a couple of minutes to recognize Denver Hawke, ten years younger than her husband. The resemblance shocked her for a moment before she realized they were half-brothers, same dad, but different moms. "You son of a—"

"Come on, Heather. You like *my* momma." He flashed what he obviously hoped was a charming smile that warmed dark blue eyes. "I told Durango we could wait until September. Then I'd have two or three guys back from Afghanistan and one would be a good team leader."

"Throw him under the bus often?" Heather pointed out the window to the green four-by-four. "Some of his crap is in my truck. Unload it. When he's back in CONUS, call me. I'll have Ransom pick up the rest."

"Heather, you married him."

"Actually, he married me under false pretenses." Heather looked Durango's cousin—no, his half-brother—up and down. "He said he was ready to be a husband. He lied. I'm seeing my lawyer as soon as I leave here and seeking an annulment."

"But you're pregnant."

"I know, and I already have two daughters." She brushed her hands together. "It's done, through and said. Now, get his crap out of my truck."

Turning, she stormed from the office, followed by Denver Hawke, who babbled excuses for Durango's behavior. Halfway to the rig, she saw Dray MacGillicudy. The teen bolted toward her. "What?"

"It's Cat. She's having the baby right now. You gotta help."

"Where is Rob?"

"Cat sent him and Jassy to take the kids for a trail ride. If Rob hovered over her for five more minutes, Cat was going to shoot him. She was making me a sandwich and peed all over the floor."

"Her water broke." Heather pressed the button that unlocked the pickup. "Help Denver take Durango's stuff to the office. Denver, find me an Army medic. You must have some with Nighthawke. Send him or her to the house to help me. Have you called the O'Connells yet, Dray?"

"No, I didn't think of it."

"Do it now. Use your cell phone or the landline in the Nighthawke office."

Leaving the men, she jogged to the house, across the porch, and in the front door. She found Cat hunched in a chair. "Hey, I hear we're having a baby."

"You think?" Cat looked up at her, sweat beading on her forehead. "My back's been aching most of the day, but the contractions haven't started yet."

"They will soon." Heather helped the other woman stand. "Let's get your clothes changed. Where is your suitcase? The O'Connells will be here soon to transport you to the hospital."

"I don't need a cop."

"You're not getting one. They also run the volunteer fire department. I told Dray to find me a medic so if the kid decides to come early, we'll be prepared. I wish I'd brought Kate with me instead of leaving her at home."

Heather guided Cat toward the master bedroom off the kitchen. "Where are Rob and Jassy riding with the girls?"

"We have a loop trail." Cat glanced at the clock radio on the nightstand. "They'll be back in a half hour or so. We'd arranged for the girls to stay with Reverend Tommy and Virginia, but they went to Seattle for the day."

"No worries. I'll take them home with me and they can have a sleepover with my twins."

"You need to contact Margo and arrange for the veterans' meeting to take place at the church tomorrow."

"I've got this." Heather led the woman to the king-size bed. "You focus on having a baby. We'll be fine."

Instead of driving into Lake Maynard to see Brazos, Heather called her sister-in-law from the guest ranch, promising to stop in at the law office the next day so the lawyer could initiate the paperwork for the annulment.

"Don't you want to file for divorce, Heather?"

"I won't give him the satisfaction," Heather retorted, supervising the emergency medics while they prepared Cat for transport to the hospital. "I'm having it annulled so people will think he's all sorts of a loser."

"Glad to hear you're not emotionally devastated by his antics," Brazos said calmly. "Okay, I'll get started on the forms. I need to send flowers to Cat. Where are the O'Connells taking her?"

"Lake Maynard Hospital."

An hour later, Heather loaded up Cat's and Rob's nine-year-old twins as well as their two collie mixes in the pickup. The girls chattered away about the new baby sister they expected. Heather promised to take them to the hospital the next day to visit. Meantime, they'd stay with her for a while. When she arrived home, her daughters dashed to greet the older girls, followed by their puppies. Surprisingly, all the canines got along after a few sniffs and woofs.

When she looked amazed, Sophie, a petite redhead, explained, "We told Laddie and Lassie they had to be on their best company manners."

"I didn't hear you say anything to them," Heather said. "When did you do that?"

"Before we got out of the truck," Samantha said, looking at her twin. "We do picture talk with them, and they tell us what they're thinking."

"I see." Heather ushered the kids and dogs toward the house. "That makes perfect sense."

"How come?" Dallas asked. "Most people can't do that."

"The O'Leary family has special gifts." Heather opened the back door.

"If you're lucky, maybe Samantha and Sophie can teach you how to talk to your puppies, and then you'll be able to understand any other animals we have."

"We'll try," Sophie said, "but it doesn't always work."

"Fair enough."

Once the girls had snacks, Heather took them into the living room to watch cartoons. Then she found Kate doing laundry. "Cat's having the baby and we're taking care of her and Rob's kids until tomorrow or the next day, depending on when she comes home."

"Sounds like you may need to plug in the landlines around the house." Kate folded a pillowcase. "Otherwise, Rob won't be able to call and share the news."

"I don't want to talk to Durango."

"Then hang up if he calls," Kate said. "You know as well as I do, he'll convince you to give him another chance when he comes home."

"No, I won't. We're done. When we're in Baker City tomorrow, I'm going to the hardware store and get new locks for the doors."

"Do you want Fenn to change them?"

"No, because he'll just give a key to Durango, and I don't want him to have one."

"You are pissed."

"You are right!"

Margo Endicott called that night to say they wouldn't be meeting at the church in Baker City but at the new veterans' center instead. She suggested they drop all four girls at the nearby daycare where they could play with Ann's daughter and other children. When Heather knocked on the door, she recognized the petite silver-haired woman in her polyester slacks, flowered top, and sandals.

"Wow, Mrs. O'Connell. I'd thought you'd have retired by now." Heather smiled at her. "These are my daughters, Dallas, Ally for short, and Galveston, but we call her Toney. Girls, this is Mrs. O'Connell. I used to come here sometimes when I was your age."

"We like to help Mrs. Janine," Samantha said. "After lunch, we get to play with her dog and practice what we learn at doggie school."

"What is that?" Heather asked.

"Obedience classes." Janine O'Connell smiled, then drew Heather into a quick hug. "I'll find the information for you. Devon Sweeney-Barrett tells me that your girls have puppies who need to learn everything that her pup does, so they'll all be good dogs when they're grown up."

"Great idea." Heather kissed her daughters, reminded them to behave, and went to join Kate in the truck.

A few minutes later, Kate parked the truck in front of a blue and white, two-story house. As they crossed the parking lot, Heather saw a small cardboard sign taped in one of the downstairs windows. It read, *Welcome Home, Brothers and Sisters!*

Tears stung and she hugged Kate's arm. "Looks like we're welcome here."

"About time," Kate said. "I remember hearing stories that women who served during the Vietnam War weren't so lucky, that they weren't considered veterans because of their gender."

"I'm glad things have changed." They climbed the steps to the front porch, and she spotted the U.S. flag along with the distinctive black and white POW/MIA one. A plywood sign, this one in red and white, hung by the door, the *Ward O'Neill Veterans' Center.*

"Who was he?" Kate asked. "A hero?"

"Not according to most people. A guy from here. He enlisted. He went. He served. He came home. He committed suicide."

Inside, they found a table covered with brochures in the entry. A staircase led to the second floor and a door to the right opened onto what would have been a living room in a private home. Heather went into the parlor and found Dray sitting behind a desk. "What are you doing here?"

The teen ran a hand through shoulder-length, curly black hair, narrowing bright blue eyes. "My mom says that my biological mother intended to go in the Army after high school. She wasn't ready to raise a kid when she was one. I don't know if she ever enlisted or if she served in Iraq or Afghanistan, but if she did, I'd like to think someone welcomed her home."

"I hope so, for your sake and hers." Kate smiled at him. "Where do we find our group?"

"In the conference room upstairs." Dray handed each of them a clipboard. "Mindy MacGillicudy is our acting counselor for now and she's handling intakes. She's talking to Ann Barrett right now. You're next, Heather. Fill out these forms while you wait. Do you want coffee? We have decaf and pastries from Twila Garvey's bakery."

"Sounds good." Heather went to a chair. "Put cream and sugar in mine, please. I've been missing coffee. I should have bought decaffeinated. I will on the way home."

It didn't take long to complete the paperwork and Heather headed into the kitchen for a refill on her coffee. She wasn't the first arrival. She found an elderly white-haired woman who still looked amazing good in jeans, a cowgirl shirt, and lace-up riding boots grabbing a maple bar.

Heather nodded a greeting. "Would you believe me if I told you, I'm not sure why I bother coming to these meetings other than to enjoy the company of Ann, Cat, and their friends, Mindy?"

"Of course I would." Mindy smiled over the top of her coffee cup. "You're lucky to have each other. When I got back from Vietnam, I didn't have anyone. How are you and Durango doing?"

"He's pissing me off. We eloped, but he's not taking our marriage seriously."

"Are you? It's a two-way street, Heather. Both of you have to give sixty percent."

"Wait a second. Why sixty percent? Why not fifty-fifty?"

"If you give a little more, then it works out to half and half. Let's go chat in my office about post-traumatic stress, Heather."

"Do we have to?"

"Yes. I skimmed your paperwork. You wrote you'd been coping with depression, nightmares, and flashbacks. What about feelings of isolation? Rage? Alienation?"

"I'm a McElroy. We're known for our 'rigging fits,' what most folks outside of Baker City would call inappropriate rages." Heather walked beside the older woman toward her office. "I used to have temper tantrums before I went to Iraq."

"Did you?" Mindy closed the office door behind them. She urged Heather to take a seat in one of the visitor chairs while she sat in the other, behind an old table covered with papers. "Tell me about one that you had in high school."

"Come off it, Mindy." Heather stared at her in disbelief. "The only time I lost my temper back then was if Durango and I had an argument."

"Okay. What about college? I heard you moved up to live with your grandparents because you weren't getting along with your folks. Why not?"

"My mom thought I was still a little kid and kept telling me what I could and couldn't do. We argued all the time."

"So, you yelled, screamed, and threw things at her?"

"Of course not!" Heather laughed. "It would have proven her point about my immaturity." She sat still for a moment. "I couldn't control my emotions when I came back from Afghanistan the last time. Somewhere, I lost me."

"Then we have a lot to talk about," Mindy said gently. "If we'd opened a place like this when Ward came home, maybe he'd still be alive. It's too late to save him, but not for the next guy or gal."

"Is his mother involved with the center?"

"She's letting us have the house rent-free," Mindy said. "She's on the board of directors. She worries she didn't hear Ward when he needed help, but he wouldn't talk about his experiences with her."

"You can't be serious." Heather shook her head. "Ward planned his suicide so the Liberty Valley cops would find him, not his mother, not anyone in Baker City. He didn't want her to see him after he blew out his brains. It's why he asked my dad to identify him, not her."

"I'll ask Art to talk to her. We'll talk statistics later about women who serve in the military, Heather. What else is bothering you?"

"I hear voices, Mindy. I hear soldiers talking, asking, begging for help. Last week, I found myself outside trying to find a wounded Marine."

"Tell me about it."

"He wanted me to find his brother." Heather drank some of her coffee. "It was a mass casualty situation. I'd come off my shift, gone to bed when the choppers started arriving with wounded."

"What kind of shift had you worked?"

"Twelve hours on, twelve off—six days a week was the norm. It didn't matter when we got slammed. I ran to triage, began assessing the wounded. The first boy was an expectant."

"Expectant? What's that?"

"Expected to die." Heather rose and paced from one side of the room to the other. "Severely brain-damaged, he'd lost both legs, an arm. I gave him morphine, moved on to the next injured soldier."

She almost felt the condemnation in the air, although Mindy hadn't spoken. "We couldn't save them all. If we tried to save an expectant, four or five others would die."

"And the boy who wanted you to find his brother? What about him?"

"He wasn't hurt too badly." Heather spun on her heel, continued pacing. "His brother died. I had to go back and tell him— Damn it!" She slammed the cup down on the table. "Other times, all we had to do was fill out forms to send with the bodies. We didn't have to tell family members. He cried for the next three days. And I was the one who killed his brother. I gave him the morphine. I moved on. It was me!"

"Was it? How many wounded were there?"

"At least seventy. Maybe closer to a hundred. I don't know. I don't remember. I just remember those two boys. We didn't have the capacity to treat the one. We couldn't get him out to the hospital ships. He was brain injured. By the time we got him evac'd, he'd have died."

"So, you did your job. You didn't tie up the operating room to try and save someone who'd have died, anyway. Isn't that what triage is all about?"

"I played God over there. I was only twenty-six the last time I went. What gave me the right to decide who would live and who would die?"

"Your job. Your training." Mindy met her gaze. "Tell me about it again, Heather."

"What will it prove?"

"You're angry with the boy who mourned his brother. What happened to him in three days? Did he escort his brother home?"

"I don't know. I think he went back to his unit. I never knew what happened to him. I wish I knew if he made it home to his family at the end of his tour."

"Tell me again." Mindy's tone was soft but matter-of-fact. "Did you cry with him? Did you grieve too? Or did you just bear the guilt of knowing you'd done the best you could for a dying boy?"

"I got one of the doctors to look at him. The surgeon agreed there was nothing we could do, not without losing other patients, and I arranged for a corpsman to stay with him."

"Sounds to me like you did everything right. Now, tell me again from the beginning."

"What the hell do you want from me?" Heather yelled. "I've already talked about it."

"I want to hear it over and over and over." Mindy gestured to the chair. "Sit down and talk to me. I want you to tell it until you understand how tragic it was and you allow yourself to mourn, not only for those soldiers, but also for you. Tears can't stay bottled up inside you. It's time to come home, Heather."

# CHAPTER THIRTY-EIGHT

During the next two weeks, Heather visited Cat and Claire, the new baby girl at the guest ranch, almost every day. Either she or Kate took Dallas and Galveston as well as Sophie, Samantha, and Devon to day camp at Janine O'Connell's preschool in Baker City when they went to therapy with Mindy. Talking to the therapist helped Heather develop coping strategies, and she started sleeping at night.

She rode Satan around the ranch, which irritated Fenn, a bonus because her uncle's unstated support of Durango annoyed Heather. It also provided opportunities to check on the boundary fence and Jeff's crew from Hawke Construction. Shopping for ponies with her mother, attending rehearsals for her cousin Ann's upcoming wedding, and refusing to answer phone calls from Durango's family in Texas took up more time.

He was lucky she didn't go through with the annulment. She'd see his sister, her lawyer, and start the legal separation when he was back in CONUS to pitch a fit. Meantime, he could suffer since he never contacted her when he was in South America. She stood over Dray while he changed the locks on the house and at the bunkhouse, monitoring the number of keys. She eyed her cousin. "Durango doesn't get one of these until I give it to him. *Comprehendes*?"

"Yeah, I got it, but I like the guy. While we built the playground for the twins, he listened when I talked to him about college. Nobody else did. They kept saying I had to choose a university."

"Why didn't you?"

"Because it costs a bloody fortune, Heather. I don't know what I want to do, so how can I ask Grandpa or Mom to pay for me to figure it out? When she and my dad divorced, he fought her on custody. It wasn't because he wanted me. He didn't. He said I wasn't really his, because I was adopted. He never paid the child support or saw me. Hell, the guy didn't even send a card when I graduated from high school in June. There's no way he'll chip in for college."

"It's why you apply for student loans, Dray."

"Yeah, but they're called loans for a reason. You have to pay them back. I got good grades, but I didn't win any athletic scholarships and only a few small academic ones." Dray removed the old locking mechanism on the back door. "Grandpa doesn't make a fortune at the café. There's a reason why Mom runs a cleaning service, started catering out of the restaurant, and works her butt off. She intends to help me and I'm not letting her kill herself putting me through college. Those scholarships won't even cover a year's tuition. And no offense, but I'm not joining the military."

"So, what's your plan?" Heather handed him a screwdriver and waited. "You've got one, don't you?"

"I'm going to work part-time at Hawke Construction and attend classes at the community college in Everett for the next two years. After I have my associate degree, I'll have a better idea of what university I want to attend, and I'll have saved money to help pay for it. I owe you. Before he left almost three weeks ago, Durango said you were the one who wanted him to talk to me."

She nodded, struggling to ignore the heat warming her face. She wasn't about to tell her young cousin that the discussion about his future was a way to allow her so-called husband back in the house after she lost her temper. Now, she had different ideas. If Durango wasn't willing to be an equal partner, she wasn't going to hurry up and wait for her man to get his head together any longer.

---

The trip ended early. Barely three weeks after he left Baker City, Durango returned to his father's home outside Abilene, Texas. After a celebratory steak dinner, they headed into Quentin's study for the usual debriefing.

"Did you find Waco?" Quentin asked.

"I don't know. I didn't get a good look. Six captives staged a breakout and escaped on an old Cessna. We provided cover fire, blew up two warehouses, and kept the insurgents busy fighting us as a distraction."

"When Bendigo gets back, I'll have him check in with his contacts and see what he learns." Quentin swirled the whisky in his glass. "Your stepmom tried touching base with Heather, but she's avoiding all of us. Denver said she dropped off your belongings at Cedar Creek."

Durango winced, eyeing his father—his *real* father—a big, burly, muscled cowboy in jeans and a white shirt. He was sixty-five but didn't look it with his salt and pepper dark hair. "She was pissed when I left."

"Vicky read somewhere that anger comes from fear, hurt, and pain. Any chance that's what Heather feels?"

"Probably all of them." Durango glanced around the paneled room with its overstuffed leather furniture and massive desk. "I don't know what to tell her."

"You're thirty-eight. It's time to grow up, son. There's an old saying—'A man can pretend to care. He can't pretend to be there.' You're either in Baker City with your wife and family, or you're not. Your decision."

"Didn't you tell me Nighthawke had a policy of not sending married men into hot zones?"

"We do, but I can't stop you from being a jackass. Choose your life. I chose mine. I'll advise your brothers to make wise choices. Do you want me to contact Gus and have him fuel up the company jet to take you to Washington in the morning?"

Durango nodded. "Faster than flying commercial. Thanks...Dad."

"Sort things out with Heather. We want to visit Baker City next week for her birthday."

"I'll do my best."

———

August sunshine, iced tea clinking in their glasses, Kate and Heather sat on the side porch watching the twins climb the ladder on the log playground. The puppies tussled over a ball in the grass.

"Your birthday is next week and Twila said your mom is talking to her about a cake." Kate leaned back in the Adirondack rocking chair. "Do you want to have a gathering here or let Cat and Rob host it at the dude ranch?"

"Their place."

Galveston scaled the log staircase at one end of the playground, bypassing the banister as she tiptoed and twirled from one step to the next in a pretend ballerina dance. The twins knew they were supposed to hold onto the rails but didn't always follow the rules.

Heather stood, put her glass on the rail, and started toward the porch stairs to run parental interference, calling over her shoulder. "If we're at the guest ranch, baby Claire can sleep in her crib, and if Cat wants a rest, she can have one too."

"Sounds good."

A shriek split the afternoon air as Galveston tumbled onto the grass. Heather ran toward her daughter. The four-year-old wasn't moving. The little girl lay crumpled on the ground, her left arm tucked beneath her at an odd angle.

Heather dropped to her knees, felt the pulse in the child's throat. The steady beat provided comfort and relief. Her baby was alive. "It's okay, Toney. Mommy's here. You'll be fine."

"M–m–m–Mommy?"

"Right here." Heather gently straightened Galveston's small legs. "I promise you'll be okay."

"I fell."

"You sure did." Dallas squatted by her twin, both puppies crowding near, Purple whining softly. "I told you dancing on the stairs was a dumb idea."

"Be quiet, Dallas." Heather guided Galveston onto her back, holding the injured arm.

"Whoa. You oughta see your arm, Toney. The bone's sticking out. It looks gross."

"It hurts, Ally." Tears poured down Galveston's face.

"Yes, but I'm going to make it better." Heather scanned the compound fracture, assessing the bloody tip of a bone poking through the skin above the wrist. She looked at Kate kneeling beside her. "We need to splint this. See what you can find."

"I'm on it." Kate rose to her feet. "Come help me, Ally."

"I'm staying with Toney. We're twins."

"Go with Auntie Kate and help her put away the puppies," Heather said firmly.

Dallas reluctantly obeyed, trudging toward the back porch with frequent glances over her shoulder, the two puppies trailing behind.

When she and Galveston were alone, Heather said, "Toney, your arm is broken. I've got to fix it. Then I'll take you to the doctor."

"Will it hurt more?"

"No," Heather lied in her best nurse's tone. "I won't let it, baby."

Taking care of people had been her profession for a long time, sixteen years. This was *her* child. It felt so different to be entrusted with her medical care. Heather smoothed the soft red-gold curls. "I love you so much, sweetie."

The little girl stared up at her with trusting, dark blue eyes. "I'm not scared no more, Mommy."

"Good. Now, close your eyes." Heather rested her hand on Galveston's forehead and eyes. "Relax, Toney. Take deep, easy breaths like you do at naptime."

While her daughter obeyed, Heather loosened the tight hold she had on her muscles. Time to be a professional, she thought, not lose her breakfast and self-control because this was *her* baby, not a stranger's. She wiped damp hands on her jeans and went to work.

A few moments later, Kate arrived with bandages, rulers, and magazines. "How is she?"

"She fainted." Heather stroked the little girl's hair. "She'll be fine."

"The bone's not sticking out no more," Dallas reported with awe on her small face. "Mommy fixed it."

"Yes, I did. Now, go get me a bowl of ice, Ally."

"But I wanta stay with Toney."

"Now, Dallas Waco."

Heather waited until Dallas obeyed, scuffing through the grass toward the back porch. The twins loved playing with the ice maker on the outside of the refrigerator. The chore would keep Dallas busy for a few minutes.

"Shall I splint this?" Kate asked, "or do you want me to assist?"

"Assist."

The two of them were an experienced team, and it didn't take long to splint the arm using magazines and rolled bandages. She'd barely finished when she heard a truck engine. Turning her head, she saw Fenn driving the green four-wheel-drive into the yard. He parked as close as possible to them.

"We'll carry down a mattress from the twins' room," Kate said. "I'll grab your purse and mine. I locked the puppies in their crate."

"Collect blankets and pillows. Call Doctor MacGillicudy at the clinic in Baker City and tell him we're bringing in Galveston."

"Got it." Kate was on her feet, following directions.

Heather had finished bandaging the arm when Dallas arrived with the bowl of ice. "Thank you, Ally. I'm taking Toney to the doctor. I want you to stay home with Uncle Fenn."

"Whobody is that?" Galveston asked.

"We only gots Unca Laredo and Unca Jeff, not Unca Fenn," Dallas said.

"I'm your Uncle Fenn. I'll take you to town, Rusty. You sit in back with Toney."

"I'm going too," Dallas announced.

While Fenn went to help with the mattress and bedding, Heather studied her daughters. "I don't know about that, Ally."

"But I need her." A tear slipped down Galveston's cheek. "We're twins."

"Okay." Heather focused on Ally. "Dallas, you can come and stay with us, but if you pick on Toney, I'm sending you out to wait in the truck with Auntie Kate."

"I'll be good."

"Let's go." Fenn gathered Galveston into his arms. "Heather, you and Kate get in the back to keep her still. Dallas, carry the ice over there. Then, get in your car seat."

Heather had dreaded the trip to Baker City. The dirt track to Cedar Creek would jar Galveston. Fording the creek would be worse as the truck bounced over rocks. Then, they had to transverse the bumpy driveway to the highway.

However, Fenn had spent many summers logging in the back country of the Cascade foothills. He knew just how to drive on the dirt and gravel roads and avoid any unnecessary bumps.

Galveston drifted in and out of consciousness on the nearly hour-long trip to town. Heather found herself praying her daughter would be all right. Yes, she attended Reverend Tommy's church in Baker City, but somehow, she'd lost the strong religious ties of her family. Right now, she desperately needed the comfort of her faith, and she wasn't sure if she'd find it again. Mentally, she added it to the list of things to discuss with Mindy MacGillicudy next week.

Fenn parked the truck in front of the clinic, a neatly restored Victorian on a quiet corner in town, and came around to the tailgate. "I'll carry her inside."

"We can do it if you'd rather disappear," Heather said.

"The kid's family. I'll take her." Fenn shared a glance with Kate. "Besides, I've got to stop running sometime." He eased Galveston into his arms. "Let's go."

Heather nodded, forcing a smile, and looked at her friend. "Seems like you found another lost soul."

"It could be a two-way street." Kate clambered down from the truck bed and Heather followed her.

Doctor Mike MacGillicudy, a mountain man in black pants, a red flannel shirt, and orange logger suspenders, loomed in the doorway. Silver hair hung to his shoulders. "What do we have, Rusty? A compound fracture?" He smiled reassuringly at Dallas, clinging to Heather's hand. "Don't worry, twin. Your sister will be fine. My goodness, Rusty. Do you know how many sets of twins have been in your family? You're carrying on a hundred-plus year tradition."

"Thanks, Doc." Heather felt a genuine smile tremble into life. Doctor MacGillicudy had been the only physician in Baker City for years, ever since his parents retired. His father had been the local veterinarian while his mother was the town doctor. Once there'd been another doctor from Liberty Valley who moved into the small town, but he'd been unable to compete with the MacGillicudys.

They accepted cords of firewood, sides of homegrown meat, farm-fresh fruits and vegetables, and volunteer labor for their medical efforts when patients didn't have cash or insurance. Mike's mother delivered babies, took care of injured and sick children, patched up loggers after drunken brawls, and was there for the dying while her husband looked after their animals alongside Heather's father, who lectured part-time at the community college.

Doctor MacGillicudy led the way into an examining room. "When did you get home, Fenn?"

"Two years ago, after I escaped from where the cartel held me."

"The Army look you over before you came here?"

"No. I figured if they left me there, they didn't have a need to know when I got home."

Heather gasped. "He means—"

"I know exactly what he means, Rusty. Don't worry. I'll check him out after we take care of this young lady. You talk to George O'Connell, Fenn. He may as well use that law degree for something besides toilet paper."

Fenn chuckled and helped Galveston sit on the table. "Will she be all right?"

"Fine." Doctor MacGillicudy began to unwrap Heather's temporary splint. "Nice job, Rusty. You looking for work?"

"I'm planning to train horses, raise beef cattle, and sing on weekends at

Pop's," Heather said. "I'm tired of nursing, Doc." She rested one hand on Dallas' shoulder and drew Kate forward with the other. "This is my best friend, Kate Flanagan. She's a better nurse than I am."

"Are you looking for work?" Doctor MacGillicudy eyed Kate hopefully. "Every nurse I hire leaves for the big city or to work in Liberty Valley where they can earn more money."

"We'll talk about it," Kate said. "Heather's pregnant and someone's got to keep an eye on her."

Dallas tilted her head, gaping up at them. "Does that mean Mommy's having a baby?"

"Yes, but not for quite a while," Heather said. "I wanted to wait to tell everyone until I was really sure."

"You'd best stay off those broncs you like to ride." Doctor MacGillicudy winked at Galveston. "Especially since you're not as brave as this youngster."

"Mommy is brave," Galveston spoke up. "She was a so-jer."

"Not when she was little," Doc MacGillicudy said. "Once she fell out of the hayloft at the McElroy farm and broke her arm. She cried the whole time I put a cast on it."

"That was your fault." Heather defended herself staunchly. "You were the one who said I couldn't play with the new kittens out there for two months and by then, they'd be grown up enough for Grandma to give them away."

"Another time, she and her friend were riding a horse double. Your mom got pulled off by her friend and slammed the same arm against a tree."

"Did it break again?" Galveston asked. "The arm, not the tree?"

"Yup, and she cried when I put another cast on it."

"It was because you said I couldn't ride until my arm healed."

"We only cry when we get hurt," Dallas said. "I cried when our daddy gave me a time-out."

"Really?" Galveston stared at her sister. "I didn't see you."

"It was when you were s'posed to play without me," Dallas explained. "Did Mommy cry other times?"

"When she grew up, she fell off the barn roof and broke her leg. She walked on it for three days until Durango brought her to see me. She cried when I put on a cast. I'm old school and I like plaster casts to stabilize bones."

"What a wuss." Kate poked Heather in the ribs. "And here I thought the same thing Toney did, that you were a brave soldier."

"I always told her folks and grandparents she was." Doctor MacGillicudy collected the materials he needed from a cupboard. "Her grandpa always took your momma to the mercantile for a big ice cream cone after I saw her."

"Mommy, will you take us?" Dallas asked.

"I'm sure she will, twin," Doctor MacGillicudy said. "Either that or your Uncle Fenn will after I look at him."

"Or I will," Kate said. "We can do it when your mom is talking to the doctor about the new baby so he can make sure it's okay for her to tell people about it."

"Good idea." Doctor MacGillicudy grinned at Galveston. "We're going to give you the best kind of cast, honey. You and your sister can draw on it with markers."

"Awesome," Galveston whispered, smiling back at him.

# CHAPTER THIRTY-NINE

Since Jeff was tied up with a project at Hawke Construction, Laredo picked Durango up at Paine Field, the airport in Everett. Durango glanced sideways at his younger brother while they headed north toward Baker City. "You're quiet. What's on your mind?"

"Heather said Uncle Quentin is your bio-dad." Laredo focused on the busy traffic around them. "The girls and I decided it had to be real."

"It is. What else?"

"You need to hear this from me. Brazos arranged for one of her friends at a lab to do D.N.A. tests for us. We're fairly sure Heather's right and the senator isn't our father either."

"All hell's going to break loose when he finds out."

Laredo shrugged. "Tell it to someone who cares. We've always known he uses the three of us to promote his career, but at least we'll start learning where the bodies are buried. Once we know who we are, Brazos wants to raise hell about his pedophile ring."

"Okay. Count me in for that. Payback's a bitch and we'll teach that to the senator and his disgusting friends." Durango leaned back in the passenger seat. "We need to stop by the Cedar Creek Guest Ranch so I can pick up the rest of my clothes. Heather was annoyed when I left."

"How are you going to smooth things out?"

"First things first. We had a deal. If I got her cousin to go to college, she'd back off on me sleeping in the bunkhouse. I did that. Now, I have to

355

convince her this was my last trip out of the country for Nighthawke. I promised her I'd stay home for good when I found Fenn and Waco. I'm pretty sure I have."

"She's not going to believe you."

"I know, but I'll keep talking until she listens."

"Good luck with that." Laredo pulled out his cell phone. "Check my gallery. There's a video you should see of her singing with Jassy and Kate at Pop's Café last time. The song should give you a clue."

---

After ice cream cones at the mercantile, they returned to the ranch. Heather scowled when she saw Tex Hawke's pickup parked next to Durango's classic truck in front of the house and him sitting on the porch swing. She glanced at her uncle. "If you want to melt into the woods, go for it. I wish I didn't have to talk to the arrogant slimeball. Durango said he'd given Tex his walking papers, but obviously the guy is a typical politician who doesn't think rules apply to him."

"No worries, Rusty. I'll carry Galveston upstairs and help get her settled."

"Thanks for all your help, Fenn. You sure made it easier for me." Heather waited until her uncle came around to the passenger side of the vehicle and helped Galveston out of her car seat. "Kate, will you go with them and get her into her p.j.'s? I'll be up as soon as I get rid of Tex."

"Works for me. Come and help us, Ally."

"Okay, I don't like that mean man."

"None of us do, honey." Heather waited until the others trooped around to the back steps and the kitchen door before she advanced on Tex. "Why are you here?"

"Estelle wanted me to stop by. She's worried about you. Nobody's seen Durango at his company in weeks. We wanted to know you were okay."

"Really?" Heather folded her arms, swept the man with a scathing gaze. "You should have asked Jeff. You'd have found out Durango's on a business trip for Nighthawke Security."

"Are you sure? We thought maybe he went somewhere with his son's mother."

"Wow, you're a piece of work." Heather gestured to the waiting truck. "Time to go, Tex. Keep pissing me off and I'm going to tell the rest of your kids again to take D.N.A. tests to find out who their fathers are. They can't count on you to tell them the truth like you told Durango about Quentin."

Shock swept across Tex's face. "He told you?"

"Yes, and I did a happy dance. I don't want you or your wife who is as sick as you are, or that Bible-thumper friend of yours, Eli Roberts, anywhere near my children." Heather paused. "Decent people don't pimp out their kids for political favors, Tex. Hit the road. Trespass again and I'll have Dick O'Connell throw your sorry ass in jail because he doesn't care for pedophiles, either."

Tex sputtered. "Nobody will believe your lies."

"Don't bet on it. They will when Estelle's other son and daughters back me up, even if she won't admit she whored around Liberty Valley, Texas, and the other Washington to get you the political support you wanted, Senator. You pimped her out before you started with your kids."

He was off the porch, and heading for his truck. Heather went upstairs to check on the twins and found both snuggled in Galveston's bed, sound asleep. She heard footsteps and turned to see Fenn and Kate muscling in the other mattress. She helped make the bed and then the three adults went downstairs to regroup.

A short time later, the three of them settled on the porch with iced tea and homemade chocolate chip cookies.

"What did you do with Tex Hawke?" Fenn asked. "Tell him to go to hell?"

"I threatened to have Dick arrest him because Tex is a freaking pervert who goes after little kids. It probably wouldn't work because we're outside of town, but nobody in Baker City likes the guy. So, it might." Heather picked up the phone and called Brazos at the law firm, leaving a message for the attorney. "Like I told Laredo, I think all of the other kids should do some investigating and find out who their *real* fathers are."

"You're such a witch and I mean that in the best possible way." Kate bit into a cookie. "Afterward, they can send out press announcements to the local media."

"You got it."

An hour later, Fenn went up to Kate's apartment to use the phone to call George. A short time later, she followed, claiming she wanted to know the resolution of the discussion. Personally, Heather doubted her veracity, but she didn't say as much. Purple woofed from the puppy corral, and a moment later, Bluey joined in on the yapping chorus.

Heather walked around the corner of the house to the front porch. In a few minutes, she saw Laredo park his rig. She stood like a statue and watched Durango open the passenger door. He reached in the back, picked up an olive-green military duffel, slung the strap over one massive shoulder, and strode toward her.

She lifted her chin. "I threw you out."

"Good luck with that." He put down the bag on the porch and pulled her into his arms. "I'm home to stay."

Tears burned, and she bit her lip. "I don't believe you."

"You should. It's over, Heather. I'm all yours. I promised you I'd quit when I brought them home. Fenn's here and I think Waco's on the way." Durango lowered his head and his mouth claimed hers.

The warm pressure of his lips demanded a response. She struggled to remain cold under the magic of the kiss, but she couldn't keep from surrendering. Her mouth opened under his and she clung to him, hating herself for yielding.

"Kissing and hugging," Dallas announced behind them. "Does this mean you aren't mad at Daddy no more, Mommy?"

Heather pushed Durango away, glaring up at him before she glanced over her shoulder at her daughter. She forced her tone to remain calm and polite. "I'm not mad, honey. Where's Toney?"

"Upstairs. I comed to get you 'cause she needs help to dress. I helped her go potty."

"You're a very good sister." Heather pulled free. "I'll help her now."

"Daddy, guess what?" Dallas ran to hug him. "Toney broke her arm."

"What?" Durango scooped her up into a warm hug. "Heather, what happened? Why didn't you call me?"

"Because I didn't know you were in CONUS, and I wasn't going to try your cell phone if you were out of the country." She shot another glare at him. "I didn't want to interrupt your business."

He winced. "I had that coming, baby. I'm sorry. I tried calling last night, but nobody answered."

Heat swamped her face, but she refused to admit that unplugging all the extensions had bitten her in the butt. Instead, she turned and headed into the house, aware he followed, talking to their daughter.

"How did Toney break her arm?"

"She was dancing on the stairs on our fort, and she fell. You shoulda seen her arm, Daddy. The bone was sticking out and Mommy had to put it back inside Toney."

"Wow, your mom can do anything."

"And Unca Fenn took us to town and the doctor. Toney got an awesome cast. We getta draw on it with markers now that naptime is over."

"Sounds fun."

"Doctor Mac said Mommy was a crybaby when she was little, but Toney was super brave. We gots ice cream cones, big ones at the merc-tile."

"I like those too. We'll have to go again now that I'm back."

When she entered the twins' bedroom, Heather found Toney sitting on the bed, her shorts and flowered sun-top beside her. "Hey, pumpkin. Daddy's home."

"Did you tell him 'bout my arm?"

"I did," Dallas reported. "But you can tell him lots more."

"Okay." Galveston wriggled off the bed and hurried into Durango's embrace. "It hurt, Daddy, but Mommy made it stop."

"Your mom used to do that when I felt bad." Durango lifted her gently into his arms. "I guess I better fix up the fort so you girls can't get hurt."

"Not gonna happen. The playground's fine. You added plenty of safety features when you built it, more than the company requires." Heather smoothed the sheets and blankets on the single bed. "If Toney had been holding the banister like she knows she should, she wouldn't have slipped and fallen. It was an accident."

Galveston heaved a sigh and wrapped one arm around Durango's neck. "Mommy says no climbing until my cast comes off. Tell her I can still play on our 'ground, Daddy. She's mean."

"Nope, not happening, princess." He kissed her forehead. "We do what your mommy says in this house."

"But you're bigger than her," Galveston pointed out.

"Yes, but she's meaner than I am." Another hug and he placed her on the bed. "Now, let Mommy help you change clothes while I put away my things and find the presents I brought you."

"We still get presents?" Dallas beamed at him. "And Doc Mac said no climbing too, Toney. And no riding the horses either, but we can still play with our puppies and the kitties."

"That's right." Heather eased the pajama top over her daughter's head. "We'll just be very careful and follow all of the doctor's directions, so you heal up fast."

"Everybody's mean, 'cept Ally." Galveston pouted. "I love her best."

"I'm glad." Durango rested a hand on Heather's shoulder. "Looks like the next six to eight weeks are going to be a fun time on the homestead, baby."

She tipped her head back to look up at him. "Yeah, you may want to call your dad and beg for a ticket to some hot zone, Marine."

"Not happening anymore. I told you already. I'm home for the duration."

"I hope so." She didn't add she'd believe him when he stuck around for more than a few days or weeks or months.

---

He found Kate making French toast when he entered the kitchen the next morning. He headed for the coffee pot, pausing to hug the twins who watched from the table. "Where's Heather?"

"Upstairs getting ready to go to the Madison place to help set up for the wedding reception tomorrow and I'm looking after the girls." Kate flipped the egg-soaked bread on the griddle. "What's your plan for today?"

"I have to go to Hawke Construction." Durango poured a cup of coffee for himself and topped off Kate's. He made a mug of peppermint tea for Heather and put it on the table for her. "Do we need anything from Lake Maynard?"

"Only a few groceries," Heather said as she came into the room and chose the seat next to Galveston's. "You need to stop by Bree's office and sign the paperwork so she can keep Tex and Estelle from visiting. He was here yesterday, and I don't want him back."

"No worries. I'm on it, baby."

"Good." Heather took the plate from Kate and put it in front of Galveston, spreading butter on the slice of French toast and then sprinkling it with sugar. "Call Rob at the guest ranch and see what you're supposed to wear when you stand up with Ann's groom tomorrow at the ceremony."

"Got it. What are you wearing?"

"My green dress. Ann liked it better than any of the bridesmaid ones she found online, and it totally pissed off her sisters when she and her stepmother told them to match it, so it's a win-win."

"I remember the last time I saw you in it." He watched a blush sweep across Heather's face and grinned when she narrowed her eyes, glowering at him. "Maybe we'll make some new memories tomorrow night. Aren't women supposed to be sentimental at weddings?"

"You wish, Marine. You wish."

He walked around the table and leaned down to kiss her, murmuring. "Payback, baby. You'll get tired of sleeping in the guest room."

"Don't bet on it."

"I already won our last bet. Dray's going to college next month. You're just too stubborn to admit you lost."

Heather sniffed derisively. "My grandma used to say there was many a slip between lips and cups. We'll see what happens in September."

---

After the wedding at the church in Baker City, everyone headed for the reception at Frank and Ginger Madison's stable. The distinctive carved wooden sign reading Majestyk Morgan Farm was decked out in white and blue bunting. Durango turned into the long, sweeping paved driveway lined by white board fences, which also separated the pastures, paddocks, and outdoor arenas.

Most farms used gravel to maintain their entrances, but not Heather's uncle. Frank Madison ran a high-class operation. Not only the main driveway was paved, so were the parking lots and other people areas. Durango walked around the Ford 150 and helped Heather out of the passenger seat, then the twins out of their car seats.

"Daddy, look." Dallas pointed toward a brightly painted carousel and eight decorated ponies in vibrant nylon bridles with matching blankets and western saddles. "There's ponies. Can we ride them?"

"That's why they're here," Heather said, waving to Darla Connors. "My uncle didn't want anyone bothering his fancy purebred Morgans, so he arranged for her to do pony rides for the kiddoes. You'll need to hold Galveston in Velvet's saddle."

"I'm a good rider. Daddy said. I steer Cinnamon myself."

"Not with a broken arm, Toney. Either Daddy helps or you don't ride at all. And you wear your helmets, girls. They're in the back seat, Durango."

Heather ignored the pouting child and walked away, leaving Durango to deal with the upcoming temper tantrum. He claimed he intended to 'stick and stay', so let him man up and handle the four-year-olds. Kate was helping Ginger, Ann's stepmother, set up food on the buffet tables, and Heather jumped in to assist them.

"Where are the girls?" Kate asked, arranging sliced fruit on a plastic tray. "I know they were with you."

"They're talking Durango into pony rides. Darla Connors brought her carousel for rides and two of the ones she's using are the pair that Durango and I are thinking about buying for the twins."

"Should Toney be riding? Won't the cast unbalance her?"

Heather gestured to the little paint mare. "Durango will hold her on, and he'll probably have Darla lead Velvet."

"I thought you were looking for a purple pony," Kate said. "That one is brown and white."

"Actually, she's a tobiano," Heather said, "and she probably has a better pedigree than either of us. And don't say a word to Toney. I refuse to dye the poor little thing's hair."

"What a stick in the mud." Ginger, a lovely blonde who didn't look old enough to have three adult stepdaughters, a son, and numerous grandchildren, laughed. "Don't mention it to Frank. People go all out at the big national shows where he competes, and frequently dye the horses."

"So not my thing," Heather said.

The reception lasted through the afternoon and into the evening. Heather avoided alcohol, opting for the sparkling cider Pop offered, but enjoyed most of the activities along with the other guests. Races, pony rides, and coin hunts through a giant pile of straw entertained the younger set. Teens and adults enjoyed throwing darts at little balloons, other carnival games, and air-gun shooting competitions with stuffed animals for prizes.

Live music began after dinner, and she joined the O'Connell men for the first set. After numerous requests, including one from the bride, Heather capitulated and belted out a rousing version of Deborah Allen's signature song, *Baby I Lied*, with help from Naveah and Chantrea Murphy. A short time later, the bride and groom left for their honeymoon, but the party continued.

When Heather left the homemade stage after the last set, Durango met her. "I'm never leaving you again. What will it take to have you sing that for me later?"

She stared up into his dark blue eyes. "Are you serious, Hawke?"

He drew her close. "Hey, I'm not stupid, baby. I've learned my lesson."

"What is that?"

"A guy can promise to care, but he can't promise to be there when he's not. I'll be there. I'll be with you. Always."

"I'm trying to believe you." She laced her arms around his neck, kissed him. "I really am."

"I had a heart to heart talk with Liz and Art today. I told them I'm done leaving CONUS. I'll stick and stay now."

Heather measured the sincerity on his features. It must be true or he wouldn't have shared those plans with her parents. When she'd seen Jeff earlier, he mentioned that Durango had let the personnel at Hawke Construction know the same thing. It's real, she thought. It's finally real. "Where are the girls?"

"Your folks and Kate took them home. Liz wanted to show Darla and her husband our place. They already heard from Summer O'Neill about the feed, from Dick that we're not animal abusers, and from Laredo who promised to keep them up to date on hoof care. Of course, your dad will be the ponies' veterinarian."

"Does that mean we're adding to our string? Are we going to have two new additions, Velvet and Flicka, in the barn tomorrow morning?"

"Hopefully, and yes, I'll take care of them." He winked at her. "I remember everything you said when you arrived at my office the first day."

Recalling the way he touched her when they were alone in his office, sent heat sweeping into her face. "Everything?"

He leaned closer and whispered, "Oh yeah, baby. Everything."

"Then come on." She caught her breath, grabbed his hand. "I think it's time for that road trip you promised me."

"What?"

"I've told you too many times, Hawke." She pulled him in the direction of the pickup. "I love you, and when I'm pregnant, I get horny. So, if we're doing forever, I want my man."

"Oh, we're definitely doing forever, baby. It's our turn."


THE END

---

Keep reading for a sneak preview of Josie Malone's upcoming *Kindred Spirits*, book five in her *Baker City Hearts & Haunts* series!

Don't miss out on your next favorite book!

Join the Satin Romance mailing list
www.satinromance.com/mail.html

# KINDRED SPIRITS

BAKER CITY HEARTS & HAUNTS ~ BOOK FIVE

# CHAPTER FORTY

*August 2019*

Master Sergeant Debbie Ramsey stopped halfway across the parking lot in front of the warehouse to watch the August sunlight paint Mount Rainier's snowcapped peak with golden rays. No matter how often she'd seen it in the last year she'd been stationed at Fort Clark, the sight always made her feel at peace, that everything was right with her world. Yes, she knew the ancient mountain was a volcano, sleeping before it erupted again, and part of the Pacific Ring of Fire. Sometimes, she felt like that herself.

She drew a deep breath of the warm afternoon air and continued to stroll toward the large building where she'd work for the next three days until her current enlistment ended. She'd taken two weeks off in April to close the deal on the riding stable she'd bought near Baker City in the Cascade foothills, then taught horse camp for two weeks in June and three more in July. She was running out of leave, but that didn't actually matter. On Saturday morning, she'd be free to follow what she'd often thought of as an impossible dream. Now, she'd have to find a way to share her upcoming departure with the soldiers she supervised.

They'd be fine, but what about her commanding officer? He'd certainly notice she was gone when he wanted something. He'd begun complaining about her using up her leave in what he called "dribs and drabs" rather than taking it all at once, but she'd told him it was easier to pick up the slack after short spurts rather than cleaning up various messes when she was gone for an extended period of time.

She smiled and hurried up the concrete stairs near the end of the long building. Inside, she paused long enough to remove her camouflage cap. She glanced swiftly at the loading area and breathed a sigh of relief when she noted the last delivery from the night before had already been stored.

One less hassle, she thought, and headed for the hallway that led to the offices at the far end of the warehouse. She'd barely reached the entry door when a familiar bellow assaulted her ears. Debbie grimaced. She'd only been away for two hours. How did hell break loose so quickly?

"Damn it, Petrie. This is bullshit. Where's Ramsey?"

"She left for an appointment." The other man speaking sounded perfectly calm. "What was I supposed to do when the MPs showed up, Major Sinclair?"

"It's bullshit, Petrie. You're giving me bullshit."

Debbie pushed open the door, catching a glimpse of the vintage sapphire and diamond claddagh ring she always wore. She stepped into the large room that doubled as her office and that of the young company clerk who thankfully had a dentist appointment and wasn't here to see the major make a fool of himself. Silently, she watched the broad-shouldered man in combat fatigues rampage toward her desk, still chanting his favorite word.

A taller, slighter, younger officer with perfectly styled black hair wearing the Army service uniform, their version of a business suit, turned to face her. Lieutenant Petrie annoyed her on so many levels, not the least of which was his insistence on refusing to wear the same uniform—camo fatigues that she and everyone else did to work in the warehouses. He nodded in greeting, then added, "Sergeant Ramsey, do something with him."

"Is that an order, sir?" Debbie opted for her most professional tone but didn't wait for an answer. Instead, she walked across the room, stopping where she'd be in the commander's way.

For a moment, she allowed herself to admire the way he filled out his fatigues and then met his golden-brown gaze when he swung around to face her. "Excuse me, sir."

"Ramsey, where have you been? Don't you know better than to leave a college-trained moron in charge of my warehouses? He can't even keep the latrines stocked in toilet paper. It's bull—"

"Major Sinclair!" Debbie gasped, pretending a shock she definitely didn't feel. "You wouldn't swear in front of a woman?"

Red seeped into his rough-hewn features, edging the strong cheekbones and once upon a time, the broken nose. "Sorry, Ramsey. I forgot you were female." Rex Sinclair ran a hand through his short, salt and pepper hair. "Where were you? That damned Petrie—"

"Major!" Debbie hoped she sounded as stunned as she had the first time. One of these days, Sinclair might catch onto the fact that she could out-swear any and all of the soldiers working in the supply company, but luckily, he hadn't yet.

"I'm sorry." Rex repeated his apology and fired a glare in the direction of his so-called aide. "Lieutenant Petrie had me called off the golf course. I had to leave the general before we finished our game and it made me irritable."

"Yes sir." Debbie sank her teeth into her bottom lip to keep from laughing. "I'm sure the first lieutenant didn't remember how much the general depends on you, sir."

"Watch it, Ramsey." Humor replaced the anger. "I may have been making a fool of myself, but you don't have enough rank to tell me so."

"It's never stopped me before, sir." She met his gaze and smiled up at him.

He wasn't a big man, only four inches taller than her five feet, six inches, but he carried himself as if he were ten feet tall and bulletproof. Just by looking she could tell he was a warrior in every sense of the word, the kind of man who picked himself up when he was knocked down, ready to fight again. At 42, he wasn't a spring chicken, but then again at almost 35, neither was she. No wonder she preferred experience.

She folded her arms, keeping her attention on him. "I don't know what's going on here, sir, but I'll take care of it."

"I know you will." He paused. "Where were you?"

"My current enlistment ends in three days, sir. I was at the Recruiting and Retention Office for my appointment with the non-com in charge there. I asked the lieutenant to let you know if you returned before I did, but—"

Rex nodded. "Did you get everything you wanted in your re-enlistment contract? A bonus, a guarantee that you'll stay here instead of being transferred or sent overseas, a promotion? Do you need me to make some calls to ensure you get everything you want?"

"It will be fine, sir. There's quite a bit of paperwork to finish so I get what I need, but we can discuss that later." Debbie glanced at the junior officer waiting by the door to his office. "Why don't you get back to your golf game? Like I said, I'm here now and I'll stick around to handle any problems that arise."

"All right." Rex frowned thoughtfully before he stepped around her, his attention on the exit door. "Wait for me to make the command decisions, Ramsey. If the general could discuss this in his office, he would."

"But the two of you can't be overheard on the golf course." Debbie inclined her head in acceptance. "We both know how this game is played, sir."

"I couldn't do it without you, Ramsey." He flashed the sudden smile that always charmed her, although he didn't realize it. "I'll be back for closing formation. If I'm not—"

"I'll handle it," Debbie repeated.

"Thanks, Ramsey. I can always count on you." Rex started for the door.

"If I'd known how important the game was, I wouldn't have had you paged, Major," Lieutenant Petrie said. "I'm glad Sergeant Ramsey was able to use her womanly wiles to calm the situation."

Before Debbie could respond, Rex did with a bark of sharp laughter. "Ramsey doesn't have any of those, Petrie. She's been in this man's army longer than you have—seventeen years—and has more combat experience. When she tells you to do something, I suggest you try listening to her and actually do it before you end up in a pine box." He strode out the door, closing it behind him.

She could tell by the bewilderment on Petrie's face that he didn't take the major's recommendation seriously. Little wonder she preferred Rex Sinclair's rawboned features to the pretty boy staring at her who figured he was smarter than anybody else on base. The major was a grown man, and he could certainly take care of himself. He'd proven it in more than one warzone, although she'd spent the tour here watching his proverbial six.

It was a deal they'd made eight years ago, covering each other's backs since neither of them had anyone else they could really trust. Granted, he'd have a fit and fall in it if he knew the rest of the enlisted had disrespectful nicknames for the junior officer. Debbie had corrected them enough that they carefully avoided saying "petri-dish" or "that petty looey" or "chicken-shit loser" around her.

"I'm sorry I wasn't here to help with the MPs, sir." She wouldn't point out he could have contacted her on her cell phone, and she was far closer to the warehouses than the major. "What's wrong? Did one of the delivery drivers get lost on base?"

"No. Two of Major Sinclair's kids showed up at the front gate and the guards brought them here. Since he hadn't left directions for their visit, I had the major paged. Come to think of it, Master Sergeant, there was nothing you could do."

Anger at his contempt for her position as the ranking non-commissioned officer swept through her. What had this idiot learned in R.O.T.C. at college about sergeants and their business? Obviously, nothing!

Debbie struggled to control her temper. *Sometimes, I feel like Mount Rainier, and I just want to explode. Venting isn't enough. Three more days. I can deal with this supercilious jackass for three more days.* "Thank you, sir. If you'll do the afternoon walk-through of the warehouse now, sir, I'll deal with this situation, sir."

Before he responded, she entered Major Sinclair's office, careful to close the door behind her. She paused to study the two girls sitting on the chairs in front of the desk, backpacks and two roller suitcases parked nearby. The nearest child, a small, plump one, had lovely ash-blonde hair. She huddled in her seat, clutching a huge toy bear wearing camo fatigues and combat boots. The other girl, a teen in fashionably torn, faded jeans, a pink, ribbed, shrunken T-shirt, and flip-flops, had shoulder-length ebony curls. Debbie waited until the pair had finished giving her a solid onceover.

"Hello, I'm Master Sergeant Ramsey. I'm sorry for all the confusion, but none of us expected you. Did your dad?"

"We wanted to surprise him," the younger child admitted.

"I see." Debbie smiled at her. "That's why I didn't put your visit on his schedule. How nice for him."

"He didn't think so," the older girl snapped, all teen angst. Tears sparkled in the dark brown eyes so much like her father's. "After the cards and gifts he sends he should have known we wanted to see him regardless of what our mother says."

"He has a lot on his mind." Debbie crossed the room and leaned against the large wooden desk. File cabinets lined two of the walls and the blinds were closed on the windows to block the heat. "The general called him this morning with a special assignment and it's all Major Sinclair can think about right now."

"We don't want to bug him." The little blonde girl sniffled, then wiped at the tears trickling from her sky-blue eyes. "It's just that he hasn't called us back and we don't want to go to boarding school. Our stepdad, Gary, is sending us next week. I don't wanna go to New York by myself or be there all alone."

"Oh, my Gawd," Debbie muttered. This added proof to her private philosophy that no good deed ever went unpunished. When Major Sinclair's divorce was finalized eight years before, she'd started a mission of sending the five children appropriate gifts because their father didn't. He blamed them for their mother's errors in judgment regardless of how it made the kids feel.

"I don't understand," Debbie said. "Why would your mom let your stepdad make a decision like that?"

"Because R.C. left for college last week with Dave and Scott," the blonde explained, picking at a hole in the knee of her jeans. "And Gary says he's done putting up with us."

"Who are they?" Debbie tilted her head to one side. "I don't recognize those names."

"Our older brothers." It was the brunette's turn. "We're all stuck with names that begin with the letter 'R,' and it gets confusing. Dave and Scott started using their middle names. Penny and I do the same thing."

"Well, that will make my life easier." Debbie reached for the box of tissues on the desk and passed it to the younger girl. "And you're—?"

"Rebecca Evangeline. Vangie."

"Okay. First things first." Debbie waited while Penny wiped her face. "Let's go have lunch. Your father won't be back for several hours, and I run the warehouses when he's away."

"You're not calling our mother or sending us back to California?" Vangie eyed her warily. "Why not?"

"It isn't my place," Debbie explained. "All I'm supposed to handle are the major's professional problems, not his personal ones. Of course, if they affect the situation and the enlisted troops here, I do have to get involved."

"And then what happens?" Penny blew her nose. "Do you call our mom?"

Debbie shook her head. "No. If I'm enmeshed in your piddly little issues, I fix them in my fashion, and you won't like it. Neither will the major. Luckily for you and your sister, I spent three years in a boarding school before I enlisted. I wouldn't recommend a place like it for either of you. I learned quite a few skills I'm sure your father would prefer you didn't know."

"Like what?" Vangie stared at her with obvious fascination. "Will you share them over lunch?"

"Don't be silly. I don't know you well enough to tell you how to hot-wire a car or pick locks or shoplift wine and clothes without being caught on film at eleven." Ignoring the giggles behind her, Debbie led the way from the major's inner sanctum to the outer office. She looked toward the opening door and the lieutenant before spotting the stocky young man who followed him. "Private Baxter, what are you doing here?"

Lieutenant Petrie answered for the enlisted man. "I told him to come back after his dental appointment since you weren't here to answer the phones or check in the deliveries. He needs to do his job."

Debbie counted silently to ten while she listened to the company clerk's garbled speech. If she couldn't understand what he was saying, how would anyone else? "Did you bring back the slip from the clinic like I asked, Baxter?"

Baxter nodded and handed her the paper he held. "Doctor said ..."

"I can read, Baxter. Spare me the gibberish." She winced at the sight of his cheeks, still swollen like a chipmunk's from the extractions and the bruise on his jaw. "The dentist has assigned Private Baxter to quarters for the next two days, Lieutenant. I'm sending him to the barracks. Major Sinclair doesn't want his people to work if they're not in top shape."

"What about the phones? Who's going to answer them?"

"It's why we have junior enlisted, sir." Debbie focused on meeting Baxter's gaze. "Stop on your way out and tell Sergeant Nelson to send someone here to answer the phones and check bills of lading. I don't want to see you until Friday morning and only if you're able to work. If not, call in and rest up over the weekend."

"Thanks, Sergeant Ramsey."

Lieutenant Petrie glowered at Debbie as the other man hurried from the office, before glancing at the teenager and tween beside her. "And what do you intend to do with Major Sinclair's children?"

"They've had a long trip here, sir. I intend to feed them and then take them to their father's house." She looked over her shoulder at them.

Backpack on one arm, suitcase towed behind them, teddy bear held tight, Penny pressed close to her older sister's side and Debbie realized the girl was definitely still a child, despite the pretense of confidence. Vangie had on enough makeup for an entire cheerleading squad, plus three pairs of earrings, a ring in her belly-button, as well as a tiny stud in her nose. "Let's see. Penny, you're ..."

"Almost ten and Van's fifteen. We'll be okay by ourselves, Sergeant Ramsey. We've stayed alone every night since Mom and Gary left for Hawaii 'cause the housekeeper goes home at six."

"Well, that's over." Debbie lifted her chin, measuring them with her gaze. "I don't believe in leaving kids by themselves. Heaven only knows what could happen."

"How do you expect to get them in the house, Master Sergeant? Do you have a key?"

Actually, she did, but she wasn't telling the lieutenant that. "Don't worry, sir. We should be able to get in with the cleaning service or I'll talk to the neighbors. Major Sinclair arranged for one of the local boys to take care of his new puppy and the cat when he's gone."

That issue resolved, Debbie ushered the girls toward the door. "Thanks for being concerned, sir, but I can handle everything. It's sergeant's business."

"What kind of puppy does my dad have?" Penny asked as soon as they were out of the office. "I love dogs, but Gary's allergic so we can't have pets anymore. The housekeeper had to take my cat home with her."

"That's too bad." Smiling, Debbie lowered her voice to a whisper. "To tell the truth, Shasta doesn't belong to your father. I found her in a parking lot last May and I couldn't abandon her, so I brought her home with me. I can't have her in the BEQ, so she lives with your dad."

Vangie's eyes widened. "That's really nice of him."

"It is." Debbie led the way to the parking lot and her 2014 blue Jeep Wrangler. "I don't know what I'd have done if he hadn't come through for me. I couldn't take Shasta to a shelter."

Vangie nodded. "Dogs die there."

"Exactly," Debbie agreed. "No matter how grouchy your father gets, remember he's a good person. He never hesitates to help out others whenever he can. He didn't owe me or Shasta a damned thing after he took in my tuxedo kitten, Bandit. And your dad would go to hell and back for the three of us."

Penny caught her breath, staring up at Debbie. "You just swore, and you made him apologize when he did it."

"That's because she didn't want him to keep acting like an idiot in front of that jerky lieutenant," Vangie explained. "He's as bad as Gary."

"Does anybody like the lieutenant?" Penny asked. "Why don't you get rid of him, Ramsey?"

"I'd like to." Debbie heaved a sigh as she unlocked the Jeep and waited for the girls to climb inside. "Unfortunately, your father has to sign all the paperwork when someone requests a transfer. He thinks he can make a good officer out of Petrie and he's not willing to give up on the man yet."

Vangie eyed her from the passenger seat. "I bet you have a way around that."

"Of course, I do but I only use it for emergencies." Debbie started the engine. "Forgery was just another life skill I learned at Celestial Faith Girls Academy for Troubled Teens. Now, what do you want to eat?"

While the girls discussed the options they'd seen on their cab ride to the base, Debbie focused on the traffic. Damn it! She was due to take over the riding stable bright and early next Monday morning when the new session of horse day camp started. *I don't have time to rescue the major's sorry ass, but I'll just have to suck it up and do what needs doing one more time. It's sergeant's business, isn't it?*

## THANK YOU FOR READING

---

Did you enjoy this book?

We invite you to leave a review at your favorite book site, such as Goodreads, Amazon, Barnes & Noble, etc.

### DID YOU KNOW THAT LEAVING A REVIEW...

- Helps other readers find books they may enjoy.
- Gives you a chance to let your voice be heard.
- Gives authors recognition for their hard work.
- Doesn't have to be long. A sentence or two about why you liked the book will do.

# ABOUT THE AUTHOR

**Josie Malone** lives and works at her family's riding stable in Washington State. She's taught children to ride and know about horses so long that she often discovers she's taught three generations of their families. Her life experiences span adventures from dealing cards in a casino, attending graduate school to get her Master's in Teaching degree, being a substitute teacher, and serving in the Army Reserve all leading to her second career as a published author.

*Contact Josie at:*
josiemaloneauthor@outlook.com

*Find her on Online at:*
www.josiemalone.com

*Join her Newsletter:*
https://sendfox.com/josiemaloneauthor

**f** facebook.com/JosieMaloneAuthor

**y** twitter.com/josmaloneauthor

**◎** instagram.com/josiemaloneauthor

**g** goodreads.com/shannonkennedy

**a** amazon.com/Josie-Malone/e/B006HC9VMI

## ALSO BY JOSIE MALONE

**Baker City Hearts and Haunts**

My Sweet Haunt

More Than A Spirit

Family Skeletons

Ghost of the Past

Kindred Spirits (Coming Soon!)

———

**Liberty Valley Love**

A Man's World

Cowboy Spell

The Marshal's Lady

Hero Spell

A Trail Through Time

Time In Between

Kitchen Witch (Coming Soon!)

www.ingramcontent.com/pod-product-compliance
Lightning Source LLC
Chambersburg PA
CBHW072303020726
47501CB00002B/376